THE CROCODILE PRINCESS

By Robyn Paterson

CONTENTS

This book is dedicated to my companions of many adventures.

Ron Dickieson
Chad Hicks
Don Chisholm
Graham Maclean
Dave Irwin
Dave Collins
Michael Horsepool
Charles Dowswell
Cindy Dowswell
James Wegg
Glenn Jupp
Michael Armstrong

With Special Thanks to:

Fiona Thraille
Yi Weng

And of course, my wife, Connie. My own Crocodile Princess.

Dramatis Personae

Little Gou (rhymes with toe).
Sister Cat

<u>The Mao Family Armed Escort Agency</u>
Crocodile Mao (rhymes with cow)(chief)
Old Gan (lieutenant)
Mao, Meiyu (May-yuu), the "Crocodile Princess"

<u>The White Tiger Armed Escort Agency</u>
Master Bai (rhymes with sigh)

<u>The Cho Family Armed Escort Agency</u>
Snowtop Cho (rhymes with slow) (chief)
Spider Chan

<u>The Jin Hua (Golden Flower) Armed Escort Agency</u>
Merciful Beauty (chief)
Miss Jia (rhymes with law)
Miss Lily

<u>The Nine Trees Armed Escort Agency</u>
Madam Lin (rhymes with pin) (chief)
Lin, Wuyun, also called Dancing Cloud
Lin, Wudao, also called Dancing Blade

<u>The Black Dragon Armed Escort Agency</u>
Master Yi (rhymes with see) (chief)
Kicker Bo

<u>Others:</u>
Master Bai (rhymes with lie)
Iron Mountain Hua (rhymes with claw)
Green Mountain Cai (pronounced "sai")
Last Brother Shou (pronounced "show")
Copper Kettle Xiao (shi-ow, rhymes with cow)
Fighting Red General Mah (rhymes with law)
Lady Moonlight

Notes about Names:

In general, I have used the Pinyin system for writing Chinese names in English because that is the current standard. The exceptions are Cho, Chan and Mah. These should be Zhou, Chen and Ma in Pinyin romanization, but I wanted to make them easier for English speakers to remember and pronounce, so I went with these alternate spellings. Please forgive me.

Also, the "u" at the end of Gou and Shou is silent (like the "w" in Snow and Show), I could have omitted it but I like the look of "Little Gou" better than "Little Go", as it seems more Chinese. And "Sho" looks too much like "Cho", so I kept the silent "u" there as well.

CHAPTER ONE

The Gambler

Luck, Water and Love.
Which of these can a man live without?

The old Chinese man flipped over his Mahjong tiles, displaying them for all to see.

"Kong! I win!"

At this, the three other gentlemen at the gambling parlor table sighed the deep breaths of those who had just lost a great deal of money.

"Old Ho, you've got the luck tonight." One of them commented.

"Why thank you, Brother Yang." Replied the winner as he gathered his silver. "It's this new charm I bought from a priest last week by the South Gate- ever since I purchased it from him, it's been nothing but good fortune my way! Why, just yesterday my third wife informed me the midwife says my newest child to be is a boy!"

"That's wonderful, Brother Ho! Please, let us buy you a drink to celebrate!" Commented another.

"No, no." Old Ho shook his head sadly. "I must be getting home. It's already quite late and I've stolen enough of your money for the night. Please forgive me, won't you all?"

"But a single drink?"

"Ahh Brother," Ho sighed. "I wish I could, but my first wife will scold me if I show up with anything stronger than tea on my breath, and I wish to keep my skin. Can we do it another time?"

All the men laughed. "Of course! Of course!" They all chanted, and wished Old Ho a safe journey home.

After the old man had left the upscale gambling parlor, the balding man whom he had addressed as Brother Yang made his excuses as well and left his companions to their fates. Brother Yang was, by those who knew him, and rarely to his face, called "Superstitious Yang" for his reliance on charms and divinations in everything he did. Even the nights he gambled were ruled by numerology and the leaves of his tea as foretold by his personal fortune teller- for you see Superstitious Yang was a rich merchant who had made luck his business. And, in turn, his business had been nothing but lucky, at least, until recently when the tea leaves seemed to have gone sour and the charms he surrounded himself with had lost their potency.

As Yang left the parlor, two men fell into step behind him, one large and imposing with a scar across his right cheek and a pair of hand-axes hanging at his hips, and the other tall and slender, with a bright-tasseled short spear strapped across his back. These were his bodyguards- Iron Mountain Hua and Golden Tassel Nan, two of the most dangerous men money could buy. For Superstitious Yang didn't always rely on luck, he also relied on strength to get what he needed. "Hua," Yang hissed.

"Sir."

"Do you know where Old Ho lives?"

Hua grunted he did.

"How long will it take him to get home then?"

The man considered, "A joss stick, maybe less."

"Could you catch him before he arrives?"

Hua didn't even think about it. "He has only been gone a short time. Even Brother Nan could catch him."

Nan raised a pointed eyebrow. "That," he sneered. "Is like suggesting the hare is in the same race with the turtle and the snail."

"I don't care." The older man snapped. "Old Ho's got a new charm that's bringing him luck. Go get it from him, and get my silver back while you're at it."

"And his life?"

"His family's had enough good luck." Yang said, and then added with a little smile at his own wit- "Time for a little bad."

* * *

At the same time a short distance away, Old Ho was himself whistling as he wandered through the night-time streets of the city of White Fox Town. Ahead of Ho, a man stumbled along, reciting loudly to himself the story he planned to tell his wife when he arrived home, but beyond him there were few people to be seen except those inhabiting the ubiquitous food stalls that never seemed to close and lined every twisting lane between point A and point B in the city.

It was those food stalls that eventually wore his reserve down, calling to him as they did with their myriad of scents, and cheered on by the coins filling his pockets. There was only so much a man who had skipped dinner and had spent the night living on tea and dried fish could take.

"Noodles and stinky tofu." Old Ho slid onto a wooden stool at one of the stalls. "Oh, and are those steam buns fresh young man?"

The seller laughed. "Fresher than you are at least, sir."

Old Ho wrinkled his nose, but his stomach got the better of him. "Reheat that one on the end, won't you?"

"You got it." Said the seller, cheerfully tossing the chosen bun into a bamboo steamer. "Tofu'll just be a minute, I need to cook the noodles."

"Take your time. Take your time." Old Ho echoed, and then surveyed the stall's other occupant, an ill-dressed young man staring deeply into a bowl of noodle soup. Ho smiled as he recognized that look.

"Bad luck tonight, youngster?"

The young man shrugged his tanned shoulders. He was of average height, with a muscular but slender build, and had his hair draped down along his back in a long simple braid. Shaggy and unkempt, Ho judged him to be in his early twenties. After a short pause, the young man sighed and said, "Can't be helped."

Not sure if the young man was talking to him, Ho's curiosity got the better of him. "What can't be helped, youngster?"

"Luck. Old Man." The youth said, still not looking at Ho. "When you don't care, it comes like the Plum Rains, but when you need it, why then it's a dry day on the plains." As he finished, he paused and considered a moment. "Hey, that rhymes."

"You missed your calling, young man." Ho chuckled. "You should have been a poet."

"Yeah, Long Ting would be proud." The youth took a swig of his wine.

Ho was surprised to hear this shabbily dressed young man mention such a prestigious name. "Long Ting? Of the Seven Sons of Wu poetry society?"

"The same." The young man sighed. "It's his fault you see me like this. He told me it would work, and now look at me!"

Ho wasn't sure what to say. "Did he...Fire you?"

"Fire me?" The youth smiled at that idea. "Fire me? Well, I suppose he did, but not in the way that you mean." Then the young man turned and regarded Ho. "Do you want to hear a story, old man?"

"Well..." Ho thought about it. He wasn't sure what he'd wandered into, but in the end, he was too curious by nature to decline. "What happened?"

In a flash, the young man and his noodle soup had both hopped over a stool and were sitting next to Ho. It happened so fast it made Ho jump a little.

"Do you know the Crocodile Princess, old man?"

Ho thought a moment. "You mean the daughter of Old Master Mao?" He answered, surprised again at this youth's social connections. White Fox Town sat at a crossroads between the Central Plains of China's North and the Riverlands of the South. This, combined with its proximity to a major trunk of the Grand Canal, had made the small city into a hub of trade where goods were exchanged and caravans met. As a result, not only was it the home of many rich merchants, it was the home to many *biaoju* families.

Biaoju, also called Armed Escort Agencies, were societies of martial artists who banded together to do security work- escorting travelers and caravans from place to place in a land filled with bandits and thieves. While some were as small as a few men with strong backs, the larger ones involved networks of hundreds of men and women dedicated to seeing any cargo they were charged with through to the end of any journey.

Old Master Mao, better known as Crocodile Mao, was the head of the city's largest *biaoju*- The Mao Family Armed Escort Agency. The Mao Family was one of the oldest and most prestigious of such agencies, and he was a very powerful and respected man. It was said that when bandits saw the deep green banner of the Mao family, they turned and ran like the devil himself was chasing them, which might not be far from the truth given Mao's legendary temper. Ho had used their services more than a few times, and was a friendly acquaintance of the Old Master.

"The same!" The youth answered. "Have you met her?"

Ho nodded. "Yes. Yes. I have indeed had that fortune. She's a beautiful, fair skinned young thing. Small framed with the most charming habit of putting yellow flowers in her hair. I remember the first time I saw her was when I was having tea with her father- when she appeared to serve us, it was like a fairy had come down from the mountains. A beautiful sight. Why, if I was any younger, I would have asked Old Mao to let me marry her, but I just took a new wife not long ago and you know how women are."

He saw a look of pain flicker in the youth's bright eyes for a moment, and then it was gone and the young man smiled mischievously. "Obviously, you didn't hear her speak."

Ho shook his head. "No. I don't recall she did."

4

The youth chuckled to himself. "If you did, you wouldn't have been so quick to get her home. But, let's not worry about that for now. So, to be straight with you, sir- you know the object of my affections."

"I guessed as much." Ho nodded.

"And knowing that, maybe you can start to see my problem. I mean, look at me? Do I look like someone who could court a woman from such a high and lofty place in society?"

Ho hesitated.

"Exactly," the youth said, catching the look in Ho's eye. "So, I came up with a plan. I would court her through poetry. I went to my friend, the poet Long Ting, and I asked him if he could write a poem for me that would charm the goddess of beauty herself."

Ho leaned forward, interested. "Did he do it?"

"He did."

"So," Ho asked. "What was the problem?"

"Time. Long Ting said it would take him six weeks to complete. And, while at first I was really upset, I thought about the future we'd have with each other, and I decided I could wait. So, I told him he had his six weeks."

"And he finished it?"

"To the day."

"And you took it to her?"

The youth shook his head. "Of course not. Well, not right away. I had to make it special, didn't I? So, I planned a whole day of it. I planned a trip to the flower gardens of the Baishan Temple in the morning, and then a picnic lunch at the winery in the noon, and finally a stroll up to the lookout pavilion to see the whole land from here to Five Hawks Crossing. And there, I decided, I would read her the poem under the sun while we overlooked the gods' beauty and ask her to be mine."

Ho was vaguely aware of his jaw hanging slack as he stared at the young man, his feelings stuck somewhere between awe and surprise. Not only was this young man well connected, he was obviously rich to afford to do what he did, and must be the scion of a wealthy family. Why then was he so shabbily dressed? No, he must be a liar, Ho thought as he pushed his mouth back into place. Still, he seemed so sincere, and Ho was curious, so he asked the next logical question.

"What went wrong? Didn't she want to go with you?"

"Worse."

"Her father was against you meeting with her?"

He laughed. "That never stopped her before! No. It was worse than that too."

"Her mother dislikes you?"

"Not at all. She treats me like her own son whenever we meet on the street."

Ho paused, trying to guess his way through the possibilities. He had been young once, and remembered his own struggles with romance. Then, he hit upon one that he was sure met the target.

"Miss Mao was away."

"Kong!" The young man slammed his hand on the countertop. "While I'd waited for the poem, my flower had been carried away by the wind! I'd been working and planning, and the Old Master had sent her to the capital for her education."

"Ahh." Ho nodded sagely and then paid the seller as his late-night snack was slid onto the table in front of him. "Well, cheer up young man! You haven't lost her, and it could have been worse."

"How?"

The old man fished out clean chopsticks from a nearby wooden holder. "Well... She could have been married off."

"She might as well have been. It's been many seasons since I last heard from her."

Ho patted him on the shoulder. "It'll be okay, young man. Everything works out in time. Look at me. Last month I was ready to sell the business to one of my rivals, but recently my luck is so good I'm thinking of expanding!"

At that moment, the stall owner, who had been quiet throughout the young man's story, suddenly perked up. "Someone's got himself lost."

Ho and the youth both turned and followed the seller's gaze to a large man standing nearby in the street looking around anxiously, he had two hand-axes swinging on cords from his hips.

"That fella's run by here twice while you two have been talking. First one way, then the other- now he's back again. Looks like he's looking for someone."

The young man made a thoughtful noise. "It's Iron Mountain Hua. I wonder what old Mister Superstition's got him doing now?"

"Oh." Said Old Ho. "Maybe he's looking for me. I was just with his master tonight and he might have sent Hua to escort me home." Ho stood up and yelled to Hua, waving his hand.

Hua jumped slightly when he saw the old man, and then hunched his shoulders and walked over to join them.

"Were you looking for me, Hua?"

"Yessir." Hua nodded. "The master...asked me to take care of you."

"Oh, well that's most thoughtful of him." Ho nodded and smiled. "I'm sorry you had to run so much while looking for me. I just stopped in for a quick bite to eat and got to talking with this young man."

Hua turned and looked at the youth for the first time, one of his eyebrows going up and a look of consternation falling across his face. "Little Gou." He said it like he'd just swallowed something sour.

"Hello Hua," said Gou with a smile. "Long time no see."

CHAPTER TWO

The Cart

Iron Mountain Hua's eyes were pure ice as a he looked at Little Gou. "Not long enough, gambler. Are you bothering my master's friend?"

"Me?" Gou said with a casual shrug. "I don't bother anyone. I'm just keeping him company on a cold evening while he eats. Care to join us? You look like you could use a drink."

Hua blinked, a calculation running through his bald head, and then he stepped forward and took the seat on the other side of Old Ho from where Gou was. "Hot wine." He told the stall-keeper.

While that man busied himself with heating the wine, Ho began to play the host.

"I must say it's awfully kind of Brother Yang to send you," Ho began. "But he really needn't have bothered, I could get home just fine on my own."

"Well, you know the master." Hua replied. "He thinks about all kinds of stuff."

"He most certainly does." Ho said cheerfully. "Well, just give me a few moments to eat, and then we'll be on our way. I'm sure my first wife is already waiting at the door for me- she worries so."

"Don't eat too fast, Master Ho." Gou commented with a glance at Hua. "It could be bad for your health."

"Thank you, young Gou." Ho said between mouthfuls of noodles. "I must say, you surprised me quite a bit with your story."

"Really?"

"Oh my, yes!" Ho paused. "To think I almost believed you! You certainly fooled me! I had no idea which way was up listening to you! But, now that I know my companion is White Fox Town's most famous storyteller, it all becomes clear! You really do have quite the gift for fiction, young man- quite the gift indeed!"

Gou laughed. "You got me, sir. It was a boring night, and I wanted to see how long I could keep you going. Please forgive me."

"Nothing to forgive, my boy. Nothing to forgive. You've got the soul of romance in you, you really do. Wait until I tell my second wife all about this! She really loves stories like that."

"If she's young and beautiful, let me stop by some time, and I'll tell it to her personally." Gou winked.

Ho laughed. "You rascal! I bet you'd charm her in no time. I can see why everyone always talks about your wit. I keep meaning to drop by the Sunset Pine and hear you talk, but I never seem to find the time."

"You're always welcome, sir. I'm sure my big brother will be happy to find a table for you whenever you want to join us."

"I will." Ho nodded as he sucked in the last of his noodles. "I will indeed. Well Gou, it's been nice meeting you. I'm afraid I have to be off now. Please forgive me?"

Ho slid off the stool, and Hua did the same, moving like a looming shadow. But, before Ho could take a single step, Gou reached out and grabbed the old man's arm.

"Mister Ho, before you leave. Can I ask you something?"

Ho gave him a curious look. "Of course, my boy. What is it?"

"Did you by any chance win a little of Superstitious Yang's silver tonight?"

"More than a little. Why?"

Gou slid some coins onto the table and hopped off his own stool. "I was just thinking that for a rich man, two guards are always better than one. You never know what might happen on the dark streets during the night."

"Are you saying I'm not good enough?" Iron Mountain rumbled.

"Oh, no." Gou shook his head. "Of course not. But, why trust to chance what could be guaranteed by a little thinking ahead?"

"I'll take your head. If ya don't get lost!" Hua waved a fist.

"Now, now." Old Man Ho stepped between them. "Gentlemen, there's no need for such troubles. Gou, although I feel more than safe, you are very welcome to walk with us as my guest, not my guard. How does that sound?"

"Sounds good, sir." Gou answered and grinned up at the big man.

Ho turned to the growling bodyguard. "And you, Hua?"

"Fine." Hua spat. "Let's go."

* * *

It was late into the Hour of the Ox, and only the sound of an occasional cat or cricket could be heard as the three men's footsteps echoed through the stone city streets. But, after the trio had been walking in quiet thought for several minutes, they began to hear a most peculiar sound. Gou was the first to notice it, since Ho was old and Hua was too preoccupied to hear much of anything, but as it grew louder all three stopped walking almost simultaneously.

"Horses." Said Gou.

"A carriage." Agreed Hua.

"It's had a wheel come off and the horses are dragging it." Ho shook his head. "I could never forget that awful sound."

As he finished there was a loud crash from a nearby laneway, and then a solitary horse, free from its harness, came dashing out across the intersection before them. Panicked. Terrified. Racing away into the night.

Gou took off running without thinking about it- clearing the distance to the corner with incredible speed and sliding to a halt as he saw the scene. The carriage the horse had been pulling was on its side, and there were three more wounded and crying horses trapped in its limbers, struggling to be free of their harnesses. On top of the carriage itself, a man dressed in fine blue clothes stood carrying a dark box under one arm and a sword in the other hand. He was slashing his blade furiously at a group of eight black-clad swordsmen who had surrounded the carriage.

Ho and Iron Mountain were beside Gou moments later, Ho gasping in surprise as he surveyed the scene.

"Bandits! In the city!" He exclaimed.

"C'mon, Hua." Gou shouted as he took a step forward. "We've got to help him!"

But Hua stood as still as his nickname and shook his head. "Not my problem."

Gou hesitated, suddenly faced with a dilemma. He didn't trust Hua with the old man, not in the slightest, but at the same time he knew he needed to do something to help the other man on the carriage. If he helped the courier, however, Gou would be outnumbered and Hua would be free to do whatever he wished and probably blame it on the bandits. This would be especially true if anything happened to Gou, who was one of the few who knew to connect Hua and the old man.

It was a win-win situation for Hua, so of course he didn't want to help. But it was a lose-lose situation for Gou, as he'd regret not helping the fighting man, and he knew he'd regret leaving Ho just as much.

So, Gou did the only thing he could think of at the time- he spun around and grabbed the old man, then leapt with him into the middle of the fight!

The bandits didn't know what was happening. At first, they were trying to finish off a single wounded courier, and then suddenly there was another man in their midst carrying an old man in his arms and using the man's feet as a weapon! Two were down before they had time to react, and Gou began to dance and weave with incredible skill among them. With the terrified old man in his arms limiting his movements, fighting defensively was the best Gou could do, but Gou's incredible nimbleness and dexterity were keeping them safe for the moment.

Despite his renown for mental dexterity and laziness, Gou was in fact one of the best students his martial arts school had turned out. Nominally a swordsman of the Sliding Water Grass School, Gou still possessed the inner-strength of a high-level martial artist who had studied many forms of kung fu. It was only his lack of interest in his studies that had taken him from the martial path and kept him from progressing to real mastery of his art. He was more than a match for most opponents in a fight, although nowhere near the level required to face off with most of the martial arts world's stronger members.

Still, it was enough to take some of the pressure off the man on the carriage, who saw his chance and took it, striking down one of the bandits who'd been distracted by Old Man Ho's cries of fear.

Unfortunately, the shock of the new situation only lasted so long, and soon the tide turned again against Gou and his charges. Gou was having to work harder and harder to stay out of the reach of the blades that seemed to come from every direction and which missed by smaller and smaller measures each time.

But, just as Gou began to worry, he might need to retreat and leave the courier to his fate, everything changed.

Gou didn't see Iron Mountain Hua enter the battle- he felt him. Felt the vibrations through the ground at his feet as the giant stepped into the fray, and felt the sudden shift in his enemy's movements as they became aware of what was happening. He also felt the pressure wave of the axe a moment before it cleaved open the back of Gou's head like a ripe melon, and dropped to avoid it in the nick of time. The axe blow catching one of the bandits right in the face and not slowing in the slightest as it continued on out the other side.

"Hey! Watch it Hua!" Gou quipped, taking advantage of his lowered position to sweep another bandit off his feet with a well-placed kick. "You almost got me too!"

"Yeah." Hua commented as he flattened another bandit. "So sorry about that."

"Apology accepted." Gou spun and weaved his way out of the fighting area, putting as much distance between Hua and himself as he could. Dropping a dizzy old man onto the ground nearby, he leapt back in to help deal with the two remaining bandits- who were now suddenly on the defensive.

Then it was all over, and the bandits were a broken and bloody pile of moaning bodies on the ground around the three combatants. The finely dressed man from the carriage slumped against the body of his transport, and slid down to the ground with the box still in hand. It had all been too much for him, and his many wounds were finally catching up.

Gou dropped to one knee beside him.

"You okay, sir?"

But, the man shook his head and waved Gou off, so the smaller man stood up and turned his attentions back to Hua, who seemed confused and unsure of what to do next.

"Hey big guy! Lighten up! You're a hero!"

Hua shot Gou a dirty look, but then it changed to a confused expression again, like Hua was truly out of his element in this situation.

Too much thinking has hurt his brain, Gou laughed inwardly as he looked around with concern. For while the problem of the bandits was resolved, there would be no help coming from the city guard or anyone else for some time. The guard didn't venture out after midnight unless forced to, and the city's good citizens, who were undoubtedly all watching them from cracked open windows and doors everywhere, wouldn't raise a hand to get involved either.

That left Gou in charge of eight dead or wounded men, an assassin, a wounded courier and an old man who was just trying to get home to see his wife.

All before the Hour of the Tiger.

"Good hero," a weak voice called out, and Gou turned to look at the wounded courier again.

"Can you help me?" He begged. "I need to get to the Bai Manor House. I can pay you."

The Bai family were another *biaoju* family, and not a small one either; if he was going to them, then Gou could guess how valuable the box must be.

Gou nodded, "Hey Hua, c'mere a minute!"

The giant lumbered over.

"This guy's just offered us a big reward to get him to Bai Manor. Work with me, and we can split it half and half."

Hua looked down at the man, then seemed to consider a moment before nodding his head. "Yeah. Okay..."

"Great, you pick him up and carry him. I'll see to the old man, and then we can get out of here."

And before Hua could reply, Gou was gone to check on Ho.

"My boy, that was incredible." The old man beamed as he got to his feet. "I haven't felt so alive in years!"

"Glad you enjoyed it, sir. Sorry about that, but I needed your help to move that mountain." Gou said. "I knew if he was ordered to protect you, he'd have to come if you were in danger. Of course, you weren't in much real danger, I just want you to know that." This wasn't entirely true, of course, and he hadn't been sure Hua would help at all. But, if the man was here to recover Mister Superstition's silver, as

Gou suspected, then Hua had needed to help them unless he wanted to have to fight the attackers by himself later.

The old man nodded, accepting Gou's word. "What's next then my boy?"

"Well sir, now we go get that man to his destination. Sorry, but I'll have to ask you to stick with us a little longer. I know it's past your bedtime, but you'll just have to come with us, it's too dangerous for you to be out here alone."

"Yes. Yes, I can see that." Said the senior, dusting himself off. "It's quite alright, young man. I'm ready to go when you are."

Gou turned and looked up at Hua, who was approaching with the courier on his back. The courier still had the small gilded wooden box, and was clinging to it with all the strength he had.

Okay, thought Gou, *one step down, now let's hope this is as easy as it looks.*

$$* \quad * \quad *$$

"Whoa! Hold up!" Gou motioned for the others to step back against the building behind him.

"What is it?" Hua hissed.

"I didn't think those guys were ordinary bandits to hit a courier inside the city, and now I'm sure of it." Gou took another glance. "Ten more of them, on horseback. They're waiting on the main route a carriage would take to the Bai Manor House."

"So, what do we do?" Hua asked.

Gou couldn't help but smile, how easily Hua was willing to work together now that there was money involved. "They're expecting a carriage, not men on foot. We'll just have to take another route."

Hua looked around. "What other route?"

Gou raised a single finger and pointed at the sky.

"How's your lightfoot kung fu?"

Two minutes later, Gou was running along the stone rooftops of the city houses with Old Ho in his arms and Hua close behind. Hua wasn't very nimble, or skilled at lightfoot kung fu, the advanced art of making yourself as light as a feather, but he did his best to keep up.

So far, they'd passed two sets of horsemen, neither of whom had noticed them as they'd sped by, but each one they'd seen made Gou more and more concerned about their opposition. Whoever they were avoiding wanted this courier badly enough to deploy so many men that even the city guard would probably be hard pressed to deal with them all, so what other tricks did they have up their robe sleeves?

The dark roof of the Bai family estate loomed several blocks ahead of them when the answer came in the form of more black-clad men, this bunch running on the rooftops of the other houses to their right, with more to their left. They were being paced, but the men didn't seem to be moving to attack, just...hem them in.

Gou came to a halt so suddenly that Hua almost ran into him, the big man only barely avoiding knocking both of them off the rooftop they stood on to the ground three stories below.

"What's wrong? What's going on?" Ho asked nervously from Gou's back.

"We can't go forward."

"Why in the hells not?" Hua cursed.

"Because, if we go forward, we're walking right into the tiger's mouth." Gou gestured to the men on the other rooftops, who had also stopped and were watching them from a distance. "They're not attacking because they're driving us to something, or someone."

"I'm not worried. I can take 'em." Hua sneered.

Gou shook his head after considering a moment. "You might be able to, but the rest of us will probably have nice funerals. We need a plan." He tried to get his bearings. "Let me think. Where are we?"

"Why, I think we're above Zhao the Butcher's place." The old man said, peering around. "I recognize Miss Jong's flower shop over there across the street."

"And which way is south?" Gou continued.

"There." Hua stabbed a huge finger into the sky. "The Pole Star will tell us. Don't you know how to find your way around the city?"

"Not by rooftop, usually. Back alleys, sure. But not rooftops." Gou considered all this information and looked around, then he nodded to himself.

"We need to go that way." He pointed to the left. "We need to be on that row of rooftops. This one is no good."

"Looks dangerous to me. There's men over there." Ho observed.

"We can do it," Gou took a deep breath. "We have to. It's our only chance. We'll use that street gate ahead and leap over to the other row. We'll just have to hope we can get past them. Once we're there, it's back on the straight course."

"This is crazy," Hua shook his head.

"No," grinned Gou. "It's strategy."

Then he took a deep breath and spun around, running a few steps before leaping off over the abyss.

CHAPTER THREE

First Blood

As Little Gou expected, the men in black didn't attack the pair of *xia* as he and Iron Mountain Hua bounded over the street entrance gate from one row of tile rooftops to the other. They just hung back, waiting to see where the duo were going with their charges. When their quarry resumed course for the Bai Manor House, they just followed from a distance.

This, of course, made Gou even more certain they were being herded into some kind of trap, but there wasn't much he could do about it. He had his plan, and hoped he'd timed things right. Hoped that they could reach the one residence he needed to reach before the trap was sprung.

Then the tiles fell away again as he leapt from one rooftop to the next, and landed– careful not to let the terrified old man on his back slip. The old man was shaking, and Gou regretted being forced to bring him along, but there wasn't much he could do about it and it was better for the old fellow to be scared than dead.

Hua's cursing brought him out of his train of thought.

Up ahead, Gou saw what he'd been waiting for– three men were standing on the rooftop block in front of them, waiting. Gou considered his options– they could dive aside and try to go around, but men on horseback swarmed with torches on the streets below. He could try to move to another row of rooftops– but that angle too had been cut off, and they were only two blocks away now from the Bai Family Manor House. The only other option left was to offer the man to them and hope they'd let him, Hua and Ho free, but he didn't consider that option safe or appealing.

So straight ahead it was.

Gou brought them to a stop a rooftop away from the trio, close enough to see each other in the light of the new moon, but still far away enough they needed to raise their voices to be heard. He took advantage of a nearby ledge to gently set Ho down before he faced the men. Hua did the same with the courier, putting him in the old man's care.

"Good evening, sirs." Gou said in loud, friendly voice. "A beautiful night for stargazing, isn't it?"

Unlike the men in black, these three eschewed the anonymous clothing of bandits and thieves and Gou could see they dressed in proper attire. The obvious leader was a thin-faced man whose gold-embroidered dark silk clothes glittered in the light of the torches from the riders below. He had gaunt features and pulled back black hair that hung in a ponytail over his right shoulder. In his left hand, a slender *jian* sword rested in a finely gilded scabbard, held up in front of him as though it was his badge of office.

Behind him, the other two were an obese man whose body was barely contained in his robes, and a towering figure in dark armor carrying a *guandao* halberd.

"Give us the box," the leader's voice was soft but powerful enough that it still reached Gou's ear as though they were next to each other.

"Well sirs," Gou said apologetically. "I'm sorry, but I can't do that until I know who I'm giving it to."

"You don't need to know that."

Gou shook his head. "I'm sorry, but I do. How can I give it to you unless I know you're the rightful owners of the box? For all I know, you're a bunch of bandits trying to steal this poor man's charge. Tell me who you are, and then we'll discuss it like honorable men."

"You might as well tell him, Shou." The fat man chuckled. "He's not going to be talking to anyone."

"There we go!" Gou added. "Civility to the end, that's the way my master told me an upright man should behave." Thus, implying that they weren't upright men if they didn't answer his question, a challenge no member of the *jianghu* martial arts underworld could go without answering.

Faced with this, the leader gestured to his fellows with his still sheathed sword.

"This, is "Copper Kettle" Xiao," he indicated the fat man who was indeed shaped like a copper kettle used for holding hot coals during the winter. "And this is Mah the Fighting Red General", he said of the taller man, who bowed courteously. "I am "Last Brother" Shou, the leader of this group. Now, I say to you again, give us the box and surrender your lives to us."

"You know them, Hua?" Gou whispered to his companion.

The Iron Mountain shook his head. "Never heard of 'em."

"Me neither," Gou stared at the three men. "Last Brother there has r's like fishhooks in the way he talks though, so it's a safe bet he's from near Hebei Province, up in the North."

Hua just nodded as he continued his own calculations in the equations that determined the answer to the question that ruled whenever two warriors met- a simple answer to a complex question- "Can I win?"

For Gou it was a lot easier, he didn't have any aspirations or lofty ideas about his skills in the face of these men- he just hoped to keep his neck attached to his head for as long as he possibly could. So, Gou did what Gou did best- he talked.

"Sorry boys. Never heard of you." He announced.

This would have been a great insult for most martial artists, who would have at least expected the opposition to pretend to recognize their names, but instead of being angry the three just shrugged it off as if it was normal.

"We met your request, now give us the box." Came Shou's steady reply.

"I still can't do that."

Shou let the scabbard slide gently down in his hand until it was just under the hilt of the sword. It was a classic position that would allow him to free the sword from the scabbard with a flick of his thumb so his other hand could easily draw it and attack. That he hadn't done it already meant this gesture was Gou's last chance.

"If I gave you the box, my friend here would lose face." Gou continued. "And, we'd rather die than lose face to a bunch of unknowns like you."

Gou didn't need to look to know that Hua was now staring daggers into his back- he'd just made Hua front and center in this conflict.

At this, Copper Kettle let out a loud cackle and leapt forward, landing in the middle of the roof between the two sides.

"If your friend wants proof of our skills, he can fight me first!" Copper Kettle announced, and flexed his broad arms in a show of strength.

"I should've killed you," Hua said under his breath as he readied his axes.

Gou glanced back at him. "Look. You're the best fighter of both of us, and this way you'll get to face them one on one. If we fought all three, it'd be three to two, but this way the fight's fair."

Iron Mountain just growled and leapt forward onto the roof, balancing like Copper Kettle Xiao did on a narrow peak barely wider than a single foot. He extended his arms, an axe now in each hand to balance his weight, and took a combat stance to face off with Xiao. It was a show of their skill than these two heavy men could not only balance where they did, but not damage the roof with their sheer weight.

"Oh. You're an axe expert, I see." Xiao commented cheerfully. "Perfect for me. Once I get my hands on you, your own mother won't recognize you."

"I'll split your fat gut open like a dumpling." Hua retorted. "Stop talking and fight with me."

"Oh, very well." Copper Kettle said as he dropped into a battle stance. "But don't say I didn't warn you."

Then Xiao was rushing at Iron Mountain in what seemed a suicidal move- coming unarmed straight at a giant with his axes at the ready. Hua was a little surprised, but inwardly pleased, and determined the man must be all talk to attempt such a feat, or stupid- both would work to his advantage.

Once the large man was close enough, Hua brought his axes together in a scissored attack designed to catch his target from two sides- one coming in high and the other coming in low. But, when the axes should have met their target, they met air! Xiao simply wasn't there to be hit- having suddenly leapt off the peak to the right. Caught off guard, by the time Hua could rebalance and turn, Xiao had rebounded off a nearby chimney flue and was flying right back up at him!

For an inexperienced fighter, this surely would have been the end. Such a fighter would have naturally tried to block Xiao, which would have resulted in him being knocked back off the roof to his death by the impact. But, Hua wasn't an inexperienced fighter, and he realized this would happen in time to instead drop to the side while swinging an axe upward. This simultaneously got him out of the way of the attack and launched a counterattack against a surprised Xiao who was flying past the point where Hua had just been.

The axe struck Xiao right in the side with full force, sending him hurtling across and downward to slam into the roof with a mighty crash of shattered clay tiles as he cratered the roof.

Meanwhile, Iron Mountain found himself in a tricky spot as his own momentum caused him to fall off the peak and start to roll down the roof on the other side! Thinking fast, he slammed his free axe into the roof, cutting into the tiles and turning the axe into a hook that kept him from rolling further.

Once Hua had himself steady, he maneuvered around so that he could use his skills to send himself flying back through the air with his kung fu to land on the peak again. At first, he faced Xiao's two companions, expecting them to make a move, but neither seemed to be planning to do anything of the sort.

Then Hua heard the crinkling of tiles behind him, and turned to see Xiao also flip back up onto the rooftop peak, this time between himself and Gou. Miraculously, Xiao seemed to be completely unharmed by the blow Hua had been certain he'd struck with his axe or the impact into the hardened clay roof tiles. Hua didn't know what to make of that, but he wasn't the type to let it worry him much- he'd never met a man he couldn't cut down by the second blow.

Now the two faced off again, much the same as before, but unlike before, Xiao approached Hua with careful steps. Edging closer with caution instead of running at him, watching Hua's movements and waiting for his attacks. He still had that smile of confidence he always bore, but now he was a bit more focused, as though he'd decided that Hua was indeed a capable opponent.

Iron Mountain watched him come, and then, just when Xiao was outside the range of his weapons, he made his move. Hua threw out his hands to either side and let go of his axes, as though he was throwing them away in a bizarre suicidal gesture, but the axes both stopped a short distance from his hands. They were each tethered to his wrist by the cords he used to hang them from his belt, and once they reached the end of the cords, they became swinging bladed weapons.

Following through against his surprised opponent, Hua brought his hands forward in a practiced gesture that swung both of the axes at his enemy from different angles. In this single display, his reach had now suddenly been doubled, and Xiao was easily within his kill-zone. With amazing speed and power, he brought the axes in on Xiao, this time certain of the kill.

But Copper Kettle Xiao was himself a tricky opponent, and when Hua attacked him Xiao didn't bother to dodge but lunged forward. This move exploited perfectly the one weakness to Hua's attack- by extending his reach he left himself unable to defend against opponents who were up close. Suddenly Xiao was nose to nose with Hua, and driving his hands upwards into the muscles below Hua's biceps with such power that there was a loud pair of cracks for all to hear as Hua's bones were literally shattered.

But, that wasn't all Xiao did.

As the surprised Hua staggered backwards, and before he could lose his balance and fall off the roof, Xiao brought another hand up and struck Hua in the forehead. This too made a resounding crack as it split his opponent's skull- delivering a killing strike.

The broken and now limp body that was Iron Mountain Hua tumbled off the roof and was claimed by the shadows below.

At the same time, Xiao was already acting.

He spun right around during the moment of shock and came right at Gou. Since Gou was the only other obstacle it was a natural choice, and deadly hands blurred as they sped at the unprepared gambler.

They never made it.

Instead, the living weapons met the pole of an ironwood staff and there was a loud "KLANG!" as the two powerful forces met and rebounded off each other.

Surprised, Xiao leapt up and back, giving himself room to deal with this new threat.

"It's about time you woke up!" Gou complained. "Wasn't I making enough noise for you?"

In front of Gou had appeared a Buddhist nun, although not an ordinary nun, as ordinary nuns weren't giants like General Mah, nor did they have the determined look of a warrior in their eyes as this one did. The bald warrior nun, clad in her flowing blue and grey robes glanced back at Gou with an expression of bemusement.

"Brother Gou, I can assure you that the hillside monks are also awake, and perhaps a few of their ancestors."

"Well, we could use them right about now." Gou gestured across the rooftop. "These guys are tough customers."

The nun nodded, shifting her focus back to Xiao.

Xiao, for his part, decided to play it polite and shifted to a more casual pose.

"Honored nun," he called to her. "I am sorry you have become involved in this matter, but since you are, could I have your name?"

The nun straightened and bowed to him with pressed hands.

"I am Sister Cat, of the Order of the Perfect Golden Dragon. Pleased to meet you, honored sir."

"Order of the Perfect Golden Dragon?" Copper Kettle wondered aloud. "Never heard of it."

"We're a modest monastic order," Sister Cat replied. "Very likely not worthy to reach sir's ears."

"Still," Xiao continued. "Your kung fu's pretty good. Not many people could block my Copper Hand attack, and to force me back shows some skill. I really don't want to fight you, Sister, so why don't you just leave now?"

Cat shook her head. "I'm sorry. But I cannot do that. Gou is my close friend, and I will protect him with all of my ability. Also, you have disturbed the peace of this city and woken my slumber- this I cannot accept."

Xiao didn't seem pleased with her answer, but his expression changed to one of resignation.

"Xiao! What's taking you so long?" Last Brother Shou called out from the other end of the roof. "Finish them and be done with it! The longer we wait, the more trouble will come."

"I'm sorry, Sister. I have no choice." Xiao said as he dropped back to an attack stance.

"Buddha's name be praised." Cat answered as she too readied herself. "If it is our destiny, then we cannot change it."

"Watch out Cat," Gou commented from behind her. "This one's hands are like knives, and he's tough as a rock."

But Gou's words were already lost in the noise as the two lunged forward at each other, the Sister's ringed staff vanishing into a series of moves that Xiao countered, and Xiao's hands never quite being able to reach the Sister. There was a difference in skill level, and this time it was on Sister Cat's side; she was clearly superior in her techniques to Xiao. Also, as they danced through their moves and counter-moves it became apparent that Xiao was somewhat winded from his earlier fight with Hua, and this was also making his movements slower than perhaps they could have been. Combined with Cat's almost flawless balance, which was nothing like Hua's ungainly maneuvering, it was clear Xiao was very much at a disadvantage in this fight.

That said, Xiao still managed to hold his own. Much as Gou had suggested, when Cat did land blows on him Xiao simply seemed able to ignore them. It was this seeming invulnerability that was keeping him in the fight even as his energy seemed to slowly be fading.

Eventually, after nearly two dozen moves had gone by in the blink of an eye without results, there came a shout from Xiao's end of the roof.

"Fool! Stand aside!"

At this Xiao retreated, skipping a single jump back, bowing quickly to the sister, and then retreating the full distance to where his impatient companions stood.

"Fighting Red General, you deal with her." Shou ordered.

The armored man passed Xiao without a word and stepped out onto the roof. Now, as he drew closer in the dim light, Gou could see he was a younger man than expected, perhaps Gou's age. His hair was long and draped down over his armored shoulders like a burial shroud, and his handsome features were emotionless and impassive. He looked like a statue of a warrior god from a temple, and there was an aura of power to him that made the hairs on the back of Gou's neck rise.

"Careful Cat," Gou whispered. "This one's pretty good too."

Sister Cat didn't reply, only nodded as she watched her new opponent's movements, looking for anything that might indicate a flaw or disability- she found none.

Mah seemed to be doing the same, and then when he had reached his own conclusion, he nodded to himself and lunged forward. He ran across the rooftop with a mighty war cry, twirling the two-handed *guandao* in his hands in front of him in a blur of motion that made it almost impossible to track where the short halberd's bladed end was at any time.

Despite being faced with this fearsome sight, Sister Cat didn't hesitate for a moment, and she too shot into action with her own staff twirling in front of her. She flowed across the roof in a series of intricate twists and movements that carried her right up to the point where the two warriors met.

Gou felt his heart leap to his throat as he watched a conflict as old as the martial arts themselves come to life. Hard versus Soft. Aggression versus Defense. Yin versus Yang. It was a conundrum that martial arts masters had struggled with for centuries, and now it was about to be realized in this one single brutal moment.

Behind him, the forgotten old man and the courier both gasped from their watching place as a blow was struck home and blood flew.

Sister Cat began to fall.

CHAPTER FOUR

Resolution

Sister Cat began to fall, then caught herself by pinging the end of her staff off the red clay roof-tile and using the recoil to cancel the downward motion while at the same time dropping to a crouch to sweep her opponent with her leg.

The Fighting Red General saw it coming and retreated to avoid her sweep, giving her the time she needed to fully right herself and come back up to a combat stance.

Cat's right shoulder stung from where Mah's blade had struck a glancing blow, the *guandao*'s menacing copper blade having slid down her staff when she'd blocked it and cut her shoulder before she could thrust it away. It had lost most of its power at that point, but its sharp edge still broke cloth and flesh before it had been stopped just a hair away from shattering bone.

First blood was Mah's, but the fight was far from over.

Gou watched the pair again assess each other, standing stock still while they each ran through the moves in their minds. For high level martial artists, a fight was not unlike a game of Chinese Chess, where there were a limited number of moves and it was possible to run through whole fights in your head without moving a finger. The more you knew about your opponent's abilities, the more accurately you could predict how they would move and what they could do. A fight wasn't just a physical conflict, it was a game of strategy where you had seconds to process a huge amount of information and come to a conclusion that brought you victory. Of course, your opponent was doing the same, and all else being equal the ability to out-think your opponent was often the deciding factor in who would win.

Sister Cat wasn't the smartest person Gou knew, but she was no fool, and when it came to the martial arts, she had a genius level talent for both the mental and physical aspects of combat. Her *qi* was focused, her form nearly perfect, and her abilities with that ringed staff of hers were second to none. These, in combination with her large size and strength, made her a formidable fighter on any battlefield, and she and Gou had fought on many already in the short time they'd known each other.

The fact that this Red General seemed to be her equal was both disturbing and telling about where these three had come from. They could only belong to some very advanced martial arts brotherhood and were some of its top fighters. At least, Gou hoped they were top fighters of that society, because if they weren't, then he shuddered at who might be in charge if these were the lieutenants! What was Last Brother Shou, the man with such a sinister martial title, capable of as their leader and likely the strongest member of the trio?

It was clear now to Gou that even Cat's timely appearance might not be enough to get them out of this one, regardless of this fight's outcome.

Mah began his move, and a fraction of a second later Cat began hers, each of them launching into their planned sequence of attacks, feints and parries as they sought to find the weakness in the other's skills. The battle was blindingly fast, but Gou's senses were sharp enough to follow it, and he saw something that disturbed him greatly in the General's movements. The Fighting Red General was putting as much pressure as possible on Cat's right arm, making her use it whenever possible and making the cut he'd already inflicted become worse and worse.

As the veins that had been severed pumped out her blood instead of delivering it to the limb which needed it, her arm would begin to fatigue and lose power. As it lost power, her fighting ability with her two-hand staff waned, and slowly but surely the General gained the advantage in what was otherwise a close to equal fight. If Sister Cat didn't manage to find a weakness in his defense soon, she would be worn down and finished off.

Gou saw what looked like a ray of hope when Mah failed to counter a blow and Cat struck him in the leg with a force he had seen turn other men's legs into pudding. But the General's armored legging seemed to take it, and he didn't falter at all- somehow, he'd managed to take the impact without feeling its true effects. Like his companion Copper Kettle Xiao, General Mah was indeed a master of receiving pain as well as inflicting it.

The fight continued for what seemed like an eternity, each opponent exhausting move after move and trick after trick on the other while Sister Cat got progressively weaker a bit at a time. Soon she'd miss a move, be too slow to parry, and it would all be over.

Gou's thoughts raced- he needed to find a way to bring this fight to an end fast, but how? His eyes darted around, looking for something that he could use. There had to be some way he could get help... Then his eyes came to rest on the men in black on horseback down in the streets, and their torches.

He had an idea.

Cupping his hands to his mouth, Gou yelled at the top of his lungs the one word that he knew would get the people of the city around them out of their homes and moving.

"Fire! Fire!" He called into the night. Then he glanced over at Old Man Ho and the courier, gesturing to both of them. A moment later, they joined him- all three of them shouting the panicked cries of fire.

The people of White Fox Town wouldn't open their doors for thievery, murderers, banditry or cries for help, but the one thing that would inspire terror enough to take action in a city where the buildings were half wood and mostly connected to each other was the threat of fire. Fires spread like the wind in places like this city, and could reduce whole blocks or sections of the city to ash in matters of hours. So, when they heard this call, the people of the city took it very seriously.

Doors were flung open, windows unshuttered and people raced into the streets, all of them searching for the source of the cries and trying to see if it was their home that was one in danger. In moments, the night-time streets were alive with activity and light, the latter being something that Gou suspected these men desperately wanted to avoid.

The sudden chaos was enough to make even the Fighting Red General pause, giving Sister Cat the breathing room she too needed.

No one was sure what to do.

Nobody, except Gou.

Taking quick action, he spun around and grabbed the courier from the ledge, throwing the man over his shoulder and leaping off the rooftop towards the nearest hanging sign. Bouncing off the sign, he flew right at one of the men on horseback! The man was so focused on the crowd he didn't even see Gou coming until the martial artist's foot was impacting into the side of his head. Gou landed and stood on the rear of the horse while the rider fell off unconscious.

"Sister!" Gou cried up at the surprised people on the rooftop. "Grab Mister Ho and retreat to the city guard office! I'll take care of this!" Then he dropped onto the horse and grabbed the reins, kicking his heels into the animal's sides.

"Hyah!" He shouted, getting the horse moving as quickly as he could.

Realizing what was happening, the other men in black tried to react, but it was too late and the crowd too chaotic. Gou shouted his way through a patch of people and then was free of the crowd and gone with only a few of the black riders in pursuit.

By the time Last Brother Shou looked back across the rooftop, Sister Cat and the old man were gone as well, and the Fighting Red General stood like a lone guardian statue on the roof.

From beside him, Copper Kettle Xiao chuckled. "I have to hand it to that guy, he's a clever one. He turned our trap around, and then escaped using our own horses! Don't think I've ever seen anyone like that before."

"You can tell that to the mistress," Shou told him levelly. "You see how funny she thinks it is."

Xiao stopped laughing.

*　*　*

With three riders in hot pursuit, Gou didn't even bother to slow the horse when he got to the Bai Manor House. With the courier still over his shoulder, Gou just leapt from the horse as it shot past the front gates and up onto the surrounding outer wall. There were large metal spikes atop that wall to keep out thieves, but Gou nimbly avoided landing on one and then leapt down into the gardens of the manor's front courtyard.

The poor guard dozing his way through night duty woke up just in time to see the martial artist running towards the house and scrambled to hit the large copper gong- sounding the alarm. By the time Gou reached the front door, it was flung open, and two dozen servants with spears came rushing out to surround him.

These were followed by the master of the house, Lord Bai, a tall imposing man with a long moustache and his first wife, a chubby small-eyed woman. A gaggle of servant girls peered at them from windows on the second floor, but Gou resisted an urge to greet them out of appreciation for the seriousness of the situation.

"What is the meaning of this?" Lord Bai asked in deep imposing tones.

"Your turn!" Gou put the poor courier down, and then spun the poor man around to face the lord. He was still clinging to the box with the last of his strength.

Lord Bai's eyes narrowed when he saw the engraved wooden box, and he stepped forward, holding out his hand.

"May I?"

The courier nodded, stumbling forward a step and extending his charge out to give to the man. His duty fulfilled, the courier collapsed, some servants rushing in to catch him before he fell.

Lord Bai stared at the box, checking its seal, and then tucked it under one arm. He ordered the courier to be cared for, and then contemplated Gou.

"You seem familiar. Are you one of our escorts, young man?"

Gou shook his head. "'Fraid not, sir. Well, now my duty is done, so if you'll excuse me, I have a friend to check on and an old man to get home before his wife has him killed. Good luck with your box, I hope it was worth it. A lot of people were hurt or worse tonight because of that thing."

Lord Bai nodded. "Then you shall be rewarded accordingly. I'm sorry it caused you so much trouble."

"I don't need too much, sir." Gou answered. "Just enough to pay for a funeral and buy a round of drinks. It's the least I can do."

* * *

As the sun rose and the Hour of the Rabbit came to an end, Old Man Ho was delivered home to his anxious wife. His luck and his life were both still intact, but he swore it would be a long time before he spent a night gambling again.

"Sharp Eyebrows" Yang, the city guard's lead police inspector and an old acquaintance of Gou's, had seen to it that the guard were roused and dealt with the damage caused by the night's events. The soldiers even searched for the men in black and the mysterious trio, but they had faded away like a bad dream. Even the bodies left by the various battles were gone, not even a scrap of black cloth left to mark their passing.

Inspector Yang had also seen to it that Sister Cat had been tended to by the guard's on-call physician, and when Gou had first arrived to find her, she had been in the middle of having her bloody arm sown together with a copper hook and string. It was beyond painful, and she looked like a ghost, but she'd smiled and simply greeted him like nothing was wrong. Gou thanked her by telling her the real story of the night's events and she'd offered to say a prayer for Iron Mountain Hua, whose funeral arrangements Gou had started before he'd arrived at the city guard station.

In the end, they both agreed the whole matter was best left undisturbed and forgotten. Government officials and secret orders went to war and had dark dealings with each new day, the less embroiled they became, the better.

* * *

It was two weeks to-the-day later that the large men arrived to deliver Gou an invitation that he couldn't refuse...

CHAPTER FIVE

The Invitation

As Little Gou and Sister Cat stepped across the threshold and into the courtyard, green tasseled spears were suddenly crossed in front of them and two men in gold embroidered jade tunics appeared to block their way.

"Invitation?" Said a stern looking older clerk, who obviously believed that the duo had arrived at the wrong place.

Gou reached into his own marine blue tunic and began to fish around for the invitation, then not finding it, he began to slowly search elsewhere on his person- checking his grey baggy pants and black leather boots for it. While he did this, the clerk became progressively more and more annoyed, and it was only when the clerk was about to speak and tell the guards to throw them out that Gou suddenly produced a yellow envelope from the first place he'd looked.

The man stared at Gou, who offered an innocent smile. Sister Cat suppressed a laugh.

"Here you are, good sir," said Gou as he handed it over.

The older man checked it three times, just to be sure he was looking at the right document, then he gave it back. His manner now much more polite as he motioned for the guards to back off.

"Welcome, Mister..." The clerk began, but Gou raised a hand.

"Just Gou's fine, don't worry about it. Has the party started yet?"

The older man indicated it had not. "We are still waiting for a few of the guests to arrive. Please, this gentleman will show you into the hall." He gestured at another servant who appeared from an alcove to lead Gou and Cat through the compound's lavish courtyard towards the manor house.

"A beautiful garden, and so much art." Sister Cat commented as she peered around at the large collection of statues that adorned the yard. Unlike Gou, she was still dressed in her daily blue and grey robes, although since those were in good repair and had not a speck of dirt on them, they were as good as any for a formal event.

Slowing down, Gou let their guide get a little ahead of them so they'd have some privacy.

"Crocodile Mao loves statues and brings them back from his journeys across the Central Plains and beyond. But, Meiyu's mother hates them and won't let them be put anywhere inside the house, so they all sit out there. He had the garden built up to accompany his statues, not the other way around. I used to hide behind that one over there when I snuck in to see Meiyu sometimes." He pointed out a large marble statue of a pouncing tiger. "I'd throw rocks from there through her window. You can see it up on the second floor."

"You're sure that's not the reason you're here today? Some jest of her father's?"

"He doesn't like me enough to joke with me, and the guys who delivered his letter weren't being friendly about it. They said if I didn't come that I'd regret it, and escort types don't exactly get picked for their senses of humor."

"I would imagine not," the nun agreed. "Is that why you invited me, then? Brother Gou? To be your escort?"

Gou laughed. "If you were my escort Sister, I'd have to get you drunk and try to seduce you. You don't want that, do you?"

"I...um...I..." The nun stammered, turning bright red.

"Sir!" The guide raised his voice and gestured ahead. "This way inside, sir."

"C'mon Sister, the party awaits."

✳ ✳ ✳

The manor's opulent grand hall was filled with people mingling, drinking and chatting as soothing *liuqin* harp music drifted through the air. Smells of fresh flowers and fine sandalwood swirled about, with just a touch of food smells lurking in the background to hint at the sumptuous meal being prepared close by. It was a fine event for the gentlemen of the city, and the people here were of some of the highest standing White Fox Town had to offer.

Then there was Gou.

Never one to be intimidated by ideas such as class and wealth, Little Gou walked among them with the ease of a man at home in any situation. In point of fact, he actually knew a great many of them already- the gambling tables of any city are perhaps the most egalitarian places in the world. Anyone may join in as long as they have the money, and the lucky poor often rub shoulders and share sorrows with the unlucky rich. Gambling was one of the bonds that joined this fraternal society together, and Gou was one of the most well-known of the city's gamblers for being as entertaining as he was unlucky.

Nearly everyone liked Gou, and Gou liked nearly everyone- so he had a great many friends and few enemies except those who offended his sense of justice or didn't share his appreciation for wit. He was a man as rich in friendship as poor in wealth, but somehow it seemed to work for him.

"So Teng," Gou said casually to the man who held the actual title of richest man in White Fox Town. "How's the new wife?"

Tenacious Teng gave a high-pitched laugh and fluttered an orange silk fan in front of his face. "Oh Gou! She's wonderful! Simply wonderful! I can't imagine ever not being married. You really should try it! Do you know she actually ordered me to come home at a decent hour tonight? Ordered! Me! It's simply delightful."

Gou blinked. "Well Teng, I've never quite heard it put that way before. I'm glad to hear you're enjoying it."

"Oh yes. Yes, indeed!" Teng chattered enthusiastically. "This whole rules of the house business is fascinating. Did you know breakfast is normally served at the same time every day? Family members actually eat together and even wait for each other!"

"I'd heard that, yes." Gou nodded while keeping a straight face. "You didn't have a lot of rules growing up in your home, did you Teng?"

"Well no." Teng reflected. "Why do you ask?"

Gou smiled and shook his head. "No reason. Have you seen our host around?"

"I did earlier, but he seems to have disappeared. I must say, I was surprised to see you and the good sister here. This isn't at all the type of party where I'd expected to find you at all."

"You and me both, Teng. You and me both. Please excuse us and say hello to Little Bei for me, won't you?"

Saying their goodbyes, Gou and Cat left Teng to converse with the next nearest person while they moved off into the room. Gou peered around, unsure and uncertain of what was happening, but sure he probably wasn't going to like it.

"I don't have a good feeling about this, Sister." Gou commented. "We've been here half the night and we still have no idea why we're on the guest list."

"Perhaps this is related to the help you gave Master Bai a short time ago, Brother. He could have asked the Old Master to invite you here today."

"Maybe," Gou agreed. "But I haven't seen him around either, which is odd since I know he and the Old Master are close. Bai is married to one of Master Mao's cousins."

The Sister regarded him, wide-eyed. "You really do know people."

"I just know the local gossip. Always good to keep an ear open."

"Really?" Said a man's voice from behind Gou. "And what do they say about me, then?"

Gou didn't even bother to turn around, he just sighed then answered. "Nothing that I can repeat in the good Sister's company, I'm afraid Cho."

A young man about the same age as Gou stepped up to join them a moment later. He was regal and refined looking, wearing a black silk robe embroidered with a white flower brocade and a white jade fastener. He was muscular, fit and handsome enough to make even the good Sister's heart skip a beat for a moment, but the thing that was most striking about him was his hair- it was pure white.

"Good evening, Sister." Cho raised a wine cup to the nun. "And good evening to you too, Gou."

"Sister- you know Snowtop Cho." Gou introduced him without enthusiasm. "Scion of the Cho Family Armed Escort Agency, and an even worse gambler than me."

Cho laughed after exchanging bows with the Sister. "Oh. I wouldn't say that Gou. It looks like my luck has changed tonight."

"Found a blind man to gamble with, did you?" Gou said with a smile.

Cho was clearly in too good a mood to be tempted by Gou's baiting, and ignored the spirit of his remarks. "Not at all. You see, I know why Old Master Mao has invited me here tonight."

Gou had wondered about that. Cho was the first son of the Mao Family Armed Escort Agency's main rivals in White Fox Town. While the two agencies weren't enemies, they weren't on the best of terms either- each group tending to pretend the other didn't exist. There was only one connection between the two right now that Gou knew of, and it made a shiver of ice run down his spine to think of how that could involve Snowtop being here.

"There's going to be a big announcement." Cho continued. "And my connections tell me that the Mao family just commissioned Hong the Goldsmith to begin work on a wedding necklace. Since they have only one unmarried daughter of wedding age, we both know who it's for. And, then I received that special invitation to the party...Well, you can see where it's all leading."

"You really need to lay off the opium, Cho. It's doing wonders for your imagination." Gou quipped, but Sister Cat noticed her friend's hands had started to shake.

"My imagination has nothing to do with it," Cho said with a grin. "The Mao family has finally decided to accept my marriage proposal, and tonight will be the announcement. Our families will finally be united, and Meiyu will be where she belongs- with me."

"You're still dreaming, Cho. Why don't you go get some tea and wake yourself up?" Gou forced a smile. "Too much wine has rattled that pale brain of yours."

Cho laughed a confident laugh and patted Gou on the shoulder. "We'll see, old friend. We'll see. Excuse me, Sister."

And with that, he left.

Sister Cat frowned as she watched Gou suddenly sag- it was as if all the air had gone out of him. She almost thought she was going to need to carry him off to a more private space, but he stayed on his feet, staring at some unseen point on the ground ahead of him in thought.

She really didn't know what to do. Being raised in a Buddhist Nunnery didn't prepare one well for the rocky road of romance as either a participant or a spectator, and she had only been in the outside world a little less than a year. She glanced around furtively for a familiar face to help, but finding none, she decided it was up to her to deal with the situation.

"Brother Gou," she whispered. "He could just be taunting you. Even he has no proof of what's coming tonight."

"They've ordered a wedding necklace, Sister." Gou replied without looking at her. "Even if Snowtop's not the groom, it means she's getting married. Her father must've invited me here tonight to let me know the truth firsthand. He probably wants to see the look on my face when he makes the announcement."

Gou's whole body was shaking now, and it seemed to the Sister as if he was almost ready to cry at any moment. She had never seen him like this. They had faced pirates, warlords, bandits and killers together without him showing a care in the world. Gou was a rock, and it seemed like he could weather any emotional storm that came his way.

But this was different. This was love.

"Cho's chased her for years. The three of us grew up together, and he asked her to marry him a few times. She always turned him down, though- said she wasn't ready to get married to anyone. But, I knew if I just tried a little bit harder than him, I'd have a chance, that she'd give me a chance. Now...it's over."

Gou let out a deep sigh, and then turned and began walking unseeing towards the door. The crowd became a blur, and his mind a haze as he stumbled along, the Sister apologizing for him as he bumped into people on his way out. He was just a little drunk, she told them, nothing to worry about, sorry for the trouble.

He was almost to the side door when the bell rang out so loudly across the hall it knocked him out of his stupor and made him turn around and look. It had been rung with incredible force from a balcony on the second level, the near shockwave of it silencing the party and bringing all eyes to the hulking bearded man who stood like a god looking down on the assembled peoples below. Clad in reds and greens, he wore a medallion of pure gold the size of a dinner plate on his chest, and it still didn't cover a quarter of his width. Around the powerful looking man was a plump woman dressed in similar but more genteel red and green silks and a few other men who looked like they'd be more at home in a bar-fight than they were on such a regal platform. The exception to them was Lord Bai, who was dressed in his own fine blue and purple robes and stood looking no less noble to the imposing figure's left.

"Is that...?" Sister Cat asked.

"Old Master Mao, the Crocodile himself." Gou finished.

Crocodile Mao set down the iron mace he'd used to ring the bell and turned his attention to the audience. Not a whisper sounded as he looked across the assembled throng and smiled a big toothy grin.

"Good Evening, my friends!" His voice echoed. "And welcome!"

A murmur rose up, and people smiled, but nobody dared to speak.

"I'm sorry to keep you waiting for your dinner, but before it's time to eat I need to make an announcement. It does me good to see all of you, for you have all been keen friends to my family and seen us through times good and bad until we reached this station in life. Five of my daughters have been raised under your eyes, and four have been married in banquets you have attended.

"Well, tonight I am proud to announce to you that the marriage of my fifth daughter, my beloved Meiyu is...is...."

Old Master Mao stopped speaking, the twin pinecones he called eyebrows furrowing and his expression becoming one of confusion. A series of whispers ran through the crowd, and people at the front began to crane their heads to look around- to find the source of what had brought his speech to a halt.

The crowd at the back of the hall began to split, with the people moving aside as if being pushed by an invisible wave. A laugh rang out from the back of the hall. It was a young woman's laugh- shrill, loud, piercing and haughty. Arrogance framed it, but in all who heard it, the emotion it caused was fear- primal fear.

Into the center of the hall came a short black palanquin, the silk covered box carried by two large muscled men- one at the front, and one at the back. Each had the dark red skin and black hair that marked people from the far south lands, and they were clad only in ballooning white pants with white sashes adorning their broad chests in lieu of a shirt.

Around the palanquin walked three men, one tall, thin and stern; one fat wearing orange robes; and the last a giant wearing red armor and brandishing a shining golden halberd. Last Brother Shou, Copper Kettle Xiao and Mah the Fighting Red General!

The assembled guests ringed the newcomers, but kept their distance. Men who were obviously fighters pushed their way to the front of the crowd as hidden weapons were handed out. In seconds, the black palanquin and its escorts were completely surrounded by men carrying swords and short spears.

Gou, recognizing the trio, moved quickly to get a good vantage point, and finding himself unable to get through the crowd settled for a perch at the back atop one of the decorative vases. Sister Cat stood beside him, but needed no help to see over the crowd and watch the proceedings

"I bring greetings," Last Brother Shou announced to the balcony. "From my mistress, the Lady Moonlight, to the Mao family on their day of celebration."

"Who?" The crowd murmured in consultation. None of them had ever heard this name before. But up on the balcony, Gou noticed Old Master Mao and Lord Bai's faces both go cold as marble when Shou spoke it.

Lord Bai was first to speak.

"What gives the Lady the right to intrude on our party uninvited? You're not wanted here, go away!"

"My lady," Shou answered, "Is here to deliver a message to the Old Master, and will leave when she's done."

"What," Mao rumbled gravely, the wooden railing before him cracking under his grip. "Is this message?"

Shou shook his head. "Before she can give it, she wishes to make a request of you."

"What is it?" Lord Bai asked.

"My Lady wishes you to assemble your ten best fighters here around us, with the exception of you two, my lords."

"What? Why?!?" Bai frowned.

"My lady wishes to see if your house is worthy of her message."

Mao and Bai looked at each other in surprise as the men around them on the balcony suddenly exploded to life, taking it on their own initiative to answer the Lady's request. The rough and tumble looking group of fighters and martial artists that made up the elite of the Mao Family Armed Escort Agency were suddenly leaping down and rushing to surround the intruders. The Mao family had over 500 men in their employ, and these were the best of those- Mao's lieutenants and top fighters who had fought off bandit clans and faced outnumbered odds time and time again.

"Tell your lady to have a good damn look at us!" Cursed a man who had the martial title of "Bloody Hook" Lo, raising his signature weapon in challenge. "It'll be the last thing the wench ever sees."

The men around him cheered and made ready to fight.

But, from inside the palanquin came a beautiful voice, so different from the laughing one heard earlier. "Shou?" She asked through the silk curtains.

"My lady?"

"Withdraw and leave me."

Shou gave a stiff bow. "Yes, my lady." Then he motioned to his two martial brothers and the three of them turned and marched back out from the hall the way they'd come, the crowd letting them pass.

"Well," announced Lord Bai once they'd gone. "How long does the lady plan on making us wait? Does she think she's a queen?"

Laughter rippled through the guests.

"It's a lady's prerogative to make gentlemen wait, is it not Lord Bai?" Came a sweet toned reply. "But, as there are no gentlemen in this room worthy of my attentions, I shall wait no longer."

A slender hand cleaved the black silk curtain.

CHAPTER SIX

Lady Moonlight

The slender white hand cleaved the black silk curtains in two, and the crowd gasped collectively as the occupant stepped into the light of the ballroom.

The woman, although many would argue later about her age, had the beautiful powdered features and large almond shaped eyes found in paintings of The Four Beauties. Her ebony hair was so long it touched her ankles, and tied off in a ponytail that was kept straight along its length by a series of pure snow-white silk ribbons. In fact, everything she wore, from the flowing silk robes to the shoes on her feet were as white as the moonlight she took as her name.

Even Little Gou, who had seen a great many beauties in his time from common farm-girls to the ladies of the Imperial Palace, was taken aback by her, and it was obvious to him and all who saw her that the title "Lady" which she used was no mere affectation- they really were in the presence of royalty. The only questions were what sort of royalty and why was she here?

Lady Moonlight let her appraising gaze sweep over the lieutenants of the Mao Family Armed Escort Agency like a queen surveying her honor guard. She looked at each in turn, and even at the anxious row of men who stood behind them holding their spears and clubs. These lieutenants were some of the biggest and roughest men in the area, but she showed no fear of them, and in fact it was they who had lost all their bravado in the face of her!

At last, she turned and looked up at the balcony where Old Master Mao stood with his wife and Lord Bai, her lips becoming a gentle smile and her large eyes gaining a friendly look.

"Honored hosts," she said in a sweet voice so at odds with the laughter they had heard from the palanquin. "I have come to deliver my message to you. So please, hear my words and carry them close to your hearts. Begin."

The last word she said was not directed at Lord Mao and his family, but at the two palanquin carriers who had let down their charge and now walked to the far edge of the ring. One carried with him a flute, and the other a *liuqin* that he began to play, the one with the flute joining in after a few beats to produce a gentle melody.

As they played, Lady Moonlight began to hum to herself and from the folds of her robes she produced a long slender *jian* sword of obvious high quality. Swaying in time with the rhythm she began an incredibly graceful sword dance that had her moving in sweeping motions around the empty circle. It was like a fairy had come down from the mountains to entertain them, and the guests all watched in rapt fascination as she moved across the floor. It wouldn't be right to say she stepped or danced, it was more like she floated across the ground- her motions so elegant, so refined, that as she moved anyone who disturbed her would have felt they had committed a crime. She danced in front of each of the lieutenants as they gazed at her in wonder, and even paused to smile at the guards and some members of the crowd.

If she had asked them to, there was little doubt most of the men in the crowd would have let her cut off their arms and legs with that sword just to be able to gaze at her a little longer. Even a thrust to the heart might not have seemed too high a price for a kiss from her plum colored lips.

Finally, she swept back into the middle of the circle where she had started and touched the tip of her sword to the ground in a gentle motion to indicate her dance was done.

The music stopped.

There was silence for a moment, and then old Master Mao began to clap.

"A fine dance! A fine dance indeed! I don't think I've ever seen better!"

The Lady smiled, and bowed her head in a sweet and humble manner.

"The Old Master's words are kind, and I thank him for them." She answered with grace. "But, I'm afraid there is a price to the dance I just gave."

Still smiling, Master Mao nodded. "You want a chance to speak with me? Do you wish to do it in private?"

Lady Moonlight gently responded that she did not. "I will deliver it here, old sir."

"Well then," snapped Lord Bai, who wasn't as taken in by any of this as his friend. "What is it? Be quick about it!"

"You have in your possession a box. It was delivered to Lord Bai's two weeks ago, and since hidden away. Will you not give it to me?"

Lord Bai laughed. "So, you're the one who sent those ruffians to attack my men."

"I am." Replied the Lady.

Old Master Mao's face lost all its shine in an instant. "You dare!" He thundered. "You dare come into my house after what you did? Who do you think you are?"

"I am your superior, old man." Lady Moonlight answered, a haughtiness slipping back into her tone. "I am your superior in every way, and I will have that box or every last member of the Mao family will die by my will before the Hour of the Rat a fortnight from now."

"You think so, do you?" Mao said in a disbelieving tone. "Well then, I thank you for delivering yourself to us before such a thing could happen. I don't think your men will be so quick to harm my family with their leader in my care. Guards! Take her!"

The old master had barked that last command to his men, who indeed had Lady Moonlight surrounded, outnumbered and at a disadvantage in every way possible. It seemed like there was no chance for her to escape this fate, all the Mao family's ten best fighters had to do was take a step in and she was theirs.

But they didn't. Not an inch.

Crocodile Mao's voice was like thunder and echoed throughout the hall loud enough to wake even the most drunken sleeper. But it was still not enough to make his men move, for they remained standing still like statues.

Mao paused, looking around, uncertain.

"I'm sorry, Master Mao." Lady Moonlight said, raising a hand to cover her mouth. "But your men have all lost their spirit to fight. In fact, they've lost all their spirits."

As she laughed some of the people in the crowd crept forward to check the fighters, and a cry of horror went through the room. They were dead! All of them! Every last one of the fighters, every guard, and not a few of the audience had been dead for over a minute now and not a single person in the room had seen it happen! As she'd danced, without spilling a single drop of blood she'd struck down each of them with her sword, not only killing them but using their pressure points to paralyze their bodies so they hadn't moved or been able to cry out!

This petite fairy who looked like a goddess from the mountains was in fact a devil from the depths of the darkest hells.

"Now, to finish our business." The Lady added once these facts had time to sink in, and the crowd dropped to silence to hang on every word. "You may contact me by coming to the South Gate and wearing a white cloth around your arm. Do this when you are ready to give me the box."

Then she sheathed her sword and got back into the palanquin, which the two red skinned men picked up again and began to carry out the way they'd come. Sister Cat began to move, but Little Gou stopped her, shaking his head.

Nobody else tried to interfere- nobody dared.

When they were almost out of the hall, however, Lady Moonlight's voice came floating back in.

"Oh, and before I forget. Congratulations on your upcoming wedding, I hope nothing happens to the bride. It is such a long trip, and one never knows, do they?"

This was followed by laughter that seemed to hang in the air long after the palanquin had vanished into the night.

* * *

Not long after the majority of the guests had also quickly disappeared, Lord Mao stood among the bodies of his men and their weeping comrades.

"Witch!" Master Mao cursed to the heavens. "In one strike she's crippled us and put us at her mercy."

Lord Bai nodded solemnly. "It's doubtful any of the others will help us now after that display, and these were our best men. Even the ones off on missions are no match for her. Perhaps we should give it to her, old friend."

Mao sneered and shook his head. "Never! I swore an oath to see that box to the gathering next month, and that's exactly what I shall do."

"But, your family..." Lord Bai gestured at the women and children who wept nearby. "Surely it's not worth all this?"

"Bai," Old Mao said with conviction. "This family was built on its reputation. We have never failed to deliver our charges to their destinations safely, not once in thirty years. If I give her that box, this family is as dead as if they die by her hands."

"Then what next?"

"Next..." Mao thought a moment. "Messengers! To me!"

Servants came as called.

"Take word to my daughters and their families. They are all to come here as quickly as possible. Tell them they are in great danger, and I will send men right behind you to escort each of them here." Then he looked at Bai again. "We will make our stand in this place, old friend. There is no place safer than here together. If we can weather the storm, then her boast will be shown for the hot air it is and we can gather allies again."

Lord Bai nodded, agreeing. "I will bring my family here as well. We will stand together."

The old warriors grasped each other's arms in a tight grip to seal their determination.

* * *

A deeply troubled Little Gou walked with his companion among a garden of headless statues. Lady Moonlight's men had left not a single one of Mao's collection undisturbed in a clear effort to drive home their message.

"What bothers you, Brother Gou?"

"Sister, have you ever seen an engagement party without the poor kids on display?"

Sister Cat considered this a moment. "I'm afraid I have only attended two parties since I came to this city, but both did have the bride and groom in attendance."

"And who did you see tonight?"

"Only the parents."

Gou nodded. "Exactly. Where were the people getting married tonight? They should have been on full display, but they weren't. Then there's what Lady Moonlight said..."

Sister Cat looked at him, confused. "Is that important?"

Gou gestured for her to follow him. "C'mon! I need to check something."

Taking a quick jog to the rear of the building, they entered the busy stables where Gou searched around until he found what he was looking for. Dodging the frantic stable boys, he ran up to where a horse was being prepared to leave, waving to its rider.

"Kam!" He called out. "Hey Kam! Hold up!"

The rider, a pock-faced man turned to look at him in surprise, then when he saw it was Gou his expression became a worried one.

"Oh! Ah. Hey Gou!" He said, trying to look busy. "Sorry, I don't have time to pay you right now. I've got messages to deliver."

Gou indicated he didn't need to worry about that and got straight to the point.

"Kam, why wasn't the Master's youngest daughter Meiyu here tonight?"

"Oh, her? She's still coming down from the capital up north! They just sent for her a few weeks ago, so she can't be more than halfway here by now. Why? You think something's gonna happen?"

Gou faked a smile. "I hope not. Where're you off to?"

"We're delivering messages to the Master's family telling them to all come here for their own safety. I hope nothing's happened to them yet!"

Gou patted the side of the horse. "You said it. Ride careful, okay? I want my money."

Kam laughed and said his goodbyes, then rider and horse were gone like a shot.

"She wouldn't," said Sister Cat.

"She said his whole family, and mentioned Meiyu specifically." Then after a short pause he added. "Sister, I've got to go find her. You don't need to come- it's going to be a long ride and I know how you feel about horses."

The nun smiled. "Brother Gou, I will manage. You will need my help, and I no more like being a bystander than you do."

Gou nodded. "Thanks Sister, that means a lot. Okay, next we have to get ourselves some horses. She might've just added that last part to make Old Mao divide his men, but I'm betting she's already sent people up to meet Meiyu's caravan."

"Can we catch them?" The Sister sounded concerned.

"If we move quick enough, then maybe. She might not know where the caravan is any more than we do, so they'll have to find her first. We just have to make sure we're a step ahead of them." Then he turned and started to run. "Sister, grab what you need for the trip and meet me at the Sunset Pine in an hour."

"Where are you going?"

Gou's voice echoed back before he vanished around a corner- "To get the fastest horses in town!"

* * *

Snowtop Cho was not a happy man.

With hunched shoulders, he walked down the laneway, kicking a rock out of the street as he made his way home. He'd considered going out and getting drunk after his big moment had been ruined, but he was too upset to even drink. He'd finally thought his luck was turning around, and what had happened? Everything had fallen down around him, as usual.

After drinking a great deal, Snowtop had been forced to step out to relieve himself during the party, and when he'd returned, he'd found many dead and the rest in shock. The announcement of his pending engagement had turned to ashes before his eyes.

He'd rushed to offer his services to the old lord, but Master Mao's servants had kept him from talking with the Old Master himself, even though he'd been desperate to ask about Meiyu. He could forgive a lot, but this was certainly a shabby way to treat one's future son-in-law, even under these circumstances.

That young witch's parting words bothered him a lot, and he would have offered the resources of his whole family's agency if only they'd given him the chance. The Cho Family *biaoju* had over 300 men in its employ, and some of the best relay riders in the province. While the Mao family had set itself up based on skilled armsmen as security, the Cho family had taken the approach that speed and intelligence were the keys to avoiding bandits. Whenever possible they routed clients through safe areas or delivered packages using the fastest mounts they could find. Few in the central plains had more mobility and intelligence resources than the Cho Family Agency.

In this mood, Snowtop wandered through the front gates of his family's compound a little less than an hour after the incident at the Mao residence. His sword, *Ice Wind*, itched against his hip, and he had the intention of calling out the servants to light the courtyard and let him practice his swordsmanship on the dummies. He'd been a swordsman his whole life, and prided himself on being one of the best in the *Jianghu* martial world. Going through the *daolu* practice forms helped him to concentrate and center himself, something he dearly needed to do. And, even if that didn't work, at least he'd have the satisfaction of getting his frustrations out on the straw men.

Just as he got through the gate however, one of the servants ran up to him.

"Young master! Young master!" The older man called out, excited.

"Yes? What is it?" Cho frowned. "Do we have a contract?"

The servant was surprised. "Why yes! Yes, we do sir! Oh my. The young master is always a step ahead of us! The letter just arrived a few minutes from the Mao compound!"

Snowtop's eyes went wide and his heart was in his throat in a moment. "What? Where is it?" His words were like gasps for air.

"Here sir!"

The servant produced the letter and Cho grabbed it from his hands, tearing the seal open and reading it. The more he read, the more he smiled, and when he finally handed it back to the servant he was grinning from ear to ear! His luck hadn't abandoned him at all! In fact, it had turned him into a hero!

"Have my travel kit prepared and have Chan gather our best men and our fastest horses. We leave for the North within the hour!" He ordered. "We're going to save my bride!"

* * *

The black palanquin had been traded for a black carriage with black horses. The two red-skinned men were now its drivers, and they took it through the hills west of White Fox Town at a leisurely rate, trying not to disturb their passenger's rest.

When it reached the next crossroads, there were three men on horseback waiting for it. One tall and thin, the other fat in orange robes, and the third a silent man in red amour. The tall thin man rode forward to stand alongside the carriage window.

"Your orders, my lady?" Last Brother Shou asked.

"Ride north," came the soft voiced reply as a scroll appeared from the carriage window for him. "Deliver this."

"Of course, my lady."

"And Shou?"

"Yes?"

"Get me the bride as well."

"Ahh...Yes, my lady." Shou hesitated, as if wondering whether to add something more, and then continued. "But, can I request more men? We don't know the route she will take and there is much land to cover."

"No." She answered. "I need them for my plans here. However, don't worry Shou, I've already seen to it that you'll have all the help you'll need. After you deliver the scroll, you only need to go to the Safflower Inn at Mount Fung and wait. She will come to you."

"She will?" Shou was unable to hide his surprise.

"Yes," the Lady said. "By the ones she will trust most- the Cho Family Armed Escort Agency."

CHAPTER SEVEN

Encounter at the Inn

Sister Cat had been waiting for some time when Little Gou appeared.

He was riding a beautiful black stallion using one of the finest leather saddles the Sister had ever seen and leading another even larger horse of impressive breeding behind him. With careful confidence he led the horses up to the front stoop of the Sunset Pine inn and hopped off, never letting go of the reins.

"Good evening, Sister! Can I interest you in a moonlight ride?"

The nun laughed, stepping out from the inn's torch-lit front porch to take the reins he offered. "Brother Gou, they're beautiful!" She said in amazement as she looked at the animals. "Wherever did you get them?"

"Give me a minute, Sister. I'll be right back." Gou announced and bounded off into the inn.

Sister Cat heard a woman's squeal of delight from somewhere upstairs in the inn, and then a rather sour noise followed, all this being punctuated by the sound of something ceramic breaking against a wall. Gou reappeared carrying a bag shortly after.

"All ready to go!" He said cheerfully.

The Sister cocked an eyebrow at him. "Miss Violet? I thought you were breaking it off with her last month?"

Gou shrugged as he attached the bag to one of the hooks on his horse's saddle. "Oh, I'm pretty sure we're done now."

"Yes, I imagine you are. Duck."

The last word registered just in time for Gou to dodge a chamber pot aimed straight for his head. It splashed and clattered onto the gravel road.

"You jerk!" Miss Violet called down from the second-floor window. "You pig! I hope your children stink!"

"They don't call her Violent Violet for nothing," Gou commented out of the side of his mouth as he smiled up at the upset young woman and gave her a flourishing bow. "Sorry my dear," Gou called up to her. "Give my regards to Big Li, or was it Fat Chow whose coin purse you caressed last night?"

Violet glared down at him, her eyes filled with death, then she grabbed her window's shutters and slammed them closed.

Snickering as he lightly flipped up onto his horse, Gou looked over at the Sister, who was eying hers with trepidation. "He won't bite."

"Yes, I know. But..." The sister hesitated. "I worry I'm hurting him when I ride."

"Sister, you're big, but not that big. I asked for the strongest horse in the stable, and trust me, that's one heck of a horse. Still, I won't blame you if you want to quit now- I can have one of elder brother's kids take the horse back."

The sister, who was nearly half again Gou's height, gingerly pulled herself up and into the saddle, making her horse grunt a bit at the sudden increase in weight on its back and shift around. That only lasted for a moment however, and then it was calm again.

Gou suppressed a laugh at the poor nun, who was clinging to the horse like she expected to fall off at any moment. There were few things in the world Sister Cat feared, but riding horses somehow seemed to be one of them. He resolved to try and stick to flat roads as much as possible, at least for the first part of the journey.

"Do we have any idea where to look first?" The Sister asked, trying to distract herself.

"I got a map from Teng, and we can worry about that when we hit Green Rapids Town." Gou brought his horse around like an expert rider. "Right now, we're just going to ride north. We can't go too fast at night, but we'll see how we do."

"Oh. Tenacious Teng?" Cat exclaimed as she coaxed her horse around to face the same way his did. "Is he our benefactor?"

Gou nodded. "His new wife owes me a few favors, and she convinced him to help us. These are two of the best horses in his stable."

"His wife?" The nun said suspiciously. "And, what relationship did you have with her?"

Gou grinned. "Not the kind you're thinking. It was all business."

"Oh?"

"Yeah, and trust me- she got the better part of the deal. It was pure highway robbery."

* * *

As the sun began to rise, Gou and the Sister found themselves riding down a smaller mist-covered trade road in a secluded forested area just off the main routes.

Gou knew it to be a shortcut from his travels, and despite his efforts to make things as easy as possible for the Sister, he had decided the extra time was worth it.

With roosters crowing in the distance, the two dew and sweat soaked riders came around a bend in the road and saw a man dumping wastewater off the roadside just ahead of them. Then the man stretched and walked back into what turned out to be a medium-sized roadside inn and restaurant. Horses and not a few carriages sat in the inn courtyard under the watchful eye of a sleeping stable-boy, and a plume of white smoke puffed from the rear, carrying the smell of breakfast out to all the world around.

"Looks as good a place to take a break as any," Gou commented, and with the Sister's agreement both the sore riders dismounted and woke the sleeping boy to care for their horses.

Grabbing his bag, Gou walked inside the inn's main dining room and surveyed the place- it was a small two-story wooden affair with a large open dining area and big round communal tables. Several of these were already occupied by travelers eager to get moving with the crack of dawn.

The Sister and Gou ordered some breakfast congee, and then took an empty table in the corner near the fireplace to try and get some warmth back in their stiff limbs. While they waited for the food to come, Gou laid his head down on the table and enjoyed the moment of rest.

"I'd forgotten how much I hate riding." He complained. "I'm sore all over."

His stoic companion raised an eyebrow. "For someone who doesn't like it, you're certainly very good at it. Where did you learn to ride, brother?"

Gou turned his head to face her, but still kept his ear to the table and eyes closed. "My family had lots of horses when I was young. My uncle taught me how to ride."

Cat was quite surprised to hear this, as it wasn't Gou's nature to talk much about his past. "Really?" She inquired. "Your family was that rich?"

"Not rich, exactly. More like we didn't need to worry much about food because my father's brothers were pretty wealthy. We lived with them when I was a kid, and my father worked as their bookkeeper. That's why he pushed us all to be scholars, my brothers and I, he thought it was the road to real wealth, not just working on the farm or being a laborer. Not that I cared much, since it was all pretty boring for me. They gave me to Doctor Duan to be his apprentice when they realized I wasn't going to be any kind of merchant." Gou yawned. "He's the one who taught me most of my skills. Of course, if I'd studied them harder instead of gambling maybe I wouldn't have so much trouble settling down."

"Always my problem," he said sleepily. "Get bored too easy and never end up learning anything at all...That's what she always said..."

Sister Cat watched him drift off to sleep with a tender expression on her face, envying him a little since she too would have enjoyed a little sleep but was in far too much pain to even consider it. Instead, she turned to face the fire and let it warm her, feeling the dry heat on her face as she wondered whether she should have come on this trip. It seemed so personal to Gou, and she questioned whether her companionship would really be so welcome once Gou finally found Old Master Mao's daughter. She even questioned a little whether she'd be happy to see them together either, after all she...

The Sister was broken from her thoughts by the sound of a familiar voice from somewhere in the dining hall behind her.

"Innkeeper! Three pork congees and a plate of thousand-year eggs! Oh, and congee for my friends too!" The merry voice laughed at his own joke.

"Yessir! Right away!" The innkeeper replied and vanished into the kitchen.

Sister Cat turned her head slightly to steal a glance across the room, hoping she wouldn't find what she expected. She was disappointed in that regard.

The man who sat at the table in the middle of the room was someone she couldn't miss for a second, not with his girth or his orange robes- Copper Kettle Xiao! He was alone, but she suspected he wouldn't be for long.

Keeping her facing away from him, she let herself slide down so she wouldn't look as tall and gently began to nudge her sleeping companion.

"Brother Gou...Brother Gou, please wake up."

Gou mumbled something, then turned his head to face the other direction.

Sighing and seeing she had no choice; the nun gave him a carefully placed elbow to the side.

That woke him up.

"What? Sister? Huh?" He looked up at her groggily.

"Brother, look at the man in the middle of the room." She whispered, keeping her face towards the wall.

He swung his head around, looking about with narrow eyes. "Oh...Hey, it's.... OH!" He exclaimed and dropped his head back down in his arms again, pretending to be sleeping. He was pretty sure Xiao wouldn't recognize him since their last encounter had been in bad light at a distance, but he wasn't taking any chances.

"Are the others with him?" Gou whispered.

Cat shook her head. "I've neither seen nor heard them, but I would expect they're close by."

"We have to get out of here." Gou sat up and turned around to face the fire. "He's looking right at the front exit, so we'll need to go out the back way."

"But if I move, he's sure to recognize me."

Gou thought a moment. "Wait here."

Then he was gone, disappeared into the back halls of the Inn and leaving the Sister facing the fireplace. Sister Cat sighed and focused on the fire, trying not to move as she wondered what Gou might be up to.

More people continued to flow in for breakfast, and then she heard Xiao call out a friendly welcome. "Brothers! Have a seat! I already ordered for you!"

Stealing a glance back, the nun saw Xiao had been joined by his boss, Last Brother Shou, and the armored ever silent Mah, the Fighting Red General. She let herself sink even lower into her chair as she listened to them talk.

"That's fine." Shou agreed as they sat down. "Something quick- we need to get moving."

"What's the rush?" Xiao put in. "That escort agency's doing the hard work, all we need to do is relax and let them deliver that girl to us."

"It's not about the bride," his boss fished around for a pair of chopsticks from the central holder and began to clean them. "We've got a message for that stuck-up guy. His mansion is near here and we can stop there before we head to the meet-up point."

"Sounds good to me, he's always got a great spread to eat." Xiao agreed. "Speaking of which, where's our food? Waiter! Waiter!"

The waiter, who was rushing past with a tray of food stopped. "Sorry sir, the new boy burnt the congee, it'll be a few more minutes."

Xiao was displeased. "Ain't that congee you got there?"

"Well, yes sir." The waiter said uncomfortably. "But it's for the lady and gentleman over there in the corner. This was the last of the old batch and they did order before you, sir."

"Well, if they say they can wait can I have it?" Copper Kettle asked.

"Oh. Uhhh..." The waiter stammered. "I guess if they don't mind."

"Sure," Xiao laughed. "It'll be no problem. I'll just go ask them. Wait here."

Xiao pushed back his chair, got up, and started to walk towards where the Sister was tensing and preparing to lunge for the staff she'd propped up on the wall nearby. She listened to each heavy step, and felt the floor bend a little as he stopped just on the other side of the table behind her.

"Hey you! Baldie!" Xiao threatened. "I want to talk to you!"

In her head, the Sister was running through the least number of moves to get her out the front door and leave them surprised enough not to follow. Settling on the direct approach she began to shift her arm up to get leverage on the table behind her so she could flip it and use it as a shield between her and Xiao while she made her escape.

Xiao slammed his hand on the table to try to get her attention. "Yo! You sleeping or something?"

Cat was about to make her move when suddenly a voice cried out from behind them.

"Granny! Where are you?" Came a woman's voice. "Oh! There you are!"

Xiao turned to look as a plump kitchen girl came waltzing past him, all smiles. "Good morning sir!" She chimed. "Talking to my gran, are you?"

While Xiao thought of how to reply, the woman walked around to the bewildered Cat's side of the table and gave the surprised nun a wink. "Gran! How many times do I need to tell you to wear your shawl? You may be a nun, but it's no good for you to be out and about like this!"

As Cat croaked out an apology, the woman put a shawl over her head and shoulders, tucking it in so it covered most of her face as well. "Going to catch the death of cold you are! Didn't you feel how nippy it was this morning?" Then she looked over at Xiao. "Yes, sir? Can I help you?"

"Oh," said the suddenly obsequies martial artist. "I was...ahh... Just going to ask if your grandmother wanted me to stoke the fire for her."

The plump girl smiled and shook her head. "That's most kind of you sir! Most kind, isn't it Gran? But the fire's going well and good, thank you. Most kind of you, though."

Xiao nodded his head cordially and gave a wan smile, then returned to his seat, motioning the waiter to deliver his food to the other table.

"I ain't that hungry," he mumbled to his fellows. Shou rolled his eyes to look at the ceiling, and Mah just stared out the window, uncaring.

When the waiter arrived at the table, he gave the kitchen girl a strange look but she just smiled and waved him off. "Take the food to the kitchen, she'll get it there." Then she leaned in next to Cat's ear. "They're not watching anymore. Follow me, and try to look old."

Cat nodded, and tried to look as hunched over and shrunken as she could when the girl lifted her from her chair. She shuffled over to grab her staff from the wall, and then used it as a walking stick as the girl led her with her towards the kitchen entrance.

"Thank you," the nun whispered to her benefactor.

"Thank that sugar lipped friend of yours," the girl said with a tone that both told Cat everything and made her not want to know any more details. "Watch your step, Gran. Don't knock over that chair again."

In this manner Cat was carefully ushered from the dining room and into the back, where Gou was waiting for her just inside the door to the kitchen. He sighed in relief on seeing her and the two of them moved to the back of the restaurant where Cat informed him of what she'd just heard while the kitchen girl busied herself putting their food into a wooden travel case.

"So, they've hired thugs to find Meiyu," Gou said at last. "And these guys are on their way to meet somebody important."

"Isn't that Lady Moonlight?"

Gou shook his head. "Moonlight was there in White Fox Town, she should know everything already. This has got to be someone else. This is either someone they work for, or someone who works for them. Might even be part of the secret society they probably belong to. Three tough weirdos like that don't just gather together on their own."

The Sister nodded in agreement. "So? What are we to do, Brother?"

"I'm thinking." Gou looked around the room for a moment, his forehead wrinkling as it did when he was deep in thought. "Okay. Here's what we're going to do." He said at last. "Sister, I want you to keep riding north. Go until you reach the river crossing at Green Rapids Town and wait for me there. If I'm not there in two days, then keep riding north and try to find her on your own. Stop at the next big city you get to and ask to find the offices of the Mao Family Armed Escort Agency. Tell them who you are, and what's going on."

The Sister's face showed her surprise.

"You're going to follow them?"

"Yep," Gou said, still thinking. "I want to know who's behind all of this. Following them is the best way. I'll catch up with you after I find out. If this guy really is close by then it'll be easy for me to catch up with you before you even get close to Green Rapids. I ride a lot faster than you, remember?"

He gave her a confident smile when he saw her look of disapproval. "Don't worry, I'll be fine. I'll be on them like sticky rice cake. They'll never even know I'm there."

The Sister raised an eyebrow. "I hope you're not too much like sticky rice cake." She said dryly.

"Which part?" Gou said, curious.

"The part which is beaten into a paste and stomped flat."

CHAPTER EIGHT

Water Flower Manor

Having parted from the Sister, Gou made his way west in pursuit of Lady Moonlight's three accomplices. They were delivering a message to someone involved with their plans, and Gou wanted to know who. As each minute passed Gou questioned his choice- his beloved Meiyu was being tracked by an unknown escort agency in the employ of Lady Moonlight and every moment spent trailing these three meant a minute's delay in reaching her. He couldn't be sure that he was making the right choice, but in his gut he felt knowing more about who was causing all this misery was worth the risk.

The morning wore on, and the sun burned away the mist to reveal a blue sky and another hot day. Gou's horse had gone all night, but with the short rest it had at the inn it was tough enough to continue to ride in the day's heat at an even pace. He couldn't risk directly following them, so Gou had to hang back and ask the other people on the road if they had seen the three and which way they'd gone. It wasn't too hard really, not with the odd appearance they cut.

By late afternoon, he ran out of leads in a hilly forested area that had few farms and even fewer travelers. A ride ahead gave him an idea of where they'd vanished, but even when he doubled back, he couldn't find exactly where they'd disappeared to among the many side-roads and trails. Eventually, he decided to try a different approach and stopped at the first house he came across- a woodcutter's hovel with a creek running next to it and a line of black and grey clothes drying in the sun.

He didn't see anyone around, so he just walked up to the front door and rapped on the frame, hoping whoever owned the place was home. He heard banging around inside, and then after a minute the door opened a crack and a bloodshot eye peered out at him.

"Yeah?" Asked the eye. "Whatdaya want?"

Gou gave his best smile and poured on the charm.

"I'm sorry sir, I'm lost and I was hoping to get some directions. I'm a traveler from Hangzhou and came up to visit an old friend without really knowing where I'm going. If you could give me a little assistance, I'd be awfully grateful."

The eye continued to stare at him.

"...And be happy to pay you for your troubles."

At that point the door suddenly sprung open, and an older man stepped out- all smiles. Behind him in the hovel Gou caught sight of an older woman and a young woman about Gou's age looking nervous.

"Young man! Sorry about the reception, we don't get a lot of visitors here and many of the ones who do come through are a little rough." Apologized the woodcutter, hanging up a small axe next to the door. "Not that I'm sayin' this about an upstanding gentleman like yourself, but one can't be too careful these days!"

Gou gestured that it wasn't to be worried about, and got right to the point.

"It's quite all-right good sir. I've been on the road for the past few days and you wouldn't believe some of the characters I've seen. Now, about those directions- are there any large estates with mansions in this area?"

The old man bobbed his head. "Why yes there is, my lord! Just over this rise behind us is Water Flower Manor, it's owned by some gentleman from up north. He comes down here during the winter and sometimes during the rest of the year to relax. His caretaker pays me good money for my wood, he does."

Gou nodded thoughtfully. "That does sound like the friend I'm looking for. Do you know the gentleman's surname?"

"Yi, sir. His family name is Yi. I'm afraid I don't know much more than that, he's a private type and I try not to ask too many questions. Not healthy for our relationship, if you know what I mean."

"Of course." Gou smiled and then reached into his purse to draw out a piece of silver. It was equal to what this man might make in a season, and his eyes went wide as Gou pressed it into his hand. "And how do I get to this estate? It sounds like it might be the one I'm looking for."

The old man proceeded to rattle off a series of roads and trails that Gou might try, and estimated it would take a man on horse maybe an hour to navigate them all. Gou just listened, nodding from time to time to show he understood, and then finally looked up at the hill that backed the woodcutter's hovel.

"Could I see the mansion from there?" He asked, pointing up at the hilltop.

"Oh yes," the old man agreed. He should be able to see it if he climbed to the peak.

"Do you mind taking care of my horse?" Gou asked him. "I'm sore after my long ride and would like to see something besides just trees."

"Of course, sir! Of course!" Smiled the woodcutter and called his daughter out to go and see to Gou's horse. The skinny girl gave him a nervous look and then rushed off before Gou could smile back.

A few quick goodbyes and Gou began to follow the woodcutter's own trail up behind and into the forest. Once he was out of sight, he made use of his lightfoot kung fu and bounded up the hill like a deer, hopping from rock to rock and going up a few rock facings that a normal man would have avoided. Gou reached the summit in record time, and could see out over the slight dip in the land that almost counted as a valley on the other side.

Sure enough, there in the middle was a large estate with cleared lands and a stone walled central compound with a brown tile roof. He could see horses and cows in the pastures behind the manor house, and a few specks of people moving around that he figured for servants. It was too far to get a good look at anything however, and he still couldn't be sure this wasn't one of uncountable similar estates scattered across the land.

With a glance behind him, Gou leapt down from the summit and began to make his way down into the forest heading towards the manor house. His horse would be fine, and another piece of silver would take care of any questions the woodcutters had about his long absence. He was going to get as close as he could, and see what there was to see about Water Flower Manor.

* * *

Gou had been moving cautiously through the forest for about twenty minutes when he stopped to rest a moment under a large tree. It was a stifling late afternoon now, and the heat and humidity were starting to get to him. His clothes were dirty and soaked with sweat, and little rivers ran down his face from his forehead.

He really wasn't much of a woodsman, not spending more time away from civilization than he needed to, but his master had believed in the good old-fashioned methods of making his apprentice work to build stamina. Gou had gathered and cut more than his share of wood in his youth because of this, and learned at least the basics of moving through a forest unnoticed. There was no fun in trailing the village girls unless they didn't know you were there, after all.

These skills did not, however, include much about knowing when others were trailing you, and Gou's first sign he was in trouble was when he became aware of just how quiet the forest around him had become.

He peered about, looking but not seeing anything or anyone which might explain why things were suddenly so quiet. His gut feeling told him he was being watched, but he wasn't sure how to deal with it or what to do. After a time, he decided that unless it was a tiger his best option wasn't running.

"Hello!" He called out, and took a helpless tone. "Is there anyone there? I've gotten lost out here in these woods and need directions!"

There was a moment of silence, and then came a response.

"What's your name!" Called out what might have been a woman's voice from his left.

"I'm Red-Leaf Feng!" Gou lied. "I'm a traveler from Hangzhou on my way to Nanjing! I got separated from my caravan this morning and have been trying to find a farmhouse. Could you tell me where I am?"

"You're in trouble!" Came another similar voice from the bushes to his right. "You're not supposed to be here!"

"Oh. Well...Look, I'm really sorry. Just tell me where I am and I'll be happy to go." Gou answered, doing his best to look confused. When he heard the second voice, he began to suspect what was going on.

"No! You came in, so you gotta stay!" Came a rough order from his right. "We're going to take you in. Start walking where we tell you, and don't stop! If you do, we'll kill you!"

"Yessir!" Gou answered wide-eyed and bobbed his head. "Please don't hurt me, I'm really sorry!"

Then the voices began to give Gou orders, and he turned and walked the way they told him to. He didn't see anyone, but he heard them moving around him- at least four of them were pacing him as he moved through the underbrush and towards the estate. He tried talking to them a few times, but each time was told to shut up by the same bossy voice.

Eventually Gou came out of the underbrush and into the cleared land, walking right out into the gardens and giving two workers quite a shock. Both men came rushing over to him.

"Hey you!" They shouted, and brandished their implements as weapons. Whoever lived here was quite fierce about their privacy.

As the men ran up to him, the voice came again from the forest behind them.

"Hold him men! He's my prisoner!"

The men jumped a little when they heard this, and then relaxed as the owner of the voice exited the forest behind Gou.

"Young master!" They cried out, and then did what the boy said.

Gou turned and looked as they grabbed him, smiling inside to himself at the bravado of the three young boys and a girl who had "captured" him- not a one of them past twelve summers in age. The one referred to as "young master" being a tall freckled youth with a gap-toothed smile and short bowl-cut hair whose clothes marked him as coming from a good family. The others were dressed in simple cotton robes, and Gou pegged them as the servant's children.

"He's a thief," the Young Master announced with pride. "We caught him running around in the forest. I want to take him to father to be punished!"

* * *

Gou knelt in the manor courtyard, taking mental notes about the place while the nervous servants stood guard over him. So far, this place looked like nothing but a typical wealthy merchant's home- a kind Gou was most familiar with from his many invitations to nights of drinking and gambling.

It wasn't long before the boy appeared, a large muscled man in fine blue robes in tow. Gou knew he was a martial artist the moment he saw him, and not one of low skill either from the way he moved. He had a large handlebar mustache and bushy black eyebrows that furrowed together as he saw Gou kneeling there looking nervous.

"See father! Just as I said! I caught a thief!" The boy stopped next to Gou and pointed at the gambler.

"Sir," the father asked in a polite but commanding tone. "What is your surname?"

Gou reiterated what he'd told the Young Master earlier- he was Red-Leaf Feng from Hangzhou and had gotten lost. "I'm really sorry sir!" Gou kowtowed and let his head bang against the gravel in mock fear. "I didn't know I was doing something wrong by coming on your land!"

"You idiot!" The master of the house screamed, full of rage.

It was only when the Young Master hit the ground a short distance away that Gou was aware that the anger wasn't directed towards him. Then in a flash the master of the house was on one knee in front of Gou, lifting him up and brushing him off.

"Mister Feng, I am very sorry." He said apologetically. "I have indulged my son too often, and this is the price I pay. Please let me make amends."

"Oh, sir. It's nothing. Really." Gou answered in deep awe. "I don't want to trouble you."

"My surname is Yi, and this is my home." Yi said with sincerity. "A home in which you are now an honored guest. Dinner is just being prepared; let my servants get you some clean clothes and then you can join us. My wife and I so rarely get visitors, and I haven't been to Hangzhou in years. It would be a great favor to us if you could tell us of the recent goings-on there."

Master Yi had a way of making people feel like they were the most important person in the world to him, and even Gou was drawn in a little by the man's charm. He started to think he'd made a mistake, and was feeling a little bad for all the tales he was spinning. Still, in for a penny, in for a pound, he decided. He wasn't going to turn down a good meal so politely offered.

"Of course, Master Yi." Gou answered. "I'd be happy to tell you everything I can."

"Good! Good!" Yi clapped Gou's shoulder and summoned a house servant with a wave. "Take care of him, please." He ordered, and then returned his gaze to Gou. "If you'll excuse me, I have business to attend to. See you at dinner, dear friend."

Gou thanked him again, and then Master Yi left. The servant gesturing for Gou to follow, which he did after sparing a glance back at the Young Master crying in the dirt. One of the servant boys tried to comfort him, and got a kick for his troubles.

* * *

Gou enjoyed the long soak in the cold spring-fed manor bathhouse. It really helped his muscles relax and took away some of the soreness of the last day. The kids had gotten him in perfectly- now he just needed to ask the right questions and poke around a little on the inside. If there was any sign of the three, he would know he had the right place and be a step ahead of them. He also wondered how Master Yi was connected to all of this, but there were limits to what he could ask under his assumed identity.

Deciding it was enough, Gou washed his hair and mouth and slipped from the tub into the cotton blankets the servants used as bath sheets to dry him off. Finally, he was given brown silk robes and sandals to wear and led through the mansion to meet the family for dinner. The manor was well decorated with many hanging scrolls done by master calligraphers and Gou found himself pausing at one that looked familiar.

"An original Wu Song," Master Yi commented from behind him. "I had him write it in honor of my previous wife. She loved his poems very much, and I wanted something to comfort her towards the end."

Gou nodded. "I've seen ones done by some of his students. If you don't mind me asking, was she the Young Master's mother?"

Master Yi sighed. "Yes. He's been nothing but trouble since her death. I'm really not sure what to do with him sometimes. Please forgive him for this afternoon, won't you?"

"It's already forgotten, my lord." Gou said, making it clear he held no bad feelings. "Boys will be boys."

Yi smiled. "Yes, they will. Well, soon he'll be old enough to be sent to school for some discipline. We'll make a man out of him yet." He gestured down the hallway. "Are you hungry Mister Feng? Please come this way."

Gou followed his host down the hall, noting the other expensive art objects that were being used as simple decorations. Whoever Master Yi was, he wasn't poor by any stretch of the imagination. Gou almost wondered if he could interest him in a game of something, but that would require more time than he had.

"This is my summer and winter home," Yi told him as they toured the manor. "I come here when I don't have business to attend to in the North, or when things get too cold for my tastes. I was born in the South and can't quite get used to the winters up around the capital. Of course, it would take so long to get to my family home in Guangdong that I have to settle for a place here halfway between. It is a little secluded, but I don't mind the break from the crowds."

"Yes, of course." Gou agreed. "I never go farther north than Nanjing, and only in the summertime when it's warmer. Can I ask my lord's profession?"

Master Yi laughed. "Just a businessman, Mister Feng! So, you can stop calling me "my lord", just Mister Yi will do. I'm no noble and I don't care much for titles."

"Yes, sir."

"Now then," he said as they approached the end of the hall. "I hope you like quail, because my hunters brought back several of them this morning. I had my cook stuff and roast them for dinner. He's quite a man. I brought him down from the capital because he can make a fine meal out of anything you can name."

Then Yi pushed open the doors and led Gou into the dining hall.

"Just make yourself at home, Mister Feng. I'm sure we'll have an interesting evening, and there'll be much to talk about."

"I'm sure there will be, Mister Yi." Gou answered as he found himself staring at the three other guests at Master Yi's table, each one of them as familiar as they were deadly. "I'm sure there will be."

CHAPTER NINE

Mrs. Yi

Master Yi ushered Gou into the dining hall and began to introduce him to the other guests, unaware that Gou knew each of them already. Last Brother Shou was cold but cordial, Copper Kettle Xiao was friendly and welcoming, and Mah the Fighting Red General wasn't wearing his armor for once. He was actually quite a noble figure out of it, clad in high quality brown and green robes, and Gou wouldn't have recognized him unless he'd been introduced by name.

None of them seemed to recognize Gou, which was natural since they'd met under bad light conditions atop a rooftop some weeks earlier. There was no reason for any of them to suspect the man in front of them was the same man who had foiled their attempts to ambush a courier, or was actively working against them to protect a bride-to-be from becoming a pawn of one of their masters.

Gou didn't make any effort to hide his nervousness, and did his best to appear slightly awed at all of this and quite honored to meet everyone, including the well-dressed beauty that Master Yi introduced as his wife. She was a cool and thoughtful looking young woman, with high cheeks and a long-pointed face that ended in a sharp chin. She gave him a curious raised eyebrow as she greeted him, as though she were trying to remember something. Gou just gave her a polite nod and then was ushered into his seat next to Mah, and at Master Yi's right-hand side.

Dinner began with an exchange of introductions, and from there the talk was more general and cultural- life in the capital, business and trade (or lack thereof) and the current state of political unrest were all discussed with great gusto. Most of this was over Gou's head, but he listened intently when others talked and gave his own small opinions when he felt it appropriate. In truth, he knew a great deal more on the topics than he let on, but felt playing dumb was worth the cover it gave him- he was nothing more than a merchant's son from the bustling city of Hangzhou. That is, until the conversation took a most interesting turn.

"Master Yi," Xiao asked during the last course. "What do you think our chances are at the gathering? Will the other groups follow us?"

Gou's ears perked up.

Master Yi stroked his mustache. "I would say they will. I've been to see the other chiefs, and they have all agreed that something must be done. Many of them have pledged their support to me in the coming vote."

"I don't trust them." Shou put in. "They talk from both sides of their mouths."

Yi smiled. "It's the nature of politics, my friend. Oh, but we shouldn't leave our guest in the dark. I'm sorry Mister Feng."

Gou indicated that it was quite alright, but Yi continued.

"I am a leading figure in a trade guild, and as you must know from your own business dealings, local guilds often belong to national ones. Every year there's a gathering of guild leaders for our particular business to discuss ways we can help each other and to resolve disputes. Guilds are like any family, they need leadership, but they don't always agree on who the leader is. Our particular guild society has a change in national leadership coming, but it hasn't been decided who will be the new leaders. I've put my own humble person forward as a candidate, but another group has done the same and now we're bartering favors with the others. It's a dreadful business, really."

Gou nodded, understanding more than was being said. "With such a kind and generous man as Master Yi as a candidate," he offered. "I'm sure the other group leaders will see the light."

"Well said! Well said!" Copper Kettle Xiao and Last Brother Shou agreed, and toasts were made to Master Yi's good fortune in the coming elections.

"Now, about your problem Mister Feng." Yi told them. "My colleagues here are riding out in the morning. They'll help to see if we can't find your caravan, and if you don't, they can see you get an escort to Nanjing. Never let it be said that the Black Dragon Armed Escort Agency didn't get a man to his destination safely. I'll see you have a comfortable room for the night."

* * *

Full of good wine and good food, Gou was more than ready to retire for the night, especially having not slept in nearly a full day. This made it even harder to stay awake, but he balanced that against the thought of being forced to ride with the deadly trio in the morning and the people who were counting on him. He wanted to take a short nap, but couldn't be sure he wouldn't wake up with the cock crowing and the sun in his face.

Thus, tired but wide awake, Gou let the sounds of the manor house fall silent as its occupants drifted off to sleep and waited for his chance. When he was sure it was late into the night and enough time had passed, Gou crept to his window and peered out. The moon was high and bright, and he had a good view of the situation. He was on the manor's second floor, but it was a quick drop for him to the courtyard below and then he'd be across and over the walls in an instant. Waiting, he saw a guard walk by after a short time, checking on things, and then disappear around a corner.

Gou's first impulse was to take that moment and jump, but with his life in the balance he decided to take the safe bet and wait. He let his eyes continue to adjust, and the sounds and smells of the courtyard fill his senses. After a few more minutes, he heard a cough from a shadowed woodpile in the corner. He'd been right to suspect Master Yi of being a careful man- there was a secret security blind there, and someone was watching the yard from it. If he'd leapt down as intended, he would have been caught for sure.

Aware of this, Gou settled in and considered what to do next. He could try the roof, but there would likely be loose tiles or even traps up there to catch unwary visitors, and the idea of sliding off into some spiked pit below did little for him. He needed to think up another way out- but how?

Then, as Gou considered his options, there was a crack of light from the house to the courtyard below, and soon a figure began walking across the courtyard right towards the woodpile blind. In the moonlight, Gou could see it was a woman- a servant from the look of her robes, and she was carrying a tray.

As Gou watched she walked up to the side of the woodpile and knocked. This was followed by the sound of wood banging and a squeak as some door was opened and she began to talk to someone inside the blind.

It was a drink delivery! The guard was being given tea by one of the servants, which would keep him distracted for a few moments. Gou couldn't believe his luck! Smiling to himself, he prepared to use his lightfoot kung fu to drop down from the window without a sound and dash to the wall.

Just before he made the leap, however, motion caught his eye and he saw another shadow burst from one of the windows to his right. It floated down to the ground like a gliding bird- showing its own considerable lightfoot skills- and then moved quickly across the courtyard and over the wall.

Not missing a moment, Gou was out the window and in hot pursuit. He assumed the servant was working for whoever he'd just seen go out, and Gou wasn't one to waste an opportunity regardless of its source. He was also curious, wanting to know where the shadow was going- the more secrets of this place he knew, the better a position he figured he'd be in.

Gou followed the shadow from a distance through the late-summer fields and into the forest beyond. In the cool night it was easier to move, and Gou found the energy to keep up with the shadow welling up within him. His second wind let him get through the forest without making much noise, and although at one point he was sure he'd lost his prey, it was then that he heard a birdcall off to his left that he guessed for a secret sign.

Creeping as silently as he could through the forest, Gou approached the sound of the call, stopping when he heard low voices talking. Unable to quite make out what they were saying, he snuck forward towards them until he found himself looking out into a clearing.

Under the moonlight, two women standing in the clearing spoke to each other in hushed voices. One of them Gou recognized as the daughter of the woodcutter he'd left his horse with; the other was wearing a thin white veil and Gou was sure this one was the shadow he'd been following from the house.

"Take this message, sister." The veiled one offered a leather-wrapped scroll. "See to it that the mistress gets it. Our worst fears are realized."

"Are you in danger, my lady?" Asked the woodcutter's daughter.

"No." The woman shook her head. "He suspects nothing. If he did, I would be dead already. But I worry about the stranger that came to our house today- my husband's son caught him here in the forest and he said he's a lost traveler, but I think I may have seen him before somewhere."

The woodcutter's daughter gasped. "He said he was a friend of your husband's and left his horse with my father. We'd begun to wonder what happened to him. He was looking for your home, my lady. He's no lost traveler."

"I see," said Mrs. Yi. "I believe I will have a word with my husband about him in the morning. The right phrase and they'll drag the truth out of him quick enough. If he's from one of the other agencies here to spy on us, we'll find out who. He doesn't matter though, all that's important is that letter, so please see the courier gets it. Our mistress's life is in danger."

"It will be done." The woodcutter's daughter answered and bowed, then turned and began to make her way back through the forest.

Mrs. Yi watched her go, and then began her own return, but before she could get far snickering laughter broke the silence. Spinning around, the woman instantly had a throwing dagger in each hand and was poised to throw them at the source of the laughter.

"Show yourself!"

Gou heard a crunching of leaves just behind the bush in which he was hiding, and was stock still as someone walked right past him.

"Shou! I might have known!" Mrs. Yi spat. "Did my husband send you?"

"Send me?" Last Brother Shou asked lightly. "I'm just out for a walk. Why else would I be here? Beautiful night, isn't it?"

"Don't play the fool with me, Shou." She cursed. "Tell me what you want."

"Well now, that's the problem isn't it? My senior's wife is a spy for his enemies, and it's my duty to tell him. Unless you have something to offer me to keep me quiet?"

"You can't prove that!" Mrs. Yi asserted. "If you say anything, I'll just deny it."

From somewhere up the night-time hill, a girl screamed in horror, and then the scream came to a sudden end.

"Your letter." Shou commented. "Will be all the proof I need."

"You bastard!" Mrs. Yi didn't wait another breath before attacking with all her fury. In a split second, the throwing daggers were airborne, and so was she, coming at him right behind them with a hidden sword aimed for Shou's heart!

Shou's own blade arced out and around, knocking the daggers aside as he twisted to avoid her follow-up attack. The two of them then began to fall into a dance of moves and countermoves, but it took only a few moves to know who the superior fighter was. Despite Mrs. Yi's obvious great skill with the martial arts, she wasn't in Shou's league, and it was clear the sinister swordsman was playing with her more than fighting her.

In a few more moves, he would disarm her and then it would be over.

Unless Gou intervened, that was.

Grabbing a nearby stick, since he wasn't armed, Gou let out a battle cry and leapt from the bush at Shou as noisily as he could. Of course, Shou turned and looked at him in surprise, and that was just the moment Mrs. Yi needed to launch her attack. Realizing his position, Shou immediately used his lightfoot kung fu to leap out of the way and landed in a nearby part of the clearing to face both of them.

Mrs. Yi looked at Gou in shock. "Why are you here?" She demanded.

"To save you!" He told her. "You need to come with me."

Shou decided that was the moment to attack again, and in a flash, Gou was dodging and weaving along with Mrs. Yi, using the stick to ward off Shou's attacks and trying to give Yi the chance she needed to get a blow in on their opponent. Neither side could quite get the advantage and while the two of them were enough to keep Shou at bay, neither was enough to defeat him. It was a losing game, and Gou knew it- all Shou needed was to tag one of them and the odds would be back in his favor.

"He's got reinforcements coming. We have to get out of here!" Gou told Mrs. Yi.

"That's fine, but how?" Came her response as she barely avoided one of Shou's powerful strikes.

Gou agreed, and he desperately looked for any chance to give them the moment of breathing they needed to escape.

"You! I recognize you now!" Shou yelled. "You're that meddler with the nun! You ran away with the box!"

"Guilty as charged," Gou answered. "But don't worry, she's not here right now so you don't need to be afraid."

"I'm not afraid of her!" Shou shifted his focus to Gou again, his anger boiling over. "I'm going to send her that tongue of yours to prove it!"

It wasn't much, but causing Shou to lose his concentration got Mrs. Yi the moment she needed and she attacked- striking Shou in the hip and leaving a nasty gash in his leg that was spraying blood within moments. Shou let out a cry of pain and immediately retreated back out of sword-range again, stumbling as the pain from his leg hit him.

Mrs. Yi moved to leap in and finish him, but Gou grabbed her arm. Even wounded, this man wouldn't be easy to finish off, and he had other concerns.

"His friends are coming, and we can't beat them all. Let's go!"

Mrs. Yi cursed and turned to run away with Gou, but not before firing off more daggers which the wounded Shou still managed to deflect.

They left him screaming obscenities into the night as they raced through the forest.

"Where are we going?" Mrs. Yi demanded.

"I have a horse at the woodcutter's home. We can use it to escape." Gou told her. "We'll double back and up over the hill to the house. That is, if you're ready to leave your husband." He added that last part as both a question and a test.

Mrs. Yi snorted. "That pig. I'll have to wash for weeks just to get the stink of him off me."

* * *

Copper Kettle Xiao strolled into the clearing, carrying the unconscious woodcutter's daughter over his shoulder and the message scroll in his hand. He looked down at Shou and whistled as he saw the wound, earning him a sharp look from Shou, who was rubbing salve over the wound in an effort to stop the bleeding.

"It was that damn Feng, or whatever his name is. He was the one with the nun." Shou commented as he worked. "He must be working for the Mao family and followed us up here."

Xiao considered this, then asked, "So, what do we do?"

"Do?" Shou spat as he tied a cloth over the wound. "I'll tell you what we do! We find that spy and give her to Yi, then we get that guy and make him suffer. I promised to cut out his tongue, and I will."

"How do we find him?"

Shou pulled himself to his feet, using his scabbard as a walking stick. "He's been following us, so he probably knows about the Lady's orders. We just need to find that bride and we'll find him. No waiting for that escort agency she duped- we're going to find her ourselves."

* * *

"Where are we going?!?" Mrs. Yi shouted into Gou's ear as their horse raced along the midnight road. They'd stopped just long enough to grab his horse and warn the woodcutter and his wife to clear out- Gou had told them their daughter was killed by bandits that had attacked the mansion. It was a lie, but probably easier to deal with than the truth of her end. It also got them moving quick enough. Mrs. Yi had also given them some money before they left, showing great sympathy that surprised Gou.

"North!" Yelled Gou over the wind and thunderous hooves. "We have to meet a friend of mine at Green Rapids Town! I'll let you off between here and there!"

"Who are you really?"

"I'll tell you when we have a chance to rest!"

"Fine!" The woman yelled back, but her hand felt for the pack on her leg containing her remaining throwing daggers. She would give him a chance to explain, she decided, and if she didn't like what she heard... She slipped a dagger into her sleeve, ready for when the moment came.

CHAPTER TEN

A Roadside Meeting

After she parted from Little Gou, Sister Cat followed his instructions as best she could. Not used to traveling long distances on horseback, much less doing it by herself, the Sister took it as slowly as possible. She followed the directions other travelers gave her until she reached a main trade road by noon of the day she parted from Gou and began to follow it. It was filled with the travelers that late summer brings out- artisans, farmers and merchants all eager to sell their wares and start stocking up for the coming winter.

Farmers lined the roadside, each with a table or blanket covered in fresh fruits, vegetables, preserves and crafts they hoped to sell to make a few extra coins. Those with watermelons made quick money from travelers seeking refreshment from the heat, and others who had set up shady stalls made similar money serving cool drinks of tea and plum. In many ways it reminded Cat of a festival atmosphere, and she did her best to enjoy the sights and sounds and not think about the horse moving under her.

At last, in the mid-afternoon heat she gave into her weariness and stopped to enjoy a cool watermelon herself. Using the money Gou had given her, she purchased it and found a nice shady spot under a tree for herself and her horse. There, she sat and watched the travelers go by, wondering how Gou was doing and whether she should have gone with him or perhaps gone in his place. His going made sense- he was the better rider and better at sneaking around than she, but still she worried how he'd manage against those three if he found himself cornered. One was more than dangerous enough, but three of them would be quite the set of odds for even him to escape.

As she considered this, she heard a rumbling from up the road the way she had come and turned her gaze to join the people around her stretching their necks out to get a good look. The rumbling soon resolved itself into a tightly packed group of horsemen, perhaps twenty in number, all of them armed and wearing fierce and determined looks on their faces. But, what most caught Cat's attention was the lead rider- and his bright shock of white hair!

Upon seeing the watermelon stand, the man signaled to his riders to slow and directed them to the side of the road. One of his men, a short, ugly and misshapen man who seemed out of place with the other big, cleanly muscled riders flipped off his horse like an acrobat and bounded across the distance to the surprised farmer.

"Ten Watermelons!" The short man exclaimed and tossed coins on the table in front of him. "Cut each in eight."

The farmer hesitated. "Sir, if'n you do that you won't be able to carry them back. You sure you don't want them whole?"

The little man gave a wry smile. "I'm sure, my good man. Don't worry about it. Just place them here in front of me."

While the farmer and his son set to work cutting the watermelons, Cat watched this strange little man begin to draw thin wires from his pocket and loop them around his fingers. When the first watermelon was placed in front of him, his skinny hands suddenly swept over the chopped-up melon in a blurred motion and then picked it up. The Sister expected it to fall apart, but was amazed to see it was now again completely intact! The man then motioned back to another of the riders who came up to fetch it from him and take it back while he waited for the next melon.

Impressed by this small man's obvious martial skills, Cat was about to step forward and ask him about it when she heard a voice call to her.

"Good Sister!"

Cat turned as Snowtop Cho dismounted and marched his way over to her.

"Hello there!" He said as he rushed up. "My apologies. I didn't see you there at first! I wasn't expecting to find you here!"

"Good day to you as well, Brother Cho." The Sister stood up and bowed deeply to him. "Buddha has seen to our meeting on this day."

Cho smiled brightly. "Yes, yes he has. On a temple pilgrimage, are you?"

For a moment, Cat considered telling him the truth, but with everything that was going on she decided that caution was the watchword of the day and merely smiled and nodded. "I am indeed. There are many temples in the North I have not seen since I came to the mainland from Taiwan."

"Good. Good." Cho nodded, peering around. "That would explain why I don't see Gou with you. Got tired of him, did you?"

Again, the Sister did her best to smile. "Brother Gou is most difficult to keep up with."

Cho laughed. "I always said that Gou would tire even a saint's patience! Looks like I got proven right!" Then he noticed the watermelon being offered to him by the short man, who had now appeared at Cho's side. "Oh, thank you Chan."

"You're welcome, Young Master." Chan replied, then looked up at the Sister, who was nearly three times his height. "Young Master?"

"Yes, Chan?"

"Are fairies allowed to become nuns?"

Cho raised an eyebrow and looked down at Chan. "I don't know. Why do you ask?"

"Because I think a fairy from the mountains has taken the form of a nun and is standing before me."

"What?" Cho looked at him confused a moment, then looked at the equally puzzled Cat. "What do you...? Oh!" Cho grinned broadly as he suddenly understood what Chan meant. "Sister Cat, allow me to introduce "Spider" Chan. Chan, this nun is a friend of Little Gou."

Still not sure what had just happened, Sister Cat gave a forced smile to the small man, who grinned back up at her impishly.

"I always knew Gou had good taste in friends. Pleased to meet you, Sister. If you ever get tired of being a nun, please let me be the first to know!"

"Chan, behave yourself." Cho sighed. "I'm sorry sister. He gets this way around tall women. Don't let him bother you, he's mostly harmless."

"O-oh. I see." Said the Sister- trying to avoid Chan's gaze and turning a little red. "So. Ah. Brother Cho, where are you riding to?"

"North. Toward Nanjing." Said Cho as he produced a knife. "I have business that way. Excuse me, Sister." And with that he ran the tip of the knife across the surface of the otherwise perfectly intact watermelon. As he did there was a "ping" sound and a wire so thin it was like a silk thread suddenly dropped away, allowing the watermelon to show its cut seams again. Cho withdrew a slice and offered it to the Sister.

"Thank you," Cat accepted it, and then bent down to look closely at the watermelon's surface. All across the melon there was a network of those wires, and the melon even stayed intact while pieces were removed due to the skill of the person who put them there. Cat was awed by the skill this showed, it was far more than even she had first suspected when she'd seen Chan work. "This is truly incredible." She stated, and looked over at Chan with new admiration.

Chan, for his part, winked at her slyly. "You should see what I can do with rope."

"Oh?" Said the innocent Sister. "Are you talented with ropes as well?"

Seeing where this could go, Cho quickly put a stop to it. "Chan is from one of the mountain villages in Sichuan. They're master weavers, and he's the son of one of the town elders. If you need someone alive, he's the best there is in our business. Letting him near rope or string is like giving a swordsman his favorite blade back."

Chan laughed self-consciously. "Don't listen to the Young Master, Sister. I just know a few monkey tricks, that's all."

"Since we're all going the same way, honored lady. Why don't you ride with us?" Cho asked her as they continued to eat and talk. "It'll be our honor to escort you for a while, and you can tell me how Gou's doing. We used to be close when we were young, but we've drifted over the years."

Tired of riding alone and looking forward to having someone to talk to, the Sister agreed. However, she soon regretted her decision, as the riders were going much faster than she liked, and for some reason Spider Chan always seemed to be next to her no matter how fast or slow she rode.

* * *

As night settled, Snowtop's party reached a large town nestled into the side of a small mountain. They knew they were approaching the town from the songs and music that started as the sun had settled and echoed into the creeping night. Firecrackers popped and gongs sounded as they approached the walled town, and they could see red and gold banners bearing the double character for happiness raised high on each house as they rode through the open front gate.

"This isn't a wedding, it's a festival." Snowtop observed as they rode among the people that filled the streets. "You there!" He called down to a nearby man.

"Yes, sir?" Answered the man, nervous at having gotten the attention of this armed party.

"What's the occasion?"

Suddenly more at ease, the man laughed. "Oh! The son of the town chief is getting married, sir! He's throwing a huge party for the whole town! Hey, you fellahs need an inn? My cousin runs one over near the east gate- good food and clean rooms."

Snowtop looked at Chan, who shrugged. Then he glanced at the Sister who nodded that it was fine with her.

"Alright then." Cho told him. "Show us the way."

The man grabbed the bridle on Cho's horse and began to lead them, obviously an experienced horseman himself. "You won't regret it, sir! With so many visitors here tonight, the inns will fill up fast, and with such a large group it'll be tough to find a place once the party starts to wind down. Why, when you're done settling in, I'm sure you'll be welcome to join the party. Folks around here are pretty friendly, and everyone's happy during a wedding, right?"

Snowtop just grunted in agreement, not wanting to encourage the man and letting him talk as they were led through the stone streets of the town. Eventually they did indeed reach an inn that was neither very new nor old, and looked like the owners might be having some success in their business. Snowtop was actually surprised by this, having expected to find a place which even the town rats were too good to frequent.

The innkeeper's wife greeted them and had their horses taken to the stables in an instant, then got all of the tired men of the party rooms and meals in short order. The Sister noticed that as they drank in the common room Chan wandered from table to table, checking on Cho's men and teasing the ones who were drinking wine good-naturedly. At first, she thought he was being playful, but she quickly realized that underneath his good cheer he was in fact reminding the men not to drink too much. She'd been surprised to learn that Chan was in fact Snowtop's second-in-command, and despite the physical size difference these rough and tumble men of the Cho Family Armed Escort Agency respected him a good deal.

At last, the men began to scatter, most of them heading for the front door and out into the celebrating town to enjoy the festivities. Chan returned to the table where the Sister and Cho sat, and dropped with a thud into an empty seat.

"I told them we ride at first light, Young Master." Chan said withdrawing a small leather pouch from his tunic. "They'll be ready."

"Good work, Chan." Snowtop nodded, satisfied. "Our mission leaves little time for rest but they deserve some tonight. It was a long ride."

"Very thoughtful, Young Master."

As the Sister watched, Chan opened the leather pouch, took out a pinch of green and red dried plants and popped them into his mouth. All of a sudden, the air was filled with an overpowering spicy smell, and the Sister's nose wrinkled in distaste.

Noticing the sister's discomfort, Cho said, "Chan, must you chew that in here? On the road is fine, but not everyone shares your love for that noxious weed."

"Sorry master," Chan moved back a little. "I just need a little pick-up after a hard day. Apologies to you too, Sister."

"It's quite alright," said the nun, doing her best to ignore the smell for politeness sake. "But, what is it you're eating?"

"My own special blend," Chan said, pouring out a little more of the dried leaves into his hand to show her. "Sichuan Goat Weed and Flower Peppers. It keeps a man up all night and always ready to ride." Then he leaned in and winked, "So, if you need me during the night, don't hesitate to call."

"Ahh, yes..." The Sister said, feeling uncomfortable again, and then to change the subject, she began to make inquiries into why they were in such a rush.

"Brother Cho, can I ask the nature of your mission?"

Cho looked at her a moment, smiling wistfully. "I suppose there isn't much harm in telling you- we're riding to meet a caravan coming down from the North. A very important caravan. It holds my future, in fact."

"Oh, I see." Said the Sister, thinking a moment.

"Why do you ask?" Snowtop put in, seeing her concern.

"Well," Cat hesitated. "I was going to ask your help in a matter. I'm not sure that Brother Gou would agree, but we're in a bit of a bind and I was hoping you might be able to give us some assistance. However, if you're busy with such an important mission I can hardly ask you to take time away from it."

"Oh?" Cho leaned in, interested. "Something personal to Gou? Now, that is interesting. Tell me more Sister. If there's anything I can do for my old friend, I'm more than welcome to consider it..."

Cat hesitated. She knew Gou wouldn't approve, but Cho was an old friend of his and despite their rivalry it was clearly in his interests to know that young Miss Mao was being targeted by such fierce opponents. Cho could in fact help, after all- who better to help fight against an armed escort agency than another one of their kind? Thinking it through, Cat decided that it would be wrong not to tell Snowtop what was going on.

"Brother Cho..." She began to say to keen, waiting ears, but never got the chance to finish- one of Snowtop's men came bursting into the dining hall like there was a ghost at his back.

"Young Master! Young Master!" He cried, and made straight for the table where the three of them stood involuntarily in surprise.

"What is it, Han?" Cho asked.

"Sir," said the breathless man. "Bandits are raiding the wedding!"

Cho and Chan glanced at each other.

"My sword," Cho ordered and Chan snatched it up from where it lay on the table to offer it to his young master. Slipping the scabbard through his belt, Cho turned to tell the Sister that he'd return shortly once this mess was dealt with- but found an empty seat. The Sister was already gone!

"It seems we're late for the party, Young Master." Said Chan with a smile.

"I begin to see what Gou likes in that nun," Cho agreed as they started after her.

* * *

For Sister Cat, the man's words had barely registered before she'd grabbed her staff and leapt across the room and out the door. Her feet only tapped the cobblestones and as she raced through the town streets; she could now hear screams up ahead and the sound of men shouting and horses whinnying. It didn't take long before she reached the town square and found herself at the rear of a crowd driven to the square's edges, but too fascinated by what they saw to leave.

Luckily, Sister Cat was more than tall enough to see over that crowd and had a clear picture of what was happening beyond. The middle of the square was indeed filled with roughly dressed men that few could mistake for being anything but bandits. There were over fifty of them, and perhaps twenty of those rode on horseback- most of these riding along the edges of the open center of the square and slashing at the air in front of the crowd to keep them frightened and contained.

In the middle of the square was a knot of people- the well-dressed wedding party who had been herded there by the bandits. A fat old man stood protecting the party, likely the mayor of the town, and behind him was the groom. The terrified new bride in red was hiding behind her future husband's broad shoulders.

Already this situation struck Cat as being odd- bandits raided and attacked without care, they didn't sort and organize their targets like these men were doing. This almost seemed more like a military occupation than a bandit raid, with the troops controlling the crowd but not taking their plunder and waiting for orders from a leader before any action was made.

The leader in question, a large bushy-faced man clad in worn pieces of military armor, dismounted his horse before the wedding party.

"I am Green Mountain Cai!" Shouted the man to the surrounding crowd, waving an oversized nine-ringed saber in the air. "All of you know me! I rule the hills to the south and you pay tribute to me to let your village have peace!"

"Y-yes!" Shouted the Mayor timidly from behind him. "We pay you tribute and you leave us be! Why are you bothering us today of all days?! Can't you see there's a wedding party going on?"

Cai gave out a loud dismissive laugh. "This wedding is an unrighteous farce! I have come to deliver justice to the man who dishonored my family name!"

All around the Sister there was the buzzing sound of people talking, and even the wedding party looked at each other in confusion.

"What do you mean?" Asked the shocked Mayor.

Green Mountain Cai sneered and then thrust out a finger at the groom. "Your son took advantage of my cousin's feelings and then when he'd had his fun he turned and married that little wench. I'm here to demand he make good on his actions and restore my family honor!"

All eyes suddenly fell to the groom, who left his now-fainted young bride in her mother-in-law's care and stepped forward.

"Your cousin chased me, I told her no! There was no dishonor to your family." The groom said in a voice loud enough that everyone could hear. "This is just her revenge."

Even in the torchlight, Cat could see Cai's face turning red. "So, my cousin is a harlot and a liar, is she?" He spat. "Is that what you're saying boy?"

The other bandits laughed and the crowd continued to murmur as they waited for the now shaken and silent groom's reply. Cat wished Little Gou were here, he might have been able to figure out a way to disarm the increasingly hostile situation.

"That's not what I said!" Protested the Groom. "Your cousin is a fine and honorable woman! She is a chaste woman! She's just...angry with me! You have no reason to be..." But the man's words were cut off by the blade that suddenly rested next to his throat.

"Honor demands I kill you, or receive payment for the slights you have given me." Cai told him with a snarl, then shouted, "Who wants to pay for this man's life!!!???"

The whole crowd had gone silent now, all focus was on the mayor whose bulging eyes stared at the sword at his son's neck. Finally, the older man sighed, seeing there was no choice, and cleared his throat to speak, but before he could utter a single word, a strong voice echoed out from the crowd.

"I will!"

Everyone turned to see who it was.

CHAPTER ELEVEN

Faceoff

"I will."

The crowd, whose gaze had all been on the bandit leader and the wedding party groom he had just threatened to execute, turned to follow the voice of the man who had just spoken.

"Show yourself!" Barked Green Mountain Cai, clearly himself surprised at this turn of events.

The crowd parted to reveal Snowtop Cho, Spider Chan and half of Cho's agency men marching into the town commons. Seeing them, Sister Cat began to apologize her way through the crowd towards her companions.

"And who are you, old man?" Challenged Cai.

"Snowtop Cho, Young Master of the Cho Family Armed Escort Agency." Came Cho's calm reply as they marched up to Cai. "And I'd say I was no more an old man than you are, but now that I get a better look at you, I'd have to say that would be giving your face too much credit."

Cai took his huge nine-ringed saber from the groom's neck and put it over his shoulder in a menacing pose as he faced Cho. "You're the bunch that doesn't pay us tribute to pass through our territory."

"We pay tribute to bandit kings, not dirt farmers who think they're bandits." Cho said steadily. "I know who you are, Cai. You're the bunch who fled when the last convoy we brought through these roads didn't look weak enough for you to handle. I recognize you now- you'll have to accept my apologies for it taking a moment, I've never seen your front before."

Cai growled at Cho's insult, and took a step forward. He was a good head taller than Cho, and looked down at the younger man. "You'd better be prepared to pay, boy. There's fifty of us and only a handful of you, and that mouth of yours has just doubled my price."

Cho didn't flinch from the bandit's gaze. "No, I have more men than this. My convoy is camped just outside of town, and I've runners getting the rest of the men as we speak." He bluffed. "But as for the price, I really am willing to pay it to restore the peace- after all this is about family honor, isn't it?"

"It is." Said Cai coldly.

"Funny that," Snowtop smiled. "I've never seen a family so willing to accept coins for a daughter's innocence being plucked. But, I guess the daughters in your family come pretty cheap."

The nine-ringed saber on Cai's shoulder was in motion in an instant, coming down hard to split Cho's head open like a melon. But when it arrived Snowtop Cho wasn't there, and Cai had to search around to find the white-haired man who had simply slipped away at the last moment like a ghost.

Shocked at this display of incredible martial skill, Cai was still too angry to let it pass and lunged forward- swatting at the air again and again while Cho just dodged the attacks. Under, over, to the side, whenever the blade came at him- Cho simply wasn't there. He hadn't even drawn his own sword, and made no attempts to counterattack the bandit leader's blows at all as the crowd of people watched in amazement.

Finally, after over twenty tries, Green Mountain Cai came to a halt- air wheezing from his out-of-shape lungs. He was a leader past his prime and too used to the soft life of tribute from towns and villages that didn't fight back. He wasn't even close to being on par with a talent of the *Jianghu* martial arts world like Snowtop Cho. A fact he had just begun to learn to his regret. Still, he had the numerical advantage, and that had been the downfall of many a skilled fighter.

"Men!" He bellowed. "Prepare to attack!"

Snowtop Cho tensed, and Chan and his men got ready for the onslaught. All around them, the bandits began to close in- the men on horseback took out bows, and the men on foot readied their spears and pole-arms. It was clear this was going to turn into a slaughter, but while they gathered and menaced the smaller group, none seemed quite willing to test the agency men's skills just yet.

"Cai," Cho growled with his hand on the hilt of his sword, *Ice Wind*. "If you give that command, I'll cut you down before a single one of them comes close. You have my word."

"Then my men will see you join me." Cai answered. "Lay down your swords if you value the lives of your men."

"I won't do that," Cho answered. "We've all sworn to die together on our feet."

Cai shook his head. "Promises made in a peach grove. But, I'll wager you're up to keeping it."

"I am."

It was a standoff, both sides a moment away from mutual destruction, and neither able to back down without losing face or personal honor. If Cai gave the order then he and many of his men would likely die, but if he didn't then he'd lose the respect of the men under his command- a potentially fatal situation for a bandit king to be in with so many always looking to take his place. If Snowtop backed down, he knew he wouldn't last long anyways, and it was better to die on his feet. Both were surely as trapped as insects in the amber of this deadly situation.

Sister Cat stopped at the edge of the crowd, she wanted to stand with Cho and his men, but worried her movements might jeopardize the momentary paralysis the situation had put them in. Now she was caught in the moment like them, waiting for the next word, the next action which would determine the future.

Nobody could have predicted what happened next.

A petite figure suddenly came flying over Snowtop Cho's head and landed on the ground between the two swordsmen.

"Chan," Cho said in surprise. "What are you doing?"

"I'm sorry, Young Master." Chan told him, keeping his facing towards Cai. "But I cannot let the eldest son of the family I serve die before me."

Green Mountain Cai looked puzzled at this turn of events. "And what is your surname, little frog?" He said to the man a fraction of his size.

"My surname is Chan, honored sir." Chan said with a bow. "I am here to make you an offer."

"Oh?"

"Yes, Lord Cai." Chan said respectfully. "Please allow this humble one to take his master's place in this duel. I will fight you, and should you win my master and his men will both pay you compensation for his insults and stand aside to let you carry on your business with this town."

"I see." Said Cai with suspicion. "And, does your Young Master agree to this?"

"He does not!" Snowtop barked. "Chan, you overstep your place! Get back with the men while I handle this!"

At that moment, spun and kowtowed before Snowtop's feet. "Young Master! Please!" Chan begged. "You cannot risk our family name over such a simple matter! Your life is too important, and think of the lives of your men! If this matter can be solved in such a simple way by merely losing one man and a little coin is it not worth it? Please allow me this one final honor!"

Snowtop was in shock. He stared down at Chan in honest surprise, as though he had never seen this side of him before, and then his heart began to melt at the display of earnestness before him. At last he nodded.

"I agree to this." He told Cai, then stepped back to join his men.

"Thank you, Young Master!" Chan said with a final kowtow to his retreating superior before he got back up to his feet and turned to face Cai.

"What do you want in return?" Cai asked him.

"If I win, you will leave peacefully- all matters of honor forgiven and forgotten."

Cai considered it. The little goblin was barely half his height, and all of his bandit clan was watching his every move now. If he turned down such a fight it would again be putting a knife in his own back, and he had little choice.

"Agreed," said Cai.

That was as much warning as Chan got, and then the bandit leader's huge nine-ringed saber was coming down at him. Chan nimbly dodged out of the way- moving with a fluid grace Cat had rarely seen outside of long practiced monks and sword dancers. Then Chan leapt forward as Cai twisted to bring his blade around for another strike and sent a blow at Cai's stomach. The bandit king, seeing the blow coming, pivoted and caused Chan's strike to just miss, again bringing his blade down to follow the little man- who this time rolled forward and only just out of the way.

And so, the dance went, with Cai on the offensive and Chan dodging and rolling out of the way of each blow from a saber almost as tall as he was. Chan's only attempts at offense seemed to be occasional blows at Cai's stomach, each of which did little to nothing. It was clear that despite Chan's speed and grace he simply didn't have the hitting power to compete with a hardened warrior like Cai and without weapons he was merely a deer dodging arrows before the final bolt from the hunter struck home.

It all seemed to Cat to be quite hopeless.

Then the inevitable happened- Chan made another attempt at a stomach blow and just connected before the hilt of Cai's saber caught him across the back of the head. Chan was sent tumbling into the dirt and it looked like the end for Chan as Cai closed in on him. But then, something nobody could have expected happened- Cai suddenly stumbled, and nearly tripped over as his pants fell down around his ankles.

There was a long pause of shock, and then the villagers and many of the bandits roared with laughter as Cai was forced to stop to gather up his pants. At the same time, Chan rolled and brought himself to his feet- holding in his hands the long rope which had been serving as Cai's belt! He grinned up at Cai, and stuck out his tongue.

"You little toad!" Cai roared and lunged forward, still holding his pants up with one hand while he attacked using his saber in the other. But this time, Chan didn't dodge away like he had before- he moved in on the blow and in a single fluid motion his hands passed over Cai's wrist, leaving a knotted rope in their wake!

When Cai tied to use his other hand to grab Chan, Chan ducked under the hand and looped the rope again up and this time around Cai's other hand as well! In a flash both of Cai's hands were now bound together by his own rope-belt and Chan had the upper hand. But, Chan didn't stop there- as Cai tried to slash at the little man with his sword, Chan dove to the side and when Cai moved to follow, he was again caught up in his fallen pants- down he went!

With Cai on his face in the dirt Chan quickly swept in- looping the rope around his neck, tying it in an instant so Cai's neck was connected on one end of the rope with the looped hands on the other. If Cai tried to move his hands, he yanked at his own head and neck, and he was so confused and caught off-guard by this all he could do was roll around half naked in the dirt while the townsfolk howled in laughter.

At last, when the cursing red Cai was on his back, he saw a shadow over him and a foot came down on his throat.

"Do you yield?" Demanded Spider Chan in a now cold and cruel voice that belied his normal mirthful nature.

Cai cursed, but when Chan artfully yanked away the sword from the bandit king's numbing fingers and tossed it aside, he realized his position and finally gave in.

Chan had won.

* * *

"To Chan!" Snowtop Cho raised a glass.

"To Chan! Drink up!" Thundered the rest of the tables. They were filled with Cho's men and some of the local townsfolk who had come to join them at the inn. The escorts had refused guest of honor positions at the wedding celebration when it had resumed and had instead retreated to the inn to rest, but some of the town had followed them back anyways to make things into another private party.

At the head table Chan blushed and thanked everyone for their kind words, crediting it all to the goddess of mercy before sitting down again with Cho and Cat beside him.

"I must say Chan," Cho told him. "You really had me going for a time there. I almost didn't let you fight him. Please forgive me for doubting your skills."

Young Master," Chan answered with sincerity. "There is nothing to forgive. Besides, if you had believed me that big mountain would have been more suspicious and might not have fought me! Your sincerity was what sold him the goods and helped get him to leave. I should be thanking you tonight."

Cho gave an exasperated grin. "See, Sister? I try to apologize to this man and he ends up thanking me! What can I do with him?"

When the two men and the people around them were done laughing at this, Cat ventured a question. "Brother Chan, were you really fighting out there? If you could have done that to him, why didn't you do it right from the start instead of taking such a risk?"

"Oh. Well. How can I lie to such a beautiful nun? The truth is Sister- and I never thought I'd say this about another man- I was having too much trouble getting his pants off!"

After the laughter from that died down, Chan explained in more detail.

"When I watched him fight the Young Master, I noticed his belt, and when we reached a stalemate, I knew that if I challenged him, he wouldn't back down, because after all- I'm so small, right? But what I didn't count on was that the knots on his belt would be so tight, and because I chose to fight unarmed to sweeten the deal, I couldn't cut it free. Every time you saw me taking a shot at him, I was really trying to loosen up those knots, and for a while there I have to admit I didn't think I was going to do it. I even thought about using my wires, but I was afraid they'd accuse me of cheating and I wanted to make the whole thing as funny as I could. Finally, I knew I had to take a chance, so instead of taking a quick grab at the belt I really had a hard go at that knot- and just as he hit me it came loose in my hand. There you have it."

Cho slapped the smaller man on the back. "Well done, my friend! Well done! You're a credit to the agency!"

"It was nothing, Young Master. Just following your examples of bravery and fearlessness. Oh, am I boring you Sister?"

Those last words were directed at Sister Cat, who had just stifled a rather large yawn. She waved her hand in front of her face and apologized.

"No, I'm sorry brothers. It's been a long time since I could enjoy sleep and even this tea is not helping. Could you excuse me for the night?"

Both men told her not to worry, and after refusing Chan's "kind" offer of an escort to her room, Cat said her goodnights and made her way upstairs. It had been over a day and a half since she'd slept and every muscle in her body was crying out for rest. She was so tired she didn't even bother to disrobe; she just took off her outer traveling robes and hung them on a chair before falling onto the straw-filled blanket that served as a mattress for the bed.

She was asleep by the time her head touched the straw.

* * *

When morning broke, Sister Cat was awakened by the smells and sounds of life from the inn below her. She could hear the men and women chatting as they prepared breakfast for their patrons and the smell of food being readied. Knowing that they would need to leave soon, she dragged her incredibly sore body from the bed and began to do stretching exercises to limber up her tortured muscles. Moving gracefully, she let Qi energy flow into her body and sooth the damage the last few days had done, warming her up and at least making the pain bearable.

As she did her exercises, she determined that this morning she was going to finish her discussion with Cho about helping to find Master Mao's Daughter, Meiyu. She'd been so weary from travel she'd been silly not to mention it straight away, and every minute they wasted brought the girl more and more in danger from Lady Moonlight and her hirelings. She couldn't rely on Gou; she would need all the help she could get, and the Cho Family Armed Escort Agency was clearly both honorable and trustworthy based on what she'd experienced the night before. Yes, she felt it was definitely time to talk with them.

Her morning exercises done, Cat got dressed and headed out to find the rest of her companions. She heard their echoing voices from the main dining hall almost as soon as she stepped into the hallway and continued her stretching as she walked towards them.

"Which way do you think Old Master Mao's daughter will come, Young Master?"

Cat froze just before the point where the second-floor hallway exited out onto an open landing that looked down onto the main eating area. She'd just heard Chan speak, but didn't quite want to believe what she'd just heard.

"She'll come through the Nanjing trade route and down from there to the Green Rapids Town. It's the fastest way to go, and the Mao's have a family shrine in Nanjing she'll need to stop and visit on her way to White Fox Town as part of the marriage custom." Cho's voice answered.

Chan made a noise of agreement, then added. "That won't give us much time to find and deliver her."

"No," Cho agreed. "It won't. But don't worry, we have all our agents searching for her. We'll get to her, and nothing is going to stand in our way."

CHAPTER TWELVE

Mercy

"What are we looking for?"

The footsteps of the horse echoed through the misty morning as it carried the two riders through the narrow stone streets of the village. Around them, servants came and went from the manor-houses on their early-morning duties, ignoring the tired looking man and woman as they rode in circles around the many manor gates.

"Do you ever stop asking questions?" Mrs. Yi snapped from her spot behind Gou on the horse.

"Do you ever answer them?"

She made an unhappy noise, but then he heard her suck in a breath. "There! It's that one."

Gou followed her long, painted fingernail to a manor house gate with a large bronze plaque above the entrance- "Jia Family Manor". "Well," he commented. "That sounds promising, are there four beauties inside to admire as well?"

Mrs. Yi smiled. "Perhaps there are. Take me over there and I'll introduce you."

"Your wish is my command!" Gou took them to the large, bronze-plated double wooden doors and helped Mrs. Yi off. He knew she could easily have leapt off herself, but his gentlemanly nature made it hard for him not to be courteous, even to a woman like her- especially since she was so beautiful.

"Let me do the talking," she told him as she walked over and made use of one of the large iron rings to knock.

A short time later, the door creaked open, and a young servant peeked his head out to look them both over.

"We're here to see the Second Young Miss," Mrs. Yi told him. Then she offered him a silk handkerchief. "Please take this to her and she'll tell you how we should be greeted."

Taking the handkerchief with care, he shut the door and disappeared inside.

"The family's second daughter an old friend of yours?"

Mrs. Yi gave him a look that any man who spends enough time around women knew as trouble- a thoughtful smile that said she had a surprise waiting for him. One that Gou suspected he wasn't going to like.

"Something like that."

The gambler considered his options- he knew she was wrapped up in a secret society, and such societies guarded their membership with deadly force. This could easily be a trap that could get him much deeper than he wanted to be, and he was very soon going to have to answer some tough questions he'd so far managed to dodge. He was her savior of the evening, and she seemed to trust him, but how far and how long were both questions with potentially dangerous answers.

Still, Little Gou knew she could be his equal in a fight, and his odds of escape before more trouble came weren't good, so that kept him standing there until one of the doors in front of them swung open and a more senior servant appeared to usher them inside with great ceremony. While the servant they had met earlier fetched their horse, Gou and Mrs. Yi were led across a wide courtyard towards one of the red-roofed, white stucco buildings. There, they were seated at a long ornately carved table and offered breakfast, something they both accepted without hesitation, and told that the Second Young Miss would be with them shortly.

And shortly she did come, just as Gou was mixing pickled eggs and salted vegetables with his congee. She was a plump woman with hair down to her waist who looked to be in her late twenties and wore far too much jewelry over her fine purple and green robes. Gou knew her type well, the kind who desperately sought to overcome their physical flaws through dressing themselves up to the point of garish distraction. That also explained what a woman of her marriageable age was still doing in the family home.

She squealed when she saw Mrs. Yi and the two embraced, gushing about the time it had been and how each other looked. Then the Second Young Miss nodded at the still-eating Gou questioningly, and asked what had brought them there.

"I need to warn the mistress," Mrs. Yi said in sudden seriousness. "I learned my husband is plotting to harm her. I tried to send a message last night, but my courier was killed by my husband's men and this guy rescued me. He says he was sent to help me, but I don't know if I can trust him. He could be a trick by my husband to learn more about us."

"Then we can't let him live."

"I agree." Mrs. Yi replied. "He already knows too much. But, I'd like to know who his masters are before we kill him."

Of course, Gou was aware of all this happening across the table from him, but took the time to finish his congee before looking up- after all, he didn't know when he'd be eating again from the looks of things. When he did look up, he found two pairs of icy eyes trying to bore right through him.

"Before you kill me, can I say a few things?" He asked, acting unconcerned.

"Speak then."

"Well, first of all I don't work for your husband. Last night was the first time I've ever met him, and I'm certainly no friend of those three devils he has working for him. Second, as someone who is as skilled as you are, Madam Yi. Did any of those attacks Last Brother Shou made look fake or half-hearted?"

"No," Mrs. Yi conceded. She had to admit, there had been real bloodlust there towards Gou in the fight the night before.

"Right. So, if I was his compatriot, why was he trying to kill me?"

"Perhaps you're his rival," Miss Jia offered.

"Still not the best time to kill me, was it?"

Mrs. Yi shook her head. "No, we're getting off the point. Who are you, and who sent you?"

"I can't tell you." Gou replied. "All I can say is that I'm your friend and ally."

"And you expect us to believe that?" Miss Jia demanded.

Gou shrugged. "Not really. But before you kill me, I suggest you take me to your mistress. She'll tell you who I am."

The two women shared a look of concern. Little Gou's confident manner had them rattled, and so far, he had done and said nothing that made him seem like their enemy. Gou had put them in a difficult situation, and they weren't quite sure what to do.

It was Miss Jia who ended the standoff. She snapped her fingers and hidden doorways snapped open to allow two large men to enter.

"Take him someplace he can't escape from and hold him there."

Outside, Gou's face took on a worried look, but inside he was happy to see these men. They were larger than him, but their movements showed more muscle than skill, and so he meekly submitted to follow them from the room and out into the courtyard. He waited until they closed the door to the room with the women in it, but almost as soon as the door to the guest house closed, Gou was off like a shot.

He had no time to waste here, and the prospects for trouble were looking greater than the prospects for knowledge, so there was no point in remaining any longer. With this in mind, he easily outpaced the two guards, dashing across the courtyard and heading toward a grove of leafy trees next to the outer wall. He could use the trees to help get over the wall, and escape from there. He'd have to leave his horse and travel bag behind, but that was a small price to pay.

However, just as he reached the grove of trees, there was a whistling sound and he instinctively leapt back as a green feathered arrow stuck itself in the ground in front of him. Then he was dodging aside as more arrows began to rain down on him like the trees themselves were shedding the arrows as leaves.

Gou retreated, trying to get away from the hidden archers, and found himself facing the men from earlier. Given his options, he raised his hands in surrender. It seemed he wouldn't be leaving the Jia Family Manor so soon after all.

* * *

The light through the room's single, small window told Gou that it was now after noon, and as he lounged on the floor of the empty room, he considered his next move.

With his failed escape attempt, he would now have to rely on his bluff about the need to take him to their boss to buy him the time he needed to escape. He doubted their mistress was here in this small town, and with travel came another opportunity to get free or find help. Of course, whoever ran their secret society wasn't going to know who he was, but even if he did get hauled before them, he might be able to talk his way out of it. Buying time was something Gou was good at- it was a long-practiced skill that had kept him alive so far.

A rustle at the door was followed by a bolt being drawn.

Gou raised an eyebrow as the haughty second daughter of the house entered, followed shortly by Mrs. Yi and the two large men who'd been guarding him.

"Stand up," Mrs. Yi ordered.

"Come to your senses, have you?"

"Do it! Now!" She motioned to the two men, who moved to flank him on either side.

Gou, knowing what came next, sighed and lazily stood up, making a point of taking his time doing it. "Are we going somewhere?"

"You are very lucky." Mrs. Yi told him.

"Oh? How so?"

"My sister wished to kill you, especially after you tried to leave us so early," she said, watching him. "But while we were discussing it, our mistress arrived. So, you'll have your chance to prove your words."

Gou forced a smile.

"Oh really? That's...wonderful."

* * *

To say that Gou was surprised by what followed would be an understatement.

He was led up through the compound, and taken to one of the guest houses to the rear of the large estate- a well decorated one with inlaid fancy carvings of birds above the main entrance. There, he was marched inside and taken to a large sitting room with further ornate decorations, nothing less than what he'd expected for such a wealthy family. No, none of this surprised him- his surprise was waiting for him in the room.

Gou went in expecting a beautiful young maiden in white with an icy gaze who wielded a sword that had felled dozens in the blink of an eye.

Instead, he found a sick looking old crone who looked like a stiff breeze could strike her dead at any moment.

"I do not know you."

Her voice was rough like gravel, but not as weak as Gou expected from her hunched-over appearance. Sitting in a well-cushioned chair, she leaned forward against her gnarled old walking stick and looked Gou up and down with the two black spots she called eyes. She wore simple gray robes, and had a blue turban on her head, nothing that gave Gou any sense of her status or origins.

"Are you sure, Grandmother?"

The Second Young Miss of the house was standing at one side of her, and several other women stood behind her, but unlike Miss Jia, these women looked like they'd be able to handle themselves in a fight. All of them were tall, broad shouldered and fierce looking creatures that showed signs of long training with the weapons they carried at their sides. It struck Gou that these warrior women were more than just this old woman's bodyguards.

"I am." The old woman finally concluded. "He is not one of ours."

"There, you see?" Miss Jia sneered, then ordered, "Take him outside and kill him!"

"Wait!" Gou had opened his mouth, but a woman's voice had come out instead of his! Surprised, he turned to see it was Mrs. Yi who now stepped forward. "We don't know who he is, or why he said he was one of us."

"He's a spy, and we should get rid of him!" The Second Young Miss crossed her arms and glared at Gou. She was looking less and less attractive to him by the minute.

"Dead men tell no tales, sister." Mrs. Yi shook her head. "But they also don't give answers when they're needed." Then she turned and looked at Gou. "Tell us who you are, and none of your tricks this time."

Gou sighed. He knew he wasn't going to be able to get out of this one quite as easily as he might have hoped. So, after weighing the options, he decided that the only way out of this situation was going to be the truth- or at least a version of it.

"My surname isn't Feng, and you may call me Little Gou."

Mrs. Yi nodded at that. "Very well, Gou. Who do you work for?"

Gou considered a moment. "Well, I guess you could say I work for myself, really."

"I don't understand."

So, Gou explained. He told them that he was a resident of White Fox Town, and that several days previously he had been a guest at a party of Master Mao of the Mao Family Armed Escort Agency. This, he noticed, seemed to make their ears perk up. Then he told them of how the party was attacked by Lady Moonlight, and that the master's daughter had been threatened. Saying that he was an old friend of the daughter (not untrue), he had left to warn her, but after a chance encounter with several of Moonlight's men at an inn, he had decided to follow them to see what they were up to, and that had led him to Mister Yi's home.

Thus, Gou gave them the truth of how he came to be before them, minus a few details.

"An obvious fabrication." The Young Miss declared, turning up her small nose at him. "We should cut out this one's tongue first!"

"But sister, his words do hold some truth," Mrs. Yi protested, continuing to surprise Gou. "Those men did come to our house last night, and I have seen this Lady Moonlight with my own eyes as she came to visit my husband. She is everything he has said."

Miss Jia shook her head, and seemed to be about to again to dismiss her sister's words, but instead it was the old woman that spoke.

"Hold."

At that single word, the Young Miss suddenly found her propriety again and stepped aside, bowing to her senior. "What would you ask, Grandmother?"

"This young man's words ring true to me as well. I believe him."

"But Grandmother he..." The plump girl started again, but was quickly silenced by a look from her elder. "Yes, grandmother."

Then the old woman gestured to Gou to approach her.

"Come closer, young man. Let an old woman get a better look at you."

This surprised Gou, as the old woman had been looking at him quite a bit, but he decided he had little choice, and so did as she wanted.

However, just as Gou drew up to her, a feeling of dread suddenly washed over him, and he dropped back into a defensive stance just in time to avoid the first in a series of blows that the old woman suddenly made with the tip of her walking stick. Five, ten, twenty strikes came out at him lightning-fast from the woman's hand, and he was forced to dodge or block as many as he could, taking a few painful hits in the process. While the old woman's body might be ancient, her control over her body's *Qi* life energies was clearly still formidable, and the blows had surprising power to match their speed.

Then, just as quickly as it started, the attack finished, and the old woman nodded to herself.

"Some talent, but hardly a worry. Your martial line is from Master Liu, is it not?"

"My teacher was Doctor Duan, a student of Master Liu."

That brought a smile to the old woman's parched lips. "Ah yes, Young Duan. He is a doctor now, you say?"

Gou said that this was true, although he marveled at her referring to his former master as "young". The doctor was very much in his later years, and it was commonly expected that he would retire soon.

"Tell me, boy." She said to him. "Did Doctor Duan ever mention the name Merciful Beauty in your presence?"

Gou looked at her, surprised. His master had indeed mentioned such a name more than once. "He did, my lady. But, only when drinking. She was his master's rival."

"His master's rival?" The old woman raised an eyebrow at that. "We were many things, boy, but your martial grandfather and I were hardly rivals." She shook her head. "What nonsense is Young Duan telling his pupils? Rivals. Ha!"

Gou did his best to remain silent on this point. If this was indeed "Merciful Beauty" he faced, he most definitely needed to do anything he could to avoid her wrath. His master had referred to her name as being "half a lie" more than once, and now Gou could see that neither of her titles applied. There were many stories about this woman, and if only some were true, he didn't wish to feel her "mercy".

According to Doctor Duan, Merciful Beauty had once been a pretty village girl that Master Liu had fallen in love with. However, the master had already had several wives at that point, and his first wife had forbidden him to take another. So, the master had reached a compromise with the girl- she would become his mistress, but in trade he would teach her the martial arts. She was a spirited girl, and Master Liu had offered her a prize she desperately wanted.

However, after a time Master Liu had tired of the girl and her uncivil manners, finding them more boorish than charming, and spent less and less time with her. She had taken very badly to it, and finally Master Liu had broken it off, leaving her and saying he wouldn't return. This had devastated the girl, and not long after she left her village and disappeared.

Of course, this worried Master Liu, but there was little he could do, and the whole affair was soon forgotten with the passage of time. At least, until the day she reappeared at his school, and announced a challenge to the master himself!

As Doctor Duan told it, she had decided that if she could challenge Master Liu, then perhaps she could rekindle his affection for her. So, she had begun to seek out other fighters to teach her, and help her improve her skills. This was why she had gone, and when she returned, she declared that if she could beat him, he had to take her as his wife.

Of course, she failed. Master Liu was called the "Crashing River" for a reason.

So, she again went away, only to return the following year with the same demand.

This cycle had continued until Master Liu's early death at the age of 50, with her coming each year, and Master Liu sending her away, defeated. It was only his death that had ended their relationship, and after that she hadn't troubled the family again. When asked what had happened to her, Doctor Duan had merely shrugged and said he didn't know.

But Gou knew. Now.

Shaking her head ruefully, Merciful Beauty looked at the young martial artist.

"One of Liu's martial grandchildren in my home. Heaven is funny, isn't it?" Then she leaned in, looked at Gou with a grandmotherly smile and said with bone-chilling seriousness, "Did you know I once swore to wipe all of Liu's line from this world?"

CHAPTER THIRTEEN

Legends

"...swore to wipe all of Liu's line from this world."

The words echoed in Gou's ears as the old woman's soft eyes took on a hard, sharp sheen, and his belly felt like it did after he'd eaten bad food at a roadside stall. Gou didn't know how to respond to that, and while his legs had the sudden urge to flee, he found himself rooted to the spot, caught in Merciful Beauty's powerful gaze.

Then, the old woman's eyes softened, and she laughed.

"But, we all do stupid things in the heat of passion, don't we, boy?"

Still unsure, Gou just nodded, and let her continue.

"In fact, I owe your martial grandfather a debt of sorts." She said. "Leaving me was perhaps one of the greatest gifts he could have given me. It forced me to go out into the world and learn what a small frog in a well I had been, and how vast the opportunities are for those with the power and will to seize them.

"So, don't worry, my boy. I won't harm you as long as you don't abuse my hospitality. I am, after all, your martial aunt, since your master and I are of the same generation. It would be unseemly for me to have you killed without due cause."

Taking his cue, Gou suddenly dropped to his knees and kowtowed to her three times. "Thank you, honored aunt. Your junior pays his respects to you!"

Impressed by Gou's display of piety, the old woman let him rise.

"Now, I suppose you wonder what it is you've gotten yourself caught up in, eh boy?"

Gou considered how to reply for a moment, and then said. "If auntie would enlighten me, I would be honored."

"Just so. Just so." The crone nodded to herself. "After my days with your martial grandfather, I had acquired much skill, and once he passed, I considered becoming a nun and retreating from the world. However, it was not to be. As I walked the road, I saw what a cruel and harsh place this land is for women, and I decided I would do what I could to change that. To accomplish this, I began to take on disciples of my own and show them how to defend themselves.

"Of course, we needed money to survive. As you know, many rich men are fearful of entrusting the security of their wives and daughters to the hands of lustful mercenaries, and we began to offer a service that made them much more comfortable. It was hard at first, but over time we gained a reputation, and now our numbers are in the hundreds as our members travel across the central plains and beyond."

"You're the *Jin Hua*," said Gou, understanding. "The Golden Flower Escort Agency."

"We are."

Gou looked around the room. The warrior women, Mrs. Yi, the attitudes of Miss Jia toward him- it all made sense now. The *Jin Hua* had a reputation as fearsome fighters who strove to show women's equality to men. It was said they were even forbidden to back down from any challenge issued by a man, although Gou considered this an exaggeration.

Then he looked over at Mrs. Yi.

"You were spying on The Black Dragons."

Mrs. Yi nodded. "When the former mistress of the house died, our leader decided it was a great opportunity to place someone close to him and learn his secrets. I was chosen to be that person."

"Lucky you," said Gou.

Mrs. Yi lowered her head and looked away.

"Young Lily is one of our most beautiful members, and she has done us a great service." Merciful Beauty continued. "Without her, we would never have known of Yi's treachery. Even though your true nature was revealed, child, it was worth the cost. We are in your debt."

"There is no debt, leader. It was my honor."

Gou watched Mrs. Yi kowtow to her master, then he looked at the old woman. "I heard her tell her messenger that your life was in danger, honored senior. Does this have anything to do with the upcoming meeting of the Society of Armed Escorts chiefs?"

"It does," frowned the old woman. "Yi and this child Moonlight have conspired to take the leadership of the council. Do they think this has not been tried before?" She gave a dismissive snort.

"Leader, if I may be so bold," said Mrs. Yi. "Please do not underestimate Mr. Yi's cunning, or the support that this Lady Moonlight has behind her. Already, because of this box, many of the society heads are up in arms and allies are already turning against each other."

The old woman considered. "You believe this is a plan by Moonlight?"

"I do, leader."

At the mention of the word "box", Gou's ears had begun to itch, and now as the women paused to think on this topic, Gou decided this was his chance to fish for more information.

"Excuse me." He said. "But what's in this box that has people so ready to kill for?"

Mrs. Yi looked to her master, who gave a nod of approval for her to speak.

"The truth is, nobody knows. At least, nobody still alive."

"Well, that sounds promising."

"Do you know the tale of Master Shan?"

Gou thought a moment. "You mean the legend of Rising Mountain's Treasure?"

At this, Mrs. Yi nodded.

The legend of "Rising Mountain" Shan's treasure was a common enough story. Shan was yet another *biaoju* head who had lived two generations previous, and had commanded the Silver Mountain Armed Escort Agency. During an uprising, his agency had been entrusted with escorting a treasure convoy fleeing from the capital in the face of an onrushing rebel army. The convoy and his men had disappeared, and legend said that the agency had robbed the convoy and hidden the treasure.

Of course, there was no proof, and Rising Mountain had been well connected enough to escape blame for what happened, but he had still retired in disgrace afterward and left the martial world. He had died a number of years later under mysterious circumstances, and many believed he was killed by people who were trying to learn the location of the treasure.

Even to this day, people still searched for the hidden fortune, and Rising Mountain's Treasure was a common one for the heroes of street theater and puppet shows to quest after. It was a tale many knew, but few believed.

Accordingly, Gou just laughed when she confirmed what he'd said. "You're kidding me? The box contains a treasure map?" He shook his head. "Aren't you all a little old to be believing in those kinds of stories?"

But the looks on the faces of the women in the room didn't change, and Gou soon found his own mirth fading.

"There is more to the story that you do not know." Mrs. Yi continued. "Did you know Master Shan was the lover of Princess Yu?"

That, Gou had never heard. Princess Yu was the daughter of crown prince Yuan Zhong, and a woman famed and well known for her beauty even to Gou's generation. A famous print of her image by the painter Liu Kao was a common feature of many wealthy homes. When her father had died before he could assume the throne, she had retired from public life and few knew what had become of her.

Taking her cue from Gou's face, Mrs. Yi continued. "It is said that the two of them met when he was escorting her on a voyage to Gansu Province. After that, whenever he came to the capital, he would bring her presents. One of the first presents was a small lacquered box which was extremely difficult to open unless you knew the secret key. She used this to store the letters they exchanged."

"Letters that people think might contain the location of his treasure." Gou said, finishing her line of thinking. "Okay. I can see that. But why did the box surface now? There must be a trick here."

"Yes, I believe that too." Mrs. Yi agreed. "But, as for how the box appeared, there is no great mystery. Although not many know this, Princess Yu retired to a nunnery after the death of Master Shan, and she remained there until her own health failed. After her passing, the son of Master Bai of the White Tiger Armed Escort Agency was summoned to the nunnery."

Now there was a familiar name. Master Bai had been the one with Master Mao the night of the party. They were martial brothers and close friends, and it was to Master Bai's son Gou assumed that Meiyu was to be married.

"There, the Abbess presented Master Bai's son with the box- one of the few possessions that Princess Yu had taken with her. He was told that since this box belonged to Master Shan, who had no heirs, it was to be given to Master Bai's family to deal with, since Shan and Bai's masters were sworn brothers."

"However, as soon as it became known that the box existed, the Bai family suddenly found itself under a deluge of requests by people who wanted possession of the box. This reached its climax when the Bai estate in the capital was attacked by robbers intending to steal the box and several members of the household staff were killed. The only reason the box remained safe was that it was well hidden, and the thieves were unable to find it.

"So, unable to keep the box safe, the Bai family decided to place the box instead in the hands of the Society of Armed Escorts' head council and let them deal with this problem. Master Shan had once been a president of the council himself, and it seemed fitting that the council should decide what to do with it."

Gou nodded in agreement. This was the logical way to take the pressure off the Bai family before something worse had happened, and it passed the responsibility of the box onto someone else. As Master Mao was the current head of the council, it only made sense that he be given possession of the box, at least until the next council meeting when the group would decide on what to do with it.

This explained what had happened the night Gou had encountered box with the courier, and was pursued by the terrible trio to the Bai family compound. It was a last attempt by those who wanted to get the box before it fell into better armed hands.

It also cleared up another point.

"So, let me guess," Gou said. "Mister Yi wants to become the new head of the council, because that will make him the one who decides what to do with the box."

Mrs. Yi agreed. "Yes. He has plans to keep those who would oppose him from attending the meeting, including my master. That is why he is working with Lady Moonlight."

They probably wanted to split the treasure or something, Gou assumed. Although, there was still the question of why Lady Moonlight had attacked Mao's party and threatened to kill his family. Wasn't she going to get the box anyway if she helped Yi win the election? Why go to all that trouble...?

Even though this conversation had given Gou many of the pieces he'd needed to truly understand what was happening, he felt there were still some things that didn't add up. He was sure something else was going on here that he wasn't seeing.

At least, not yet.

"Well, this is all very interesting." Gou finally announced. "And, I wish you luck with Mister Yi and the council meeting. But, I need to warn Master Mao's daughter before the men Lady Moonlight sent for her find her."

Then he kowtowed to Merciful Beauty.

"Auntie, thank you for your hospitality. It has been an honor to meet you, and receive your wisdom. If I have your permission to leave, I will give thanks to your name."

Accepting this, Merciful Beauty gave him words of encouragement, and Gou was about to leave when suddenly Mrs. Yi stepped in front of her master and bowed deeply.

"Leader. I wish your permission to accompany this man on his journey. My mission is over. I owe him a debt for my life, and wish to have the chance to repay it."

The old woman nodded, and then looked at the startled Gou.

"Do you accept her offer, young man?"

Gou blinked, unsure. "Ahhh. Sure. If she doesn't mind a little rough travel."

Mrs. Yi bowed to her master, then to Gou.

"Thank you, brother, for this chance."

* * *

After this, Gou was taken by the Second Young Miss to look at the household's collection of swords and pick one to take with him. Mrs. Yi, however, remained behind with Merciful Beauty.

"Thank you for your kindness and understanding, grandmother." She told her master, preparing to back out of the room.

"Hold." Said the crone.

"Leader?"

"I have a new mission for you. You are to capture old Mao's daughter and bring her to us."

"Grandmother?!?" Mrs. Yi's mouth hung open, and she stared at her master in shock. "I...I..."

This bought her a sharp look of reproach from the old woman.

"Is there a problem with your hearing, child?"

Mrs. Yi hesitated, then bowed.

"No, grandmother. I... hear and obey."

Then, watching the girl. Merciful Beauty's eyes softened a bit.

"I know this may be hard for you, Lily. You seem to have honest feelings of gratitude for this young man. But, you must do this for the good of the family, and your sisters. Whoever possesses the treasure will be rich enough to dominate all of the *Jianghu*. Those who miss this chance will be slaves to the winners, and I will not let my daughters suffer that fate- ever. We are depending on you, and your skills, my child."

"Of course, leader. I owe you and my sisters everything." The she hesitated and asked. "And Gou?"

"He knows too much of this affair to remain alive."

"Yes...Mistress."

* * *

Less than an hour later, Gou and Mrs. Yi were on the road north heading for Green Rapids Town. In that time, they had been resupplied, they had both been given horses, and Mrs. Yi had changed into proper travel clothes.

Mrs. Yi, or Miss Lily, as she now told Gou to call her with her marriage being a thing of the past, was quite a beautiful figure. Even though she wore simple brown pants and a short light blue travel robe with her hair all done up into a bun under a black cap, it was hard to mistake her for a man. Her face was simply too white, and her chest too shapely for anyone to make that mistake.

"You impress me, Gou." She said as their horses trotted through the busy streets of a small town along their way.

Gou gave her a lopsided grin. "Well, the feeling's mutual, my lady. But, you first. Why?"

"You have found yourself deep within a world where you do not belong, and yet you still show little sign of concern. I know you are not a fool, so you must be a brave man indeed."

The gambler rubbed the back of his head and laughed. "Oh, I don't know. I think I can be a pretty big fool sometimes. Getting involved in this mess was definitely not one of my better ideas."

"But you still do not turn back."

Gou looked wistful for a moment. "Can't. I've got someone I care about who's going to get hurt in all this. If I did nothing, I think I'd go crazy."

Mrs. Yi listened and nodded thoughtfully. "I believe, I understand. I too had someone I cared about once, but my duty took me away from him, and now... now it is much too late."

Gou shrugged. "You're still alive, aren't you? And hey, you're single now, right?"

That earned him a wan smile from his beautiful companion. "I'm no longer marriageable, and it is likely he has long moved on. No, I will devote my life to my sisters, once I have settled my debt with you."

"You didn't have to come, you know? I'll be fine."

But she shook her head. "If I did nothing, I think I'd go crazy." She said, giving him a wink.

* * *

"Hold."

Snowtop Cho had raised his hand in front of a large, respectable looking Inn.

Sister Cat lifted her tired head and looked up. The place they'd arrived at was a large, two story affair located in Green Rapids Town near the outskirts of the city. An expansive courtyard designed to hold whole convoys and caravans was almost half full, and now as the men around her began to dismount stable boys rushed from the shade to grab their horses.

A smiling young boy reached for the reigns of her horse as well, but another hand arrived before his and shooed the lad back.

"Here you go, Sister. Take your time." Said the grinning Spider Chan, looking up at her. He'd hopped off his own horse and rushed back to hers with surprising speed.

"Ahh." Said Cat, feeling a little uncomfortable around the diminutive man. "Yes... Thank you, Brother Chan."

"No problem, my lady. None at all."

Cat dismounted with care, letting first one foot, and then the other touch blessed dirt. She'd gotten more used to riding with the practice of the last two days, but it was still anything but a pleasant experience. She was so tense on the mount, always worrying that she'd fall off or that the animal would develop a mind of its own and lead her in some unwanted direction.

Luckily for her, the horse had seemed to pick up the idea it was to ride with Snowtop's men, and simply followed along with their group at their own pace. It had given her some time to think and consider what she was going to do next.

It had been a great shock when she'd discovered that Snowtop and his men were working for Lady Moonlight. She didn't know how someone Gou had considered a friend could be so dishonorable. He'd seemed like such a good man at the wedding party, and with the incident with the bandits, that she'd almost let herself trust him.

She shuddered at the thought of almost having revealed herself and her mission. That would have been a disaster. Now, more than ever, she needed Gou's wisdom to help her deal with this problem.

"Looking for someone, Sister?" She heard Chan say, and she realized that she had unconsciously been looking out at the crowded evening street as her thoughts wandered. She gave him a polite smile and a shake of her head.

"No. Just...impressed by the number of people in this place."

Chan bobbed his head. "Travel season is always like this. Green Rapids Town is the only place around with big pull ferries. Hear that noise?"

At his cue, the Sister cocked her head and listened. Over the din of the crowd and passing animals, she could hear loud clanking sounds coming from the direction of the river. She could also hear the bleating of oxen, and the sudden exclamations of men and whips.

"That's the ferries being pulled across the river, they use animals to pull the chains so they can get them across right quick. One of the coolies told me that both ferries can cross the river almost a hundred times on a day like this. They have a great system going. You'll be impressed!"

"Oh. I see." Said Cat, then a thought struck her and she asked. "Do the ferries run at night?"

"Don't want to say goodbye to me just yet, do you?" He winked, forcing Cat to stifle a shudder. "No, they have to let the animals rest at night, so it looks like we can have one last dinner together. And perhaps share a drink?"

"I..." Cat started. "Don't drink. But do not let me stop you from enjoying yourself."

"Oh, don't worry, sister. As long as I have your company, I definitely will." He grinned, gesturing toward the inn. "Shall we??"

He began to walk to the inn, and for a moment Cat turned her head and looked back at the crowd, hoping to catch sight of a familiar face. Inwardly, she thanked the gods that it was the end of the day, and they wouldn't be able to go forward until the morning. That gave Gou one more night to catch up.

But, the nature of the crowded port also meant that if Gou didn't arrive soon, he could be trapped on this side while Snowtop and his men raced ahead. One night was so much time, and yet also seemed so little.

Sighing, Cat turned and went inside. Leaving her silent prayers hanging on the evening breeze.

CHAPTER FOURTEEN

Green Rapids Town

The sun's first morning rays glittered off the expanse of the Zhe river, framing fishing boats and their already long-tired occupants. The Zhe river was shallow but wide, and here above the rapids, where the river bottom dipped slightly, the fish were plentiful and varied. From the River Herring to the mighty Sturgeon, all could be caught here with time and patience, and then sent to the markets of Green Rapids Town, just below the rocky shoals.

Green Rapids Town was a common point of meeting for travelers between the marshy South and the plains of the North, being the only major crossing for some distance of the otherwise treacherous river. A bridge being difficult to build on a river that flooded as often as the Zhe did, the crossings were made on two cable-towed ferry-barges that connected the Southern Green Rapids Town with the smaller Kingfisher Village on the north side.

Each ferry-barge, large enough to hold fifty travelers at a time, or several carts and their oxen and attendants, plied the river back and forth in a constant monotony every day the river allowed it. From early morning until late at night, teams of oxen and slaves worked to enable this system to flow, but unlike machines, the men and animals had their limits. Only so many barges could cross each day, but the flood of travelers who wanted to do the crossing was nearly endless, especially in the high season of late summer.

The end result of this was that there was almost always a huge backlog of people waiting for their chance to cross, sometimes needing to wait for days, and the local economy had adapted accordingly. Shops, tea houses, inns, brothels and gambling halls filled Green Rapids, and the locals considered it their civic duty to see how much traveler's money they could acquire, to the point of making a near sport of it. As gloomy as it was during the winter, Green Rapids was like a constant carnival in the summer months, and a crowded mass of sights and sounds that rivaled anywhere in the Middle Kingdom.

Into this press of people, Little Gou and his companion Miss Lily walked their horses, looking for a place to stop and rest for a time. A hard night's ride was now at their backs, and their bodies demanded rest- the demand made even more acute by the fact that neither had slept especially well in the last two days.

"Where did you say you would meet your friend?"

Gou shrugged. "I didn't. I figured I'd be able to find her once I got here."

This got him a raised eyebrow from his companion. "Did you know it would be this crowded?"

"Yep," Gou said without concern. "My friend is pretty easy to find, though."

"I see."

Gou smiled. "You will when I find her. While I'm gone, why don't you go down to the dock and see how long the wait is to get on one of the ferries? Don't buy any tickets, just find out what kind of wait time we're looking at. Then come back to..." He peered around, and then picked a restaurant at random. "That steamed bun place over there with the red sign."

Ms. Lily looked at the place, and then nodded. "And where will you be?"

"Finding my friend."

"How?"

"Watch and see. Just follow my lead, and whatever happens, don't do anything to stop it."

Gou's companion looked at him, a hundred questions behind her eyes, and then she just shrugged and did as he asked.

Gou walked for a short time, casually looking around as though trying to decide which place to stay. Then, having found an interesting looking place that offered both a bed and companionship, he reached into his traveling bag, pulled out one of his coin purses and quickly pretended to count out some money. After he had done so, he frowned, shook his head, and placed the purse back into the bag- but did so in such a way that the top of the purse was still visible through the bag opening. After that, he looked around again at the local shops, sighed, and slouched his shoulders as if in acceptance of a harsh reality.

With Gou seemingly oblivious, it didn't take long before a short malnourished looking boy appeared in the crowd just ahead of them. As Gou approached, he waved and tried to catch Gou's attention.

"Hey mister, wanna buy some cooked chestnuts? Cheap!"

Gou shook his head, and waved the kid away, but at the same time he felt a slight tug on his bag as the change purse was gently pulled free. Gou had to admire the kid's accomplice, as he or she had a light touch, and would probably have a good future ahead of them in such a traveler-rich environment. But, now that they had taken the bait, it was time for Gou to play his own part.

Jerking up, Gou whirled around and fixed his eyes on a little girl just starting to fade into the crowd, her eyes going wide as they met his. Then she was gone, and Gou was shouting.

"Thief! My purse!" He howled. Then he spun on Ms. Lily, who was just as startled as the little girl had been. "Here, take this! I'm going after her!" He shouted as he shoved the reigns of his horse into Ms. Lily's hands and took off running into the crowd.

Ms. Lily was so startled, all she could do was stammer a moment, and then watch as Gou too was swallowed by the crowd and vanished.

* * *

What Gou needed was a source of information, and he knew if he wanted to find one in a place like this, the best people to ask were the pickpockets. Mostly children, he'd noted more than two dozen of them working the crowd as he'd moved along the busy streets, and knew the game well enough to pick out the standard methods they used to ply their trades.

The little girl who'd picked his purse had followed what she'd assumed to be a hidden escape route into a rabbit warren maze of spaces that existed under the tables of the roadside sellers. It was a common enough method for escape for one so young and small, and she'd probably used it many times before to escape whenever she was noticed.

But this time when she at last surfaced at the normal meeting point there was a difference, her accomplice was there as usual- but he wasn't alone. The moment she saw Gou, she jumped and tried to retreat back into her rabbit hole, but this time lightning-fast hands grabbed her before she could turn and hauled her up into the light by the back of her tunic.

She thought about kicking and screaming and crying for help, since concerned people often stopped to help a poor child being abused. But, the moment she locked eyes with the amused looking Gou, she suddenly found herself instinctively knowing he didn't mean her any harm and relaxed despite herself.

"Purse." Gou held out an open hand.

With a shy smile, the waif lifted the purse into view and set it down in his hand.

Gou looked at the purse, then back at her.

"And, the coins you just snuck out before you gave it to me."

Those too appeared in his hand after a moment's hesitation.

Then with a nod, Gou set her down next to her older partner.

"You kids want to make some easy money?" He asked before they could retreat again.

That made them pause- both of them eying him suspiciously.

"What kind of work?" Demanded the older boy, taking a business posture.

"Not the kind you usually do. I'm looking for someone and I hope you can help me find her."

"Pay first." Said the boy.

Gou reached into his purse, and tossed each of them a copper coin. "Half now, half when I find her. Agreed?"

They both did, and Gou briefly described Sister Cat to them- someone neither of them had seen before, but who were more than willing to help him find. The boy, Jun was his name, had a quick exchange with the girl, Pei, and then Gou was told to wait while they both ran off again.

By the time the famished Gou had finished two fish and ginger steam buns at a nearby seller, Pei reappeared and told him to follow her. Taking him via a series of back alleys with surprising speed, the girl eventually brought Gou to a large inn just off the main thoroughfare. Jun was waiting across the street with another boy, and approached them quickly.

"She there." Said the boy with a nod towards the inn, putting out his hand again.

Gou looked again at the inn.

"Five Safe Golden Nights Inn," read the sign in large red characters across a wooden title board.

When he saw that, Gou was both surprised and yet somehow sure that this was in fact the right place. Nodding to himself, he gave each of the children their payment and thanked them, then marched across the street towards the front step of the inn.

Casually stepping over the front door sill and into the main hall of the inn, Gou took note of the armed men who were gathered at several tables inside. They were gambling and playing dice while they drank and whiled the time away, but their presence confirmed what he suspected. The Cho family ran a series of inns that were actually waystations and safehouses for the convoys they protected as they moved across the middle kingdom, and each of these had the words "safe" and "golden" somewhere in their names to let members of their organization find these inns no matter where they may be. Green Rapids Town, being the major crossing that it was, would be expected to have a large one, and this was clearly it.

But the question was- what was the Sister doing here?

As the host approached him to inquire to his needs, Gou smiled and played a simple hunch- he asked to speak to Snowtop Cho.

The old host looked him over once, and then asked him to wait, disappearing into the back rooms of the Inn, but not before quietly telling some of the armed men to keep an eye on Gou. They did their best to look tough, but Gou just smiled and ignored their stares.

A few moments later, Gou was being hustled into the back rooms himself, and was led into a small but luxurious private hall where it appeared Snowtop was holding court. It seemed as if he'd been preparing to intimidate whoever had come to see him, for Snowtop was seated in a raised chair, and various lieutenants were standing around the room looking fierce. But the moment they recognized Gou everything changed- the group of them relaxed and Snowtop hopped out of his chair to rush and embrace Gou.

"Gou!" He exclaimed, much more warmly than the last time they'd met. "When old Yu told me, someone had come to see me I assumed...well...nevermind. What are you doing here?"

"Morning Cho, you haven't seen my friend Sister Cat around, have you? I'm looking for her."

"Brother Gou?" Came a hopeful voice from nearby, and then the tall nun stooped under a doorway curtain and stepped into the room.

"Ahh, there you are, Sister. I was worried you'd run off and joined another nunnery on me."

"Gou, it's so good to see you. What happened?"

"Nothing we can't talk about later." He said, not wanting to reveal much in front of Cho until he knew why Cat was there. "You two meet on the road?"

"Oh," said Cat, hesitating. "Yes, I was traveling and Brother Cho was kind enough to offer to escort me as I made my pilgrimage north."

"Well, that's mighty nice of you, Cho."

Snowtop shook his head. "Not at all. Always happy to help a friend in need, Gou. Although I am curious- how did you know to find the Sister here?"

"Well brother, it's like this." Gou grinned. "You have your intelligence network, and I have mine. Mine might be a little shorter than yours, but what they lose in height, they make up for in numbers."

Cho nodded, and Gou could see he was trying not to show his puzzlement at what Gou had said. That suited Gou fine, however, as it kept Cho from asking further questions that Gou might not feel like answering.

"Speaking of numbers," Gou interrupted before Cho could regain his train of thought. "Do you mind if we reduce these odds to two? I came because I need to discuss some private business with the good Sister here."

"Not at all," Cho indicated the room from which Cat had just come. "I can tell whatever it is that it must be important. We'll talk after."

In a short time, Gou and Cat were alone, and when Gou had made sure to his satisfaction there was no-one listening, he turned and spoke to Cat in a low voice.

"Sister, we need to talk."

Cat gestured for him wait, worry clear in her eyes. "Brother Gou, I'm so glad to see you. I didn't know what to do, and we have to do something."

Caught off-guard by Cat's descent into near-panic, Gou put his own thoughts aside for the moment and let his curiosity guide him. "Do something? What do you mean?"

"Brother Gou, do you remember those three villains we met at the inn said that they had an escort agency sent to find Miss Mao?"

Gou gave a sharp nod. "Of course, why?"

"Brother, the agency they talked of is the Cho family agency! He's been sent to find her caravan!"

It took a moment for the words to sink into Gou's brain, but when they did a look of deep concern spread over his face. "Are you sure?"

"Yes," she bobbed her head emphatically. "I heard Cho talking about it yesterday morning, and again later overheard his men speaking of it as well."

"No..." Gou couldn't believe it. "You've got to be wrong, Sister. Cho would do anything to get close to Meiyu, but he wouldn't work for Lady Moonlight, especially not after the other night."

"I don't know what to think, Brother Gou." She replied. "But I know what I heard."

"Maybe he was sent by her father?" Gou offered as an alternative. "But...If that's the case then why would he have the Chos do it? Hmmm...No, something doesn't add up here."

"Then what do we do?"

Gou thought about it a moment.

"Leave it to me."

* * *

Following their encounter with Gou earlier, the two pickpockets Jun and Pei had returned to their daily work. The crowd was thick, there was protection money to be paid to the gangs. Their small family of thieves also needed money to survive when the Zhe River's waters ran cold with the upcoming end of the travel season.

Clutching his bag of chestnuts, Jun scanned the crowd, looking for their next mark.

Spotting some obvious out-of-towners, Jun began his approach.

There were three of them, each leading a horse. A tall slender one with a ponytail, a large fat one who looked like a Buddha statue come to life, and a cloaked one whose travel robes stuck out at odd angles.

Coming around from the side, Jun observed them, and saw that the tall slender one with the sword had left his horse's travel back untied. It was a good opportunity, and he decided to take it. He signaled the nearby Pei to go for the bag, and then began to get himself in front of the trio for the distraction.

But, just as Jun began his pitch, and to thrust the bag of nuts forward, the words suddenly died in his throat.

The slender man had only glanced at him, but those eyes had been cold enough to reduce Jun's resolve to tatters in a split second. In that fragment of a moment, Jun knew he was looking at something that wasn't quite human, and left him certain that if he said another word it would be his last.

Letting them pass, Jun just stared, and then he remembered his partner- he had to stop her!

Spinning around, Jun looked for Pei, but saw no sign of the girl.

Where had she gone?

* * *

"Where is he? I know that you know."

Ms. Lily held the little girl by the faded white shirt she wore, making sure the little street urchin couldn't escape.

Despite the threats, Pei looked up with defiance at the woman who held her and shook her head. Then she extended an open palm.

Seeing this, Ms. Lily made an exasperated sound. She'd been waiting for Gou for some time now, and after spotting this pickpocket she'd decided to try and see if she knew where he'd gone. The problem was that she didn't even know if Gou had found the girl, much less if the girl knew where Gou was.

Finally, deciding that she didn't have much choice, Lily took out a coin and placed it in the girl's hand.

That completely changed the girl's manner, and she grinned up at Lily with a gap-toothed smile.

"You want me to take you to him, miss?"

Lily indicated that she did.

"Follow." Said the girl.

* * *

From a nearby spot of shade under an awning, three pairs of eyes watched the little girl begin to lead Ms. Lily off towards one of the side streets.

Xiao, who had noticed her first, looked at his slender companion.

"Do you want me to grab her?"

But Last Brother Shou just shook his head. "No. Let's see where she takes us."

This made Xiao laugh. "You just want to find that Feng fellow and teach him a lesson."

Shou didn't answer. He didn't need to.

"Fine, fine." Xiao shrugged, and handed the reigns of his horse to their armored companion. "Wait here."

Then he merged into the crowd with surprising speed.

Shou watched him go, squinting in the late morning sun. Despite his stoic appearance, he was quite pleased. He'd come this way hoping to find these two, and here they were. Now they could take care of this piece of unfinished business before they continued on north to get the bride.

Good luck all around.

CHAPTER FIFTEEN

Crossing Over

Sitting at a long table in the main dining hall of the Five Safe Golden Nights Inn, Little Gou leaned over and poured his friend Cho another cup of wine.

"I have to say, Cho, I'm pretty surprised to see you here, especially after everything that went on back at Mao's party. I'd have thought you'd want to stick close to town to help them out."

Cho raised an eyebrow at that. "I would have thought the same of you, Gou. You left town in an awful hurry."

Gou shrugged. "Didn't you hear? There's a big game of Pai Gow happening in Yangzhou next week. All the major players are going to be there. You should come check it out."

Cho looked at his friend and sighed. "I never knew you were so callous Gou. The Mao's could use even a man like you."

Gou leaned back in his chair. "Money is money, and the Mao's aren't about to do me any favors. Besides, who are you to say that? I thought you expected to be old man Mao's son-in-law, but here you are chasing gold just like me."

Hearing that brought a grin to Snowtop Cho's face. "Ah Gou," he said, looking with pride at his childhood friend. "If you knew, your eyes would become like jade."

"Oh, c'mon. It's not like you can't tell me."

"Well," Cho considered, and Gou could see in his eyes what looked to be ego battling with caution- ego won. "You remember the party, and the threat that devil witch made toward Meiyu?"

Gou nodded that he did.

"Well, Master Mao sent me to bring her home."

"Oh really?" Gou said, letting his actual uncertainty show. "Maybe you'll have a chance to eat at his table after all. So, he called you in and said he couldn't think of anyone else he wanted to help his daughter?"

"Perhaps he did," Cho smiled confidently. "Who else would he trust more with such an important mission?"

"You mean, besides his own people?"

Cho waved the idea away. "They're too busy."

Gou nodded, as though taking it in. "You don't mind if I see the introduction letter he sent with you, do you? It's not that I don't trust you, but..."

"Sorry Gou," the swordsman said, looking at his drink. "It's not something I can share."

Gou studied him for a time, then shook his head. "So, you didn't get it from him."

That made the swordsman stop and give Gou a sour look.

"Well..." Snowtop admitted. "No... It came through a messenger. But, it did bear his personal seal."

"Personal seals can be faked, you know?"

Snowtop's eyes narrowed, his manner now as cold as his nickname. "What are you implying?"

Gou shrugged. "Nothing. Nothing. Just checking to make sure. After all, we wouldn't want to fall for one of that devil witch's tricks, would we?"

Snowtop stared at him for a time, as if thinking, and then finally he shook his head and gave a sad smile. "Gou...I know this hurts you greatly, that Mao chose me, but please, don't be so bitter about it. Who was he going to choose? You? You're the reason he sent Meiyu away in the first place."

That struck bone, but Gou did his best not to show it.

"I just...wanted to make sure. Meiyu means a lot to me." Gou said, finding his voice showed more real emotion than he planned.

"I know she does," Snowtop's tone became more sympathetic. "Don't worry, I'll take good care of her. You have my word on it."

"Thanks." Gou nodded, and the two of them sat in silence for a time, until Gou asked- "So when are you going across?"

"Just after noon. It took some doing, but I have arranged a barge." Then he paused for a moment and added- "You'll understand if I don't have room for you to join us."

Gou looked at him, feigning surprise. "Did I say I was going across today?" The gambler smiled. "Do you know how much money I can make around a place like this with so many bored travelers?"

"But you came looking for the Sister?"

"We'd planned to meet here."

Snowtop nodded. "I see."

Gou leaned back in his chair. "Yep. Yep. You don't need to worry about me at all. I'm going to plenty busy." Then he suddenly perked up. A woman had just appeared in the front doorway of the inn, a very beautiful and familiar woman. "Speaking of which."

All attention in the dining hall turned to look at Ms. Lily, who was peering around cautiously while her eyes adjusted to the hall's dim light.

Snowtop gave a lecherous smile. "Ah Gou, you never change."

"Excuse me a moment," Gou said, and hopped off the bench to go over to where Ms. Lily watched him with her hands on her hips. "Hello there."

"Where have you been? When you didn't come to the meeting place..."

Gou rubbed the back of his head. "Yeah, sorry about that. I got busy." Then he stepped forward, placing a hand on her back and guiding her in. "Pretend we're just here to gamble," he whispered as he led her to where Snowtop and the others waited.

"Lily, this is..." He said, gesturing to Snowtop, but his words dropped off as he saw the look on his old friend's face. The young swordsman was staring at this girl like she was his grandmother's ghost.

"You..." Said Snowtop, pointed at the woman. "But, you're..."

Gou had a feeling that things had just gotten a whole lot more complicated.

* * *

Slurping back his noodles, Last Brother Shou glanced over at his silent armored companion. Mah seemed to be contemplating his meal, as if trying to decide whether to eat it or not.

This made Shou sigh. Mah was the type who was nearly always depressed about one thing or another. In Mah's case, perhaps it was somewhat justified by what the man had lost, but it was still annoying.

"You'll need your strength." Shou nudged the bowl in front of the large man. "Eat it."

Mah's head turned slowly to look at him, and then he looked back at the bowl of noodles and nodded. Reaching up a gauntleted hand, Mah removed the "death's mask" faceplate he normally wore to cover his face and set it down on the table next to him.

As Mah began to eat, Xiao appeared. He plopped right down on the wooden bench across from Shou, and waved a few pudgy fingers in the air to attract the attention of the waiter.

"Did you find him?"

The bronze skinned man nodded. "I did." Then, after yelling his order, he turned back to Shou. "They're both here, at an inn on the East side."

Shou started to rise, reaching for the sword beside him on the table, but Xiao waved him down. "Not so quick, my friend. There's more you need to know."

Shou considered him a moment, and then sat back down.

"Explain."

And Xiao did.

Xiao had followed the former Mrs. Yi and the little child across the town until the girl had led the woman to an inn. There, the child had pointed to the inn and they had parted ways, with the child returning to the streets and the woman going inside.

Staying a safe distance away, Xiao had seen the woman enter the foyer of the inn, and the man they knew as Feng come out from inside to greet her. Then they had gone inside, and while he wanted to follow, there was something about this Inn that made Xiao cautious. He had noticed many large armed men about, and the place seemed awfully heavily guarded for a normal tavern.

So, instead of approaching, Xiao had begun asking around, trying to find out more about the place. It hadn't taken him long to learn the inn's true nature and ownership, and once he'd learned that, he'd approached one of the coming and going stable boys to find out a little more detailed information. A few coins later and he'd had enough to return.

"So, he's connected with the Cho family." Shou remarked.

"Yes, he's in there with Snowtop Cho right now. He, Yi's wife, and that big nun too, along with at least a dozen other fighters."

"The lady's plan has failed." Came a third voice, and the two looked in surprise at Mah before nodding in agreement.

"Yeah, we can't rely on the Cho family to fetch her anymore." Xiao said. "We'll have to go get the girl ourselves. Of course, we were going to do it anyway, but now we really need to get across that river fast. I'm sorry, Shou, but your revenge may have to wait."

Shou considered this. He burned for revenge against the pair, but he had to consider the rewards his lady would give him if he returned with the girl. If they waited too long here, the chance could be lost, and all hope of success as well, unless...

The grave swordsman fixed the bronze skinned man with an intense look. "Do you know when they plan to cross?"

Xiao grinned, which meant he did. "The boy said they were to ready the horses just after lunch."

Shou waited while Xiao's food was delivered to the table, and then he told them his plan.

* * *

Gou grabbed Lily's arm, pulling her to a stop.

She turned to face him, and he could see tears running down her cheeks. "Let go of me!" She cried, and tried half-heartedly to pull her arm away.

Gou didn't budge, ignoring the stares of the passersby on the busy street around them.

"What was all that?"

But the young woman looked away and didn't answer, although she did stop struggling. She just stood there and cried.

After a moment, Sister Cat emerged from the crowd.

"Brother Gou?" She said, looking at the girl, and then him.

Gou shook his head. "I have no idea. I guess they know each other."

Almost immediately after coming face to face with Snowtop, Miss Lily had turned and dashed from the Inn, leaving everyone stunned. Gou had taken the chance to dash after her, and apparently Cat had done the same in the sudden confusion.

"Is anyone else following?" He asked the nun.

She indicated they weren't.

"Brother Gou, what are we to do?"

Gou considered a moment. This event might have turned out to be a blessing in disguise. It was clear Snowtop was being used, but refused to accept it because of his blind feelings for Meiyu. Now they were away from Snowtop and his men, and had a chance to try and get ahead of them. Of course, that required crossing the river before noon, and there was little time left.

Gou turned to the *Jin Hua* woman again, and drew closer to her.

"Lily, I know it's been a big shock for you, but we've got to move. Can you walk?"

There was silence for a moment, and then Lily nodded, slowly composing herself. "Let's go," she rasped.

Gou and Cat exchanged a curious look, and then the three of them set out for the docks as fast as they could manage.

* * *

If there was a single truism that held strong among the men of the Middle Kingdom, it was this- if any single group of men gathered and were forced to wait for any length of time, gambling would begin.

Thus, when Gou and the others found the string of people waiting to board the noontime ferry-barge, it took only a few rolls of the dice before Gou had three spots near the front of the line. It only took a small challenge, and the men were more than happy to offer their places instead of paying the money they now owed, despite the scolding it earned them from their unhappy wives.

So, when the two barges traded places, and the newly arrived ferry was done unloading, Gou and his companions were among the first of the passengers waiting to board. This didn't mean they actually boarded first, however. The main purpose of the barges was to carry across horses, carts, livestock, and the other components of trade caravans. Once the caravans who had booked the ferry-barges were aboard, only then were the individual passengers allowed to fill in what space was left on a first-come, first-serve basis.

Gou watched as five covered wagons without their animals were loaded aboard by dock workers, and then the animals themselves- three horses, a donkey, and seven oxen were tucked in around the wagons with expert precision. He had to admire the skill of these workers, and their ability to pack as much as they possibly could into so limited a space. He knew he was watching generations of knowledge play out before his eyes, and made a point of enjoying the show.

At last, the small caravan was all set in, and the man who guarded the passenger line received a nod from the foreman. Opening the wooden gate, he motioned for the human cattle to come aboard with a wave of his burly arm, collecting their wooden tickets as they entered.

Gou, being near the front of the line, moved as fast as he could along the side of the barge with his two companions in tow, heading straight for the front. He wanted to be in a good position to leave quickly once they arrived on the other side, especially since they'd need to hire new horses once they got there. Knowing the animals would prevent them from crossing quickly, they'd elected to sell their horses on this side in favor of getting new ones once they'd crossed. It was a large and expensive risk, but a necessary one to maintain speed.

Arriving at the front, the three hustled along the long wooden gate that blocked off the far end of the boat, and took positions at a prime vantage spot. Soon the whole narrow section was crowded elbow to elbow, and Gou made a point of placing his purses deep in his tunic's inner pockets, suggesting his companions do something similar.

"Will the crossing take long?"

Gou shook his head at the large nun, who was looking a bit cramped in these crowded conditions. "Shouldn't take too long. Just remember to breathe."

"I shall try." Said the nun, giving an evil stare to the man with the wandering hands standing next to her. He backed off fast enough once he realized the position he was in.

"How are you doing?" Gou asked Lily, who had remained quiet and downcast for some time now.

She shook her head from side to side without looking at him, her eyes lost somewhere in the river waters. "I will be fine."

"When you want to talk about it, I'm a good listener."

"I do not wish to." She said, a hint of anger in her voice.

"Fine. Fine." He said, backing off emotionally, if not physically. "Up to you."

This was an odd turn, Gou considered. It did make sense, with both being members of the armed escort world, that Snowtop and Lily might have met before, but to have such a strong reaction was a bit of a surprise. He couldn't help but smile a little though- Snowtop was so proper and upright he'd never expected his old friend could be a heartbreaker, but this clearly seemed to be the case.

It was going to be worth the couple bottles of wine it would take to get the story from the swordsman when the whole affair was done, Gou mused as he looked around. Their fellow passengers were the usual bunch- merchants, peddlers and pilgrims, no one looking especially interesting.

After a few more moments, Gou saw a yellow flag appear at the port on the other side, and there was some yelling from behind them. Then they heard the almost thunderous sounds of chains being drawn through a mechanism, and he watched as huge iron chains were drawn up from the gray-green waters of the river until they were taut, forming a direct line between the front of their barge and the port on the other side.

Soon, their ferry lurched forward, and the whole thing began to move. At the same time, Gou could see a second set of chains that extended from the other side to the port that they had just left, and another barge which was setting out from the distant port toward them.

It was all very exciting for the first few minutes, and the people around him seemed quite impressed, with Sister Cat staring at the whole thing in wonder. Even Miss Lily was brought out of her funk by the experience, looking around with some interest now as this ingenious method carried them across the waters. But Gou, having experienced this a few times before, quickly lost interest and began to look around again. They were halfway across already, and it wouldn't be long now before they reached the other side.

That's when Gou spotted him.

Or perhaps, you could say he spotted Gou. It happened at the same time.

For, standing right above them atop one of the covered wagons, looking down on the passengers, was the tall, slender swordsman called Last Brother Shou.

The gambler's eyes fixed with the swordsman.

And the swordsman gave a cold, sinister smile.

Gou felt a chill run down his back.

"Sister..." Gou said, groping for the nun's robes, and both she and Ms. Lily turned to look at Gou, the sound of worry in his voice bringing them alert.

But, when they followed his gaze up to where Shou was, the swordsman was already gone.

"Gou, what is it?"

"It's Last Brother Shou, he's on the ferry. He was right there." He told the worried nun, and started looking for a way around the wagons back to the main deck.

"Shou? Here?" Ms. Lily gasped, now completely alert. "But if he's here..."

"You can bet those other sons of turtles are as well." Gou couldn't see a way around the packed deck, so instead he began to elbow back toward the wagons, letting the passengers who were behind him move forward. The two women followed him, and they stopped when they reached the back of the wagon.

"We'll crawl underneath to get onto the main deck," Gou said, indicating the large gap beneath the wagon. "Then we can..."

A deep shadow passed overhead, causing Gou to spin around and look up just in time to see two more shadows leap from the wagon top and land gracefully on the front railing. Turning, Gou saw it was Shou and his two companions, but they were only on the railing for a fraction of a second before they leapt off the front of the boat.

Unable to see past the people between him and the front, Gou at first thought they'd jumped into the water, but after a moment he saw them again. They were running along the thick chains that connected the barge to the other side of the river!

The chains were pulled taut by the tension, but even still, they were slick with water and the trio were demonstrating amazing skill with lightfoot kung fu as they moved along the chains with incredible speed. Gou had known they were masters from his rooftop encounter with them, but this display of dexterity only further cemented his mutual feelings of awe and fear at what these men were capable of.

But these feelings only lasted a moment, and then they too were gone, shattered by the call that rose up from the main deck of the barge.

"Fire! Fire!"

Gou didn't even have time to curse before the world around him exploded into panic and terror.

* * *

"Cheer up, master!"

Snowtop Cho sighed and shook his head. "Chan, what should I do?"

When Spider Chan had returned to the Five Golden Safe Nights Inn from gathering information, he had found the place in total disarray. Even his master was drinking heavily by the hearth with everyone afraid to approach him. This was a double shock, both because they were short on time, and because in all his years with the family, he could count on a single hand the number of times he had seen Snowtop drink more than a single cup of wine.

Thus, with only a short time before their barge was to leave, Chan had quickly set about putting things into motion and getting ready for their party to make a crossing. It had been a near thing, but long experience helped him get everything together, including his somewhat drunken master. Now, the two men were riding at the heads of two lines of horses down the market street heading for the dock at a brisk pace.

"Master," Chan said, sympathetically. "If I've learned anything in my many years, it's that you can't hang your life on the ways of women. If she had wanted to see you, she wouldn't have fled like she did."

Cho's head hung like a tired dog's. "I know, Chan. I know."

"Focus on our mission, Young Master." Chan said, trying to be upbeat. "Why should you worry about the past when you've got a bright future to look toward?"

Snowtop let his head bob in agreement, but there wasn't much enthusiasm there.

Letting out a small sigh, Chan was considering telling one of his own stories to cheer the Young Master up when he noticed people in the crowd running toward the dock. He watched curiously as news was passed along, and then some people ran toward the dock while others ran off to tell more people.

Something was up, and Chan suspected whatever it was wouldn't be good.

Then the riders came around a corner onto the main road leading straight down to the dock, and all questions were answered.

"The ferry!"

There, almost halfway across the river, sat a ferry-barge almost completely engulfed in flames. Waves of smoke poured off a bright orange inferno, covering the river downstream with a thick blanket of black smoke. On the other side of the river, the opposite ferry port was also in flames, pouring even more smoke into the air.

Chan stared at the sight, open-mouthed for a time, and then turned to look at Snowtop. He had expected the young master to be equally shocked, but instead of surprised, he found the young man looking alert and determined instead.

"Young Master?"

"Chan," the swordsman said calmly. "Take a few men, and find a boatman that will take a few people across without horses. We can get some on the other side. Reserve him before others do."

"Of course, Young Master."

Then Snowtop looked back at his assembled fighters, once again the master of the Cho Family Armed Escort Agency, and yelled out- "The rest of you, with me! We'll see if there's anything we can do to help!"

Chan watched them go rushing down toward the dock, and despite the circumstances couldn't help smiling. It was good to have the Young Master feeling himself again. Then he took the men who had stayed and rushed off down a side street, heading upstream.

He pitied the people on board that barge. He'd seen such fires before in his career, and knew the death toll that went with them. He didn't expect there would be many survivors this time, either.

CHAPTER SIXTEEN

Meiyu

In a bridal caravan, there are few people more uncomfortable than the bride, especially when her father insists that she ride in a proper palanquin the whole way. While such a conveyance might offer luxurious comfort to some, to Mao Meiyu, the palanquin was a hot boring box that offered neither enough light to read by, nor enough comfort to sleep in. If there had been a method of torture more certain to drive one mad than this, she hadn't heard of it.

As she gave up trying to read for the umpteenth time in a week, Meiyu cried out for her bearers to stop. The men carrying her did as she ordered, and she whipped back the green door curtain and hopped out as quickly as she could.

"My lady, what seems to be the problem?"

Meiyu turned as her "Uncle" Gan came riding back on his horse. The burly old swordsman was one of her father's most trusted lieutenants, and had long cared for Meiyu much like a real uncle would, even following her to the imperial capital to take over operations there when she had been sent there to be educated by her father. He had claimed it was all a coincidence when he'd come to pay his respects shortly after she'd settled in, but she knew better- he was there to keep an eye on her.

"Uncle, please. Please. Please. Please! Let me ride a horse!"

The old man shook his head. "Tradition states..."

"You know damn well that this isn't tradition! I'm not going to my husband's home- I'm returning to my own!" She glared up at him, challenging him to tell her she was wrong.

"That may be," Gan said, not backing down. "But a young lady, and especially a young bride to be, cannot risk the dangers of a horse when her wedding night is so close."

He emphasized those last words to drive his point home. He had been perfectly fine with Meiyu riding a horse all these years, and in fact had overseen her being taught to do so when she'd been barely six. However, that had all ended when an old meddler of a nurse had taken him aside and whispered in his ear the potential riding a horse carried for a loss of maidenhood, and thus a ruined first night that might also be the quick end of a marriage.

Not being willing to risk being blamed for such an event, Meiyu's riding days had come to an abrupt halt, and Gan clearly had no intention of changing that rule under any circumstances.

"If my lady is feeling cramped, she is most welcome to walk." He told her, then wheeled around his horse and gestured for the caravan to begin moving. There were over fifty people in the wedding caravan, which brought not only Meiyu from the center of the empire, but also an abundance of gifts, foodstuffs and other items. Six carts and twenty pack horses worth of goods to be precise, in addition to what the servants carried on their backs.

Meiyu watched some of them pass her by, and then fell in step with the procession, her own personal maids appearing around her with an umbrella to shield her from the summer heat as the caravan threaded its way down south through the central plain towards Zhejiang and White Fox Town.

"Where are we now?" Meiyu asked one of her maids, Little Jing, who was also one of her closest friends.

"Near Xuzhou," the small, sharp eyed woman answered. "We'll be crossing the Feihuang River soon, and entering Tongshan."

Meiyu nodded. "Over halfway then," she said thoughtfully. "I wonder how he'll look?"

"I am told the second son of the Yun family is not unattractive."

Meiyu looked at her maid, and her eyes sparkled with laughter. "Oh yes. Him. I suppose he'll be good looking enough, although his younger brother has the nose of a monkey, so it does make one wonder..."

The maids laughed at that, and Meiyu grinned.

*　*　*

With the coming of dusk, the caravan found and settled at a large country inn of the kind that specialized in trade caravans between north and south. While the carriers settled and unpacked, Meiyu took the time to ready herself to be presentable for dinner. However, when she went to leave her room, her uncle appeared and barred her way.

"You will be dining in your room tonight," he informed her in a serious tone.

When she pressed for details, he finally relented and explained that several disreputable characters had been seen around the busy inn and he was concerned for her safety.

Of course, telling this to a young lady with Meiyu's temperament just made her want to attend the communal dinner even more!

She waited until he'd left, then quickly switched to some boy's clothes she'd brought for just such an occasion.

"How do I look?" She asked Little Jing as she struck a serious and thoughtful pose. She was now a handsome looking young man in blue pants, a grey long coat with white sequins, and a black cap atop her head to hide her hair.

"Kind sir, will you marry me?" Asked the maid, looking at her with big, adoring eyes.

"Sorry, my dear." Meiyu replied in the deepest voice she could manage. "The world is filled with too many beauties for a man such as myself to settle down."

"Oh, dear sir! You're so cruel!" Cried the maid in mock despair, and then they both laughed.

"Wear my dress," she told her friend. "If anyone comes to serve food, pretend to be me but don't let them in. Have them leave it just inside the door."

The maid agreed, and then after her maids distracted the guards her uncle left, Meiyu slipped out the door and down the hallway into the communal dining room.

The inn's great hall was a large noisy affair, filled with the sights, sounds and smells of over a hundred travelers taking their evening rice. Dishes of all kinds flowed around the room on trays, while wine was toasted and men and women of all shapes and sizes laughed, yelled and chattered like birds. Trays of seasoned beef in soy sauce, barbecued pork and drunken chicken made Meiyu's mouth water as their smells wafted up, and flowed in the smoky lantern light that kept the hall lit as summer evening descended.

Unable to resist, Meiyu quickly found a spot near the railing where she could look down upon the diners, and ordered up several dishes. Then she sat back with her tea and began to observe the people below her, feeling a little thrill at the power anonymity afforded her. She could see without being seen, and observe freely in ways that her school's headmistress would most definitely disapprove of.

It made her lips curl into a smile as she watched the bustle below.

Her uncle, and the rest of the guards and caravan leaders were gathered at a long table just underneath her, with the carriers and other staff consigned to eat in the servant's quarters behind the inn. Her own maids would eat in their rooms, as had been decided by her overprotective uncle.

The other tables were mostly occupied by people she judged as merchants and their companions, as one would expect at a trade crossing like this. Among them she also spotted a few swordsmen, obvious bodyguards and escorts, although none were people she knew, or who looked especially interesting or famous. In fact, as she surveyed the room more closely, she became less and less impressed with its contents. Her uncle had promised danger, but she saw none here, just boringly normal people stained with mud and wine.

Still, the night was young and there was always hope. So, she tucked into her dinner and enjoyed her meal, keeping an ear and eye open for whatever might pop up below.

It was as she was finishing the chicken, she'd ordered that her eye caught motion on the other balcony across from where she sat. Glancing over, she saw three people standing solemnly at the rail, looking down at where her uncle and the others sat below.

There were two women- one prune faced, one around her own age- and a young man who had the build and bearing of a swordsman. All three were clad in black, with each also having an article of bright green to offset their plain attire. The ugly older woman had her black hair piled up into a topknot with a bright green ribbon, the slender and attractive young woman had a bright green sash around her waist, and the swordsman wore a bright green vest with a golden slash on the lapel. All three carried long, slender Jian swords in ornately gilded sheaths.

So distinctive were they that Meiyu was positive she knew these strangers, but couldn't quite put her finger on their names. What was clear, however, was that these three were focused on her uncle, and from them she could feel a strong air of menace and malevolent intent. As she watched, the girl stepped back and left, while the older woman and the young man headed for the stairs.

Her pulse quickened as the old prune led the young man down the side staircase and through the assembled until she reached the table where the members of the Mao Family Armed Escort Agency sat enjoying their meal. She approached from behind Uncle Gan, and for a moment Meiyu wanted to yell out a warning before the old witch tried something, but just as the words started to form in her mouth the conversation at the table died and she saw hands lay on swords. Her uncle casually rose from his seat and turned to face the new arrivals while the men behind him stood up.

Meiyu now wished she'd thought to bring a sword. While she was no master of the blade, she knew how to use it better than many of her father's men and could make herself useful in the right moments. This looked to be one of those moments, and she unconsciously leaned in, expecting to see metal flash like it often did when members of the *Jianghu* martial underworld met.

Instead, what she saw was her uncle clasp his hands together and bow deeply to the old woman, and many of the other men do the same!

"Madam Lin!" Exclaimed the old swordsman. "This is a most unexpected pleasure!"

Meiyu's memory clicked the pieces into place. The old woman was Madam Lin, head of the Nine Trees Armed Escort Agency, a group that guarded caravans from the Mongol raiders up in the Northeast around Ningyuan. That meant her companions were her granddaughter, Wuyun (also known as Dancing Cloud) and her grandson Wudao (called the Dancing Blade) who had both made a name for themselves in the martial world for their refined paired style of swordsmanship. Their techniques were handed down from their grandparents, and with their parents lost to a fever they had taken a lead in the clan's activities after the recent death of their grandfather.

Even without the grandfather, the elder madam of the Lin clan was still a force to be reckoned with, and there had long been rumors that when Mongol tribes bent on raiding saw the Nine Trees flag they quickly retreated rather than risk her wrath. She was the force that made her clan a power in the escort trade, and now she was facing Meiyu's uncle with unknown intent.

"Master Gan," the old woman said with only a slight nod of her head to return the bow. "It is fortunate that we might meet here. You know my grandson, I presume?"

"Dancing Blade?" Gan said cordially. "I should hope so. The name of the Twin Dancers has carried far and wide. It is a pleasure to meet you, lad!" He greeted the young warrior, who returned his courtesy, then looked at Madam Lin with some curiosity. "I am surprised to see you here. If I may be so presumptuous, is there a special reason for this honor?"

"There is," agreed the Madam. "We are on our way to an event near Suzhou."

"Ah," Gan answered as if he understood. "Yes, you would be, wouldn't you? When I think of it, this meeting was most expected after all! Excuse this old man and his ignorance."

"Yes," the old woman said simply. "In relation to that meeting, I wish you convey a message to your master."

"Yes?" Old Gan said, surprised. "And what might that be?"

It was as she said this that Meiyu noticed something that made her look up and gasp! Standing at the balcony near the entrance to the rear rooms was Dancing Cloud, and with her was a young woman dressed in wedding finery with her hair over her face- Little Jing!

She heard gasps from below as well, and her uncle stammering in shock.

"I believe," said Madam Lin. "The message is clear enough. Tell him we wish an exchange- his daughter's life for the box."

CHAPTER SEVENTEEN

The Lin Family

"...His daughter's life for the box."

Meiyu stared at the scene in shock- her maid, her closest friend, Little Jing was only a thin silver blade away from death. She couldn't believe that the Lin family could be so ruthless or underhanded as to do something like this. Didn't they know what this would do their family reputation?

And what was this box she was talking about? What could be so important?

But Meiyu pushed aside such questions as she heard her uncle finally begin to speak below.

"Madam Lin!" Gan gasped. "This is outrageous!"

The prune faced old woman merely looked at him curiously. "Clearly you are unaware of the stakes involved. Nothing is too outrageous in times such as these."

At this, the assembled Mao family escorts wanted to lunge forward and attack, but Gan held them back with a gesture.

"Madam Lin..." He said, his voice showing the great effort it was taking to remain calm. "Whatever grievances you have with our master, the girl is no part of this. Don't sully the names of your family or shame your ancestors by engaging in such low acts as kidnapping."

"She is a member of your clan, that is enough." Said the elder. "Now, lay down your blades."

Meiyu watched as her Uncle Gan gave a deep sigh and shrugged. "Fine, if you wish there to be blood, then that's how it will be." Then at a whistle from their leader, the nine warriors of the Mao Armed Escort Agency who stood with Gan moved in a flash to surround the old woman and her grandson with their blades.

"Even with your skill, madam." Gan said in an intimidating voice that Meiyu had never heard before, "You and your grandson will not escape us alive." Then he looked up menacingly at Dancing Cloud. "The girl will not escape us either, when we are done with you. So, I offer you a trade, your lives for those of your hostage."

It was a standoff. And, Meiyu watched in rapt fascination as each side faced down the other, neither saying a word as a war of wills took place. She knew her uncle was the veteran of over a hundred caravans, and had no doubts had been in this situation many times before. However, she also knew that Madam Lin was long experienced in these maneuvers of deceit and treachery that often took place within the martial underworld.

Against another opponent, each would likely win, but against such fearsome opposition, who would be victorious was anyone's guess. Either way, the outcome was likely to be short, fast and brutal if one did not back away from the challenge...

And then it happened.

One of her uncle's fighters gave a loud groan, and doubled over.

Everyone looked at the man in shock, but then, another man did the same!

Gan gave Madam Lin a sharp look, "We checked the food for poison."

The crone smiled. "Do you know why my grandchildren are called the Twin Dancers? Because two things which are good when apart can be most deadly when they are brought together."

"No!" Gan shouted, and lunged at her with his sword, but the poison was already starting to affect him as well, and she easily avoided his clumsy attack. Then she counterattacked with her small hands in a burst of moves that left Gan, and the two nearest Mao men lying crumpled on the floor. Her grandson finished the others with equal speed, not leaving a single member of the Mao escorts standing.

Meiyu then watched as Madam Lin stood over the barely conscious Gan.

"I apologize for the methods, but we cannot have you following us. The poison is not lethal, and you will recover...in a few weeks."

Then she turned and stabbed a finger at the innkeeper.

"You."

The short, chubby man bowed nervously. "Yes, my lady?"

"Their servants, fetch them."

While the innkeeper sent a boy to do so, Meiyu considered her options. There wasn't much she was going to be able to do against this old witch, and it sounded like if she kept still these devils would be gone soon. On the other hand, if they left, they would take Little Jing, and when they learned she wasn't Meiyu they would likely kill her.

There had to be a way out of this, and Meiyu struggled to think what it was as she watched Dancing Cloud escort Jing down the stairs to join the others below. What would Little Gou do in a situation like this, she found herself thinking. If only she'd paid more attention to those ridiculous stories he always told while trying to impress her. Perhaps there would have been something there she could use.

But no, she wasn't Little Gou, she was Mao Meiyu, her father's daughter.

And she knew what had to be done.

Meiyu waited until the lead servants appeared, and then made her move.

While Madam Lin instructed the servants to take the poisoned men to their master and pass along the message of her hostage, Meiyu got from her seat and walked down the stairs.

Dancing Blade saw her coming, and perhaps concerned she might be fighter or escort he let his hand fall on his sword hilt as he fixed her with his sharp gaze.

"Begone," he said, watching her approach.

His need to speak caused the others to turn and look at her, and Meiyu saw the shock in Little Jing's eyes as her friend saw her approach. She could see the pleading look in Jing's expression, not for help, but for Meiyu to leave her be! But, this attempt at sacrifice only made Meiyu's determination to carry through even stronger.

"You have the wrong girl," Meiyu said, pulling off her black cap to let her long hair flow free. "I'm the one you want."

For the first time in the evening, even Madam Lin looked confused.

"What is this?"

"I'm Mao Meiyu," she said, standing before them. "That girl is my servant who was taking my place while I ate out here."

The elder Lin looked her over with care, then had Dancing Cloud bring Jing closer so she could be examined. Finally, the old fighter looked at the servants from the caravan she had summoned.

"Is that one," she said, pointing at Meiyu. "Your master's daughter?"

No, the three servants assured her, Jing was in fact their master's daughter, not this stranger.

Satisfied, the old woman made her decision, and at a nod from her, Jing was released and Dancing Sword grabbed Meiyu's arm.

"You resemble your mother," Madam Lin commented. "But, I needed their lies to be sure."

* * *

"Hold."

When Last Brother Shou raised his hand, his two companions brought their horses to a stop. It had been almost a full day and a half since they had stolen these mounts after setting the barge on fire and fleeing from Green Rapids Town. Now, they were searching from inn to inn, looking for any sign or trace of the Mao bridal caravan.

Having stopped for dinner, their questions had borne fruit- some merchants had seen the very caravan they were looking for to the west earlier in the day. They didn't even stay to finish their meals before they were on their hard-worn mounts again and riding, following directions to the most likely place where such a caravan would spend the night.

Now, just before midnight, they had found the Inn in question.

The three dismounted, and Shou sent Xiao to look in the stable yard.

He came back a few minutes later to indicate that there was indeed a large caravan here, including a bridal palanquin.

They had found the right place, at last.

Forming up with Shou at the lead, the three headed straight for the front gate of the Inn. It was quiet inside, but that wasn't unusual for this hour. Only a few lanterns were lit, which meant most of the people would probably be asleep.

All the better for them.

Pushing open the gate, they walked inside. The main hall of the inn was quiet, as expected, and the only occupants of the many tables were a chubby, balding man and what looked to be two servants sitting and talking over wine. The chubby man, who Shou took to be the innkeeper, jumped up and scurried to greet them.

"Gracious guests," he said, bowing slightly, "Welcome. Welcome. Do you need a room for the night?"

Shou kept his voice low, glancing about.

"I'm looking for a bridal caravan owned by the Mao family. Are they staying here?"

The innkeeper froze, his smile fading.

"Ahh...Yes..." He finally said, and something about his tone and odd expression made Shou pause.

"Have they not all come?"

The Innkeeper hesitated, and then explained...

* * *

The sun had just crested the horizon to the east and the air was still filled with the light mists of morning when the horse Meiyu was riding came to an abrupt stop and jolted her out of the half-sleep fatigue had pushed her into.

Looking up, she saw they were now on the bank of what looked to be a long but extremely straight river. Dancing Cloud was beside her, looking as tired as Meiyu felt, and the elder Lin had gone forward with the girl's brother to a very small port along the waterway. There, she could see them bargaining with some dark-skinned merchant from the South who was using his hands a lot.

"Where are we?" Meiyu asked, hoping the sister was feeling talkative.

The girl gave her a sharp look for talking, but then her face softened. She was too tired to play the captor. "It's a canal," she said in her thick Northern accent. "We're going to travel by boat to prevent them from finding us."

Meiyu nodded, but didn't say anything. Weary as she was, even she knew that wasn't correct. Maybe to Northerners, who lived in a dryer climate, water and river travel represented a way to lose their pursuers, but here in central China travel on the canals was anything but private. Not only would everyone in this village know the way they had gone, but everyone along the canal who they passed (and there would be many) would also take note of them.

Her father, Crocodile Mao, had earned his nickname because of his fondness for escorting people and goods on the rivers and canals of the central plains. The Empire was built on its ancient canals, and there was always trade passing along these busy networks of waterways. While it was not the majority of his business anymore, many of the tales Meiyu had grown up on were of jobs done on the water.

She knew the tricks of the trade here, but wondered if the Lin family did.

After a time, Madam Lin returned to the horses and ordered the girls to dismount. They untied Meiyu's hands from the saddle horn, but kept her hands tied together and Dancing Cloud led her along like a horse. The whole group and their horses were escorted to the dock, which at the moment was empty of boats, barges, or anything else resembling transportation.

Dancing Cloud put her on a stone bench and told her to sit quietly, trying the end of the rope to nearby post, and then left Meiyu alone while she walked a short distance away to see to the horses. Not that this gave Meiyu a chance to escape, for Dancing Sword was still near her, seeing to his grandmother's needs.

It seemed they were going to have to wait for the next barge. This suited Meiyu fine, as it meant she wouldn't be on a moving animal. After the night before, even the bruises on her backside had bruises, and she enjoyed sitting on something flat and stable. She leaned back against the wall behind her and closed her eyes to enjoy the moment.

She must have dozed, because the next thing she was aware of was Dancing Cloud talking to her and shoving a steamed bun into her hands. As she accepted it, the other girl sat down beside her and began to eat. Meiyu watched as the desperately hungry girl, who wasn't much older than herself, tried to find a way to eat the still too hot bun by blowing on it and taking small bites. It was all very childlike, and she began to feel that Dancing Cloud was actually a bit immature for her age, despite her stern manner.

Maybe, she thought, under other circumstances she and this girl might have been friends. They really weren't so different, not at all. Well, except for this girl having the manners of a wolf cub.

Then the Lin girl, perhaps realizing that she was being watched, looked at her crossly and gestured toward Meiyu's own bun.

"Eat."

Meiyu nodded and began to nibble, then she said. "Can I ask you something?"

The Lin girl looked at her suspiciously, but didn't say no, so Meiyu continued. "Your grandmother said she wanted to trade me to my father for a box. What kind of box?"

"It is important, that is all I know." The girl said. "Grandmother says we need it to get justice for my grandfather."

Meiyu leaned in. "Master Lin was murdered?"

Dancing Cloud gave a sad nod of her head.

"Who did it?"

"We do not know. We sent letters to the council, but they refused to help us. If we have the box, grandmother says they will listen."

"Wuyun," Meiyu pleased. "This is wrong. Kidnapping me isn't going to help bring justice for your grandfather."

"You are the one who is wrong, child." Came a voice, and Meiyu turned to look up into the angry eyes of Madam Lin. "The only thing those whore sons of the council care about is power, so we will take their precious box from them and use it to make them help us. My late husband's spirit will not rest until the blood of his enemy is poured on his grave."

A fire burned brightly in the old woman's eyes, one that Meiyu had seen many times in her short life as a member of the *Jianghu* martial arts underworld. It was the flame of vengeance, and it made a person sacrifice anyone and anything in order to achieve their bloody dreams. Seeing it in Madam Lin, Meiyu realized at that moment that there would be no reasoning with this woman or her grandchildren.

Talking her way out of this situation would be useless.

She was going to have to find another way.

* * *

It was well into the morning when the boat they were waiting for finally came. Manned by thin, bronze skinned men wearing broad-brimmed straw hats, the flat-bottomed riverboat coasted up to the dock. Almost as soon as it was tied up, the men were scampering to take down the single white sail and transfer the wide boat's cargo to the merchant's men. Busy as ants, the bags of grain and boxes of vegetables they carried were unloaded onto carts that were driven up, and then left once they were full.

Once that was done, the dark-skinned merchant she had seen Madam Lin talk to earlier motioned for them to approach, and Meiyu saw him take Madam Lin's money. The horses were taken aboard first, carefully tied in the middle of the boat, and then Meiyu and the family boarded and were given seats near the front.

The boatmen eyed Meiyu curiously as she was led aboard, but were smart enough to keep their questions to themselves in light of her armed escorts. She was again placed on a bench with Dancing Cloud as her guard, and after the boatmen loaded some other smaller cargo the ship cast off, heading south along the busy canal.

Meiyu drifted back to sleep for a time, the rocking of the boat soothing her, and was only awakened when she became conscious of the singing. Craning her neck around, she saw it was the boatman at the rudder. He had a strong, hearty voice for so thin a man, and the song was a familiar tune in one of the Southern dialects that Meiyu had heard many times. It wasn't long before the other boatmen joined in as well, and soon the whole ship was filled with harmony.

Dancing Cloud looked around at them in wonder.

"Do you want to know what they're singing?" Meiyu asked.

The Northern girl nodded.

"It's a homecoming song," Meiyu said, and then began to translate. "A husband has traveled far to make money for his family and braved many storms and bandits. Now he's coming home, and they're listing off the things he's bringing for his wife and children. The chorus is the list of things he's bringing back for them. 'A jade for my wife, pure as the sky. A dress for my daughter, to bring a tear to her eye. A peach for my mother, as round as can be. A pole for my son, to be strong like me.'"

Dancing Cloud listened for a time, then said. "The caravan men of the North sing something like that when we travel with them. But, the lyrics are different."

"There are many different versions of this song too, it changes depending on the singer and what they can come up with. Each singer will take his turn singing the chorus and add his own words to suit his song."

As they listened, one of the men at the prow sang his version of the chorus, changing it to say what he'd be bringing back for each of his three sons while the others listened and laughed at his bawdy humor.

The verse done, the rest of the crew joined in the Chorus again, and this time Meiyu joined them. Her high soprano rose up to counterpoint their baritones in a way that made everyone sit up and listen.

When it came around to her turn for a verse, her voice raised into a beautiful tremolo, the words woven with imagery steeped in an archaic dialect from her ancestors.

The boatmen hummed quietly to her melody, smiling languidly as if this were a daily occurrence, and carried on with poling the barge. They were happy to have new voice in their old song, and listened with great intent. Despite themselves, the Lin family had to admire this beautiful melody echoing like a flock of songbirds hidden the surrounding trees.

Finally, her verse done, her voice drifted off and the crew once again picked up the rhythmic bass tones of the chorus.

"You sing very well." Said an appreciative Dancing Cloud and Meiyu nodded her thanks. The Mao girl felt more relaxed now, much of her stress having been drained away by the effort of singing. She couldn't help but smile that she'd finally put her hated singing coach's long efforts to use.

The cicadas ringing in the distance, the afternoon wore on.

CHAPTER EIGHTEEN

The Happy Ox Inn

It was late afternoon when it happened.

Baking under the mid-day sun, most of the crew had retreated under the shade offered by the sail and superstructure as the ship cut through the green waters of the canal. Meiyu had let herself doze in the heat, but the Lin clan members were still up and awake around her, watching for trouble. They were an extremely careful lot. With only a few exceptions, she had noticed that they ate only their own dried rations to make sure no-one could poison them, and there were always two of them awake at any given time.

At the moment, Madam Lin was the one sleeping, while Dancing Blade watched Meiyu and Dancing Cloud ate. The dried meat and pickled vegetables had a strong, pungent odor to them that made most of the people around her move far away.

Then, without warning, one of the four horses tied in the center suddenly let out a cry and started thrashing around. Everyone who had been asleep was instantly awake, and the crew erupted into worried shouts as the animal began to kick and try to pull itself free. This also upset the other horses, who began to react by drawing away and trying to escape from their panicked brother.

Four large, upset animals anywhere is a problem, but on a boat only five arm-spans wide it could be a disaster. So, the Lin clan members leapt into immediate action, with Dancing Blade rushing for the horse which had started the problem, while Dancing Cloud and Madam Lin moved into try and separate the other three horses from their disturbed brother.

As this happened, Meiyu was watching in fascination, but then felt a hand on her shoulder. Looking up, she saw one of the boatmen, who laid a finger in front of his lips.

"You have a beautiful voice songbird, but more so, you have a clever way with verses. Child of the great Crocodile of White Fox Town, is it? We have great respect for him, and would do anything to help his child stuck in a time of need." He produced a small knife that he used to cut her bonds. "Fly, little songbird. While you have the chance."

In an instant, she was free, and she did the first thing that came to mind- she jumped up, ran to the edge of the boat and dove off.

Hitting the cool water, she took a moment to kick free of her shoes, and then swam up to the surface. The boat had already sailed past her, but there was no sign any of the Lins had noticed she was gone- yet. Seizing the moment, she began to swim as fast as she could for a clump of bushes near the shore. Once there, she used the plants as cover while she crept out of the murky canal and headed into the forest beyond.

Being Northerners from the dry plains, she considered it likely that her former captors couldn't swim, which meant they would have to get the boat to shore to follow her. That would buy her time, but even more importantly, they wouldn't know which side of the canal she was on. With just three of them, it would be hard for them to pursue her on both sides, and that gave her odds she could work with.

They would have horses, but they were also strangers to the Central Plains, which meant that the locals wouldn't be as inclined to help them as they would her. If she could just find a large enough town, she could get help from some of her family's allies.

For now, Meiyu just focused on running as fast as her bare feet could carry her.

* * *

Last Brother Shou had seen everything.

Sitting atop a horse on a nearby hilltop that overlooked the canal, he and his two companions had watched as the girl jumped from the boat and fled into the forest beyond.

They had tracked the Lin clan members to the place where they'd gotten passage on the riverboat, and spent most of the day following the boat's slow passage along the waterway. It wasn't hard for their horses to overtake the boat, and they'd been content with pacing it and waiting for it to make landfall so they could make their move.

Now that was in the past, and their quarry was again escaping them on the other side of the canal.

Shou frowned. "Is there a crossing near here?"

He looked at Xiao, and Xiao looked at Mah.

Mah said nothing.

"Then we find one." Shou said, bringing his horse around and gesturing ahead of them along the road. "She'll head for the nearest town, we'll catch her there."

* * *

"This'll do. Thank you."

Meiyu hopped from the cart and bowed a more formal thank you to the old farmer who'd been kind enough to give her a ride into town. Then she turned and looked about. It wasn't a large town, perhaps fifty or sixty families, but Willow Garden was on the caravan routes, so there was a chance she might find some of her family's allies here.

The market square was mostly empty, with the majority of the businesses having closed for the day. All that remained open were a few lantern-lit outdoor wine gardens and a couple street food sellers. A scattering of people wandered about- people strolling to enjoy the cooling early evening breeze as the sun set in the west.

Picking an older couple, Meiyu approached them cautiously and politely, brushing her hair back and arranging herself to try to make up for her disheveled, barefoot appearance. While the husband recoiled at her approach, the wife seemed more sympathetic, and after a brief conversation Meiyu learned what she needed to know. There were three large inns in the town, each of them just off the market square a short distance. The roughest was a place called the Happy Ox Inn, and it was also the largest of the three, which made it her best choice.

Making her way down the side street, she located the Happy Ox fairly easily by following the sounds of laughter and singing. It had an extensive wine garden patio, and as Meiyu passed she could see it was filled with tough looking drunken travelers and overly painted women enjoying themselves under newly lit lanterns.

To most, that sight alone would have been enough to turn them around and send them in another direction, lest the revelers took notice of them. But Mao Meiyu was a resident of White Fox Town, and the daughter of an armed escort agency headman. To her, this wasn't dangerous, it was a small touch of home.

Meiyu wandered into the inn's central hall and looked around. It was a typically laid-out country Inn, with a two-level central hall and little in the way of decoration. A bit stuffy from the lanterns and back ovens, it was not as full as outside, and the smells of food that filled the place pulled hard at her empty stomach.

As the Lins had taken her money purse, there was little she could do about that. So, she steeled herself and hoped for the best as she headed straight for the bar along the wall to her right.

A soot and cobweb encrusted placard reading "The Happy Ox" hung above the bar along with a small mounted box containing the customary shrine to the Seven Lucky Gods. She tossed a silent prayer to them herself as she eased up to the bar and caught the innkeeper's attention.

He gave a yellow-toothed smile, looking her up and down, and letting his gaze linger on her chest for just a bit too long.

"Yes? Can I help you?"

"I'm trying to find someone from the Mao Family Armed Escort Agency, or someone who knows them. Is there anyone like that around here?"

The innkeeper's smile faded to almost a frown, then he indicated the stairs at the back with a dismissive wave of his hand.

"Go the second floor, blue trimmed door on your right." He said, and then wandered off to tend to another customer.

Meiyu blinked. She hadn't hoped, but now she was so close! Her heart leapt as she turned around to head for the stairs.

And, that's when she saw Dancing Cloud.

The unhappy looking Lin clan fighter was coming around the tables to her right, between her and the stairs. And a quick look showed Dancing Blade was there as well, coming at her from the main entrance to her left.

She was surrounded!

What could she do? She was so close! She just had to find a way to get across the room to the staircase and up to her father's people on the second floor. If she got there, they could help her fend off these her pursuers- but how?

Then it occurred to her- the people upstairs weren't her only source of help.

Her eyes darted around the room, and she spotted the person she was looking for. Across the hall was the biggest, toughest looking man in the room- a hairy mountain of muscle clad in animal furs and surrounded by other rough looking fighters. They looked like a bunch of bandits in to spend their ill-gotten gains.

Perfect.

Snatching a half-empty wine flask from the top of the bar, Meiyu wound up and threw it with all her might at the lead bandit's bald head.

Out of the corner of her eye, Meiyu caught a flash of panic on Dancing Cloud's face, and the Lin girl started to move to intercept the bottle, but it was much too late. There was a resounding "crack!" as the bottle hit, and then the crash of ceramic shattering as it hit the floor.

In an instant, the whole inn was filled with the sound of chairs flying as a whole table of bandits leapt to their feet, weapons at the ready. They scanned the room, looking about for whoever had just signed their grave marker, and their eyes all fell on Mao Meiyu.

At first, they seemed a bit confused, but then at a barked order from their still cursing, wine-soaked leader they rapidly began to advance at her, throwing tables and people out of the way as they charged across the room like an advancing horde.

Meiyu looked at Dancing Cloud.

Dancing Cloud looked at Meiyu.

"I hate you." Said the Lin girl's eyes.

Then she and her brother both leapt to put themselves between Meiyu and the bandits, their *jian* swords drawn as both took up a side-by-side battle stance.

The appearance of the green and black clad Twin Dancers of the Nine Trees Armed Escort Agency may have caused a hesitation in the bandits, but it was nothing significant. No-one here knew who they were, and all they saw was a pair of finely dressed young adults with swords. Nothing to be concerned about.

As a result, the charge continued, and in seconds the first of the bandits reached the Lin fighters, axe held high and wailing from the top of his lungs. At least, until Dancing Blade's sword tip carved out most of his throat. He hit the ground in a gurgling mess.

But, even though he was down, the rest of them already had momentum, and so where he fell, five more took his place to surround the pair.

Meiyu watched as the twin combatants, clearly experienced at dealing with situations such as these, fell into a series of practiced moves. At first, one would defend while the other attacked, and then at an unknown signal, they would switch positions without losing a beat. This created an almost unbreachable wall of death that the bandits threw themselves against, and as a result, the second wave went down mere moments after the first bandit had hit the floor.

Meiyu had known the pair were good, but she hadn't realized how good, and she now knew that this distraction wasn't going to last much longer. So, leaving them to fight off the remaining bandits, Meiyu dashed around the fight and made an arc right for the back stairs- almost reaching them when something in the back of her head told her to duck.

Instinctively, she dropped and rolled, hearing the whoosh of the hand axe pass over her head and the deep "thunk!" of it burying itself into the wooden pillar beside her.

Spinning around, she saw the bandit leader coming at her, a second larger axe in his grip. Screaming obscenities, he brought the axe down at her head, forcing her to roll out of the way and dive beneath a nearby table in an effort to stay away from him.

On and on he came, flipping the tables as she scrambled this way and that, trying to avoid the axe that just kept coming. In the back of her head, it occurred to her that perhaps this wasn't such a good idea after all, and she cursed herself for underestimating the potential downside of her strategy.

Spotting a saber lying on the floor nearby, she seriously considered fighting back, but that idea died a quick death when she realized that it wouldn't be much use against the power of the axe that she was facing. She was out-classed, out-powered, and- as she dove to avoid another attack- quickly running out of places to hide.

Then she saw her opening.

The axe had become stuck in the floor after that last strike, and the bandit leader was having trouble freeing it. In that fraction of a second, she dove past the bandit in a roll and came up on the other side running. With all her effort, she bolted to the stairs and bounded up them three steps at a time.

Behind her, Meiyu could hear the thunderous steps as the bandit leader followed, and as she hit the corner on the stairs, she saw him charging up the steps right after her. There was blood on his face and murder in his eyes.

But she was faster, and she continued up the stairs and out into the hall balcony. It was filled with inn girls and their clients leaning over the railing to watch the fight. Seeing the bandit come up behind her, they began to scream and scatter, which suited her fine since she needed the way clear.

Sprinting forward, she searched frantically for the blue trimmed door- finally seeing it just ahead at the end of the corridor. With her chest heaving, she prayed that there would be some of her father's fighters inside, or at least someone who could help her escape from the giant looming up at her rear.

However, just as she was about to reach the door there was a whistling sound and pain screamed from her back as something hard and heavy struck her. She was thrown forward, slamming into the floor and everything went black for a brief moment as the world became a spinning mess.

As soon as she could even try to think, she was moving again, forcing herself to try and get up. Twisting around, she saw the bandit leader's oversized hand lift up the heavy axe from where it had struck her and stride forward. He had thrown the blunt end to bring her down, but now the gleaming blade was hanging above her as she scrambled backwards as fast as she could- her body screaming when she slammed against the door.

"You little witch." He growled. "I'm going to skin you alive."

"W-wait," she said, raising hand in feeble defense and yelling as loudly as she could. "If you harm me, you'll regret it, my father is Crocodile Mao!"

But the giant shook his bloody head, "Don't know him, but if he wants your skin, he can pay me for it."

The axe went up, preparing for a killing blow.

But, just as it did, Meiyu felt the door behind her open, and she fell onto her back, looking up at the ceiling.

From the room with the blue trimmed door, a man Meiyu had never seen before ducked and stepped into the corridor. A handsome face with sad eyes looked down at her, framed by a flowing mass of long black hair that ran down over the shoulders of red armor. Almost as big as the bandit leader, he was clad in the dress of a military man and carried a halberd.

"Crocodile Mao's daughter?" He said, looking down at her.

"Y-yes!" She gasped. "Help me!"

He nodded once, and shifted his gaze to the bandit leader. The barbarian had been so shocked by this soldier's appearance that he'd not only stopped his attack, but stared at the new arrival in wonder.

"Leave her," said the armored man.

Not quite willing to give up, the bandit leader brought his axe to the ready. "This one owes me. Are you going to pay her debt?"

But, just as he finished those words, his eyes went wide with shock, and he looked down to see the blade of the soldier's halberd embedded deep in his chest. It had happened so fast he hadn't even seen the man move, it was like it had just appeared there on its own.

Just as quickly, the halberd was gone, and the bandit leader collapsed to the floor- his huge body a twitching lifeless mass.

Meiyu stared at the dead bandit, shocked by the sudden violence. Even she, who had been right there, hadn't seen the attack until it was finished.

Who was this soldier?

She had never seen anyone like him before, and certainly would have known if her father employed such an incredibly skilled fighter.

The soldier leaned down, offering his hand to help her up.

"Come."

Hesitating, Meiyu began to reach out to take it, but then another voice called out.

"Stop!"

Both Meiyu and the soldier turned to see the battered pair of Dancing Blade and Dancing Cloud rushing along the corridor at them. It was Dancing Blade who had shouted, and both had their bloodied weapons at the ready.

"She's ours!" The Lin brother called out as the pair drew close. "Leave her be if you value your life!"

CHAPTER NINETEEN

Desperate Battle

The man called Mah the Fighting Red General stepped past Meiyu, leaving her sitting on the floor where she was, and placed himself between her and the Twin Dancers of the Nine Trees Armed Escort Agency. Between them lay the lifeless body of the bandit leader whose blood still dripped from the blade of Mah's *guandao* halberd.

"Give up now!" Dancing Cloud echoed her brother's statement. "You can't win."

But the towering soldier neither retreated nor said a word, choosing to instead remain where he was. The sad, silent fighter in red armor keeping his weapon at the ready as he watched them carefully, his body slowly sliding into a battle stance.

He was much larger than either of them, and had the advantage of reach- with his halberd being easily twice as long as their slender *jian* swords. On the other hand, they were in a corridor where Mah's head nearly scraped against the ceiling, and he could touch both sides without extending his arms to the fullest. Yes, one side was open, looking out on the main dining hall of the inn, but this whole situation offered little advantage for such a long weapon as the halberd in anything but a defensive stance.

They couldn't attack without risking him hitting them, but neither could he use his weapon to its fullest and advance. A halberd is not a spear, it is more akin to a saber with an extremely long handle, and it needed room to cut and slash at its opponent if it was to be used to its greatest effect in battle. Its focus on reach also came with a great disadvantage- if an opponent closed to inside the weapon's reach then it was reduced to a defensive weapon at best.

It was a standoff, and both sides were now fixated on each other, playing out the situation in their minds as they stood there just out of reach. Whoever found the right series of moves to defeat the enemy would have the advantage. Whoever made the wrong choices could easily end up dead.

Such is life in the martial underworld of the *Jianghu*.

Meiyu was now leaning against the wall next to the room where Mah had come from. Her back was a mass of searing pain where the dead bandit leader had struck her, and she was sure something was broken. The events of the last day were hitting her like a hammer, and she found herself growing wearier by the second, as though all the life had been drained from her body.

Still, she struggled to keep focused, taking shallow breaths to deal with the pain and watching the fighters size each other up. Neither seemed inclined to make the first move, and if she could she would have fled inside the room and shut the door. Two against one wasn't easy odds at the best of times, and the Twin Dancers were the most skilled of paired fighters.

It happened so fast, Meiyu almost missed it.

Dancing Cloud suddenly drew a pair of short, throwing knives from a pocket hidden within her tunic and threw them at Mah's head. At the same time, Dancing Blade dashed forward, he was almost half bent over and keeping low to the ground as he and his sword weaved in at Mah. The huge soldier suddenly had a choice, he could block the knives coming right at his head, or he could defend against the man and blade now coming at his lower half.

This was the deadly effect of a team attack, and against most opponents, it would likely have been effective and fatal.

But Mah was not most opponents.

Making use of the plates that covered his forearms, Mah brought his left arm up to block the small knives, while at the same time thrusting forward with the Halberd one-handed in a short arc that went out to the one side and then swept across, covering the width of the hallway. While it might have lacked power, it was enough of a threat that anyone inside that arc risked being caught by the blade or stuck by the staff and slammed into the wall as it swung to the side.

Clearly, the Fighting Red General had faced similar tactics before, and knew in an instant how to counter them.

Dancing Blade saw what was happening only a second after coming into range of the halberd, but had no time to retreat before the blade was sweeping at him. Instead, he dropped to the left and brought up his sword at an angle, so that when the deadly blade of the halberd came at him it merely slid up the sword and over its master to strike the wall above his head.

Then, before Mah could react, Dancing Blade was lunging forward again, his sword lunging for Mah's leg. At the same time, Dancing Cloud was now moving as well, leaping onto the waist-level railing and dashing forward along it like a cat, trying to flank the soldier while he was focused on trying to deal with her brother.

It was a difficult situation, but Mah still had one large advantage over the pair- he was wearing armor.

Instead of trying to block Dancing Blade's attack on his leg, Mah instead chose to maneuver so it struck his armored boot. While at the same time, he brought the halberd back over Dancing Blade's head in an arc aimed to knock his sister from the railing before she could get close enough to strike.

Dancing Cloud saw the attack coming, and unable to avoid it was forced to dive off the railing into the empty space of the dining hall and disappear below.

Meanwhile, to Dancing Blade's further surprise, Mah chose to drop the Halberd rather than hold onto it, and close to face the Lin swordsman in hand to hand. While the halberd wasn't effective in close fighting, a sword has a similar problem with close combat, and suddenly Dancing Blade felt the crushing grip of a gauntleted hand close on his sword arm.

Mah didn't so much as punch Dancing Blade as pull him forward into his mailed right fist, smashing the young swordsman's nose flat and breaking more than a few teeth. Another hit and then he slammed the dazed boy into the wall so hard he broke the plaster, and let the swordsman's unconscious form drop to the floor below.

But as the Fighting Red General started to reach for his fallen weapon, he heard the sounds of footsteps landing on the floor behind him and spun just in time to block a series of attacks by Dancing Cloud.

The girl had indeed leapt off into thin air, however, as she did, she'd grabbed one of the railing spokes with her left hand and swung her body around to grab another spoke with her foot. Hanging off the side with her sword between her teeth, she'd needed a moment to pull herself back to the railing, and had now returned- set on avenging her brother.

And avenge him she was determined to do, launching a series of ferocious attacks on the soldier that kept him on the defensive and drove him back in his efforts to avoid the rain of sword tips she was showering on him. His armor had gaps that let him move, but they were also vulnerable points, and she too showed her experience by directing each of her attacks at them. The moment he defended one point, her sword was already heading to another, and he was forced to retreat farther and farther.

She'd already pushed him back past her fallen brother, and where Mah's own weapon lay.

"I'm going to crack you open, turtle." She cursed at him. "And feed your guts to the birds!"

Then, perhaps sensing the futility of his situation, Mah did something she hadn't expected.

He stopped defending.

Her slender blade hit the gap between his left shoulder plate and his chest plate and slid right in, then he quickly twisted to the side and brought up a mailed fist to grab her sword while it was trapped between the metal plates. His strength, and the surprise of what he'd done let him rip her sword free of her hands and he threw it aside to clatter down in the main hall.

At least Dancing Cloud was smart enough not to let her eyes follow the sword, because the moment he'd hurled it away, Mah was coming at her. His looming right hand thrust out, grabbing right for her head, and now she was the one who was forced to retreat as he advanced upon her.

She grabbed for her fallen brother's sword, and managed to get it, but in that moment Mah had scooped up his halberd, and now he had the advantage there as well. She had lost the momentum, and this battle, and she could see that she wasn't going to get it back.

It was time to retreat.

But what about her unconscious brother? She couldn't leave him. What could she do?

She stood there, unable to go forward or back- caught in time.

* * *

Meiyu had watched the whole of the fight with as much interest as she could manage, and now saw the situation that had resulted. Dancing Cloud had clearly had enough, but she was unable to retreat because the soldier was standing next to her fallen brother. Leaving would save her, but it would also mark his grave.

Mao's daughter wasn't really sure how much she could influence this armored fighter, but if he really was one of her father's men, maybe she could intercede.

"Stop!" She called out. "Stop fighting."

The Lin girl, who now had her back to Meiyu, stiffened, but didn't change her stance. The soldier, on the other hand, now seemed to hesitate a bit, still keeping his guard up but looking past his enemy at her.

"Let her take her brother and go," Meiyu ordered. "They're beaten."

Her voice and words were weak, but in the pure quiet of the moment they were now in, they were more than strong enough to carry.

There was a short pause, and then the soldier left his combat stance and raised up his halberd to indicate that he was done fighting.

"Take him," he told the girl, moving back a step.

Watching her enemy warily, Dancing Cloud stepped forward, and then quickly sheathed her sword, helped the groggy man to his feet, and retreated.

She took the other hallway to retreat, not wanting to go past Mah, and in the process she passed by Meiyu. As she did, she gave Meiyu a look of thanks, and then continued on and away.

Meiyu watched them go, and then looked up to see the armored warrior was now kneeling next to her, concern in his sad eyes.

"Are you hurt?"

It seemed a strange thing to be asked by a man who had a small stream of blood now running down his chest plate, but Meiyu was in too much pain to worry about such things.

"My back," she said. "Hurts a lot."

Mah stripped off his mailed gloves, and then leaned her forward slightly to begin using his large, but gentle fingers to check her back and side. He moved with expert skill, checking her over as a doctor might to see what was broken and where her injuries were. He even checked her pulse.

When he was done, he laid her back against the wall very carefully.

"Your back is not broken, but your shoulder blade is. You need to rest and not move to let yourself heal." He looked concerned. "I will need to carry you to a bed. You must endure."

"Right," Meiyu nodded, knowing why he was concerned. This was going to hurt. "Do it."

The giant knelt down even lower and slipped his arms beneath her legs and back, carefully supporting her. Then he tensed slightly, and lifted.

There was searing pain like someone had thrust a burning knife into her back and was cutting her shoulder from her body, and Meiyu had to fight to keep from screaming.

He only barely got her inside the door before the pain became so great she passed out.

Merciful darkness swallowed her.

* * *

When Meiyu awoke, she was lying on a bed in a small dark room.

A mosquito net surrounded the bed, but beyond the thin gauze she could see the room was a simple one, with a table and chairs and little else except a few decorations on the walls. On one of the chairs a large man sat with his back to her, long flowing dark hair covered much of his back, but she could see he was bare-chested. The table beside him was piled high with pieces of armor and a small pile of dark stained rags.

There was a sour, pungent smell in the air, and she saw that he was applying herbs of some kind to long strips of cloth that he then proceeded to tie around his left shoulder. He grunted in pain as he tied them tight, but made no other sound. Then he pulled on a light gray tunic and stood up, his head turning to look at her.

For a moment, she thought about pretending to be asleep, but then decided it would be a wasted effort. What did she need to be afraid of, after all? He was one of her father's men, and he would get her home.

"Are you hungry?"

She shook her head. "Not yet." Then she started to rise, and dull pain flared to screaming life along her right shoulder, forcing her to lay back down flat. She had to take short breaths again to deal with the pain, and slowly it returned to its dull former self.

She wasn't going to try that again for a while.

Then something occurred to her.

"We can't stay." She said. "They will come back, and bring...help."

She almost said "their grandmother", but then her brain realized how non-threatening that sounded when she was trying to make him realize the urgency of the situation.

He considered a moment, and then shook his head.

"You are safe."

"But..."

"You are safe." He said again, in a strong clear voice that few would dare to disagree with. It was like she was hearing the words from her father.

Meiyu was going to say something, but at this, she decided that it would be better to keep quiet for the moment. He was certainly capable, perhaps even able to fight off all three members of the Lin clan, and she had no doubt he had friends nearby. No, she needed to rest and recover as quickly as possible. She would have to travel soon, and the better her injury was when that time came, the faster they could go.

She closed her eyes, and just tried to rest.

* * *

The next morning, she ate the pork bone congee he brought her.

The tricky part was getting her vertical enough to eat without enduring too much pain from her back. It did seem to be hurting a little less this morning, but any movement was still an exercise in extreme pain. They only managed to get her up through using large pillows and a writing board the soldier had found that he placed behind her back, it kept her back flat and unmoving as they got her up and used the pillows to prop it up.

Her back was still under stress, but it was tolerable for a short time.

He had to feed her, as moving her arms still resulted in jolts of pain.

After a few mouthfuls, she paused. "I'm sorry. I don't know honored senior's surname?"

"I am Mah," he said as he softly scraped the bottom of the ceramic spoon against the edge of the bowl.

She waited for more information, but it didn't come. She also noticed that he didn't address her in the proper manner as "Miss Mao" or "Master's Daughter" either.

"Are you from this area, Mr. Mah?"

He shook his head, waiting patiently to feed her. "From the Northwest."

"How long have you been working for my father?"

He looked into her eyes, and she into his. She saw the truth.

"But...I was told an agent of my family was here."

"A lie. I was waiting for you."

She considered this, and then asked. "Are you after this box too?"

"My mistress is."

"Who is your mistress?"

"You...will meet her soon."

Meiyu didn't like the sound of that, but there was very little she could do about it. She was well and truly trapped, and there would be no song that would allow her to escape from this situation. Then again, as with the Lin clan, she sensed that these people also needed her alive, which meant she would be safe- for now.

Finally, she asked. "When I told you to let them go, you did. Why? I'm not your master's daughter."

She saw him thinking, and then he answered. "I was wounded, and it was easier."

He's lying, she realized. There was something else.

Still, that was all she could expect to get from him for now, so she just opened her mouth and let him feed her.

She found herself fascinated by this man, and resolved to find out as much as she could about him.

* * *

Two other men came that afternoon, a tall, gaunt one who never smiled, and a fat one who never stopped smiling. Mah explained the situation to them, and the tall one wanted to get a cart and move her. But her keeper refused, saying that she couldn't be moved for now with her injury. It was too dangerous.

In the end, they decided to leave Meiyu where she was while she recovered and the newcomers left, but not before the fat one made a lewd comment about Mah enjoying his time alone with her. It was a passing joke, but it made Mah stop and frown.

It was a woman who came to serve her dinner. A tired looking woman with small eyes, she introduced herself as Little Peony, and looked to Meiyu like someone who was far more used to servicing men than women. She didn't talk much, but she was clearly being paid enough that she would do whatever was required of her, and Meiyu was happy to have another woman present.

Meiyu was still wearing the same torn and dirty men's clothes from two days before, and needed to change. Peony found her some new clothes, and helped Meiyu clean and redress herself. It was a long, slow process, and Meiyu was weak and soaked with sweat by the time they were done. The clothes were women's clothes, worn and faded pink and yellow robes, and they had a vaguely unpleasant stale smell to them, but Meiyu was happy just to wear something clean.

After she had changed, Peony left and Mah came in to check on her a short time later. He clearly intended just to stay a short time now, showing a sudden sense of propriety and not wanting to be alone in a room with this young unmarried woman any longer than he had to be. But, once he was there Meiyu gestured toward the chair next to her bed.

"Could you keep me company for a time?"

He hesitated, but then did as she asked, sitting down stiff-backed on the chair.

"I want to thank you for Peony," she continued. "I don't think she likes me much, but she's been a great help."

"You are welcome." He said formally, not looking at her. "Is there anything else the miss needs?"

"Tell me about your armor." She asked, watching him carefully.

He glanced at her, surprise on his normally passive face.

"My armor? But..."

"Please? It will give me something to think of besides the pain."

"I see." He frowned again, then sighed. "Very well."

And he began his story.

CHAPTER TWENTY

The General

Some of what Meiyu learned, she learned from Mah during that evening, the rest came from a later time when Copper Kettle Xiao was guarding her the next day. Xiao seemed to sense her interest in Mah, and was more than happy to provide details as the unpleasant man seemed to enjoy bedeviling Mah and he felt that her knowing more would only increase the General's discomfort.

What she learned was this- Mah's title of the "Fighting Red General" was in fact not just a grand style or nickname others had given him like "Mountain Divider" or "Heaven's Red Shooting Star" that men in the martial underground of the *Jianghu* applied liberally to themselves- he really was a General in the Imperial Service.

Or at least, he was once.

General Mah, for that was the only name she could get from him, was born in the province of Wuhan in the city of Green Cliff to a wealthy farming family that lived on the city's edge. The youngest of eight sons, Mah had little prospect of inheritance, and an overabundance of talent for athletics, so his entry into the military had been both natural and happened at a young age.

Once in the military, Mah had shown both his talent for the martial arts and leadership, and it hadn't taken long before he was a rising star among the provincial garrison. He had reached the rank of Captain by the age of 19, and was involved with many skirmishes against the nomads of the North and the mountain peoples of the West. In these, he became both admired and beloved by his men, and in his province few there were who didn't know his name.

Thus, it only made sense that when the Emperor sent the Crown Prince to do a survey of his future domains and he came to Wuhan, Mah was part of his escort.

This had been the start of both Mah's greatest luck, and his greatest misfortune.

The Crown Prince was a restless man who was easily bored, having reached his mid-twenties being served the luxuries of the world and with his every whim catered to. As a result, the somewhat poor province of Wuhan had little to really interest the youthful son of heaven, and once he had dispensed with local beauties and delicacies, he found himself looking for more interesting entertainment.

That was when one of the governor's advisers told the Prince about the rare Golden Condor that lived in the mountains of the Northern part of the province. To a man who fancied himself a hunter and sportsman, to say nothing of a son looking to impress his father, hearing of the Golden Condor was an irresistible temptation to the Prince. Thus, he determined that he would hunt the bird himself, and present it stuffed to his father as one of the treasures he had collected during his survey.

Hearing this threw the Governor into a panic. The hills where the Condor lived were still home to several rebel tribes, and if anything happened to the Prince the Governor had little doubts as to his future prospects for longevity. So, despite the Prince's own royal guard, the Governor insisted on sending additional men with him, and at their head he put Captain Mah.

Mah was an easy going fellow in those days, and it didn't take long after their first meeting for he and the Crown Prince to become close. Despite their vast differences in status, both had a fondness for horses and bow hunting, and Mah had a self-effacing way of telling stories about his adventures that the Prince appreciated. The prince was commonly surrounded by men who constantly bragged of their prowess, and this simple soldier who had done so much and yet gave credit to others was a rarity in the Prince's small world.

When they finally reached the Condor's territory after many days, it was Mah the Prince took with him in his small hunting party. The party's eight men, all armed with bows, ventured up to where the Condors nested and after searching for the biggest one, they could find they set up their trap for the mighty bird. Mah and his soldiers climbed down the mountainside toward the bird's nest, while the Prince laid in wait on a ledge above for the Condor to appear.

When it finally did appear, trying to defend its nest from the interlopers, the Prince fired several arrows, but all of them missed. Finally, after several of the soldiers had been sent tumbling to their deaths by the furious bird, Mah found purchase in the bird's own nest, drew a bow which he attached a short rope to, and fired- mortally wounding it.

He then climbed up to the ledge where the Prince waited, and presented the bird to the Prince as tribute.

The Crown Prince could easily have been angry, and Mah's career could have come to a swift end at that very moment. However, he instead made a joke about his own poor bowman ship and thanked Mah for his service, accepting the bird so that the party could return to the main camp for the day.

But, when they returned to the main camp, they instead found it stripped of everything and only the dead bodies of nearly fifty of their escorts left for the vultures. While they had been gone, the very rebel hill tribes that the Governor had feared had attacked and looted the camp, and now they were days away from the nearest outpost with nothing but their clothes and their hunting gear.

It was here that Mah again showed his ability, for while still showing deference to the Crown Prince, he organized the small party to help them survive and led them in a long and roundabout way toward the nearest garrison. Several times during the journey they nearly perished, but each time Mah's own ingenuity and knowledge of the mountains saved them.

In the end, nearly two weeks after they had been stranded, the small party returned to civilization, not having lost a single man.

It had been a long trip, and an educational one for the Prince, who had bonded with Mah during the trip to the point where the men had almost become inseparable. His first order to the Governor once things had been settled had been to transfer Mah over to the Prince's own guard. Then, when they had returned to the Capital after finishing the survey, he had petitioned his father for a commission for Mah in the elite officer ranks, citing Mah's own service record and bravery.

The Emperor had agreed, and Mah had been made a Colonel in the Imperial Army and was assigned to a unit commanded by one of the Prince's Uncles, who treated Mah most favorably. During this time, the Prince and Mah continued to be close friends, and it was the Prince who acted as the matchmaker in Mah's marriage to a girl from a noble family, and helped him settle in the capital. They saw each other often, and Mah never failed to bring back rare wines for the Prince whenever he went into the field, which the two would stay up and drink together under the light of the moon.

Soon Mah's commanding General passed away, and with the Prince's support Mah was selected to replace him at the age of 36, making him one of the youngest men to hold that rank in the service. It was just after his promotion that he heard that drought had struck his family farms, and he rushed there to give aid, returning to the capital with his parents so that they could live out their senior years in the comfort of his large manor house.

A filial son, a loyal citizen, and a brave leader. Mah had fostered a great reputation and was now well known in the Empire as the Fighting Red General for his unique crimson armor, but his fast rise and powerful support from above had made him arrogant. Like any commander, he had those around him constantly trying to curry favor, and more and more he let himself listen to these men and ignore those who whispered caution.

With the Prince's support behind him, he talked to the senior generals as though they were his equals, and openly criticized their plans in front of their men. He spoke publicly of his disdain for the Eunuchs who so strongly influenced the royal court, and even assaulted the family member of a powerful Eunuch who had an argument with one of his officers, telling the man what he thought of his masters.

It got so bad that even the Crown Prince himself took Mah aside and urged caution, knowing the forces which were starting to become arrayed against the rising young General. He urged him to show respect and make peace with his enemies, because life was difficult enough in the closed circles of the capital without making even more trouble for one's self.

Of course, Mah ignored this, and he continued to ignore the politics of the capital, confident that with the Prince's friendship and support he could just focus on doing his job and being a good son and husband.

"Do not worry, my prince." He told his friend. "With our twin might, we will set this land on the proper path and cleanse it of these parasites."

Then, a short time after he had said those fateful words, his whole world changed.

The Emperor became ill, and as so often happens when the throne will soon become empty a struggle for power began in the palace. The Eunuchs largest faction, led by the monstrously fat man known as Mount Shan, decided that they would strongly prefer the Crown Prince's younger brother on the throne, as he was barely a teen and would be far easier to control. Thus, with the backing of the younger prince's mother's family, they framed the Crown Prince for plotting to kill his father and had him swiftly executed before anyone could protest.

In the blink of an eye, General Mah's support was gone.

Soon after, when the new Emperor had taken the throne, Mah suddenly found himself dragged up before the Imperial Throne in chains. He was accused of conspiring with the family of the former crown prince's mother to assassinate the new Emperor, and sentenced to be executed. His lands were to be seized, and his family members sold into slavery to repay the debt he owed the state. The last thing he had seen was the smile of the Eunuch whose family member he had assaulted, and then they had locked him away with so many other political prisoners.

Lost in his own despair, Mah sat in his cell despondent, awaiting his death and reflecting how he had come to this. He had served the state and his prince faithfully, but all it had amounted to was treachery and the loss of everything he loved. He hated the Eunuchs, but there was little he could do against them, and most of all, he wept for his family who would now endure a miserable life because of him. His whole world had collapsed, and there were many he could blame, but most of all he blamed himself.

The man who was marched in chains to the sun-bleached execution grounds was not the same man who had entered the capital so many years before. He was sullen, quiet and without spirit- so much so that he didn't even notice that he was the only one whose head was being placed upon the block, or that the audience to see him die was also just a handful of nobles.

As the executioner stood above him, sword at the ready, Mah said his prayers, and awaited for the end to come.

But instead, he heard a voice say- "Is this how the Fighting Red General dies? Leaving his men and family to rot?"

The words pierced Mah's veil of darkness, and he looked up, surprised.

Aware for the first time of his surroundings, he squinted at the small group of nobles who sat under the shade of the viewing box ahead of him. They were the usual bunch of silk and jewel encrusted bureaucrats, none of them people he knew, but he focused on the one who had spoken.

That one was a white-faced young man who was so softly handsome that he might be considered pretty. He dressed in simple scholar's clothes, and wore none of the jewels of the others, but despite this there was an aura of power about him.

"So. The general does have some life left, yet."

The white-faced scholar met Mah's baleful gaze with a smile.

Mah looked down, "End me." He had no taste for this foolishness.

"Obviously," said the scholar, striding from the shade to where Mah knelt. "You have no care for your own life. But, what of your family? Does it please you to think your pretty wife will become the personal servant of another man? Or that your father will die in a pit cursing his son until the end of his days?"

"Dog!" Mah cried, and strained against the chains so mightily that it seemed they would be torn from the rocks they were bolted to.

"Good." Said the scholar cheerfully. "Now we have something to discuss. You see, I am the one who your wife will attend, and I am the one in whose garden your parents labor to pay your debts. I bought them, and I will do with them as I will. But the truth is, the servant I want the most...is you."

Mah stared at the man, confusion on his face.

"What do you say? I have need of your halberd, General. You are a man of great talent, and while I cannot restore your former glory, I can give your family a future that it certainly doesn't have now."

The words were so great a shock that Mah couldn't speak for a time, but when he did his answer was- "You will free my wife and parents?"

"No," said the scholar. "But, while you serve me I will treat them as honored guests instead of servants. If you serve me well, you will have a chance to earn their freedom."

Mah bowed his head, he had little choice.

"Then this humble one begs you take him into your service, my lord."

"You swear your loyalty to me, and only me?"

"I do."

"Then remember this, General." Said the scholar, leaning in closer. "Remember this feeling, and how close the executioner's blade is to your throat. That blade is mine, and your life is in my hands. If you displease me, it will be your wife's throat that is cut first, and those you love will follow her. So, work hard, and remember."

Then Mah was led away, and returned to his cell.

The next day, a small-eyed bureaucrat came and fetched him, taking him from the prison and to a large compound on the edge of the capital. There, he was given quarters, a bath, and new clothes before being re-united with his wife and family. The group of them just hugged and wept over their misfortune, and he told them that he would see to it that they were taken care of.

Then he was led into the back garden, where he found the other two- the gaunt humorless swordsman, and the mirthful killer. They stopped their drinking as he approached, and Xiao offered him a seat at their table- he refused and chose instead to sit alone nearby. Neither had the bearing of the one in charge, and Mah felt no interest in listening to servants.

The greatest surprise of the day was the one that followed.

Mah expected the pale faced scholar to come and talk with them, but the one who came was a beautiful woman dressed all in white. Followed by a line of servants, she entered with the grace and bearing of a queen, and then took a seat near them under the shade of the umbrellas her servants bore.

The other two men immediately dropped to their knees before her, bowing their heads and offering her greetings. Mah stared in wonder, he had sized these two up as the hardest of men, the kind who would kill at the smallest offense, but there they were acting like a pair of children before this girl younger than they.

What power did this woman hold?

Then, after accepting their welcome, the girl turned and smiled gently at Mah. The moment he saw that smile, he knew she had been the scholar of the day before, and a chill ran down Mah's spine. There was a cold power behind those soft eyes, and Mah felt his legs begin to weaken.

"Come, join us." She said, offering him a seat before her.

He did as she asked without delay.

"General Mah, may I introduce your new elder brothers. This is Shou, and this is Xiao, they too work for me, and you will be traveling together. Please be good companions with them."

Mah stood up and greeted each of them formally as his elders, but instead of accepting the greeting the two other men just laughed and told him to sit down.

Normally, Mah would have been very offended by this discourtesy, but given the circumstances he did as he was told, and the focus returned to their mistress.

"I brought the three of you together," she told them. "Because I need skilled men who can carry out my orders without delay. From this day forward, you will serve as my hands, and do as I tell you. I will promise rewards for your loyalty, and pain for your failures. Each of you owes me something, and this is my price."

"We serve at your command," said Shou. "Order us as you will."

And she did, with Mah and the others serving her for the past several years. When they were not on assignment, which was rare, Mah was allowed to visit with his family, but except for that he rarely saw them. Still, when Meiyu asked if he missed them, he just shrugged and said "They are safe".

But as she considered their story, Meiyu came to realize that both men had been extremely circumspect about one thing- who was this mysterious woman they worked for? Who was behind her, and how was it she wielded such power? She couldn't help but feel a great important detail had been left out of Mah's tale.

Given the chance, she would have hunted out those details as well, were it not for what happened the following morning.

CHAPTER TWENTY-ONE

The Rescue

It was the morning of the third day after Meiyu's injury that her three captors appeared with the board wrapped in blankets. There was no discussion of the matter, Mah simply told her "we're moving" and very gently slipped his arms under her while the other two held the board to the same height with the bed.

It was still painful for her to move, and she had to grit her teeth to keep from crying out, but knew she had little choice and didn't want to show weakness in front of these men. So, she worked with Mah to get herself over onto the board as quickly as possible, hoping that once she was laying flat on it, the pain would subside.

It did, but only slightly, and then she had to face the agony of them maneuvering her out of the room and slowly making their way down the stairs. More than once did the two men carrying the makeshift stretcher nearly drop her, and her knuckles were as white as bone from their death grip on the side of the board to keep herself from falling off.

Finally, down the stairs, they marched her across the main hall of the inn in front of a few dozen curious onlookers. On the balconies above, she could see Peony and the other women who worked at the inn watching. She tried not to look at them, as if by not meeting their gaze she could banish the embarrassment she felt.

It was when she turned her head and looked straight out into the diners that she saw him...

"Gou?"

It was just for a brief moment, in that last second before they whisked her out the front doors of the inn, but she was sure she'd seen his face. A little older, a little more tan, but in the back leaning against one of the pillars he'd been there, watching her with angry eyes.

At least, she'd thought it was him.

Then he was gone, and she was outside being spun around so they could slip her under the dingy gray cloth framework that covered the back of a cart. Mah climbed into the twilight space next to her, and near her feet the back gate was slammed up and locked into position.

"I am sorry."

She looked at Mah in the sepia toned light, and could see him frowning. He really meant it, she knew it from the tone of his voice. Still thinking of her brief vision of Gou, she didn't answer, just turning her head away from him.

Then there was the sound of a whip somewhere ahead, followed by a whinny and a sudden jerk as the cart lurched forward. Shoots of fire began to run down her back, and her chest felt like it was about to explode. But, that was only the beginning, for then the bumps began as the cart rolled along the poorly maintained road.

Her world quickly descended into one of pain as she fought not to scream with each jolt or drop. She had to endure. She would endure.

Or die trying.

* * *

Meiyu wasn't aware of how much time had passed, but at some point the cart finally, mercifully came to a stop. She was only half-conscious now, so weary from the pain and the heat of the covered space that she'd almost fallen into a stupor. But she was aware they had stopped, and was aware that Mah had left her.

Then after a time, he returned, and the cart began to move again, slowly at first, and then she was suddenly jolted awake by a large bump as the cart picked up speed. Screaming, she reached out and grabbed Mah's arm for support and something to focus on in her pain.

Instead of armor, she found rough-hewn cloth, and it surprised her enough that she looked at Mah again.

But the General was nowhere to be seen, and instead of the red armored fighter, there was another person in the dim light with her, just as big, but much softer and bald.

"Rest easy, Miss Mao." said the large nun. "You are with friends."

* * *

"Any sign of them?"

When Miss Lily indicated there wasn't, Gou relaxed somewhat, but kept the cart moving at a brisk pace. He almost felt bad for what he'd done to them- almost.

"What did you put in their food?" Lily asked.

"Well, I know how much Xiao likes his breakfast congee, so I made sure it was extra hearty."

"With what?"

Gou smirked. "You remember that dried meat we had that got soaked at Green Rapids and then sat inside the travel bag in the sun for the last couple days? The stuff that really stank?"

She indicated she did.

"They had it for breakfast."

Miss Lily couldn't help herself- she laughed. "You're awful!" She said between breaths.

Gou shrugged. "Hey, it's not like they didn't deserve it. If you hadn't suggested unhooking the oxen on the ferry and swimming with them to shore, we'd all be walking with Buddha right now. They've hurt a whole lot of people, and a little food stall belly is the least they deserve."

Inside, Gou couldn't help but laugh- remembering the image of the fearsome men running off into the forest with their hands on their stomachs like a bunch of little children. He and the women, following from a distance, had crept up at that time and stolen both the horses and cart while the trio were otherwise occupied. A simple, perfect grab that between the trio's illness and the loss of their horses would buy Gou an hour or two.

In truth, Gou had wanted to do a lot more to them, especially after learning Meiyu was injured at the Happy Ox, but he doubted that the good Sister would approve of what he had in mind, so he'd settled for giving them this little taste of hell.

For now.

Now they just needed to get as far away from the trio as possible, using every moment to their best advantage.

They were finally going home.

* * *

Sitting on the back of the cart at a roadside fruit stand, Gou looked from the Sister to the pale, semi-conscious Meiyu while Miss Lily stood there with her arms crossed in thought.

"There's nothing you can do for her?"

Sister Cat shook her head sadly. "I can block the pain by stimulating her pressure points, but little more. She is in need of rest and aid that I cannot give her. She is also most certainly not fit to keep traveling as we have been."

"Should we try to meet up with her caravan?" Miss Lily offered. "They could provide a smoother ride than we could."

Gou nodded, "I'd considered that. The problem is that it will be one of the first places they'll look. Too many people are after her, and we can't endanger the caravan when all those fighters are still poisoned."

"Damn Lins." Miss Lily cursed. "Faithless dogs."

"Given that we have just poisoned our own enemies," the Sister put in. "I don't believe we are in a position to judge their actions."

Miss Lily seemed ready to take offense at that, but Gou stopped her. The two women hadn't really gotten along well during the trip so far, and Gou had often needed to mediate between them. Cat was being her usual blunt and honest self, but that seemed to rub the high-strung Miss Lily the wrong way more often than not.

"Staying with the matter at hand," Gou said in an effort to keep the conversation from derailing. "What are our other options? I don't want to stop at a farmhouse unless we have to- too much chance of putting them in danger."

In truth, Gou still felt badly about what had happened to the farmers when he'd rescued Miss Lily, and wanted very much to avoid bringing more bystanders into this deadly affair.

Both the women agreed with this sentiment, but as they discussed it, they also had to rule out going to a town because too many eyes could follow them. Miss Lily suggested finding one of her agency's outposts, in hopes they could get help there, but Gou disagreed. They'd be in the same vulnerable position that Moonlight's men had been in while they'd stayed too long in Willow Garden.

"We can't stop, and we can't continue like this." Gou said, as much to himself as he did to the others. "So, I guess..." he paused, a thought occurring to him. "...we have just one option."

Then Gou told them what it was.

＊ ＊ ＊

"They came this way."

Dancing Blade stood up, wiping the mud from his hands where he'd just been examining the tracks along the dirt road. He'd been tracking animals since he was a child, and the cart's horses left a distinctive trace that wasn't hard to follow. One of the horses had a damaged hoof that left a clear mark.

Poor luck for them.

"Are they far ahead?" Asked his grandmother from atop her nearby horse.

"Two hours at most."

Dancing Blade walked over to his own horse, his face hung in a deep scowl. Although he knew his grandmother and sister didn't really blame him, he took this whole situation as his deep personal shame.

First, he had allowed himself to be beaten by that red armored devil, forcing his sister to sacrifice her own face and give up the girl to rescue him. Then, he had fallen asleep due to the herbal healing medicine when it was his turn to watch the inn where they'd been keeping Mao's daughter.

As a result, the devil and his companions had been able to escape in the morning with the girl, and the Lins had been unable to follow. By the time they'd learned what had happened, they were long behind, and forced to race to catch up.

When they had caught up, they'd found the red armored devil and his allies walking along the road without cart or horses. It had been a near-thing, as they had tried to steal the Lin family's mounts, but they seemed weakened and the Lins were able to put enough distance between them to escape.

Dancing Blade had wanted to go back and finish them off, but his mother had overruled him. If those men were walking, someone else had the girl, and time could be more precious than honor- for the moment.

They'd lost the trail for a time, as the road had turned to solid rock and split at many places, but now they were back on the right track.

Their single horses could go faster than a cart, and as he climbed gingerly up into the saddle Dancing Blade let a hint of a smile cross his face.

He was angry, and needed someone to vent his feelings upon.

The ones who had taken the Mao girl would do nicely.

* * *

Walking up to the open-air restaurant, Gou dusted off a stool and sat down. Cat and Lily were already there, eating their daily rice in a cold silence that told Gou all he needed to know. Beside them, the wagon sat with a single horse harnessed to it, its companion having been taken by Gou with their other horses to be sold.

A waiter scurried up to the table and poured Gou some tea to wash down the dust, and Gou ordered some rice and lamb from the hanging menu board. He then turned to his two scrupulously silent companions.

"Well, that's all taken care of. This one and the cart will be picked up from the dock when we're done with it."

Lily was the first to respond.

"Then you found a boat to take us downriver?"

"Even better," Gou smiled. "When I went down to the dock, I heard someone calling my name. I turned out to be Slow Jung, one of my old gambling buddies. You remember Jung, right Sister?"

"I do indeed," said the nun, and then she made a sour face. "Does he still smell like banana oil?"

Gou grinned. "Oh yeah. I almost didn't recognize him, but when I got a whiff of that stuff, I remembered him quick enough."

Lily blinked, "Banana oil?"

"Yep," Gou took a sip from his tea. "An old doctor told him that if you rub banana oil on yourself every day, you'll keep your joints from going hard. Lots of people in his family have stiff joints when they get old, so he's afraid it's going to happen to him too. I don't know where he gets the stuff, but you can smell him coming from over the horizon."

Lily wrinkled her nose. "Sounds lovely."

"Wait until you smell him!" Gou laughed again. "But anyways, he's a riverboat captain now, and said he'll take us, and give Meiyu one of his private cabins."

"Brother Gou, that's wonderful!"

"Yeah, they're loading up cargo now. We'll be able to board when they're done." Then he glanced at the cart. "She wake up yet?"

The nun shook her head. "I have given her some medicine to help with the pain, but it will also make her sleep deeply."

"I see," said Gou, who'd been hoping to talk with the injured girl. He hadn't even had a chance to say hello since they'd rescued his old friend, but then there would be time for that later.

It was after his meal came that he noticed Sister Cat seemed to be considering something. He let it go on for a bit, and then finally got tired and said– "Alright Sister, out with it. What's bothering you?"

Sister Cat looked up at him with a slightly embarrassed expression, like a child caught doing something they shouldn't have been doing, and then sighed.

"Brother Gou, do you believe taking her back to White Fox Town is the correct course of action?"

Gou paused a moment, cocking his head slightly to the left as he often did when he was thinking, and then looked directly at her and said "What do you mean?"

"Well," she continued with a little hesitation. "Shouldn't we head north or west? She is safe, and that is the most important thing. Returning her to White Fox Town in time for Lady Moonlight's deadline may be placing her in more danger than she would otherwise be normally in.

"I know that you wish to return her to her father so that he knows she is safe, but cannot a messenger do that as well? Also, the forces searching for her will assume we are returning to White Fox Town, so we are more likely to meet them if we travel to the south."

Now that she had finally said it, she looked relieved, but also a little concerned. Gou could see that the Sister was worried about his reaction, which was fair since Gou had been rather emotional about this whole affair.

Gou put down his chopsticks, and stroked his chin thoughtfully.

"You know something sister? You're right."

CHAPTER TWENTY-TWO

Ambush

As they crested the hill, the river's long and snakelike form came into view, and Dancing Cloud reigned in her horse. She scanned the water, and then, spotting what she was looking for, thrust out a finger.

"There it is."

Her mother and brother both followed her line of focus to a riverboat with a blue fore-sail and a green after-sail that was leisurely plowing its way through the water heading north.

"You're certain it's the right ship, brother?"

Dancing Blade nodded. "I checked with three different men. The Mao girl was loaded aboard that ship by a man, a woman and a nun."

"Why would they go north?" His sister wondered. "Aren't they trying to get her to her home?"

"Perhaps not, child." Said her grandmother. "We don't know who they are, or what group they represent. They may be taking her somewhere safe until the time of the gathering for the Society of Armed Escorts chiefs."

Dancing Cloud frowned, it did make sense, but...

Her grandmother looked at her and seeing her uncertainty, added "Also, it is the opposite direction their pursuers would expect them to go. Not the first time we have seen that trick, is it?"

This, Dancing Cloud had to admit was absolutely true. The tribes of the Northern Plains, who often raided the caravans they guarded, regularly used this kind of distraction trick. Sending horses and a single man riding in the expected direction while the rest rode another way to avoid pursuers after they'd done a raid.

"Where can we catch them, grandmother?" Her brother asked, anxious to move again.

"We will ride ahead, and ask at the towns if this ship is expected to dock." Madam Lin told them. "When it does, we will steal aboard and get the girl back."

They started to ride again, and Dancing Cloud continued to follow the ship with her eyes. Part of her hoped that the ship wouldn't dock until it was so far north that they'd given up. She knew it was bad of her to think this way, but the Mao girl reminded her of her Fourth Cousin and she considered this whole effort to kidnap a bride shameful.

Still, she had her duty, and for that duty she would follow the Mao girl to the edge of heaven and back if necessary. It didn't mean, however, that she had to be happy about it.

* * *

Gou stood on the deck of the *Lazy Dragon* and scanned the shores of the river and the hills beyond. He told himself he was worrying without cause, but something about those riders he'd just seen on the trade road to the east bothered him. They'd seemed to focus on this ship for just a little too long before they rode off ahead.

"Mango?"

Gou turned and took the red and green fruit he was being offered. "Sure, thanks Jung."

The wild looking riverboat captain stood next to him, gnawing on the pit of another mango, his thick overgrown black beard covered in bits of orange goo from the fruit. His head was also covered with a mass of black hair, and the whole thing framed his leathery nose and eyes. He wore only a pair of short pants in the summer heat, his deeply tanned skin showing off his muscled form.

A fellow native of White Fox Town, Gou had known "Slow" Jung a long time, even before he'd gotten the nickname "Slow" for his tendency to take his time when gambling. He would always hem and haw, and bring the game to a crawl while he decided whether he wanted to bet or not, and how much money he should put in. In actual truth, Jung was pretty fast and a fair fighter as well, he just tended to overthink things.

"I have to admire you Gou, to be so young and have so many wives. Even a nun!"

Case in point.

Gou stopped peeling his mango and raised an eyebrow. "Jung, you do know nuns can't get married, right?"

Gou saw a hint of panic cross the other man's eyes as he knew he'd just said something stupid. "Oh. Yeah. Sure. I knew that. So... uh...How about the other two?"

Gou shook his head in mock sadness. "Just friends I'm afraid. Seems I'm losing my touch as I get older."

Jung considered this, then said. "So, does that mean I can try my luck with them?"

Gou looked at the riverboat captain, his oily beard filled with bits of orange and white goo, and stinking of sweat and banana oil and suppressed an urge to tell him to go give it a try. It would be too cruel, although he wasn't sure who it would be cruelest to.

"Well, one's a nun, one's sick, and the third just lost her husband. Better to leave them be."

Jung hung his head and nodded. "Yeah, you're right."

Trying to change the subject, Gou looked up at the sky. "It's getting cloudy."

"Hmmm?" Said Jung, still in the middle of whatever thoughts were rumbling around in his head regarding the Sister. "Oh yeah. Looks like there'll be a storm before sundown."

Hearing that, Gou commented- "My sick friend can't take much of a rough ride."

"Oh, it's not a problem," said Jung. "We'll be tied up tight to a dock when it hits. I need to take on peaches at East Hill. We'll stay there while the storm blows over."

That may have put Jung's mind to rest, but it didn't help Gou much. Time spent docked was dangerous, and he'd rather be moving as much as possible. Still, with the coming storm there would be little chance of trouble unless their pursuers were very determined.

* * *

Copper Kettle Xiao strode back to where his brothers waited on the bench, his chins covered with the juice of the juicy peach he was eating like a starving man. He had a small sack of them in the other hand, which he swung as he walked.

"Well?" Last Brother Shou asked, his tone short.

"They've just passed." Xiao said between mouthfuls of peach. "They didn't stop here, though."

Shou considered. "They'll stop, and we'll be there when they do."

After recovering from their rounds of diarrhea, the three had managed to waylay a couple travelers and taken their horses. They'd ridden hard, but arrived at the dock town too late to catch the gambler and his friends from boarding a ship and sailing north toward Xuzhou.

It had surprised Shou to learn they were sailing away from Mao's family home, but the more he thought about it, the more it made sense. They had a sick girl with them, and taking her into the fight wouldn't do. They were going somewhere safe where they could hide out, or perhaps even planning to double-back and return using a different route.

Either way, they were close now, and there was going to be a reckoning for what they'd made him suffer. Before he took the girl, he was going to kill that gambler, and his friends, and do it as slowly as possible.

* * *

Gou had rarely heard such a ferocious storm as the one which raged this night. The thunder was almost a single continuous series of cracks, and the rain didn't so much fall as come screaming down at the earth with violent intent. It hammered the deck above him in a dull roar that sounded like the ship was caught under a waterfall.

The ship around him was tossing slightly from side to side, and jolts ran through the ship as each swing would bring the ship hard against the buffers of the dock where it was tied. This made it quite difficult for Gou to walk, much less walk and carry food, but he did his best to do so without spilling any.

Finally, reaching the cabin door he shot out a hand to knock, and then brought it back quickly to stabilize the covered tray he was holding.

"Who is it?" Asked a voice from within.

"Dinner."

"Come in."

Gou used a finger to tug the door handle and pull the door slightly open, and then used his foot to push it open the rest of the way. Inside was a small, cramped room with a single canvas covered platform that served as a bed, a shelf on one wall to serve as a table, and a single wooden stool.

On the stool, Miss Lily sat, where she had been watching the unconscious Meiyu for the past few hours under the dim light of an oil lamp. They'd been taking turns watching the sick girl, and it was time for Gou's shift to begin.

Lily looked at the tray Gou carried hungrily, and then paused, looking at Gou himself in surprise.

"You're soaked."

Gou nodded. "Yep. Went into town to get the food. Got caught in the storm on the way back." Then he handed the covered tray to Lily. "Eat up before it gets cold."

Lily frowned. "Don't you need to eat?"

"Already did," Gou said, walking over to check on the sleeping girl. Seeing her made his heart ache. She looked better than she had when they'd rescued her, more peaceful, and more color in her cheeks. "I brought that back for you."

"Oh, Gou..." Lily said, in a tone that said she found this touching. "You didn't have to. Thank you."

Gou shrugged, "Hey, it's the least I can do. This isn't your fight, and you still came to help out."

If Gou had been watching, he would have noticed Lily's soft smile faded a little at that remark, and she looked down at the food. "It is my duty and honor," she said quietly.

"Well, we're glad to have you with us." Gou said, finally looking at her again. "But, I do have a favor to ask."

She looked up at him, looking right into his eyes, surprised. "What...is it?"

"Well," Gou rubbed the back of his head. "I'm not sure how to ask this, but..."

"Yes?" She said, hopefully.

"I was wondering if you could..."

"Yes?"

"...Be a little nicer to Sister Cat."

"Oh." She said, and looked down again, slight disappointment in her voice.

Not noticing, Gou continued. "I know that she can be a little uptight sometimes, and a little blunt, but she's a good person and just wants to do the right thing. You gotta understand, she was raised in a nunnery, and she's still getting use to this society thing. Heaven knows she bugs me sometimes too, but if you give her a chance and get to know her, I think you two could really get along."

Miss Lily just bobbed her head as he talked, and then when he'd finished, she just said. "I will try." In a quiet voice that hinted at disappointment.

"Good," said Gou, still not noticing her change in manner. "This whole thing is going to be a lot easier if we can all do our best to get along. We're all comrades, right?"

"Yes." Lily agreed, and then got up and excused herself. "I need to go eat this."

"Sure, see you later." Gou said, and watched her slip outside and close the door. He smiled to himself, relieved that she'd taken it so well. It had been bothering him for a while, but he hadn't quite known what to do. Now it was over.

As Gou pulled the stool closer to the bed, it occurred to him that he'd missed another chance to ask about Lily's connection with Snowtop.

Oh well, he decided, there'd be plenty of time to ask her later. Then, as he sat down, he looked at Meiyu, and his smile became a softer one.

"Don't worry, we'll get you home." He said to the sleeping girl. "I'm not going to lose you again."

Above him, thunder roared in agreement.

* * *

The light of the storm illuminated the riverside dock where the ship was tied. The crew had all gone inside, or found shelter elsewhere, and the sail-less riverboat bucked and bobbed in the storm as sheets of heavy rain washed over it. There were a few lights faintly visible from openings along the side, but most of the ship was dark and empty looking.

Beneath the awning of a nearby building, three figures crouched and watched the boat carefully. They had been there for only a short time, but were anxious to move. Only their caution held them back.

When Last Brother Shou was satisfied, he turned to his two companions. "Follow me," he said, and dashed off across the small dockyard in the rain.

With amazing speed, he swept up onto the dock, over the side of the ship, and onto its deck. Seeing no opposition, or sign of a trap, he dashed back to the covered portion at the rear of the ship that held the cabins. He was using lightfoot kung fu to keep his steps soft and smooth, and with effort avoided making too much noise as they moved across the deck and slipped up next to the door that led into the cabin area.

Behind him, two other shadows did the same, and all three stopped at the door.

Mah was too large and bulky in his armor, and wouldn't fit, so Shou had told him to wait outside and cut down anyone who tried to flee. He also did it because he wasn't sure he trusted Mah anymore, not after some of what had happened surrounding the girl. Better to put him where he would cause the least amount of trouble.

Xiao was also large, but his more flexible bulk would still fit inside the cramped halls of the ship, and Shou would use him to cover his back.

Giving each a look to make sure that they knew the plan, Shou drew his blade and reached for the handle.

* * *

"Gou...?"

The voice was soft and weak, but the sound of it practically knocked the dozing Gou off his stool. The gambler had to grab the shelf next to him to keep from falling over because he tried to spin around so fast.

When he did, he found two of the most beautiful eyes in the world looking at him.

"You're awake!" He exclaimed, and hopped off the stool to kneel down next to the bed. "Well, of course you're awake. I don't need to tell you that, do I?" Then he took a breath, catching himself. "How are you?"

"Hurts." Meiyu answered after trying to move a little. "Where is this?"

"Don't worry, you're safe." Gou said, trying to sound as reassuring as possible. "I came to bring you home."

She took that in. "But...How?"

"Hey, you know me. Always ready to be there for my friends." He smiled. "You hungry? I can get you something to eat."

She stared at him with sleepy eyes, as if she was trying to decide whether this was a dream or reality. Then to his surprise, she reached out and brushed the side of his face with her fingertips.

"Is it really you?"

He reached up and took her hand, holding it to his cheek. Then he closed his eyes, enjoying the moment. His heart was pounding, and he felt like he wanted to cry. He thought that if his life ended at that moment, he would feel like it had been complete.

Then she said something that he'd thought he'd only ever hear in his dreams.

"I've missed you."

Gou opened his eyes, looking right into hers. She was crying now, the tears running down the sides of her face. Before he knew it, he was crying as well. It wasn't something a man should do, but he couldn't stop himself.

"Me too," he said in a hoarse voice.

"I'm sorry."

Gou sniffed, looking at her in surprise. "For what?"

"For leaving without saying goodbye. It was father, he wouldn't let me..."

Gou raised a hand to stop her. "Shhh. Shhh. I know. I know it wasn't your choice."

"I wanted to write, but thought you hated me."

Gou reached out and tapped her softly on the forehead with his index finger. "Melon head! What would make you think that? Of course I don't hate you." He said in mock anger.

"Is it true?"

The young man gave her a soft smile. "Yes, it's true. I couldn't hate you if my life depended on it."

"Gou..." She started to cry again.

Gou almost joined her, but before he could, there suddenly rang out a lot of yelling outside, and he could hear bumping and thumping on the deck above.

Meiyu started to sit up, but Gou forced her back down. "No, don't move!" He cried. "It'll be fine. I'll check on things."

Spinning around, Gou suddenly realized that the sword he'd gotten from the *Jin Hua* was sitting in another cabin. There was nothing here he could use, not even a stick.

That's when he heard the heavy footsteps in the hall outside...

* * *

Shou had never had any problem with killing. Men. Women. Children. Seniors. It had never mattered to him. People were just the moving dead- they simply didn't know it. Shou saw his job as making them aware of their situation, and putting them where they belonged.

He had earned the title of "Last Brother" when he had killed all of his master's other disciples. He had approached his master one day and asked if he would be the one to inherit the master's secret techniques. The old man had replied that it would go to the student who was most worthy of the title. Perhaps he had been trying to sound encouraging. It didn't matter. Shou presented him with the heads of his brothers the next day at breakfast.

To him, it had been the simplest way to achieve his goals, however his master hadn't seen it that way, and instead had chosen to try to kill him. After his master had died, he'd taken his master's scrolls and fled with them into the forest, where he'd lived and worked to learn the school's techniques.

In order to survive, he'd eventually fallen in with some bandits, and when their leader had become troublesome, he'd taken the job himself. It wasn't hard, and the others already feared him. Word of what he had done had gotten around, which was why everyone called him "Last Brother".

He'd gotten quite the troop together, and it took the provincial garrison surrounding his mountain to bring him down. He'd thought it was the end when they'd taken him to those execution grounds, but then he'd met someone who cared even less for others than he did. Someone more deadly than himself.

Now he killed for her, and he enjoyed it.

Flicking the blood of the last boatman off his blade, Shou dashed down the hall toward the Captain's cabin. The other cabins had yielded nothing but boatmen, and he was certain he would find his prey there.

He paused only to check that Xiao was behind him, and then he grabbed the handle, raised his sword, and rushed inside. If it didn't look like the girl, it was going to die.

CHAPTER TWENTY-THREE

Reunion

Gou came up in a stance, spinning around and ready to fight as the door slammed open behind him. He didn't have any weapons, but he braced himself to fight like a cornered dog against whoever came through that door.

He almost attacked without waiting, but luckily he didn't, as the person who came rushing through the door was a worried looking Sister Cat.

"Brother Gou!" She cried, her arm coming reflexively up in a blocking motion as she saw his stance.

"Sister!" Gou relaxed a bit, then concern gripped him. "Sister, what's wrong?"

"Brother Gou, I am sorry to bother you. You as well, Miss Mao." She gave a quick bow by means of a nod of her head toward the fallen woman. "Lightning has struck the ship moored next to us and set it on fire. Captain Jung and his men have gone to try and help put it out, but I worry that it may be a trick."

Gou gave a sharp nod. "You're right, Cat. We'd better be prepared. Where's Lily?"

"On the deck, watching the fire I believe."

"Stay here while I get my sword," he said, ducking past her and rushing down the hall.

* * *

Last Brother Shou's eyebrows knit together as he stared around the Captain's cabin of the ship. It was empty, and there was no sign of the girl or the gambler.

Growling, he spun and looked at Xiao.

"Did you check the other cabins?"

"Yes, they're not here." The fat man peered past him inside the cabin. "I wonder. Did they go into town?"

Shou nodded, it was a possibility.

He started to march for the exit, forcing Xiao to duck into a nearby cabin to let him pass. Then he started to run, as he heard the sounds of metal on metal and yells from outside.

Bursting onto the deck, Shou and Xiao found their companion Mah locked in a life or death struggle with three attackers. The armored giant was doing his best to fend off two women and a man. As the lightning flashed, Shou judged them to be the leaders of the Nine Trees Escort Agency, the Lin family who had kidnapped the Mao girl before Shou's group had.

"Give us the girl!" Shouted Madam Lin at Shou over the sounds of the wind and storm. "And we might let you live."

Shou shook his head in disgust. "Help him," he ordered Xiao. "We have work to do."

"Of course," the fat man leapt forward, always eager to fight.

That taken care of, Shou looked toward the flickering lights of the small town near the dock. Clearly the Lin family also believed them to be here, so where were they? Where had their prey gone?

* * *

"That's it, Cat. Nice and gentle."

Gou and the nun lowered the board down onto a set of prepared boxes, making sure it was secure. It was the same board that they'd used to bring Meiyu onto the ship, but it now had an extra board of Captain Jung's design added to support her back so she could sit up.

The storm had passed, and it was a beautiful day, so Gou had suggested they bring Meiyu out of the small dark musty cabin to give her a little air. She'd agreed, and with a little fiddling, they'd gotten her out; now she was on the after-deck with a beautiful view of the passing green shoreline.

It had been a bit painful, but worth it.

"Thank you, Gou." She said, adjusting the blankets they'd carefully layered behind her back. "It's good to be out of there."

"My lady's comfort," the gambler bowed. "Is of utmost importance."

Meiyu smiled. "You should have been a servant, Gou. It suits you."

"My lady, the only person I serve is me." Gou said with a wink. "And if I had a choice, I'd fire myself!"

All three of them laughed at that.

"Where are we?" Meiyu said, craning her neck around to get a better look at their surroundings.

"The Liangxi River, near the mouth of Lake Tai. Jung says we'll be out on the lake by noon."

Meiyu nodded. "They won't be able to follow us then."

"Nope. We'll be free as birds. See? Just like I said."

He smiled at her, and the smugness on his face made her look away. When he'd told her at breakfast that they were on a riverboat she'd told him that it was dangerous. As her previous experience had shown, it was too easy to track a riverboat and fast horses could easily get ahead of them.

He'd reassured her that he'd taken precautions, and told her that when they'd left the dock they'd done so after attracting a lot of attention and on another boat, which was going north. Then, after a short distance, they'd met Jung's boat, transferred over in a hidden cove, and come back south. This way, to anyone who asked around in the town they would be on another ship going the opposite direction.

She had to admit, it was a clever strategy, and one worthy of Little Gou. It was one of the things that had always infuriated her about him, he was so smart, and so capable, and yet all he did was waste time on games and drinking. He'd even been apprenticed to Doctor Duan, a doctor whose reputation went far beyond their city, and yet he'd managed to fail at that as well. Gou could be almost anything he wanted to be, and she saw nothing but potential in him, yet it was unused potential at best, and outright wasted at worst.

"Whoever is trying to follow us will be way behind," Gou continued. "If we're lucky, they'll follow the other ship for a couple days before they can turn back. That should give us smooth sailing all the way to White Fox Town. Jung tells me we might even beat your caravan back."

Meiyu looked over at the boat captain and suppressed a shiver as he smiled at her with rotten teeth and his beard full of food. She gave a wan smile and then looked away as fast as decorum allowed, ahead at the widening river.

Her caravan. Her wedding caravan. She was going back to face her future with a man who'd she'd never met. Suddenly, White Fox Town was the last place in the world she wanted to be and she hoped that this ship would become stranded somewhere so they wouldn't have to return until long after her father had given up on this idea.

This was the life she wanted- a life of freedom and adventure. She wanted to ride, and sail and see the world. She wanted to go out and live. And, she wanted to do it with...

She looked at the man standing next to her, who was vigilantly scanning the horizon. Wondering. Thinking. Hoping. She could hope, couldn't she? Maybe all this box business would change something.

Well, until then. Until she returned home. She would keep hoping, and try to forget what awaited her. For now, it was all she could do.

* * *

The next two days passed as the *Lazy Dragon* sailed south through the series of small lakes, channels and canals that connected them. They saw no sign of pursuit, although Gou eyed every ship that came even near them with suspicion, and after the previous week of events it was a restful respite for all of them.

During this time, everyone shared their stories, and Meiyu finally learned what had happened at the engagement celebration only a week and a half before. She learned about the box, the *Jin Hua*, Master Shan and Princess Yu, and the harrowing events of the crossing at Green Rapids.

The only thing Gou decided to leave out was the involvement of Snowtop Cho, which he told himself was because he wanted to protect Snowtop's reputation. He wasn't sure Meiyu would believe it anyways, so it seemed best to just let that information remain hidden.

Meiyu, on the other hand, told of her encounter with the Lin family, and her subsequent escape with the help of the riverboat crew, and then capture by Moonlight's men. Everyone was impressed by her quick wits, but she expressed a regret that she didn't know what had happened to the crew of the riverboat. She was relieved when Captain Jung told her he not only knew the ship she'd been on, but that they hadn't been harmed by the Lins after her escape. It seemed the Lin clan hadn't been sure if the crew was involved, and had simply refused to pay and left.

However, the thing that got the most attention was her story about Mah the Fighting Red General. Not only because it was a tragic tale, but because of what it revealed about the people chasing them.

"Lady Moonlight is working for the government," Lily concluded, after hearing the story. "There must be someone in Nanjing who wants the box."

Gou nodded. "The question is- why? Just for the treasure?"

Everyone looked at him, but it was Lily who asked "What do you mean?"

"It's something that's bothered me since this whole thing started- why is she doing things the way she's doing them?" Then, when that got even more blank looks, Gou explained. "Look, if I were Lady Moonlight and I wanted the box, I can completely see sending thugs to grab a messenger, that makes sense. What doesn't make sense is her appearance at the engagement party. Why make such a big show of declaring that you want the box and that you're going to kill the Mao family if they don't give it to you."

"Why, for intimidation, of course." Lily said. "She was trying to scare them."

Gou shook his head. "Scare them to do what? She must have known Crocodile Mao is as hard headed as they come. Threatening him is like trying to threaten a mule- the more noise you make the more it will fight you. All she was doing was guaranteeing he wouldn't do what she wanted.

"If she wanted the box, or to do the hostage method, she would have kidnapped Meiyu before the announcement. Or, better yet, grabbed Meiyu's mother or siblings while they weren't prepared and then used them to get it. There are many ways to solve the problem of the box, but she did the most showy and flashy one, and the one least likely to actually get her what she says she wanted."

"So?" Cat offered. "She doesn't want the box?"

"I think...she does." Gou admitted. "But I don't think it's her real goal here. The box is just a distraction, she's trying to get it, but also trying to get something else."

"Like what?" Lily asked.

Then Gou looked right at her- "You tell me."

Lily's eyes went wide in surprise. "What do you mean?"

"I mean," said Gou. "When I first met you, Moonlight's men were at Master Yi's house, and before I saved you, you told the farmer's daughter that your mistress was in danger. What did you mean by that? I didn't ask you before because I didn't think you'd tell me and it was part of your mission for the *Jin Hua*, but now I need to know everything I can if I'm going to figure out what's going on."

All eyes were on Lily now, and the young woman turned away from them. She was clearly conflicted, and having to make a choice between her loyalty to her sisterhood and their common goal of solving this mystery.

"Miss Lily, please." Sister Cat pleaded. "Many people are being hurt, and this may prevent great suffering."

At last, Lily turned around and nodded.

"I will say what I can." She said, reluctantly.

"That's all we ask," Gou answered. "That, and a little more wine. Jung, you have another jug?"

"Of course!" Said the Captain and sent a man to fetch it.

When he'd returned and Gou had refilled the ceramic cup he was using, Miss Lily began her story.

"As Gou has said, I was married to Master Yi, of the Black Dragon Armed Escort Agency. Not long after our marriage, Lady Moonlight came to see Master Yi. At first, I thought she was just a tart that some client had sent to sweeten a deal, but later as I listened in on them talking, I came to realize she was the client herself.

"She said that she represented powerful people who didn't trust the current leadership of the Society of Armed Escorts leaders and wanted someone they could rely on to take charge of the guild. They offered to support him in his bid to become president of the council, but in return he had to do what they asked of him.

"My former husband is a very ambitious man, but he is also a cautious one. He asked for proof of their power and sincerity before he would believe them. Lady Moonlight told her to give him a name, and he chose Master Lin of the Nine Trees Armed Escort Agency."

At the mention of this man's name, Meiyu said– "When I was with them, Madam Lin said she wanted to force the council to help her catch her husband's killer. You mean it was Master Yi?"

Miss Lily nodded. "Yes. They had been rivals for a long time, and there was a feud between them because of a contract that Master Lin stole from him. With the Lin family crippled, Master Yi would be able to move his business into the Northeast region."

"So, what happened?" Gou put in.

"Two months later, she came again." Miss Lily said, then paused as a look of revulsion came over her face and she wrapped herself in her arms. "I remember my husband called everyone into the main hall, and there was something large covered by a sheet. When she had one of her foreign servants pull it back, it was a giant stuffed tiger. And...in its mouth...was the head of Master Lin."

Captain Jung spit out his wine, Sister Cat looked ill, Meiyu was shocked, and Gou just shook his head. "Well, I gotta admit, that woman does nothing halfway. She really should have gone into the theater."

Lily nodded slowly, her face showing her revulsion at the memory. "We all screamed, but my husband just laughed and walked around, he said that Master Lin had gotten the fate he deserved. Then he thanked Lady Moonlight, and invited her into his study to talk. I wasn't able to hear what they talked of because I was busy calming the servants, but I know that whatever it was he and she had made some deal.

"I tried to find out from him later what it was, but he would tell me nothing. He said it was better if I didn't know too much about his affairs. I can only assume he made a pact with her to become leader of the council, although I can't say what the terms were."

"So that's why her men were at your manor house the night I met you." Gou said. "They were delivering him his orders."

"As you say," Lily agreed. "Those men came to stay with us several times. They were disgusting pigs, but I had to serve them in order to learn what they were planning. Usually they talked of small things, nothing important."

Or nothing you're willing to tell us, Gou thought.

"...But on the night you came to the house, they brought something for my husband. It was a scroll from their mistress, and when my husband read it, he was overjoyed. He asked them several times if this was true, and they said that it was, and then he took them aside for drinking. He was in a very happy mood, which is why he was so kind to you when you arrived that night. Normally, he didn't like trespassers on his land."

"Well, I was a very charming trespasser."

She gave him a faint smile, and then continued.

"After the dinner when we met, he took them into his study and they drank and talked. When they were done, my husband was very drunk, so when he had gone to bed I snuck down into his study and went to the secret places where he kept his scrolls.

"It took me some time, but I found the one he'd just received and took it to another room where I could read its contents. I had to be very careful, because the alcohol hadn't seemed to affect those three monsters at all, and they could be lurking about. What I found was shocking!

"The scroll said that before the next gathering the three heads of the council- Master Mao, Master Bai, and my mistress Merciful Beauty, would all be dead, and that he would be able to take his place as council president. It also said she had the support of many of the council members already, but that he would need to move quickly to secure his place once the three elders were gone.

"In trade, he was to pretend to ally with Master Mao, and then turn on him at an appointed time. He would also give her the box."

"D-did it say when that would happen?" Stammered Meiyu, who had turned white as a sheet. She had reached out now, and was grabbing onto Lily's sleeve, almost as if it were a life line. Perhaps to her it was, Gou knew, Master Bai was a close uncle to her, and to lose both he and her father would be a terrible blow.

The other woman looked at her sympathetically. "No. But, it said that they would be executed for treason."

"Treason? No!" Meiyu gasped. "How!?! My father is no traitor!"

"I'm sorry," Lily said, putting a hand on Meiyu's shoulder. "I truly don't know."

"I do." Said Gou.

Everyone looked at Gou in surprise.

CHAPTER TWENTY-FOUR

The Plot

"Based on what you've just said," said Gou. "It all makes sense now."

"Gou!" Gasped Meiyu. "What do you mean? How?!? I don't understand."

Gou sighed, and shook his head. "Now that I think about it, it's really very simple. It even explains why she went to your family house that night, and tried to have you kidnapped."

"Brother Gou?" Cat also looked unsure. "Can you explain?"

"Okay," Gou said, starting to pace around the deck as he talked. "Let's look at it from the point of view of whoever is behind this. Let's say you want to dispose of a very rich and powerful man who has an army which spans across the empire. A man you might even be afraid of. How would you get rid of him?"

"I'd frame him for treason." Said Meiyu. "Say that he was planning to rebel against the empire, and then send the army to arrest him."

Gou stopped and stared at her. "What were they teaching you at that school of yours?"

The girl gave a shrug, "You learn a lot about such things in the capital. It happens quite often."

"Remind me never to get on your bad side," he remarked, and then continued. "You're right, that's usually what they'd do. But in this case, you'd have a special problem- as I said, he has an army of highly trained and very loyal soldiers, and they're scattered everywhere. If you arrest him, they're going to try to free him at best, or become rebels and come looking for revenge at worst."

"No," Gou continued. "You can't arrest him without making more trouble for yourself. That is, unless you can manage to get him to gather everyone important in his organization in one place at one time. That way, you can arrest them all in one single catch."

Meiyu stared at him. "The box."

"The box," he agreed. "She made him gather all of his family and top agency men in one place to defend a box he's sworn on his honor to protect. That's why she gave him two weeks to do it, enough time for most of his forces to gather. She also counted on Lord Bai being his sworn ally, so he'll be there with his men as well, so it'll be hitting two birds with a single stone.

"Both men will then be charged with plotting against the Emperor based on fake evidence, and everyone in their organizations will either be killed or enslaved. Their property will become part of the state, a treasure even bigger than Master Shan's several times over, and many people will become very rich in the process." He shook his head. "Like I said, simple. Although, there are a few tricks to it."

"Such as?"

"Well, you're going to have an extremely large number of highly skilled fighters in one place. You can't sneak up on them with an army because they'll just flee, and you likely can't arrest that many fighters without a sizable fighting force. You need some way to make them lower their defenses..."

"Master Yi!" Cat exclaimed.

"Exactly," Gou nodded sadly. "Master Yi will likely pretend to join Mao and Bai in the defense, but in reality, he's going to betray them. I'm sure he and Lady Moonlight have come up with some plan where Yi will help her people get through the defenses and keep the people there from escaping. That, and he'll be needed to keep the whole Society of Armed Escorts calm when news of this gets out."

"But Gou," asked the nun. "If that's the case, there is still something I do not understand. Why would she want to kidnap Master Mao's daughter? Why not just let her arrive and be captured with the other members of the family?"

"You're right, Sister." Gou frowned. "Unless she wanted her as insurance in case something went wrong. Remember that she only sent someone to get Miss Mao after the party, and she initially sent someone else to do her dirty work. She may only have mentioned Miss Mao at the party just to rattle her father and keep him distracted. Remember, this is all a game to keep Master Mao from realizing that he's walking right into her trap."

"Gou," Meiyu said, her voice trembling. "Is this all true?"

Gou sighed and nodded. "Yeah. As near as I can figure it, that's what's going on. It makes the most sense out of all the possibilities, especially when we assume Lady Moonlight is a government agent. We know the government is afraid the armed escort agencies will rebel, so they're looking for ways to get rid of them."

"Then...we have to hurry back!" Meiyu cried. "We have to warn father!"

"No."

The word hung like a sign in the air as everyone stopped and stared at Gou.

"B-but..." Meiyu stammered.

Gou raised a hand. "We'll warn them, yes. But as far as going back, that's the last thing we're going to do. Our job is to keep you safe, and putting you into the pot with all the other dumplings isn't going to do that." Then he dropped to one knee next to her so he could look her right in the eye, and took a softer tone. "Meiyu, I know you want to go back and help, but in your condition, you can't do anything but get in the way. We'll let your father know you're safe, so he can stop worrying and start focusing on what he needs to do- protecting your mother, brothers and the rest of the agency.

"That's not going to be easy, and having you there as you are won't make it any better. You're just going to have to sit this one out."

All this effort bought him was her angry glare. "I thought I could trust you, Gou."

"You can," He sighed. "More than you can trust yourself right now."

She looked away. "I'm tired. Take me to my room."

Knowing when to quit, Gou shrugged, and motioned for Sister Cat to help him do as Meiyu wanted.

She just needed time to think, he decided, then she'd understand. The last thing they needed to do now was return to White Fox Town.

* * *

Meiyu threw a pillow at the door when it slid shut, and immediately regretted it as pain raced down her back. Gasping in agony, she laid herself down on the flat bed and breathed shallowly to let the spasms of pain slowly subside.

She was finding her back wasn't hurt as much as she'd feared at first, and she'd begun to think the damage was more to muscle than to bone. Still, if she exerted herself at all the pain would make spots dance in front of her eyes and she'd be unable to do anything but try to force herself to relax.

But now, the tears that streamed down her face were because of the pain she felt within as much as from her body. She was scared that she would never see her family again, and that she'd never hear her father's laugh or see her mother's kind smile. She'd treated them so shabbily when she'd met them last, and now they were going to be lost to her when they'd done nothing wrong.

She also felt hurt at the idea that Gou wasn't going to try to help them. She knew Gou and her father had never been fond of each other, it was no secret that she'd been sent away to keep her apart from Gou. Her father had been worried she might just give in to the gambler's charms. But, she couldn't believe Gou would just let her family be taken prisoner.

Even as she thought it, she knew it wasn't true. Gou was going to send a messenger, he said, and was going to warn them as best he could. The rational part of her commented that maybe what Gou was doing really was the best way. It hurt, but what could she really do?

She could do something, dammit! She would do something. She would find a way. She had to.

In this state, torn this way and that, she slowly fell asleep in the warm darkness of her cabin. Her last thoughts were of the distant voices she could hear talking through the open window.

Gou's voice.

Traitor!

She wasn't sure when it was she awoke, although it was still very much dark outside. What she was aware of was that there was someone else in the small cabin with her, a shape standing over her in the darkness.

She almost cried out, but a firm hand suddenly clamped over her mouth and a soft female voice whispered "Shhhhh."

Unsure, Meiyu stopped struggling and after a moment she realized this was the other woman Gou had brought with him, the one called Miss Lily.

There was something about this woman Meiyu didn't like, and hearing her background earlier in the evening had made this feeling even stronger. Still, Gou seemed to trust her, and she was a capable woman who had helped rescue Meiyu from her captors.

"I am here to offer help," the woman said. "Will you cry out?"

Meiyu shook her head, and the hand was removed.

"I apologize for coming like this," Lily said, sitting down on the edge of Meiyu's bed. "But, I have something I need to discuss with you, and I had to wait until Gou and the others had fallen asleep."

"What do you want?" Meiyu asked, unsure.

"Despite his appearance, Gou is an honorable man, and he's doing what he believes is right." Lily said. "But, that doesn't mean he is. I worry that if Gou sends a messenger, your father will ignore them. If that happens, your family will be wiped out, and my sisters and master will also suffer the same fate."

Hearing this, Meiyu couldn't help readily agreeing. "You're right, we need to change his mind!"

But in the dim light, she could see the other woman shake her head. "It's no use. I tried already, but he refuses to see logic. His affection for you is blinding him to what needs to be done."

Meiyu sighed, and she could feel the tears start to build again. This time tears of frustration and helplessness. If she was well, he wouldn't treat her like this, and he couldn't stop her from leaving the ship to do what had to be done.

She felt a hand on her arm.

"Sister, don't despair." Lily said. "There is a way. This boat has a second smaller boat, one it tows behind it. I heard the crew say it's for emergencies, but they need to put it in the water occasionally to keep the wood from drying out and splitting. We can use it to leave and warn your family, if you're able."

Meiyu gasped. Was this possible?

"I know how to sail," she said quickly. "If you do not, I can tell you what to do."

"Then you will do it?" Lily asked. "Will your injury allow you to travel?"

"Of course," Meiyu lied. "It wasn't so bad, and thanks to the nun's care I am much better. We need to risk it."

Hearing that, the other woman agreed. "It is just after midnight now, and all are sleep except for the man who is piloting the boat. I will give him wine to make him sleepy, and when he is drunk, I will come to get you. You will need to ride on my shoulders."

"I can do that." Meiyu said, forcing down her fears. It would be agony, but she had to do it. "Just come get me."

Then the one named Lily was gone, and Meiyu was alone with her thoughts. She had to do this. She just had to. Gou would understand.

She hoped.

* * *

As Miss Lily stepped from Meiyu's cabin and slid the door closed, she too found herself filled with conflicted feelings. On one hand, she had pledged to help Gou in his mission to save Miss Mao and return her home. On the other, she was sworn to the *Jin Hua* and their master, and she needed to do whatever would benefit the sisterhood.

If Gou's theory was correct, as it likely was, the box could be merely a trick, and the Mao Family Armed Escort Agency would soon be crushed. But, on the off chance the box was still of value, and that Mao may have hidden it somewhere, then holding his daughter could be the key to gaining its contents and any secrets it might hold.

She would escape with the girl and head for the nearest outpost of the sisterhood. Once there, the girl would be safely in their care, and taken care of. She would personally see that no harm came to Meiyu, and that she would be a protected guest while she recovered from her injury, safely away from the manipulations of Lady Moonlight and her masters.

In that way, she would fulfill both her pledge to Gou, and her duty. Once everything was over and done with, they would either trade her for the box, or if it was lost, release her to rejoin her family.

However, there was still one other point. Her grandmother's orders hadn't stopped at acquiring Meiyu- they also included Gou. She felt the daggers inside her robes. He was asleep on the deck above, and it would be a simple thing to finish him without alerting the others...

* * *

Gou had bad dreams that night.

He dreamed someone was chasing him through a house, he didn't know who, but whoever they were was enough to make him afraid. Each room he ran into had another door, and each door revealed another room in a seemingly endless succession. He knew he had to get outside to escape and be free, but no matter what direction he went the house never ended.

Finally, he came to a door and wrenched it open to discover a finely dressed woman sitting in the middle of a room facing away from him. He rushed forward, trying to warn her of what was coming, and put his hand on her shoulder.

Miss Lily turned and looked at him, her face smiling gleefully, and then he felt the sharp pain as she drove a blade right through his chest.

Gou woke up gasping for air, with his hands trying to staunch invisible blood. The pain of the blade was still there, but quickly fading, and he sat rocking himself on the main deck of the ship.

Well that was unpleasant, he decided. He wasn't one to have nightmares, but this business, and perhaps too much to drink, had brought them out. Rubbing his chest, he stood up and looked around.

It was still late at night, but the ship was lit by oil lanterns that hung fore and aft, and these provided some light to work from. He could see Sister Cat, Jung, and several crewmen sleeping on the deck. It was a warm night, and better to be outside than in some dank stateroom. He'd wanted Meiyu to be out as well, but doubted she'd take him up on his offer.

The ship's sails were still up, and the wind blowing from the Northwest was filling them and carrying the ship south. Jung had said they'd reach Manshan Island by mid-day tomorrow, and be moving closer to shore. Gou planned to stop at a town there and send off some messengers to White Fox Town, and then have Jung carry them west.

He had friends who owed him, and he planned to collect on those debts. They had places he and the others could stay until this blew over, and at the same time he could enjoy a little time at the tables.

It was a win-win situation all around.

He knew Meiyu wasn't going to like it, but this was the way it was going to have to be. He wasn't stupid enough to take on the government, and this wasn't his fight. He just wanted her to be safe. This had never been about crazy *biaoju* politics or even crazier government thugs, it had always been about Meiyu.

He might have played with others since she'd been taken from him, but they'd never stayed with him long. They could always sense he'd been holding back from them, and sooner or later they moved on to men who were more devoted that Gou seemed to be. He couldn't help it, he cared for them, but there was always that spot in his heart that no-one could touch.

No one but her.

He took a deep breath and looked out over the darkened lake at the ship's lights reflecting on the water. With he and her, it was like they had been friends for a hundred lifetimes. They had talked like old friends on their first meeting, and the conversations had only gotten deeper the longer they'd known each other.

It was an intenseness Gou had never known with another human being, a closeness and naturalness that he knew instinctively was something rare and to be cherished. Those around them had sensed it too, and that was why Meiyu's father had sent her away rather than let it go on any longer. He had greater plans for his daughter than some street rat of little background or fortune.

Gou had never really blamed the old fighter for that, and it was hard for Gou to hold a grudge against anyone. But by the same token, he didn't owe him any more favors than what decency and honor required. They were both *xia*, and both lived by the codes of the *Jianghu* martial underworld, and that's why Gou would warn him, but little more.

His resolve firm, Gou sucked in a deep breath, blew it out his mouth, and turned back to the ship and the moment at hand. Instinctively, he looked around for Miss Lily. He didn't believe in dreams as the future or visions from the gods, but he knew it meant he was concerned about her. He'd accepted her help because he'd needed it and she seemed quite sincere, but there was a part of him that never fully trusted her.

Maybe this dream was a reflection of that.

Not seeing Lily about, he wandered to the after-deck of the ship, the raised section where the pilot stood manning the rudder to keep the ship on course. Or at least, was supposed to be manning it. Instead he found the rudder shaft tied to keep it straight, and the crewman asleep on a coiled rope with a jug of wine next to him.

Gou frowned, some good this would do if they were blown off course or heading for some rocks. He shook his head and kicked the lightly man until he woke, trying to save him from the Captain's wrath.

"Hey, wake up." He said as the crewman started to come around. "If you want to sleep, get someone else to watch the ship."

The crewman made an unintelligible noise and scratched himself, then looked around.

"Where's the girl?" He asked.

"What girl?"

"The pretty one who keeps her hair up like a man."

A memory of a grinning woman's face suddenly appeared to Gou, laughing at him.

* * *

Some distance behind, in the ship's rowboat, Meiyu turned to look at her companion. She'd been watching the direction the ship had gone for any sign it might have turned around– that someone had noticed their escape.

There was none.

Now, the worry fading along with the pain from having been carried onto the rowboat by Miss Lily, she began to relax.

She could only barely see Lily in the moonlight, sitting facing her, working the oars. The woman was surprisingly strong for her size, and had carried Meiyu to the rowboat with little effort.

"Where are we going?" Meiyu whispered, as though they could still hear her aboard the distant ship.

"Away from the ship's path, in case they return." Lily told her. "We'll wait until it's light, and then head for the lakeshore to find a fishing village. We should be able to head inland, and get passage south from there."

A sensible plan, Meiyu thought in agreement.

A part of her thrilled at the thought of seeing her family again. They had to hurry, but she would be there when the time came. She would see her father and mother, and they would face the future together.

Not even Gou could stop that now.

CHAPTER TWENTY-FIVE

Turnabout

It was just before dawn when the ship found them.

Meiyu guessed later that Miss Lily must also have fallen asleep, as her first memories were of strong men's hands grabbing her and hauling her up from the rowboat. Of course, with her injury, the moment they did this her shoulder was wracked with pain and she started screaming.

By the time she could focus again, she was laying on the deck of a larger ship with men gathered around her. She could hear Lily cursing nearby, and there was a lot of shouting and yelling going on.

Then suddenly the men next to her parted, and a handsome clean-shaven young man with white hair appeared.

"I told you to be careful with her!" He cursed at the men, and then his expression softened as he looked at her. "Miss Mao? Are you injured? You're safe, it's me- Cho."

* * *

"Any luck?"

Captain Jung shook his head. "None, I'm afraid."

Gou sighed and looked at the horizon. They'd doubled back to try and find the rowboat after Lily and Meiyu had been discovered missing, but now it was late into the morning and still there was no sign of them.

"It's a big lake," Jung commented. "Lots of coves and villages they could have gone to. We're not likely to find them unless the gods see fit."

"Right," Gou agreed, chewing on his lower lip. Then he turned and looked at Sister Cat, who was standing nearby. "Well Sister, what do you think?"

"I believe," said the nun. "They are attempting to return to warn Miss Mao's father of the danger. If we want to find them, we would be better served by doing the same."

"She's right, Gou." Jung put in. "That girl of yours was howling last night when you told her she couldn't see her family again."

Gou couldn't argue with any of this- he knew both of them were right. He also knew that this meant there was really only one thing left for him to do.

"Get us to the nearest place we'll be able to get decent horses." Gou said to the Captain. "We need to send off a message. And then, the Sister and I are going home."

* * *

Mao Meiyu awoke to find herself once more in the cabin of a ship, but this one was much bigger than the one she'd been on before, and more sumptuously decorated. Multicolored silks hung around the room, and the smell of sandalwood fixtures and statues fought to bring a sense of civilization to the cabin that was nowhere to be found on a common trading vessel.

As she was studying this place, the cabin door peeked open a crack and someone looked in at her. While she watched, it closed, and then moments later she heard the sound of quick footsteps and there was a knock at the door.

"Come in," Meiyu said, not seeing she had many other choices.

At this, the door opened and Snowtop Cho swept into the room- stock straight, muscular, not a single white hair out of place. As the door was closed behind him, he marched over to where she lay and dropped to one knee, bowing his head.

"When we reach your family, this humble one will take any punishment that my lady sees fit." He said, not looking at her.

Meiyu blinked. Surprised.

"Brother Cho...What are you doing?"

"I failed in my mission to protect you, and allowed the men of this ship to harm you after we found you in the water. At your command, I will discipline them in any way you wish for the treatment my lady suffered." Then he looked her directly in the eye. "Please let this one know your thoughts, my lady."

Meiyu let herself smile. He was still as stiff as ever.

"Brother Cho, your men didn't know I was hurt. You can't blame them for what happened. Let them do their duty."

"Is that what my lady truly wishes?"

Meiyu indicated that it was.

"Then they will be pardoned by your mercy." He said, bowing his head again. "I will let them know that you forgave them out of the kindness of your heart."

"It's good to see you, Brother Cho."

The young swordsman looked up at her, surprise in his eyes. "It... It is good to see my lady as well."

"Call me Miss Mao."

Snowtop's brows furrowed. "That would be too much of an assumption."

"Not if I order you to."

They looked at each other, and she could see the wheels turning inside his head. He wanted to be more friendly with her, which was natural since they'd known each other for many years, but his sense of duty and decorum was holding him back. At last, he made his choice.

"Can I bring Miss Mao something to eat or drink?"

* * *

Once food had been brought, and she'd managed to wear his demeanor down to something slightly softer, Meiyu and Snowtop began to discuss the issue of what had brought them to this odd place and situation.

While she ate, Snowtop showed her the letter from her father he carried, which she saw bore the clear mark of her father's *hanko* chop. Then he told her of how he had traveled to the crossing at Green Rapids Town and been stymied when the ferry-barge had been burned and the whole affair turned into a mess.

Since it would have taken too long to wait while the ferry-barge was repaired, he and his men had been taken across by fishermen's boats. Not wanting to leave their horses, it had taken quite a bit of time, but they had managed to get back on the road and raced to meet her as quickly as they could.

When they found the wedding caravan, however, it was already on the way south without her, and they learned what had happened at the inn with the Lin family. They also discovered that Gou and his companions had met with the caravan before them, and while Snowtop was happy to hear they were alive, he was shocked to learn that they too were also looking for Meiyu.

Snowtop commented that he supposed Gou was jealous when he'd learned that Miss Mao's father had sent him on this mission, and was trying to steal some of the glory. It was shameful, but then Gou had always been a little bit unreliable and self-centered.

To this, Meiyu said nothing.

After Snowtop and his companions had gone searching for the Lin family, they'd eventually caught rumors of the deaths of the bandits in Willow Garden and recognized descriptions of the Lin clan. Rushing there, they'd been too late, and found she'd already been taken away in a cart by the three men who he'd seen accompanying Lady Moonlight.

Explaining that his man, Chan, was an expert tracker, they'd managed to follow the cart because of one of the horse shoes and this had led them to a riverside town. In that town, they learned that it hadn't been the three fighters that had brought her, but instead Gou and his two companions. They also learned that the Lin clan and the three fighters had previously been there, asked about the boat she'd left on, and gone.

It was here that Snowtop smiled, and she could hear the pride in his voice. For while the others had asked the locals what ship Meiyu had been taken aboard, Snowtop's man learned who Gou had talked to. When he'd heard that the captain Gou had met was one who smelled of banana oil, he'd known immediately it was Slow Jung. Then, when he'd learned Gou didn't get on Slow Jung's ship, he'd guessed it was a trick, and followed the stinky captain's ship instead.

They'd ridden to the mouth of the river, and then chartered the largest ship they could find to set out in pursuit of Jung's vessel. Fortunately, the port they'd gone to was a large one, and Snowtop was able to use his contacts there to get a good ship from a wealthier client who used his family services.

They'd worried they might have lost the trail when they spotted the rowboat adrift in the morning, and been shocked to discover who the passengers were. Snowtop then paused, and asked how it was Meiyu and Lily had ended up in that boat. Also, what had become of Gou and Jung's ship?

Meiyu thought a moment, and then said "Brother Cho, will you give me your help?"

"Without hesitation", Snowtop answered. "In anything my lady asks."

Then Meiyu proceeded to tell Snowtop what had transpired for her since that fateful encounter with the Lin clan. However, when she got to the events of the previous night and what they had uncovered of Lady Moonlight's plan, she faltered. If she told him the truth, wouldn't Snowtop act just as Gou had? To avoid the danger of White Fox Town, and try to put her somewhere safe while merely sending a messenger?

She decided she couldn't risk the possibility.

"Gou has discovered the secret of the box my father keeps for the Society of Armed Escorts leadership council, but he didn't want to take me home for fear that Lady Moonlight might be waiting for me. I need to get that message to my father as quickly as possible, and I can't trust anyone to write it down. So, Lily helped me leave the ship while the rest of them slept, but we became lost until the kind brother found us."

Snowtop nodded. "I can commend Gou on his wits and caution," he said, and for a moment Meiyu's heart started to sink. But then he added, "But, with such vital information to be held back for caution would be a mistake."

"Then you'll help me, Brother Cho?"

The very question seemed to surprise the young swordsman. "My lady doesn't even need to ask. We'll make port as quickly as we can, as we can make better time over land. If my lady is able to take riding a horse, that is." He looked at her with concern.

"If we can get a cart, I will manage."

"Then, if you will excuse me. I will have a word with the Captain." He bowed, then added. "We will get you home, my lady. As swiftly as possible, I promise you."

* * *

"You look happy, Young Master."

"Really, Chan?" Cho smiled down at his lieutenant. "Am I not always happy?"

Spider Chan smiled back. "Only if you don't count the past few weeks."

Snowtop laughed. "Yes, I suppose I have been very focused, haven't I?"

"Well, the Young Master can't be blamed. This has been a trip of ill fortune from the start." Both men were standing on the command deck of the *Golden Repose*, the ship which Snowtop had borrowed from a wealthy client. It offered a beautiful view of the green lake waters, and the shoreline that was just starting to fade into view along the horizon to the east. "I am almost surprised we had such luck and found her at all before she'd returned home."

"Well," said Snowtop, a hint of wistfulness coming into his voice. "That we found her is enough."

"Not just her," Chan said, eying his master. "We also found her companion."

Chan saw Snowtop noticeably stiffen at the mention of the other woman now kept under guard in one of the ship's rooms. This only confirmed what he had already suspected.

"It seems the Young Master is having a bountiful catch from the lake today."

"Chan," said Snowtop, the mirth gone from his voice. "Heaven is cruel."

"Oh really?" Said the short, homely Chan.

"On the same day, it has reunited me with two women who have touched my heart, and left me unable to choose."

"It seems to me, Young Master." Chan said, helpfully. "That before you have a choice, you have to see where you stand with each of them. You have yet to talk to the other one yet. She may have different ideas than you do."

"I want to, Chan. But, I'm afraid."

"Afraid of her?"

"Afraid of myself. Even seeing her brings back many feelings, not all of them pleasant or honorable."

Chan thought about this a moment, then said- "Master, we will arrive at a port before dinner, and we must decide what to do with her before we're to ride out. If you wish, I can see that she's left with some money and a way to find her way home when we leave her behind." He saw Snowtop flinch at that idea, and added. "Or, she can ride with us, but we can't take a prisoner with us when time is so important.

"The Young Master must make a decision."

* * *

Lily sat on a barrel in the corner of the storeroom, her knees pulled up tight against her chest and her face buried between them. She had been crying, but now her tears were long dry. The day she had long feared had finally come, and there was no escape, she was going to have to face her past.

She had known it the moment she'd seen the ship that had picked them up had been Snowtop's, and she'd almost been tempted to jump overboard when she'd seen him on the deck. Only her will to live, and sense of duty to her sisterhood, had kept her from doing so.

Then they'd locked her here alone in this warm, dark room, with only a tiny hole for light and fresh air. It had given her time to think about what she could do, or what she could say when she saw him. He, who she had cruelly betrayed in the worst manner possible.

"May I enter?"

The words came from behind the door, and before she could think she'd already heard herself say "Yes".

He stepped inside, hands clasped behind his back, shoulders erect, and face neutral.

The lock behind him clicked into place.

They were alone.

"Are you well?" He asked in a general tone.

"I am," she replied. Watching him look around the storeroom at anything but her.

"Good." He said, and then finally looked in her direction. "I must say, I was surprised when I saw you with Gou in Green Rapids Town. Have you known him long?"

She shook her head. "Just met him."

"Ahh." He nodded. "He's a good fellow, but a little unpredictable. You need to watch him."

"I'll remember that."

"I should thank you..." He started, then paused as if he wasn't sure he wanted to finish the sentence. "For taking care of Miss Mao. She says it was you who helped her leave the ship. We wouldn't have found her without you."

"You're welcome. Is she well?"

"Well enough, we're going to take her home."

Well, that was it then. Her mission was finished. Lily leaned her head back against the wall behind her- eyes up at the ceiling. "She'll be happy about that."

There was a long silence, as both were frozen in place, and for a moment Lily thought he was going to turn and leave.

"Can I know the reason why you left?" He finally said, an edge audible in his voice.

"Does it matter?"

"It does." He said, and she could feel his eyes staring at her. It made her angry.

"It's not your concern," she said bitterly. "I made my choice."

"But why?"

Part of her wanted to tell him, to say that she'd been selected by Merciful Beauty to become the wife of the Black Dragon Armed Escort Agency's leader. That she'd had no choice, and that it was a decision that had torn at her every day of her life since. But, there was another part, one that resented being put in this position where she couldn't explain herself. That part was angry and frustrated, and too strong to resist.

"Maybe you weren't enough for me," she finally said. "Always following me around like a puppy dog. It was cute at first, but then I got tired of it. I wanted someone who earned his position, not a little boy who got it from his father."

"I... see." His voice was cold with anger, and she could see the emotions playing on his face. "Well, if that's how you felt you made the right decision for both of us." He turned away, toward the door. "When we leave, you will remain on the ship for half a day. Then you will be released unharmed, and allowed to go about your business."

As he knocked on the door to signal the guard outside, a thought occurred to her- hadn't Gou said that Snowtop was being tricked by Lady Moonlight? If that was true, he'd be taking the girl into a trap, and worse, walking into one himself.

"Wait!" She said, as the door opened.

"Goodbye, Ming," Snowtop said as he stepped through. "Have a good life."

"No, wait!" She jumped off the barrel. "You have to give her to her father, don't give her to anyone else!"

But, even as she said it, the door closed behind him.

And he was gone.

* * *

The ship made port that afternoon, and after taking time to buy a carriage with a good suspension, Snowtop and his men loaded Meiyu aboard. He noticed she was quite pale once they got her inside, but she seemed to be making a good show of it, and he again felt quite moved by her strength and determination.

After Chan had formed the men up into lines, Snowtop took a final glance back in the direction of the ship, and then called out for them to follow him as he led them in a gallop out of town. Their horses were re-energized after being able to spend the time aboard the ship resting, and they fell into step around the carriage, which was going as fast as it could reasonably manage.

In this way, Snowtop took Meiyu south along the main trade roads, and they wound a path down toward White Fox Town. The port they'd docked at was only a full day's ride from their home city, but with the carriage and Meiyu's condition it took them a day and a half until they were able to feel like they were on familiar ground.

It was then that Snowtop reviewed the letter he had received from Miss Mao's father and its instructions. He was to take her to the Safflower Inn on the edge of Mount Fung, where agents of the Mao family would meet them and lead them to one of the agency safe-houses.

Snowtop knew the inn, as it was a famous one for a bloody fight between two rival gangs a few years before, and led the party there. It was nearing dusk when they saw the lights of the inn ahead of them, and brought the carriage up in front.

After informing Miss Mao of where they were, and reassuring her of how close they were to home, Snowtop left Chan and some men to guard the carriage while he went with some others inside.

It didn't take long before they found the person waiting for them.

CHAPTER TWENTY-SIX

Betrayal

"Master, a word."

The man called Crocodile Mao gestured to the servant to wait, and continued with what he'd been saying. "I have runners occupying every corner with orders to look for her approach, we will know the minute she appears. Keep the men where they are."

He finished that by looking around the table at his lieutenants to make it clear this was the way it was going to be. He wasn't going to split up his forces and let them get picked off by this witch and her men- he would make her come to them.

The lieutenants who had been advocating a more proactive approach all found something interesting about the table in front of them, and Mao considered the matter closed.

"Now stay alert," he said, and turned away, indicating for the servant to follow as he stepped from the table. Around the hall, he could see over thirty of his best men and kinsmen, all of whom had answered the call and were dressed for battle. They were joined by Master Bai's kinsmen, and a few other fighters who were loyal to either Mao or Bai and had chosen to throw in their lots with the old agency heads. Nearly fifty men in total, a room full of men about whom tales were told from Guangdong to Urumqi.

They were going to give this upstart witch a fight she wouldn't forget if she made the mistake of starting one.

"Speak." Mao said softly, leaning down and in to hear the servant. He was not a small man, and the servant had to stand on his tip-toes to reach the master's ear.

"Sir, a man has arrived saying he must speak with you. They say it's about today's deadline."

"Indeed?" Mao tugged at his beard and nodded. "Where is he?"

"In the second garden, sir."

With the servant in tow, Mao strode off to the second of the manor's five gardens. Mao's eldest daughter was a gardener of some skill, and she had taken what had been largely neglected gardens built by the previous occupants and turned them into beautifully landscaped areas.

This one in particular was the most beautiful, and thus the place he often received guests. Orange Calla Lilies lined the edges, with white and blue Chrysanthemums mixed in to bring out the greatest effect. Flowering vines with purple flowers grew up over a stone gazebo in the garden's middle, and there was a carved stone table and seats hidden within that allowed for private conversations.

Mao couldn't see who was awaiting him as he followed the stone path to the gazebo, but when he ducked inside, he was shocked to discover it was someone he knew well.

"Ahh," he exclaimed. "Lord Yi!" And, clasped his hands together to bow to the other man.

Yi did the same, "Master Mao. It has been too long." Clad in an elegant long blue robe, Lord Yi had his hair tied back into a long braid. He smiled at Mao and gestured toward the seat across from him.

"Indeed it has," Mao said as they both took their seats. "Was it that business with the Persians in Nanjing?"

Lord Yi laughed. "Your memory is as sharp as always. That was quite a while ago, but I'm sure you remember it like yesterday."

"No. No." Mao waved a hand in front of his face. "You flatter me. I only remember because it was such an unusual situation. I have fought for many contracts in my time, but to actually fight using our best warriors to prove who was worthy of a contract was most peculiar. I am sorry of any loss of face our victory caused you or your organization."

Mao was both somber and serious, but Lord Yi again just waved it off. "It was nothing. Truly, I owe you for taking that contract from me. To escort a caravan all the way to Persia was an incredible undertaking, and I later gained a more valuable contract with a local merchant. It all worked as heaven's will intended in the end."

Nodding, Mao relaxed slightly. "I should have known that Lord Yi was not such a small-minded man. Forgive me my ignorance."

After a servant had brought them tea, and a bit more small talk had passed between them, Master Mao was beginning to feel the time and said. "I am sorry that I cannot talk further, but this is a most busy day in my household and I have many duties to attend to. Is there some small way I can help my honored guest?"

"Yes," Lord Yi said, his face becoming earnest. "Allow me to aid you in this time of crisis."

"Lord Yi?" Master Mao said, surprised.

"I have heard of your situation, old friend. The threat that this witch has placed upon your household, and I have come to offer the aid of myself and my men to your cause. My men wait nearby, and I need only order them to come and stand beside you tonight."

Master Mao, coming out of his surprise, immediately told Lord Yi that the offer was most generous, but that in fact unnecessary. They had prepared for almost two weeks, and Master Mao had both men and weapons at the ready.

Still, Lord Yi insisted, and in the end Mao relented.

"Well, then." Mao said with a grin. "Order your men to join us. And tonight. we will dine together as the witch howls in frustration outside our doors."

* * *

In the shadow of Mount Fung, a single rider brought her horse up to a halt and peered around a forest clearing. Clad in men's riding clothes, she was nonetheless so mud-stained and disheveled that it would be hard to match her to either gender at the moment.

Dismounting, she walked over and tied the horse to a low-hanging branch before starting to survey the scene.

The clearing was a mess of churned mud, blood, bits of clothing, broken weapons, broken amour and the bodies of dead horses. The remains of a terrific battle. However, as she passed through the scene, she noted there were no bodies anywhere to be seen.

Where had they gone? Lily wondered.

After she had escaped from the masters of the *Golden Repose*, Lily had stolen a horse and set out in immediate pursuit of Snowtop and his entourage. It had taken some effort, but she had followed the signs until she'd reached an inn on the edge of town early this morning. There she'd learned that Snowtop had arrived at the Inn the night before, met a man the innkeeper didn't recognize, and then left with him in this direction.

What had happened here? She wondered, walking about and looking at the tracks in the ground. Hoof prints showed where a group of men on horseback had entered this clearing from the east. Footprints showed a mass of men emerging from the forest to surround the horses, and there had been fighting. Finally, the attackers had dispersed in several directions.

But only one of those directions showed the long narrow grooves of wheels in soft earth.

That was the one Lily chose to follow.

* * *

As the old brown walls of White Fox Town came into view, Gou couldn't help but give a sigh of relief. He had wondered if they were going to reach the city in time, but now, on the day of Lady Moonlight's terrible decree, they were within sight of their goal.

"Nothing like the smell of home, is there sister?"

Sister Cat, riding on the trotting horse next to him, wrinkled her nose. "It is indeed memorable. Although, I believe I preferred the air out in the countryside."

"Ahh, too much fresh air will go to your head. This is the smell of civilization."

"Are you saying that civilization stinks?"

Gou laughed. "Maybe it does. All I know is that I do after being on the road for two days straight."

The nun nodded. "I as well. But, we had best hurry to the Mao family home. It may already be too late."

Gou gestured toward the crossing ahead of them, which was ringed with stalls selling the harvests of late summer. "Mao's estate is on the outside of the city near the Northwest gate, if we take the road to the right we'll be there before dinner."

"Brother," the nun said, gesturing at the sun sinking in the west. "Have you considered that we may be too late?"

With a bob of his head, Gou indicated that he indeed had considered it. In fact, it was something that had pushed them and their horses to the limit during the last day. If they were late, he could only hope that Meiyu had arrived first and warned them in time.

If they weren't too late, he hoped there would still be time to convince Crocodile Mao of what needed to be done. The jaws of the trap were closing, and it would take all of his effort to get out of it with all his limbs intact.

* * *

Mao Manor was ringed by a wall a little more than double the height of a man. This wall had three entrances, one for the directions east, south and north, with the south gate being the main entrance. The other two were made for servants and workers to use, although now they were completely barred shut and blocked with piles of large stones.

"A wise precaution," Lord Yi nodded as Mao gave him a tour of the defenses. "She may only enter through the main gate, where most of our forces are. And, you have lined our fighters up in a ring around the manor house as well. Most sensible."

The coolness of the evening had started to descend on the land, and the first hints of stars had begun to appear in the Eastern sky. By the time they finished their inspection tour, the servants were lighting the oil lamps and distributing them to the many hooked poles placed around the compound. The whole effect was of stars appearing both on heaven and earth at the same time.

Only the moon had yet to rise.

As they walked back to the main hall, Lord Yi stopped to note the empty expanse of grass laid out in front of it. "It looks like there were statues here. Were they cleared away to make things more open for our men?"

Master Mao stiffened, but only said "More of the witch's work. Pay it no mind."

Then he led Lord Yi into the manor house's main hall where their best fighters sat at the long tables that cross-crossed the cavernous room. The tables were filled with savory dishes of beef, and pork and duck, and the men were toasting each other and laughing as they exchanged stories. The whole place had an atmosphere more like a wedding feast than it did a place where warriors waited before a battle.

"It still seems a waste that you won't let them drink the wine I brought," Lord Yi commented as they made their way through the men. As they went, man after man wanted to toast Master Mao, who reciprocated with the grace and speed of long practice.

"Wine is for after the battle, my friend." Mao said, pausing to pat an old comrade on the shoulder. "I learned long ago that juice from apples makes a better companion for warriors than wine. Have you tried it yet? I get it from a local grower."

"Perhaps later," Lord Yi said without smiling. "You may not drink the wine, but I still prefer it."

"As you wish," Mao said, and finally led Lord Yi up to the head table. There, Mao's wife was entertaining several of Mao's lieutenants, along with Lord Bai and his wife. Lord Bai was a tall, slender man with a long wispy white beard that flowed down across his chest like a morning fog down a hill.

Guiding Lord Yi to the head of the table, Mao offered him the seat to his left, across from Lord Bai. Lord Yi ceremonially refused such a prestigious position, but then finally accepted and took his place.

"I must say, I am surprised you joined us." Lord Bai commented. "I never took Lord Yi as being someone who made risks in his business."

Mao accepted the juice his servant poured for him, and watched Bai carefully. He knew his best friend didn't approve of him accepting Lord Yi's help, and was more than a little suspicious of the Black Dragon master. He hoped Lord Yi wasn't going to be storming out before this dinner was through.

But if Lord Yi was offended, he showed no signs of it. He merely smiled and said "You are quite correct, and if I had any doubts as to this night's outcome, I would certainly not have come." Then he raised a glass and said "A toast to our benefactor! *Ganbei!*"

At that, everyone at the head table, and more than a few of the other tables called out "*Ganbei!*" in the traditional drinking salute and all raised and drained their glasses in a toast.

Once that was done, the assembled began to eat heartily, and as they did Lord Yi asked— "So, tell me honestly Master Mao. What is the story behind this box the witch wants? Why do you think she desires it so badly?"

Mao paused a moment, chewing his mutton, and then said "The box was the property of former Princess Yu, who retired into seclusion many years ago. She has asked that our guild council dispose of it for her, and sent it to me for safekeeping until our coming gathering in two weeks.

"As for why she wants it, I cannot say. Have you any thoughts on the subject, Master Yi? You are a man of resources and have many ears across the land."

At this, all eyes turned to Lord Yi, who nodded.

"I have indeed given this matter a great deal of thought, and I have reached the conclusion that there must be a great treasure inside that box. I do not know who this Lady Moonlight is, but that she could exist at all without anyone knowing of her skills is strange indeed. I almost wonder if she is an agent of the kingdoms up beyond the Great Wall."

At this, many of heads around the table nodded. It did seem most plausible, and explained a great deal. But, there was one who didn't nod.

"So, what should we do with the box, then? Lord Yi?" Said Master Bai, watching him with careful eyes.

But Lord Yi didn't take the bait. "That is not for me to decide, but the council, I'm afraid. I will agree with whatever decision they make."

"Just so!" Mao thundered. "We are merely escorts, are we not? Our job is to get our cargo to its destination, and once there, it is left to others to distribute it."

"Our host is too humble," Lord Bai commented. "As the president of the council, you have the ability to decide on the box at any time. The council will always stand beside your wishes."

But, Mao shook his head. "The box was left to the council as a whole to decide, and it would be too presumptuous of me to make such a decision. Besides, what if the box did contain a treasure? Should I then keep it for myself? What would others say of my agency or family if we did such a thing? How would that make us better than the bandits we have spent our lives guarding against?

"No, the box stays closed until the time comes when we all may examine it."

"Most sensible! Most sensible indeed!" Lord Yi agreed, clapping his hands in admiration. "Master Mao again lives up to his reputation for fairness and honor."

Again, many heads around the table nodded.

"However," Lord Yi asked. "Are you sure the box is safely stored? If it is out of sight, then some sneak thief would be able to take it. Can I not offer more guards to defend it?"

At this, Lord Bai and Master Mao both exchanged an amused look, and Lord Yi also noticed several others around the table doing the same. Not sure what the joke was, and feeling somewhat uncomfortable, Master Yi's black eyebrows furrowed and he looked around unsure.

"Is there something I should know?" He said.

"The box," Lord Bai said with a knowing smile. "Is guarded by every man in this room." Then he raised a finger, and pointed upward.

Following the direction he was given, Lord Yi tilted his head back. Then gasped. For high among the beams in the room's vaulted ceiling a black lacquered box hung suspended from a chain. There was no visible way to get to it, nor was there any way a man could leap that high.

"Incredible." Lord Yi grinned. "Simply incredible. Master Mao again lives up to his reputation."

Smiling modestly, Mao waved the compliment away. "It is merely an old trick for keeping things safe from wild animals. I am afraid it was the best I could think of."

"Still," Master Yi raised his wine glass. "I am most impressed. Every man in this room is both a suspect and a guard at the same time. It would take a master thief to steal that box, or a genius."

"Luckily none in this room are either," Master Mao laughed, and the others joined him. With the exception of Lord Yi, who smiled a very private smile.

* * *

"You better not be yanking my chain, Gou."

The large man, who went by the name Bronze Faced Sun, glanced down at the smaller man who he was leading through the series of checkpoints toward the main hall. Gou and his companion had shown up at the front gate a short time earlier, and Sun had been called from the main gathering to come and vouch for the gambler.

"How many of these men work for Lord Yi?" Gou asked, glancing around at the knots of soldiers who lined the inner wall.

"Maybe a third," Sun shrugged. "We're lucky he brought so many."

He didn't notice Gou and the nun exchange a worried look. "Yeah, lucky." Gou said, and smiled at some men who were eying him with suspicion.

Finally, the three of them arrived at the short hallway that led to the main dining hall and marched into the brightly lit room beyond. A room with so many occupants that one would have expected it to be filled with the noise of feasting and merriment, but which was now as silent as a tomb.

All three of them stopped and stared in wonder at the sight before them—for every man in the room was now lying face down on the tables or sprawled on the floors unmoving.

All except for one, who stood on one of the tables in the middle, looking up. As they entered, Sister Cat gasped and the mustached man turned to look down at them.

Lord Yi smiled.

"Ahh. Mister Feng. I was wondering when we'd meet again." He said to Gou.

And behind them, out in the yard, a scream went up, and then another. The sounds of battle.

Gou felt the jaws of the trap close around his neck.

CHAPTER TWENTY-SEVEN

Eye of the Storm

Gou, Cat, and Bronze Faced Sun stood looking in shock at the scene before them. The entire leadership of both the Mao and Bai agencies lay strewn about the room unmoving, and only their poisoner, Lord Yi, remained.

"What happened here?!?" Demanded Bronze Face Sun, drawing his saber and stepping forward to level it at Lord Yi.

Lord Yi gave a simple shrug. "I told them to drink wine, but they chose not to listen to me. Not that it would have made much difference- you never know what people put in juice these days."

"Wretched dog!" Bronze Faced Sun leapt forward, jumping onto the long tables and running across them at the smiling master of the Black Dragons.

"Oh?" Lord Yi began to roll up his sleeves to reveal corded muscles. "Will I get to dirty my hands after all?" Then he scooped up a sword from a nearby fallen warrior and flicked off the sheath with a single motion. "Let's see how long you last."

Bronze Faced Sun hit the end of the table and arced up through the air, bringing his blade down at the smiling lord. The gentleman casually blocked the frenzied warrior's saber while at the same time stepping aside and striking him with his free palm. The fighter howled in pain as he was thrown sideways to smash into the head table. Cutlery and dishes flew everywhere, and he tumbled a bit before coming to a halt, chest heaving, and face and hair covered with wine and food.

Lord Yi was on him almost immediately, and it was only at the last moment that Bronze Faced Sun was able to slide out of the way and begin an attempt at a counterattack. It was clear to Gou, however, that Bronze Faced Sun was no match for Lord Yi, and in fact, he seemed to be getting slower by the moment.

"Sister," Gou said, starting his own dash forward. "The drug must be taking effect on Sun too, we've got to save him, but make sure you leave that son of a turtle in talking condition."

The huge nun, who had legs even longer than Gou, rushed past him with her staff at the ready. "I will do my best!" She declared, and then let out a loud war cry that startled Lord Yi enough to get him to back off his victim for just a moment.

But that moment was enough!

In that time, Sister Cat covered the distance and launched her attack, the tip of her ironwood pole lashing out with lightning speed at Lord Yi. He was forced to retreat to defend himself against the weapon, which had a much greater reach than his sword, and the two began a deadly dance across the floor.

Meanwhile, Bronze Faced Sun, who was still standing, started to lumber forward, determined to avenge his fallen master. But, as he raised his sword hand, Gou appeared in his way, grabbing it.

"You need to sit this one out, Sun." Gou said, taking the man's sword with ease. "You've been poisoned."

"Out of my way!" Sun screamed at Gou. "Or do you stand with that wretch too??"

Gou didn't even bother to answer, he just gave Sun a shove and the large man tumbled back onto the stone floor. His eyes rolled back into his head, and he lay there unmoving.

"Sorry Sun, you'll need to sit this one out."

Turning back to the fight, what Gou saw surprised him.

Lord Yi, a renowned fighter and master of a national escort agency, a man in his prime as a fighter and feared by many, was losing badly against the young nun. Gou had known that Sister Cat was formidable, but even he was taken aback by her skill as she led the older warrior around like a puppet with her staff. The difference between her and this man was clear, and after backing him against a support pillar, Cat casually disarmed him and then pinned him by the throat to the stone support.

As Lord Yi's borrowed weapon clattered nearby, Gou patted his friend on the shoulder. "Nice work, Sister."

"You..." She said through gasps of breath. "...Are welcome...Brother."

Stepping between them, Gou looked at the still-struggling man whose face had begun to turn red. "I wouldn't resist if I were you," he said, beginning to run his hands along Lord Yi's clothes. "It won't be good for your long-term health."

Perhaps sensing the truth in Gou's words, Yi relaxed his hands, but the nun still kept him pinned while Gou began to work his way through the lord's pockets. "My men...will be here soon," the trapped lord hissed.

Gou, who was doing his best to ignore the sounds of the battle raging outside, just nodded. "Yep. I imagine they will." Then from a hidden pocket in Lord Yi's sash he produced a handful of small, folded paper packets. "We'll just need to be done by then. Now, which of these is the antidote?"

"The antidote to the poison?" Cat asked from behind him.

"Yep. There's no way a careful man like Lord Yi here would poison this many people without making sure he had some antidote at the ready. So, which is it, my lord?"

Yi, for his part, just glared at Gou. "Try one, and find out." He told the gambler.

This brought a smile to Gou's face- a sinister grin that he reserved for only special occasions. "How about we try them on you first? The way I figure it, the one that doesn't kill you will probably be the one we're looking for." Then he held up the packets, which variously bore the characters for "*Han*" and "*Liu*" written on them.

Lord Yi's eyes went wide. "You can't!"

"*Han* it is!" Gou said gleefully, and ripped the top off one of the packets. "Hold him, Sister." Her ordered, and approached the struggling man. Naturally Lord Yi refused to open his mouth, so Gou squeezed his nose and when Yi finally gasped for air, Gou poured the powder in and held the mouth shut.

After what he judged to be long enough, Gou released the gagging man's mouth and let him cough and gasp for a minute. "You wretch!" Yi cursed between coughs. "You little wretch, I'll skin you alive!"

Gou smiled. "Right on the first try."

"Are you sure?" Asked Cat.

"His first words weren't 'give me the other packet', and he seems more angry than scared, so I'd say it's a safe enough bet. Tie him up."

With that, Gou ran off to find some water, and mixed the contents of two packets into it. Then, just to be sure, poured a bit of it into a silver goblet to see if it would turn black. When it didn't, Gou returned to the head table where Master Mao and the other top fighters were splayed out.

"I'm sorry to do this to you, Mao." He said, "But if I don't then you're dead anyways." Then Gou tilted the man's head back and poured a little of the water down his throat. Then, not waiting for a reaction, he began to do the same to the other men present.

He was just on his third man when Sister Cat let out a yell of alarm. A group of armed fighters wearing the symbol of the Black Dragons on their shoulders had come into the room. As soon as they saw Gou and Cat, they let out a battle cry and with weapons raised began rushing across toward them...

Knowing she could handle it, Gou continued to work quickly on the fighters and let Cat deal with the men. When he looked up, they had all been rendered unconscious, and the Sister looked more concerned than winded.

"There will be more coming, and we may not defeat them all." She said. "Brother, I dearly hope you have a plan."

Deciding he was out of time, Gou ran for the main doors. "Help me get these closed." He said, and the two of them shut the doors and put a thick wooden bar across them. Then they began doing the same thing to the other doors to the room, blocking them off as best they could. The windows were barred, which would help as well, he hoped.

"That will delay them," Gou said. "Although I doubt it will last for long."

As if on cue, there was banging at one set of doors, and then another. They were surrounded, and there seemed to be little avenue of escape.

It was then, when Gou looked up to check for other points of entry, that he noticed the box. He'd wondered what Lord Yi had been looking at when they'd entered, but had been too busy to check. He pointed it out to Sister Cat.

"Clever trick," he said, unknowingly echoing Lord Yi's sentiment from earlier.

"Should we try to take it down?" The nun asked. "Perhaps we could use it as a bargaining tool?"

"Maybe," Gou said, cocking his head in thought.

Then there was a loud thump at the main doors, and the whole hall seemed to shake for a moment. Then came another, and Gou could see the doors bending inward.

"Whatever we do, we'd better do it fast."

* * *

Outside the main hall, a knot of Lord Yi's men had gathered, and were using a stone statue of the goddess Kuan-Yin to try and break down the wooden doors.

"Do it again!" Their leader yelled, and the group rushed forward- stone hitting wood with the sound of a thundercrack.

Still, it held.

But for how long?

As the men pulled back, preparing for another try at it, there was a yelling noise behind them, and all turned to look.

Three figures were striding across the front garden, and as they came into the light of the many lamps, they revealed themselves to be Last Brother Shou, Copper Kettle Xiao, and Mah the Fighting Red General.

"What's happening here?" Shou asked, eying the door.

"We're locked out," reported the Black Dragon leader, a man who went by the name of Kicker Bo. "They were all supposed to be drugged, but somebody's barred the door."

"Did you try the other doors?"

"All locked."

"The windows?"

"Barred and covered. We can't even see inside."

Shou considered this, and then looked at his companions. "Help them."

Xiao and Mah strode forward, and the Black Dragons quickly scattered in front of them. Then the two big men each took a side of the statue, lifted it up, and proceeded to ram the stone against the wood so hard that the goddess of mercy's head fell off.

It only took three more tries, and the wood split apart with a mighty crack, the two doors crashing inward so hard that one of them fell off its hinges.

Shou was first through the door, and his partners came after, with the other men fanning out behind. But, what they saw made them come up short.

There on a table on the raised dais, on the far side of the room, Lord Yi stood upon a chair with a noose around his neck. The noose was attached to a chain thrown over one of the ceiling beams. Next to him stood Little Gou, his foot on the chair, ready to push it out and send Lord Yi to meet his ancestors at a moment's notice.

"Good evening, gentlemen" Gou called out. "I'd suggest you stop right where you are."

The Black Dragon men halted, but Shou and his companions didn't seem bothered in the slightest.

"Finish him," Shou answered coldly. "It will save us the trouble later."

But beside him, Copper Kettle Xiao whispered caution.

"Shou, the mistress said we need him." He whispered with concern. "She won't be pleased if anything happens."

"Yes," Mah agreed. "He must live."

Shou looked at the other men, and for a moment it seemed he was going to draw his blade and attack them, but then he refocused on Gou.

"If he dies, so do you."

Gou smiled. "You say that like you're not going to kill me anyways. No, if you want him alive, you're going to have to do what I say."

"What do you want?" Xiao said, stepping forward.

"All of you, out of here." Gou announced, and gestured back to the way they came. "Once you're gone, then we'll talk."

"We'd better go," Xiao said, and motioned for the men behind them to leave. Then he looked at Shou. "The mistress will come soon, let her decide. You'll get your chance, and we won't have to take the blame."

Shou, who was almost grinding his teeth, threw a final glare at Gou, then turned and walked back out. Xiao and Mah followed him, with Xiao stopping to say "You won't have long. We'll be back once our mistress arrives. I suggest you kill yourselves now and save yourselves a lot of pain."

* * *

Gou watched the trio leave, and then looked up at Lord Yi. "See, you're worth something after all." Then, ignoring the other man's growling, he looked over at the nun. "How're our patients doing?"

The sister, who'd been holding the wrist of Master Mao, said "His pulse is getting stronger. I believe the medicine is working. However, even if they awaken, I doubt they will be in any condition to aid us in our fight."

"I know," Gou mused. "We might be fighting a losing battle here, but a room full of people who can walk is better than one full of sleepers. You keep an eye on the door while I give more of them the medicine."

The nun agreed, and Gou started to administer the antidote to the others in the room, starting with the biggest and toughest looking men. He hoped their systems would throw off the drug the fastest, and they could be used to carry out the rest if need be. He didn't have enough of the drug to help everyone, and this was the best he could do.

It was while he was doing this that Sister Cat suddenly called out for him to come. There was a commotion happening outside one of the side doors, and Gou anxiously pulled the cover off a window to look out.

There, next to the door, he saw Snowtop Cho, along with his assistant Spider Chan and the *Jin Hua* fighter Miss Lily battling against a group of Black Dragon fighters. The three were clearly superior, but more Dragons were coming, and Gou worried the three killers would soon join the fight.

"Quick, help me unbolt the door!" He cried out, and he and the Sister pulled away the table they'd used to block the door and pulled back the bolts to fling it open.

"Cho!" Gou yelled from the open door. "In here! Quick!"

The three fighters, seeing Gou, immediately made a rush for the door, and dispatched several of the Dragons as they ran. Then they hurried inside and helped Gou and Cat block the door again, to the frustrations of the men outside.

Once they were safe, Gou immediately turned on Miss Lily. "Where's Meiyu? What did you do with her!"

Miss Lily shrank back at his accusations, but Snowtop intervened. "Wait Gou, if there is blame to be placed here, let me take it. Miss Lily was attempting to help Miss Mao warn her father."

This made Gou stop and stare at him. "You followed the letter, didn't you? You gave her to Lady Moonlight!"

Snowtop's shoulders sagged and he nodded. "Yes."

Gou was incensed. "You stupid son of a pig!" He railed against his friend. "I told you! I told you the letter was a fake! But no, Master Cho can't be wrong! Master Cho has his pride!" Then he punched Snowtop, a right cross that sent the swordsman tumbling to the floor. "Master Cho is a spit drooling idiot!"

With blood dribbling from his broken lip, Snowtop looked up at Gou, not in defiance or anger, but with an expression of shame and regret. "You are right."

Gou almost kicked him, but instead held his anger and turned to Chan. "Are there more coming, or is it just you three?"

It was then that Chan related the details of how the three had arrived at the Mao Estate, from the ambush the night before to their rescue by Miss Lily. In the ambush, only Snowtop and Chan had managed to avoid being wounded, and they'd been moved with Snowtop's men to a guarded house on the edge of town. There, Miss Lily had found them, overcome their guards, and helped them to escape, but not before Meiyu had been taken away.

After Miss Lily had explained the situation to them, Snowtop had sent his wounded men back to the Cho family estate to get help, while the three of them had rushed to warn Master Mao. But, just after coming over the wall and approaching the Manor House they'd been attacked, and that's where Gou had found them.

"The Old Master will send men as soon as he hears," Chan said, but there was a tone of doubt in his voice. "However, it will take time to gather them."

"Time is something we don't have," Gou told him. "When the big witch herself arrives, she's not going to be as easy to keep away as her stooges."

Then Gou told the new arrivals the full situation, and how he and Cat had come to be locked in the main hall of the manor house. "We need to hold them off until the drug can start to work and wake these people up."

Snowtop, who Gou noted Lily had tenderly helped to his feet, was the first one to speak. "We need to reduce their forces if we're to have a chance."

Gou looked at him, surprised. "You're an idiot, but don't get suicidal."

"Brother Gou," Cat put in, "I believe that Brother Cho is right. If their forces are reduced, then they may reconsider this attack."

"Beauty and brains in one package," Chan said, making the nun blush. "I gotta agree with the Sister."

Gou considered it, it was risky, but there was possibility there. Then, he looked over at the dirty and disheveled Lily. "What do you think?"

Lily shrugged. "You know I enjoy surprises."

"All right then," Gou nodded. "It's a heck of a gamble, but it's also something they'd never expect. Let's do it- let's take the fight to them."

At this he looked to Spider Chan and said- "When it comes to this kind of thing, you're the most experienced one here. You have any suggestions?"

The older Chan hesitated for a moment, glancing at Snowtop. But, his master merely shook his head. "He's right, Chan. You have been on many campaigns with my father, if anyone knows how to survive this, it will be you."

Chan bobbed his head. "You sell yourself short, Young Master, and trust me, I know all about short. But, if it were me in charge, here's what I'd do..."

When he was done laying out his plan, everyone looked at Gou, who nodded in agreement. "I like it, but there's one thing I need to change- you're going to have to do it without me."

CHAPTER TWENTY-EIGHT

Challenges

"More people got inside."

Xiao looked at Kicker Bo, the Black Dragon squad leader. "How many more people?"

"My men say three." Bo explained. "We caught them trying to sneak in, but before we could trap them that guy and the nun opened the door and let them in."

Xiao frowned. "I don't like this."

Shou looked at the Black Dragon man. "Do we have a description of them?"

"Three men. One was a swordsman in black with white hair, another was a dwarf, and another swordsman who was dressed like a beggar."

"Sounds like Snowtop Cho got loose," Xiao commented. "That'll be him and that damn dwarf that follows him around. I don't know the beggar, though."

"If Snowtop Cho is here, more men may come." Mah commented.

Shou nodded. The General was right, and Lady Moonlight still wasn't here with the rest of their forces. Damn that arrogant Yi for starting the assault early—he'd thrown off their timing. Killing him was starting to seem more and more like a good idea to Shou, regardless of the consequences.

Then, as they stood considering the circumstances, something unexpected happened. From the front door of the manor hall, a small ugly man in green and orange strode out into the courtyard. He put his hands on his hips and peered around nonchalantly at the many fighters, chewing his Goat Weed and standing like a farmer surveying his lands in the morning.

"I'm told there is a fat pig out here named Copper Kettle Xiao that can barely move without his bottom scraping on the ground." Chan announced. "Is this true?"

There was snickering from the crowd of soldiers, and Shou looked at Xiao, whose face was turning red. Then Xiao got up and stepped out into the circle of light from the many oil lanterns, the Black Dragon soldiers pulled back and left the two men facing each other on the stone patio.

"You speak loudly, goblin." Xiao said with false joviality. "But clearly your brain is too small and simple to know what you're doing. Why not tell me your name so I can find your mother for you?"

The small man laughed. "I'm not sure I should. You look like you ate the last animal whose name you heard."

That earned another round of laughter from the crowd, and Xiao lost all of his faux friendliness. "I am Xiao, called Copper Kettle because I have mastered the Iron Skin technique. Maybe you've heard of me?"

The small man cocked his head and winked. "Really? I'd heard they called you Copper Kettle because you were full of hot air. Call me Chan, nickname Spider."

However, Chan barely had time to finish saying his name before one of Xiao's deadly Copper Hands was driven straight into his throat. Or at least, that was how it should have been, given the speed of the hand that lashed out, but at the last moment Chan's body shifted slightly so that the hand passed harmlessly by his face.

As the hand continued past, Chan reached up and touched Xiao's wrist, then ducked backward as the big man's other hand came up from below. This too he touched lightly on the wrist, and then he jumped backward and away from the larger fighter, spinning his hands around in a rapid series of movements that looked like a cat trying to bat mosquitoes from the air.

It was then that the most amazing thing happened- Xiao's hands moved like they were guided by puppeteer and suddenly slammed together with a loud clap. There was a gasp from the audience, and Xiao's own eyes were wide with shock as he tried to free his hands- but they would not move. They were sealed together, as if by an invisible force.

"What have you done?!?" Howled Copper Kettle in frustration, waving his arms about.

But while Xiao had stopped in shock, Chan was still very much in motion. He ran past the bigger man, running around him with his hands trailing low to the ground until he'd circled around Xiao twice. Then again, he began pulling at the air in a series of motions until not just Xiao's hands were together, but his feet were suddenly forced together as well. Not just that, they were now linked, so that when Xiao pulled up his hands, he yanked his own feet out from under himself and toppled over.

The soldiers present howled in laughter as Xiao rolled around like a ball on the ground. Xiao, for his part, stood with one foot on the big man's back, standing like a great hunter over his kill.

"Thank you, you're too kind." He said, bowing to the audience.

Last Brother Shou let out a low growl. "Free him," he ordered the armored giant standing nearby.

"Wait." Said the giant, watching intently.

"For what?"

That's when it happened- with a loud grunting sound, Copper Kettle Xiao suddenly burst free of the invisible bonds that held him tight. After that, in the surprise of the moment, he grabbed onto Chan's leg and began to roll, pulling the little man down with his weight and rolling on top of him.

Chan let out a horrible scream as Xiao shifted around so he was sitting on top of the little man and ripping the last of Chan's wires free from his wrists.

"Your tricks don't work on someone with Iron Skin, little monkey." Said Xiao with venom in his voice, then he struck the pinned Chan's right shoulder.

A loud cracking sound mixed with Chan's screams echoed throughout the makeshift arena as the bones shattered.

* * *

From the entrance to the main hall, Sister Cat and Snowtop Cho watched the events unfolding outside.

"Brother Cho," said Cat with worry. "We need to help him."

But Chan's Young Master shook his head. "No, honored lady. He made the plan, and knew the risks. If we go out there, it will turn from a duel into a war, and we can't afford to stray from the plan."

"But Brother..." The young nun gripped her ironwood staff tightly, watching as Xiao rained down a series of punches on the prone man's head. Then turned away, unable to watch any longer.

Snowtop was right, she thought. Chan knew the risks when he made this plan, and when he volunteered to be first out. They needed to buy time and keep the attackers distracted, and a duel with the top enemy fighters seemed the best way to accomplish this. Rather than make it a formal challenge, Chan had said it needed to be an informal challenge based on pride and honor. If they didn't accept the first challenge, the whole thing would fail, and who could turn down a challenge from a man the size of a child and claim to be a top fighter?

So, Chan had gone first. Knowing the danger, and that he might very well be outclassed by the man he faced. She had told him what she knew of Copper Kettle Xiao from their earlier encounter, and he had seemed confident in his abilities.

Now it looked like that might not be enough.

Then she heard Snowtop gasp, and unable to stop herself, she turned to look. Her heart plummeting from what she saw.

* * *

Xiao wrenched Chan's body from the ground and held it up in the air like the head of a lion he had just taken. Holding on to the small man's neck, he raised him high and shouted "Look at your crowd now, little monkey! Where are you funny words, now? Eh!"

The bloody Chan, his twitching left arm hanging limply at his side and his other limbs seemingly too weak to move, said something in a voice too weak for anyone to hear. And Xiao twisted him around so they were face to face.

"Say that again?" Xiao snarled, his voice filled with a killing lust.

He had just long enough to see a smile pass across Chan's eyes, and then there was a "whhffft!" sound as suddenly Xiao's world turned into burning blackness. Releasing the smaller fighter, Xiao clutched at his eyes, screaming and howling for water.

Chan, now freed, came to life again, and landing on his feet, he stepped aside and let the larger man run screaming from the field. Then, taking a single bow with his working arm, Chan skittered back into the manor house the way he'd come.

When he returned, he found a teary-eyed Sister Cat and a concerned looking Snowtop Cho waiting.

"Good work, Chan." Snowtop commended him.

Chan just shrugged with his right shoulder, and winced at the effort. "Sorry it took so long, Young Master." He said through gritted teeth, his breath had a strong spicy smell to it now. "The pig wouldn't stay in the pot."

"What did you do?" Asked the Sister, leading the small man over to a bench and sitting him down.

"Sichuan Flower Peppers, Sister." Chan said, giving a gap-toothed smile. He'd lost two of his front teeth, and had three more chipped by Xiao's pounding. "Hottest kind around. I mix extra with my chewing leaf before I go into a fight. I'm used to them, but a fella gets them in his eyes- he's likely to go blind." He winked.

"You were most brave, now let me set your shoulder." The nun told him. "If it's not done soon, you will lose the use of your arm."

But Chan used his working arm to push her away. "No. If we lose the momentum now, we won't get it back. You need to get out there."

"But..."

Snowtop put a hand on her shoulder. "He's right sister. We have to stick to the plan."

* * *

Outside, Last Brother Shou watched in disgust as Xiao plunged his head into a fountain again and again crying "I'm blind! I'm blind!"

"Simpering fool," he cursed. He would never have allowed a live enemy to get so close. As far as he was concerned, Xiao had let his impervious skin make him weak and careless, and now he was paying the price he deserved. He had failed to kill those Lin clan fighters they'd met on the boat, and now this disgrace.

Xiao had always been the weakest of the three. A former monk turned gang enforcer in the capital, he was used to dealing with men much weaker than himself and showed it with his nonchalant manner. This overconfidence is what had gotten him caught by the capital militia after he'd killed a minor official over gambling debts. Sentenced to death, Xiao had taken a new position under Lady Moonlight to avoid the slow torture that awaited him otherwise.

In a way, Shou hoped the blindness was permanent, at least that way Xiao would no longer be fit to serve with them, and he wouldn't have to listen any longer to Xiao's incessant chatter or his thunderous snoring.

The leader of Lady Moonlight's men turned back to look at the manor entrance just in time to see a new figure emerge. This one he didn't have to wonder about as she hopped down the steps and onto the stone patio.

He already knew her.

Sister Cat reached the middle of the makeshift arena and spun her staff before pointing its tip at the armored figure of General Mah.

"Fighting Red General, I challenge you to a duel!"

Mah looked at Shou. He seemed perplexed. Then he put on the helmet he carried under his arm and grabbed his *guandao* halberd from where it lay propped up nearby.

Shou frowned. The previous fighter may have been taken as bravado, or stalling for time. This was something else. There was a plan at work here, and he began to think it through. Then after a moment, he motioned for Kicker Bo to approach.

"Yeah?" Bo said, leaning in.

"Reinforce the men around the other exits, and make sure we have a rotating guard." Shou ordered. "This might be a distraction while they try to sneak Mao out."

"I was just thinking the same thing." Bo agreed, and began issuing orders.

Then Shou turned to watch the fight. This was the second time these two had fought. The first time, the nun had only escaped with her life when a trick by that damned gambler had forced them to retreat. Now, there would be no tricks, and no escape.

Here, she would meet her end.

* * *

Sister Cat watched her opponent stride onto the field, his *guandao* at the ready and his red armor almost black in the light of the oil lamps. With his pale face visible beneath the helmet, he looked like a god of death, coming to claim another soul for the afterlife.

So, there they stood, the noble nun clad in her light blue and grey robes, and the dark soul stealer. Heaven and hell incarnate, once again battling for the souls of men.

"General," Cat said in a voice that only he could hear. "I have heard your story from Miss Mao, and I want you to know my heart goes out to you. However, can you not see that these actions disgrace you and your family name? You aid evil ones who seek to kill the innocent and twist the state for their own ends. I will not ask you to turn your blade on your comrades, but could you not stand aside and leave this battlefield?

"You showed mercy to Miss Mao, so I know it is in your heart. Now please again, show mercy to the people she loves and allow justice to prevail."

Her words spoken, the Sister watched the other man carefully for any small sign that they had any effect. To her surprise, as she watched tears began to stream down his cheeks.

"Nun," he said after a moment. "I spared Miss Mao because she reminded me of the wife who sits in chains far from here. Seeing her, the heart I thought dead was reminded for one brief shining moment of what it felt like to be with the one I loved.

"I bare no malice to you, or to the people who you try to protect, but my family suffers every day for my sins. If killing you will bring my family freedom, as a dutiful husband and son I can do nothing else. I am sorry."

The two of them stood silent for a time, and then each bowed to the other in understanding. Heaven had decreed this battle would happen, and mortal thoughts or desires had little say in the matter. Each knew their place in the great wheel of destiny.

Coming up from her bow, and filled with new determination, Sister Cat struck a long-practiced stance and stood at the ready.

This time, she would not lose.

* * *

Deep in the manor hall, Little Gou paused from what he was doing. From the shouts that now rang out, he knew the second round of the fight had begun- Cat's turn. Not a religious man, but Gou still prayed hard for her safe return. He had witnessed their last fight, and knew where his friend's skills stood in comparison with the armored giant's. It was going to be close.

Nearby where Gou sat, Lily worked to minister to the fallen warriors of the Mao family. They'd had enough medicine for almost half of the assembled in the end- the rest would have to place their fates in the hands of the nun out there risking her life.

And Gou.

No pressure.

He wiped his brow with the back of his hand, then he went back to work- if he was right, everything tonight would depend on what he did now.

* * *

The battle which danced across the stone patio area was one which had been played out throughout history, and which has occurred endless times since. Two opponents equal in skill, one possessing superior armor and weaponry, but lacking mobility, and the other having speed and maneuverability, but lacking the ability to strike a decisive hit.

The open space of the makeshift arena gave Sister Cat a mobility she lacked the first time she faced off against General Mah. Then, they had been on the narrow spine of a rooftop, and she had been forced to contend with his power and defense in a way that put her at a severe disadvantage. Even when she hit him with her staff, his armor took the blows, but the same could not be said about her. She had been fighting a wall with a stick.

Here, the situation was very different. The same armor which made him proof against her blows also slowed him down, hindered him, and limited his ability to react to the strikes she was raining down upon him. It was an advantage that she had been counting on when she took this challenge again, and which was one of the things in her favor.

The other thing was that she had spent a great deal of time thinking about their last encounter. It had been hard not to, as her mostly healed shoulder still ached from the gash he had given her that time. In her meditations, she had replayed the battle countless times- always looking for something she could have done better, something she might have missed.

Now, with the real man before her, and the advantage of motion returned to her, she wasn't going to make the same mistakes again. This she demonstrated as he tried the same trick he had before, letting his shaft ride down her block and pushing in to try to strike her shoulder.

This time, she twisted away when he went for the push, leaving him pushing against air, and bringing the other end of her own staff around to slam hard against the back of his helmet in a blow that would have crushed in many men's skulls.

Mah was sent stumbling forward, off balance and disoriented as she now drove the other end of her staff into the unarmored back of his knee. This knocked his leg out from under him, and the armored giant toppled over backwards to crash like thunder onto the hard stone.

Moving to finish the battle, Cat leapt up into the air and with a mighty cry brought her heavy ironwood staff down onto Mah's chest. She intended to beat him decisively, and had no intention of allowing him to rise again.

But, Mah's reflexes were still intact, even if he was disoriented, and somewhere in his mind the simple equation of "stillness = death" had been etched in place by time. So, as the Sister's blow came down hard it only struck bare chiseled stone instead of armor and flesh.

Even worse, the bladed end of Mah's *guandao* was now sweeping out at her own foot, and she was forced to leap back and away to avoid losing it.

By the time she was ready to move in again, it was too late- Mah was up on one knee, his weapon at the ready to block her attack. The chance had been lost, and he was ready for her.

Still, Sister Cat let herself smile. The first round had gone to her. Now they would see who was truly the better fighter.

CHAPTER TWENTY-NINE

Fallen Heroes

A *guandao* is a specialized form of halberd weighing anywhere from eight to fifty kilograms with a thick knifelike blade attached to one end of the pole and a sharp spear tip mounted on the other. Named for the War Saint himself, Guan Yu, the weapon was originally designed for mounted riders to stab and slash at enemies in battle.

It is a weapon which requires great skill or great strength to use effectively, especially if the user isn't mounted. In the hands of a master it is a weapon of awful power and lethal effectiveness.

The Staff, on the other hand, is derived from perhaps the oldest of all weapons- the stick. It has remained an essential part of man's arsenal since the dawn of time, and its simplicity is its strength. In the hands of a skilled user, the staff is not only a good weapon for offense, but a highly versatile means of defense as well.

Yin and Yang. Speed versus Power.

Sister Cat versus Mah the Fighting Red General.

Both warriors spun and leapt around the patio area like a pair of whirlwinds, their lethal weapons clashing again and again. Thrust. Parry. Strike. Block. Sweep. Leap. The dance continued in all its many forms over and over again, each one looking for opportunity or weakness.

Sister Cat noted that Mah was moving less as the fight went on, and seemed to be favoring his right leg where she'd struck at his knee. His armor, designed for the Northern battlefield, was starting to wear him down in the oppressive humidity of the South in August. Even though it was now evening, his skin wouldn't be able to breathe in that armor, and his greatest asset would slowly become his greatest enemy.

Cat, on the other hand, was both used to the local climate, and dressed lightly in a single layer of nun's robes. Slicked with sweat, she was breathing hard, but in no way tired out by the exertions. To her the cooling night air was a friend, and it aided her in this war of flashing lights and darting shadows.

The way things were looking, all she needed to do was to keep going and outlast him- let fatigue take its course and he would soon falter.

Of course, Mah knew this as well, and as a result her opponent was starting to become more aggressive. He was pushing her more, trying to catch her in a corner or with her back against the crowd where an enemy soldier might take advantage. If she had to watch her back and front, it would make it harder for her to defend against him.

His time was running out, but he was determined to finish her before that happened.

* * *

"Prop me up, so I can watch, Young Master."

Snowtop glanced from the battle to the nearby bench where Spider Chan lay recovering. "Stay where you are, Chan. I'll tell you how the battle develops."

"Is she winning?"

The swordsman paused to consider the two dark shapes darting around the torch-lit battlefield below. "It's too close to tell yet. Perhaps I should have taken this one."

"If one of us faced more than one opponent," Chan said, laying his head back on the cool stone and closing his eyes. "We'd be too exhausted to fight if they try to take advantage or when it's time for the next step."

Snowtop nodded, "'Point at the Mulberry and Abuse the Cicada.' You never cease to amaze me, Chan. I had no idea you were so well read in military strategy."

"The Young Master could easily surpass this humble one if he only applied himself as much to his learning as he has his swordsmanship." Chan said dryly. "I'll find you a copy of the 36 Stratagems of War when this is over."

At this, his master smiled. "No need. My father gave it to me when I was twelve. I'm sure it's on my shelf somewhere. My shelves have a natural talent for collecting both books and dust."

"If your brain isn't filled with one, it will be filled with the other." His servant told him. "Best to decide which before you're an old man like me."

"Chan, you're only six years my elder."

"I feel much older."

"You look it too, now...rest." Those last words had an edge to them that made Chan look up.

"It's finishing?"

"Yes." Snowtop answered gravely.

* * *

Sister Cat had made a mistake.

In the world of shadow and light on the battlefield below, it was easy to miss a movement or misjudge the distance between things. The two fighters were often fighting on instinct, but instinct wasn't always perfect or accurate.

In blocking General Mah's last sequence of attacks, Sister Cat had misjudged the last strike as a feint, and as a result Mah had added another cut to her with his blade- this one a gash in her thigh.

She couldn't tell how deep it was, but from the pain it would have to be pretty deep. Her leg was starting to stiffen up a little, and each motion seemed to be more painful than the last one.

Now she was the one with time as her enemy, and she cursed herself for her own clumsiness. This was turning into a repeat of their last battle, and try as she could, she couldn't think of any way to stop it.

Mah was pushing down on her even harder now, with his blade coming at her from all directions, forcing her to block again and again. Each shot hit harder, each blow became trickier to deal with. She felt her bones rattling as instead of guiding the enemy weapon away, her staff was taking the powerful blows and transferring the force back into her arms and back.

Then it happened.

She'd parried a blow, and went for a hard counter-attack when he'd brought up the *guandao*'s blade just in time to block.

There was a loud cracking sound.

Nearly a third of her wooden staff came to rest on the stone some distance away.

Then the other end of Mah's *Guandao* was impacting into the side of her head. It was the spear end, but it came from the side so instead of killing her, it hammered into her skull and sent her reeling.

Another blow, this one a kick to her chest, and she flew backwards to skid to a halt on the patio, the world around her a blur of light.

By the time she'd regained her bearings, he was above her, the blade of the *Guandao* raised and there was nothing she could do the stop it.

She feebly tried to bring her arm up. To defend herself. She had lost and would pay the price.

With what strength she had left, Cat said to him. "Please, Brother Mah. I am resolved to my end, but do you want Ms. Mao's family to become like yours? Sold into slavery? Their lives destroyed in the name of corruption and greed? Once you have ended me, please think of this."

These were her last words before he brought the blade down in a killing stroke.

* * *

Little Gou looked up.

What was the sound he had just heard from the front of the manor hall? Why was it now suddenly so quiet?

His first instinct was to jump up to run and check, but he stopped himself. The results of what happened outside were only part of the story- he had to find the rest.

They were fighting for him, and he couldn't let them down.

"Gou!" Lily called out, and he turned to see her helping a big man to his feet. He could hear the sounds of groaning, cursing and retching all around the hall now as life began to return to the room.

Seeing this, Gou turned. He was sitting on the dais near the head table and Master Mao was the first they had given the antidote to, so he should be waking up just about...now.

Angry eyes met Gou's. Eyes filled with murderous intent.

Gou smiled weakly.

He could explain. He hoped.

* * *

Mah's blade dripped blood, the droplets falling to land on Sister Cat's nose and run down her cheeks.

It was her blood.

But she was still alive.

The blade had stopped centimeters from her head and now hung suspended over her- unmoving.

Looking beyond the weapon to its master, she could see two eyes staring out at her from beneath the helmet. In them, there was uncertainty. Then resolve.

The blade disappeared, and the Fighting Red General looked down at her.

"You have lost." He said, and turned away. "Go. Now."

Still in shock, Cat just watched him open-mouthed. Then she heard a voice from within the manor house call out. "Sister! Hurry!"

That was when instinct kicked in, and Cat pulled herself to her feet. Limping, she moved as fast as she could up the stairs and back into the manor house where Snowtop and Chan were waiting for her.

She was crying by the time she reached the inner foyer, although whether from shock, or pain, or frustration she couldn't be sure.

"Brother Cho," she said to Snowtop when she saw him watching her with concern. "Don't fail."

Their eyes met, and an understanding passed between them.

"Just rest, Sister." He told her. "I will finish this."

* * *

"What's wrong with you?!?" Last Brother Shou shouted as Mah approached. "Why didn't you kill that bald witch?"

Mah only gave him a glance as he passed, but for the first time since they'd met, Shou knew fear. It wasn't an emotion Shou felt often, but without a doubt Shou knew that if he continued to push Mah his own life would be considerably shorter.

The armored giant kept walking, and didn't stop until he'd left the estate. Leaving the remaining forces staring after him.

"What's this, then?" Kicker Bo asked from beside Shou. "Where's he going?"

"Doesn't matter." Shou cut him off angrily. "How's Xiao?"

"See for yourself."

Shou glanced over to see Xiao slumped down in front of the fountain, sobbing over his lost eyesight. This was going horribly bad, he was now down his two best fighters, and the lady still wasn't here yet. Not that the people inside could go far with over forty of the Black Dragons surrounding them, but it was still not a comfortable situation.

Perhaps he should just rush in and take them. He could blame Mah now if Lord Yi was killed, and finishing the job had just become more important than any single man's life.

He was about to tell Bo just that when his attention was drawn by the crowd to another man coming down the steps from the manor house- Snowtop Cho!

The young white-haired swordsman marched across the patio to stand in the middle, looking right at Shou.

"I am here to challenge Last Brother Shou to a duel." He announced.

All eyes moved to Shou.

The gaunt swordsman looked over at Kicker Bo. "Enough of this- kill him and we'll storm the place."

The Black Dragon men began to look at one-another, and whispers rippled through the crowd. They were all part of the *biaoju* culture, and there were few among them who hadn't heard the name Snowtop Cho before.

Nobody moved.

When Shou realized that none of them planned to follow his orders, not even Kicker Bo, he frowned. Shou knew Snowtop had a reputation as a top-flight swordsman, but to see this many capable men intimidated by one young pup was too much.

"Fine." He growled, and grabbed his sword.

This wouldn't take long.

"Brother Cho," he announced as he strode out to face the younger man. "I have heard you have some ability with a blade. I would like to see it."

Snowtop bowed, but didn't take his eyes off Shou. "You flatter me, sir. I hope this one's talent with the sword can live up to your kind words."

Arrogant little wretch. Thought Shou, and dramatically lifted up his sword and scabbard so they were horizontal in front of his face. Drawing the sheath back to reveal the slender blade he said "I took this sword off Master Lin of the Nine Trees when he came to take me for abusing his friend's daughter. I kept it to remind myself that titles and reputations have little meaning in this world."

"Then we have something in common," Cho said. "My own *jian* was forged by Master Wei, the same smith who forged the sword that you carry. In his final years, he forged eight masterpieces. If I am not mistaken, the blade you hold is *Eclipsing Heart*."

"It is." Shou answered, honestly surprised that Snowtop knew this. "I am told that Master Wei would only forge a sword after he had judged a candidate worthy. Is that your father's sword?"

This idea seemed to amuse Snowtop. "You have heard correctly, but it was I that went to Mount Red Deer and met with Master Wei, not my father."

Shou snorted, "You? You're barely a man."

"I was sixteen when I went, seventeen when I returned. However, senior is correct, I am still somewhat inexperienced. Perhaps you could instruct me?"

Noting that Cho had yet to draw his own sword from the sheath looped at his hip, Shou shouted "As you wish!" Then he launched into a quick strike designed to cleave Cho's belly open. His speed was incredible, and there were none watching who doubted that such a cut would have been the end of them.

None, that is, except for Snowtop Cho, who simply stepped back and outside of the swing.

Undaunted, Shou continued his attack, slashing, stabbing, and cutting at the younger swordsman. But, each time the white-haired youth simply dodged or avoided the attacks, making none of his own, and not even drawing his blade.

Seeing this made Shou even more angry, and he became more and more aggressive in his attacks until he was dripping in sweat and panting from the effort. How could this young man keep avoiding him? This wasn't possible. He'd cut down swordsmen by the measure, and none had shown him ability like this.

And he hadn't even drawn his sword!

Finally, Snowtop raised a hand, and Shou halted, more for his own need to rest than out of respect for his opponent.

"Did you hear that?" The youth asked.

Shou paused, confused. "Hear what?"

As Shou listened there came the sound of an owl call from nearby.

At this, Snowtop nodded to himself and bowed.

"I thank senior for the lesson. Your style is one I have rarely encountered before, and it has been interesting to see what you have done with it. I will end our lesson here today."

Then Snowtop turned and began to walk toward the manor house steps, leaving an astonished Shou staring after him. But astonishment became anger, and anger became rage, and Shou surged forward, ready to cut down the other man from behind...

He wasn't sure when the white-haired man vanished, but once again Shou's sword cut only air. However, this time there was a difference- a cool, stinging sensation that ran across Shou's belly and into his chest.

"Its name is *Ice Wind*," Snowtop's voice said from somewhere behind him.

An appropriate name, Shou agreed.

Then he died.

* * *

Snowtop flicked the blood from his sword, then sheathed it and reached down to take *Eclipsing Heart* from where the other man had dropped it. He picked it up reverently, feeling the perfect balance of the weapon.

Should he survive this, he would need to return the sword to Master Lin's family. They would sleep more soundly knowing the fate of their master, and his assassin.

Then he turned and ascended the manor house steps, stopping halfway up to turn and look at the silent crowd of Black Dragon fighters.

"Brothers," he said loudly. "The Mao family is under my protection. If you leave now, I promise your master will have a fair trial before the ruling council of the Society of Armed Escorts."

"Forget that!" Yelled Kicker Bo, running forward with a saber raised. "If we let you have him, the Master is as good as dead."

There was a rumble of agreement from the crowd, and the ones with long weapons like spears and pole-axes began to rush forward. Snowtop may have been an expert swordsman, but even he could only do so much against so many long weapons. Behind them, the others advanced with swords and axes, all of them intent in cutting down whoever they needed to in order to get back their master.

Then, as they advanced, Snowtop saw the determination on their faces turn into a look of shock, and then a look of fear.

They weren't looking at him anymore, they were looking past him. Where, at the entrance to the manor hall, now stood Crocodile Mao in all his glory, and around him were arrayed his top fighters, each of them carrying weapons and looking down upon the Black Dragons with vicious contempt.

Snowtop looked back at them, nodding to Sister Cat, Spider Chan and Miss Lily, who were standing with the assembled warriors of the Mao clan. Then he looked to the Black Dragons again.

"Leave. Now."

In an instant, the Black Dragons turned into a scrambling mass of bodies trying to climb all over each other to escape. They flowed out of the main garden and disappeared beyond the outbuildings as fast as they could.

After the last of them was gone, a collective sigh of relief when through the assembled warriors, and not a few of them had to be helped down to the steps. Even Crocodile Mao, who had started down to thank Snowtop, quickly found himself unsteady on his feet and it was only thanks to the intervention of Sister Cat that he didn't go crashing down the stairs.

"Thank you, Young Cho." He said once they'd gotten him sitting down. "I owe you and your family a deep debt of gratitude."

"No. No." Snowtop bowed to the older man. "It was nothing. I am merely happy to see that the Old Master is on his feet again."

"Well, trying to be, anyways." The pale Old Mao joked. "I doubt any of us will be in fighting condition for another day or two. If your father has a few men he could spare, I would greatly appreciate it."

By referring to his father as the master of the family agency, not Snowtop, Master Mao had inadvertently insulted the young man, but the Young Master took it in stride. "There should be some men coming now. We will do what we can to help make sure the Mao and Bai families remain safe."

"Good. Good." Said Mao, trying to rise. "I should see to my servants then."

But, just as he'd started to unsteadily get to his feet, the air was filled with the sound of war horns. And, to the shock of everyone on the stairs, soldiers began to pour into the yard before them. Not a disorganized crew of Black Dragon Escort Agency soldiers, but trained members of the Imperial Army filed into the yard.

At their head, an army colonel in resplendent green armor rode, and beside him on another steed was a slender pale-faced young man in scholar's clothes.

"By order of his Imperial Majesty, the Son of Heaven," the armored Colonel called out. "Everyone in this dwelling is hereby placed under arrest on the charge of rebellion against the state. Surrender or die!"

CHAPTER THIRTY

Standoff

"Surrender or die!"

The words echoed through the estate, backed by the sound of armor clanking and marching boots. One group of enemies had been replaced by another, one twice as numerous and inescapable under heaven.

Crocodile Mao slumped back down onto the steps, and most of the men behind him also let their legs buckle beneath them. The wind of good fortune that had saved them had now blown them straight into a whirlpool with no bottom in sight. Not a one of them doubted that to surrender also meant death, just of a slower and more painful kind, but there was nothing they could do about it.

"Do you surrender?" the Colonel asked.

Mao looked to Snowtop, who stood looking out at the rows of spears with his jaw clenched and muscles tensing. "Flee now," Mao said. "You owe us nothing more. Take your friends and go. I will do my best to delay them here."

But Snowtop held fast. "If I abandoned the Old Master in this hour of need, how would my men ever follow me in the future?"

Mao started to protest, but then stopped. "You are a good man, Young Cho. Your father raised you well." Then Mao looked at the Colonel and opened his mouth to give his surrender, but before he could there was yelling from their right.

From around the right side of the manor house a group of armored figures appeared, making the soldiers on that side retreat. Bearing the symbol of the Cho Family Armed Escort Agency, and led by the plump figure of Old Master Cho himself this new group of fighters marched into view.

"The Cho Family has arrived!" One of the newly arriving fighters called out, and Old Master Cho raised a sword to point at the Colonel.

"The Cho Family stands with the Mao Family."

"Father!" Called Snowtop, and the two Cho men exchanged a nod.

Crocodile Mao nodded to Old Master Cho, and the other man returned the gesture. Mao was amazed that they had come, but in his heart he feared it just meant more souls he would have to pay a debt to in the afterlife. The Cho men were still nowhere near enough to hold against the Imperial Army forces, despite their bravery.

Then, as he was trying to think what to do next, there was another commotion on the left side of the manor house. The soldiers there also pulled back as another large group of fighters marched into view-- this one entirely composed of women!

"The *Jin Hua* also stands with the Mao Family!" Boomed an old woman's voice, and Mao watched as the wizened figure of Merciful Beauty walked into the light. She looked very small, surrounded by the armored Amazonian warriors that flanked her, but there was no doubt of her presence, or her power.

Stunned, all Old Master Mao could do was try to keep his jaw from dropping as he returned her nod of greeting. How was this possible? He wondered. He had a cordial relationship with the *Jin Hua*, but this was an incredible turn of events.

Even the Army Colonel seemed surprised by this. He had obviously been told he'd be merely picking up a group of drugged men, but now he was facing off against two forces of highly skilled fighters as well. Mao saw him turn and look at the scholar, who had been watching silently through all of this.

The scholar said a few words to the Colonel, and Mao could see the military man stiffen. Then the Colonel announced with an almost panicked sound to his voice-- "If you persist in this action, you will all be declared rebels and your lands seized. Retreat now, and the Son of Heaven will be merciful and overlook this transgression. Stay, and you will become enemies of the state!"

This made Mao take a closer look at the scholar, who the Old Master had thought looked familiar from the moment the soldiers had arrived. There was something about the young man's face that denoted not just nobility, but a certain...femininity.

Lady Moonlight!

It was the witch herself, disguised as a man!

Angered, Mao forced himself to his feet.

"This household has always paid our taxes and dealt honestly with the state." He yelled. "We have neither cause nor desire to rebel, and are innocent of all the false charges that may have been leveled against us. However, if the state is unjust, with heaven as our witness, we will stand against it until our dying breath!"

Then he pointed his sword at the Colonel, willing himself not to let it shake. "Come to us at your peril."

From behind him, shouts of agreement went up from his men, and now both armies stood ready on the brink of battle. The defenders still the weaker of the two in numbers, but willing to risk everything to stand up to the larger Imperial Army force.

The armed escorts had skill, the Imperial Army had numbers, and the result was guaranteed to be bloody. Mao could only hope that this would be enough to make the Colonel back down. He could see the hesitation now in the Imperial soldiers, and even the Colonel himself was looking around, worried.

That was when Lady Moonlight spurred her horse and rode to stand between the two groups, facing Master Mao.

"Master Mao," she said. "We have already captured your youngest daughter, and many members of your household." Then, at a gesture from her, the soldiers split to reveal a group of people in chains. Mao's heart sank as he recognized not just Meiyu, but also Old Gan, and a number of his senior fighters from the north who had been coming down with the wedding caravan. "Surrender now, or we will behead them all here in front of you."

Then the prisoners were thrown down onto their knees, and soldiers came up with large bladed sabers to stand beside them- at the ready to perform the execution.

"You witch!" Mao screamed at her. "You stinking whore!"

Lady Moonlight raised a hand, and a blade fell.

Smiling Wu, a cheerful honest man Mao had trained since he was a boy, died.

"Any word you say which is not "I" or "Surrender" will kill another one of your people." She said plainly. "Do not waste their lives."

Mao's sword dipped down as anger fought despair in his heart and finally lost.

"I..." He said, letting the blade slip from his fingers to clatter down the stone steps. "I..." And he started to say the word "surrender", but what he heard was a voice that wasn't his say...

"Excuse me!"

* * *

All eyes searched for the source of the voice who had just spoken. Where did it come from? Who was it?

Then, at the top of the stairs Little Gou appeared, carrying under his arm a black lacquered box wrapped in yellow ribbons. Smiling confidently, he walked down the steps past Mao and Snowtop, and came to stand before Lady Moonlight on her horse.

"Good evening, my lady." He gave a short bow.

She regarded him with suspicion. "You are the gambler Shou spoke of- Gou."

"I am."

Then she smiled cruelly. "If you're here to bargain for their lives with the box, you are mistaken. It was a tool for my uses, nothing more."

Gou laughed, and then said in a low voice that only she could hear. "Well, we both know that isn't true, don't we- your highness?"

For a moment Gou saw something resembling concern flicker across the woman's eyes, but then she returned his smile. "It doesn't matter if you know, a man with no tongue tells no tales."

At this, Gou nodded in acquiescence. He knew she could kill him at any moment, but to do so would start a fight she might not win. He intended to press his advantage as far as it would go. "You're right of course, but we'll get to that in a moment. First, you should know that this box contains a collection of letters between Princess Yu and Master Shan. I think you suspected that already, but I just wanted to let you know. Second, having just read pretty much all of them, I can tell you that there is no treasure map in any of them or references to a hoard of any kind.

"But, of course," he continued. "You never really cared about the treasure anyway, did you? The bigger score was this whole organization, you wanted to bury the Mao agency."

She snorted. "*Xia* are vermin to be exterminated."

"Really?" Gou cocked his head and looked at her. "You sure employ a lot of vermin then. What does that make you?"

"Perhaps I'm just using rats to catch each other." She said with a smile.

"Does that make you a cat?"

"Come closer and tell me how sharp my claws are."

Gou smiled back. "A good dog knows not to let his nose get too close to a cat's claws."

"You are very clever."

"My momma told me so," he answered, and then shrugged. "But then, you know how moms are. They always want the best for their children, and don't want them hurt."

"I wouldn't know."

"You should," he said, his friendly demeanor becoming something more serious. "Your mother sacrificed everything to give you a good life and a good future. Living in the palace for her was hell, but she wanted to make sure you had a chance to have a good future."

Lady Moonlight snorted. "A good life? Do you know what kind of life I had in the palace? My father hated me, and my mother cared more about social politics than her own daughter. Thanks to her, I never knew my father."

"Well, you're right about that."

"What does that mean?"

"It means you didn't get your talent for martial arts from the imperial line."

Her face turned red- "That's a filthy lie!"

"Not according to your moth..."

Gou's problem as a gambler was that he occasionally gambled a little too much and went a bit far. When this happened, he usually lost his money. However, this particular time it nearly cost him his life.

The words were barely out of his mouth before the sword appeared in her hand and was cleaving its way toward Gou's throat. She was astoundingly fast, with a level of skill Gou had only seen in Snowtop and a few others. And, at the moment, all that skill was directed at a single purpose- silencing him!

His long years of training kicking in, Gou tried to block the attack, but the only thing he had in hand was the box.

The air was suddenly filled with paper as the box exploded from her attack. All Lady Moonlight could do was watch in horror as a lifetime of unrequited love ballooned up into the air to be carried by the breeze and scatter across the courtyard.

"No! No!" She cried.

"Oh, I wouldn't worry about it." Gou said, standing in the middle of the mess. "The important letters aren't even here."

"What?" She stared at him. "What do you mean?"

"I mean, the ones which describe your true parentage are already in the hands of the agency heads." Gou gestured back toward the manor house. "I had them distributed while we've been talking." Then he grinned. "Now, I suppose you might get Old Mao, he's kinda drugged up. Same with Old Cho, he's pretty fat. But, if you think you're going to get that letter away from Merciful Beauty, well...I wish you luck."

"You!" She cried, seeing her whole plan unravel before her eyes. "You little wretch!"

"I bet you say that to all the boys." Then he pointed to Meiyu and the other captives. "Now, release the prisoners and tell your army to turn around and start walking."

For a moment, he wasn't sure if she was going to do it, and as he watched her expression of shock turn to one of anger and her jaw set into place. Finally, she looked down at him and said. "I will remember this."

"I hope so." He agreed. Then he reached into his tunic and pulled out one more piece of paper. Handing it to her, he said "This is for you."

Looking at it, she asked. "What is this?"

"A letter to you from your mother, it was in the box." He said plainly. "I guess she expected you to find it. Don't worry, I haven't read it."

She stared at it for a time, and then shoved the piece of paper into one of her robe's inner pockets. "I don't care." She said, and turned around to leave.

"Sure you don't," said Gou, watching her ride away.

Then he walked over to where the prisoners still knelt on the ground. Meiyu looked up at him, stunned.

"Gou?" She said. Her face was worn and she was shaking.

He dropped to one knee in front of her. "Don't worry, they're gone." Around him, other members of the Mao family were rushing up to help. "Get some smithing tools from the stables." He told the first man he saw, then looked back at her. "We'll get you free as soon as we can."

"Gou!" She cried, wrapping her arms around him. "I was so scared!"

"Shhh. Shhh." He told her, holding her gently. It wasn't proper, but propriety was the last thing on anyone's mind at the moment.

"I'm so sorry. I just wanted to warn father. I just wanted to help." She sobbed. "Lily said she'd take me, and I met Snowtop and..."

"It's okay. It's all okay." He reassured her. "It all worked out in the end, right?"

Then he noticed some of the household maids were kneeling next to him now, and slowly started to pull away. When he did, she resisted and buried her head in his chest. "No!"

"Look, I'm not going anywhere. Alright? They're going to take care of you. I have things I need to do."

It took a bit longer, but eventually she reluctantly agreed to let go of him. "I'll see you soon, okay?" He told her, and then her ladies in waiting took over.

Getting up, Gou found Crocodile Mao standing behind him.

"Gou, thank you." Said the older man. "I'm sorry about what I said earlier..."

But Gou shook his head, "Hey, you found me reading your precious letters. I can understand why you were mad. Don't worry about it."

"Yes," the older man said, sounding unconvinced. "My whole family owes you a great debt, Gou. If there is anything I can do to repay you, it is yours." Then, seeing the look on Gou's face he asked- "What is it? Name it, and I will give it to you."

But Gou just shook his head again and smiled his self-deprecating grin. "We'll talk later. I have to see to my friends."

"Of course," and the big man clapped him on both shoulders so hard Gou thought he felt a rib snap.

Making his way through a crowd that all seemed personally determined to thank him, Gou found Sister Cat up in the manor house with Snowtop Cho, and Spider Chan. She was setting Chan's shoulder on one of the tables, and as Gou approached, he heard a crack that made him wince and a whimper of pain from the smaller man.

"There, it's in place." The nun said, and started to tie on the makeshift splits she'd made from torn strips of her robe to keep the bones from moving.

"What a touch," Chan said feebly. "You sure know how to handle a man, sister."

"Hmph." Said the nun, and continued her work.

"I'm surprised you didn't rush to help Meiyu," Gou said to Snowtop.

"It's your night, Gou." Snowtop said, patting Gou on the already sore shoulder. "I didn't want to interrupt."

The two men regarded each other. "Thanks," said Gou. "I appreciate it."

"Will she be okay?" Cat asked.

Gou nodded. "Her family has her, she can't ask for better care."

"Good."

"Hey Gou." Chan said. "I got two questions."

"I got two answers, so we're even."

Chan smirked. "Funny." Then he said. "How come the *Jin Hua* are here, and what did you say to that witch to make her go away?"

Cat and Snowtop looked at him as well.

"Well, you'll have to settle for just one answer tonight. I'm tired." Gou told them. "The *Jin Hua* are here because I asked them to come. I sent a messenger to them after Slow Jung let us off at port."

"But Gou," Snowtop frowned. "What did you say that would make them want to join our cause?"

Gou smiled. "It wasn't hard. I just pointed out that if Lady Moonlight got Master Mao and the Box, they were going to be next. It was in Merciful Beauty's self-interest to come. Also, and this is between you and me," he winked. "I think she's kinda sweet on me."

"I... see..." Snowtop answered, clearly not happy with the image that conjured in his head.

"Speaking of sweeties," Gou indicated to his left with his chin, where Miss Lily waited a short distance away. "I think someone's looking for you."

Snowtop blushed. "Chan, will you be...?"

"I will, Young Master."

"Good." The swordsman straightened. "Sister. Gou." He said, and then walked off to where Lily stood. Gou chuckled as he watched Snowtop's grace disappear in the face of a beautiful woman.

"Same old Cho." Gou mused, and then he looked down at the nun. "How are you doing, Sister?" Gou asked, taking note of the red stained temporary bandage on his friend's hip. "When you're done with him, we need to have someone take a look at you as well."

"Thank you, Brother." The tired nun said. "I will be fine."

"Will you?" He said earnestly, looking her in the eye.

"In time." She answered in a way that meant they'd talk about it later. Then she added. "And you? You look troubled."

"Yeah..." The Gambler said, looking down in thought. "Master Mao offered me whatever I wanted in thanks."

"Oh?" She said in understanding. "That's...Wonderful. I'm so happy for you."

"Yeah," Gou answered. "Me too."

The nun frowned. "You do not sound happy. Is there something wrong?"

Gou sucked in a deep breath and let it out slowly. "I've got a lot of thinking to do, is all. Now, if you'll excuse me, I've got a beauty to see."

"Miss Mao?"

Gou winced. "No, the Merciful kind. I hope."

* * *

Gou found Merciful Beauty resting with her attendants in one of the estate guest houses. Her retinue included the plump Miss Jia, who had taken such a dislike to Gou in their earlier meeting, but who now was much more cordial. She met Gou at the entrance and led him inside.

Inside he found Merciful Beauty sitting in a chair waiting for him, and he came and knelt in front of her.

"Your Junior comes to pay his respects to his Martial Grandmother." He said, bowing respectfully.

She watched him with cold eyes. "Did we dance as you expected us to?"

Keeping his eyes on the floor, Gou answered "I only acted in Martial Grandmother's best interests. As I explained in the letter, this was the best time to make a stand."

"You're a clever one, Little Gou." She said, some warmth returning to her voice. "I can see why Duan chose you."

"Thank you, senior. I merely try my best."

"Well, clever dog, our help does not come without a price. We have aided you, now you must do the same for us."

"I will serve senior as best I can."

"You are unmarried, are you not?"

Gou looked up, startled. "Umm. Yes. That is true."

The old woman's lips curled up. "It happens. I know a girl in need of a husband."

CHAPTER THIRTY-ONE

Decisions

"She wants you to what?"

It was late afternoon the following day, and Gou was sitting at a table in the ante-room of the Sunset Pine Inn with Sister Cat. She had come looking for him when he hadn't come to the brunch Master Mao had served for his guests the following day, and found him here drinking alone.

"She wants me to marry Lily."

"But Brother Cho... And Miss Mao..."

Gou sighed. "She doesn't know about them. She just thinks Lily is nearly unmarriageable, and is looking for someone to take care of her."

"That is a noble goal, but to force you to do so is most unreasonable."

"I would agree." He sighed again and reached for the wine jar to pour himself another cup. "I'm not going to do it. But, that's not the real problem."

"You're worried about Brother Cho?"

"Only if he finds out before I say no."

Her face took on a confused look. "Then what?"

"If I refuse to marry Lily, then I can't turn around and marry Meiyu without offending the *Jin Hua*. The last thing the Mao family needs right now is bad blood with another agency."

"Oh. I see." Cat had seen firsthand how a promise of marriage casually broken could lead to violent disputes.

"If Meiyu wasn't officially engaged, it wouldn't be a problem, but apparently she's supposed to get married into the Yun Clan in a few weeks. Another family the Mao's can't afford to have mad at them right now. It's going to be awfully bad timing if that gets broken off and I pop up as the new groom right afterward."

"Could you not delay it? Have her stay unmarried for a time, and then when all is forgotten you may marry her."

"I thought about that," he agreed. "We'll have to see if she'll agree to it. Actually, the truth is that I haven't even talked to her father about this, he might still refuse- but I wouldn't bet on it. As far as he's concerned, I've saved the whole clan, so their lives are mine."

"That is a great deal of responsibility." Commented the nun, who then quickly regretted it when Gou glared at her. "I'm sorry."

Relaxing, Gou shook his head. "No. I just hadn't considered that it went both ways. You're right, it is a lot of responsibility."

"So, what will you do?"

Gou downed his glass and set it down with a bang as he stood up. "What I always do when I can't think of an answer- hit the tables. I'll let you know how it turns out."

* * *

Meiyu awoke late the next morning to find herself in her old bed, the sun shining in on her and the birds outside chittering away. Looking around the room, it was all so peaceful, and she felt like she was sixteen again, waking up from a dream.

It was only when she moved and the pain in her back returned that she was reminded that the events of the past week were something more real than a nightmare. Her wrists too, bore the red marks where she'd been tied, and she stared at them for a time.

She hadn't seen Gou since the night of the assault. He had promised to come back to her, but had disappeared and no-one seemed to know where he'd gone.

Where was he now? She wondered. Out celebrating his great victory? Maybe drinking with her father? Or out gambling?

"You look better."

Startled, she clutched the blankets to her chest and looked around. There on her windowsill sat Little Gou!

Relaxing, she shook her head.

"Hey, you're the one who taught me how to climb up here. Don't blame me if I come to visit."

"No, silly." She said, wiping a stray tear from her eye. "I'm happy you're here."

"After the other night, that makes two of us." He hopped down and walked over to her bed. He was wearing a fresh light green sleeveless tunic now that was open down the middle to show off his muscles, with clean black pants and slippers. Suddenly, she started to feel a little faint.

"How are you feeling?" He asked, squatting down next to her bed. "You doing better?"

She nodded that she was. "Are you okay?"

"Me?" He smirked. "Oh, I'm fine. Nothing a couple night's sleep can't fix."

"Gou, thank you." She shook her head, starting to tear up again. "I can't believe what you did. It's all so incredible."

"Well, for you- anything."

She stared at him for a time. "You really mean that, don't you?"

"I do." He answered, his eyes never leaving hers. Had they always been so beautiful? Maybe she just hadn't noticed before...

Meiyu felt herself starting to blush and turned away. "Gou...I..." She said, her voice suddenly husky. "Was wondering..."

"Yes?"

"...What you said to her to make her go away." She found herself saying, then cursed herself inwardly for being a coward.

"Who? You mean Lady Moonlight?"

"Uh-huh."

"Well..." He thought about it a moment. "It's a bit complicated, but I guess you could say that I know something she doesn't want anyone else to know. Your father and the other agency leaders have proof of this secret, which they can use to keep her in line if she causes trouble again. So, I don't think she'll be back anytime soon." Then he laughed and scratched his ear. "It's funny, really. The thing she wanted she didn't think she needed, and the thing she needed she didn't think she wanted."

"Gou, that makes no sense."

He shrugged. "Yeah, I guess not. But the point is, she's gone and she won't be back. So, I guess you can have your wedding after all."

Meiyu's eyes dropped to her hands. "Yes. My wedding..." Then she took a deep breath. "Gou, I've been thinking and I've decided that I don't think I want to marry him."

When she didn't hear anything, she looked up to see Gou staring at her with a shocked expression on his face. She couldn't tell if he was happy or sad, or just...anything.

"Well? Say something."

"A-are you sure?"

"Uh-huh." She nodded, watching him carefully.

Gou chewed on his lower lip, then looked her in the eyes and said. "Meiyu. Don't call off the wedding."

She was shocked. She couldn't believe he was saying such a thing. "W-why not?" She stammered. "It's my choice! I can marry who I want to."

Gou's eyes hardened. "Well, you can't marry me."

She stared at him, unbelieving. Was this the man who'd come halfway across the empire and risked his life to save her? Was this the man who'd stood up to the Throne of Heaven to protect her family? Who she'd known since childhood?

Tears started to stream down her face. "You're a bastard."

He nodded. "Not the first time I've heard that."

Her face was red and puffy now, her eyes filled with tears. "Will you at least tell me why?"

Gou looked at her, and for a second, she could see conflict playing out on his face. There was something there for a moment, but then it was gone and he smiled. "I'm not the settling down kind. I like my life, and I don't want to change it. Not for you, not for anyone. Actually, the funny thing is, your dad was right about me. He was right to send you away."

"I'm not asking you to change!" She protested, but he just stood up and shook his head.

"Yeah, you are. I live in an inn with thieves and sing-song girls, and I waste all my money every day on the tables. Do you really think you can live with a man like that? We're from two different worlds, and all we'll do is make each other miserable. You know it. I know it. So, let's just accept the truth."

"But...if we just care for each other enough..." She said, the words sounded hollow in her ears even as she said them, but she wasn't willing to give up so easily.

"Caring won't feed a family," he answered. "And I'm not ready for that kind of responsibility. You need to start having children, and I'm not ready to be anyone's father now, if ever. So, go marry someone who is."

"Gou..." She said, her voice down to a hoarse whisper from crying.

"Goodbye, Meiyu." He said, heading for the window. "Have a good life."

* * *

"How was it?"

Gou looked over at the person who'd just sat down on the stool next to him. She barely fit beneath the awning of the steamed-bun stall, being forced to duck slightly to keep her shaved head from touching the greasy fabric.

"I did what needed to be done." His voice sounded tired and old, even to him.

The nun nodded. "I'm sorry, Brother."

"Hey. I just told her the truth. That's all it took. Funny that. I wasn't going to have her end up like Princess Yu- living for a man who she could never be with. We saw how well that kind of thing goes."

"Yes," agreed the nun. Then she asked, "Did you speak with her father?"

"Yep." Gou patted the money pouch in his inner robe pocket, which made a full sound. "Paid off my debts, and I still have this. I figure I can have a heck of a run with it."

She nodded. "I hope you enjoy yourself."

He gave a wan smile. "I'll do my best." Then sighed. "I'm going to need to keep a low profile for a bit, between Lady Moonlight and Merciful Beauty. I'm thinking of going south to one of the gambling pagodas. Want to come?"

Sister Cat clucked her tongue. "I think not. My leg is not fit for traveling, and I have much study to do to improve my skills."

"Fair enough, we..." Gou started, and then from somewhere nearby on the street, a cry rang out that made both their heads turn.

"Thief! Thief!" Cried a man's voice, and they watched as a black clad figure leapt from atop a nearby carriage onto an awning, and then scrambled up the side of a building like a monkey.

Gou looked at Cat. Cat looked at Gou.

No words needed to be said.

When the steamed bun seller looked down, both of his stools were empty, and only a few coppers for the bill remained.

FIN

EPILOGUE

Upon her arrival home, Lady Moonlight found the manor staff repairing damage from what had obviously been a large fight.

"A tall armored soldier came and took several of the servants." Her man at arms told her. "We attempted to stop him, but he was too strong."

He looked like he was expecting to become about a head shorter as he told her, but was surprised when she waved him off with nothing more than a disinterested "Yes. I understand."

Instead, she retreated to her study, where she placed a thin letter written on rice paper on the table and walked over to look out the windows at the spectacular mountain lake beyond.

She was troubled and uncertain. She would have to report to her master that the plan had failed, and he would not be pleased, but that was not what bothered her the most. She had lived her life thus far based on a set of goals and ideas, but now she had begun to question them.

Who was she really? She wondered. What was she?

Her life had been one filled with certainty and determination, and she had never failed at anything before. Yet, here she was, and what was she going to do now?

In this labyrinth of uncertainties, there was however one thought that burned brightly in her mind- she was going to have revenge on the one who had made her feel like this.

The one named Little Gou.

Want to know when my next eBook will be available? Want updates?

Go to Robynpaterson.com to join my mailing list!

I promise no SPAM, and to only contact you when something I think you might be interested in is released.

WHAT IS THIS "WUXIA" THING ANYWAYS?

Every culture has their heroic warriors of history- the Americans have Cowboys, the British have their Knights, the French have their Musketeers, the Japanese have their Samurai, and the Chinese have their Wuxia. Despite the different cultural backgrounds, each of them has countless tales of romance told about their heroic deeds in times of trouble, and how they fought duels of honor to save friends and loved ones from the forces of evil. How they served masters, both good and evil, and how their names became legend.

Of the fighters on the list, however, the Wuxia are the most nuanced and hardest to pin down. Yes, they had a code of honor (many of them, in fact), and yes, they generally fought to protect the innocent and uphold justice, but at the same time while some were noble generals, just as many were thieves and bandits and pirates. In this sense, the Wuxia are closest on that list to the American Cowboys- each Xia is different, and trying to make his way in the world as best he (or she) knows how with their weapon at their side and their pride on the line.

While it has older roots, the genre of heroic Wuxia tales is actually a relatively modern genre, and has most of its foundations in the serialized Chinese pulp novels of the mid-20th century. Novelists like Jin Yong, Liang Yusheng and Gu Long took influences like Alexandre Dumas's Three Musketeers, American Westerns, and Gangster films and then combined them with historical Chinese figures and events to weave incredible romantic stories about heroic martial artists and swordsmen that have transcended fiction to become cultural icons. The Condor Heroes, Jin Yong's most famous novel, is arguably one of the most popular and well-known books on the planet- just not in the English-speaking world.

Eventually, this genre translated into film, and while thousands of films have been produced, most Americans only know a few examples like Crouching Tiger, Hidden Dragon, HERO, and the House of Flying Daggers. Of these, Crouching Tiger is probably the best example of the genre itself, as the other two were primarily art films. Crouching Tiger has elements of an art film as well, but it has more of a balance to it between art and the special subculture the Wuxia inhabit called the *Jianghu*.

The *Jianghu* (lit. "Rivers and Lakes") is again much like the wild west world inhabited by the cowboys- a fictional romanticized subculture where everyone is a master of some martial art or weapons skill, people fight duels at the drop of a hat over everything, and the most important thing is maintaining your own personal honor and reputation. It's made of up respectable monks and armed security escorts (like we see in this novel), disreputable bandits and gamblers (like Little Gou), and everyone in between who claims to follow the martial codes. Strange criminals with secret lost martial arts lie around every corner, secret societies are always trying to rule the Empire, and there's always some weapon that everybody and their brother has to have or die trying.

Welcome to the world of the Adventures of Little Gou.

Cultural Note:

The term "Xiao"(lit. "Little") in Mandarin is often put before people's names to connote "cute" or "little", and is most often put in front of women's names as a sort of familiar nickname by friends or family. (Similar to putting "-chan" behind women's names in Japan.) However, it can also be put in front of men's names to have a similar meaning, and this is the case with Little Gou's name, which is actually not his real name, but a nickname he is commonly known by in the *Jianghu* martial world. (Gou himself is in his early 20's.)

Little Gou first appeared in a series of Audio Dramas on the Kung Fu Action Theatre podcast. You can hear Little Gou's full-cast audio adventures for free at http://kungfuactiontheatre.com/.

About the Author: Rob is a teacher, writer and blogger based in London, Ontario, Canada. He is a teacher at Fanshawe College and the founder/producer of the Kung Fu Action Theatre audio drama group (kungfuactiontheatre.com). He is married to his amazing wife Connie, and owned by his dogs Winston and Penny.

Connect With Me Online:
My blog: http://robynpaterson.com
E-mail: rpatersonca@gmail.com
Twitter: http://twitter.com/rob_paterson
Goodreads: http://www.goodreads.com/author/show/4580354.Robyn_Paterson

Thanks for reading! Zaijian! 88!

www.ingramcontent.com/pod-product-compliance
Lightning Source LLC
Chambersburg PA
CBHW020601180626
46810CB00007B/2596